The Way West

Also by A. B. GUTHRIE, JR.: THE BIG SKY

A. B. GUTHRIE, JR.

The Way West

WILLIAM   SLOANE   ASSOCIATES
Publishers   *New York*

To
HARRIET

MAPS

The Way West

Chapter - - - - - - - - - - - - - - One

THE DAY dawned clear, but it had rained the night before, the sudden squally rain of middle March. Taking a look out the kitchen door, seeing the path lead down to the muddy barnyard and the tracks of his shoepacks splashed in it, Lije Evans was just as well satisfied that things were wet. It gave him an excuse not to work, even if he could be mending harness or fixing tools. Not that he minded work; it was just that he didn't feel like working today.

"Likely I'll go to town, Rebecca," he said, closing the door.

"To talk about Oregon," she said, not quite as if she blamed him.

"Why, now," he answered, smiling at her while he lounged over to a stool, "I hadn't give a thought to what I'll talk about. I'll talk about whatever comes up." He knew she saw through him, and he didn't care. She always had seen through him.

"I don't know why everyone's gone crazy all of a sudden," she said while she wiped the last of the dishes and hung the towel on its peg. "Everyone talking about Oregon, and it so far away you can't think where."

"Not everybody. Not as many as will be."

"It'll blow over. You wait and see." She got the broom out of the corner. "I declare, that dog does track things up."

Evans looked down at Rock, who had let himself fall in the middle of the floor after leaving the marks of his big pads on the worn wood. "Rock's a good dog."

At the mention of his name, the dog lifted his head and got up slow and came over and put his chin in Evans' lap. He was getting old, Evans told himself, seeing the muzzle graying and the eyes beginning to shine dim with years. Rock was half hound and half no-one-knew-what, but he was a handsome dog, white and blue mixed, and a good one, too. "Reckon it's too much to ask him to wipe his feet before he comes in," Evans said.

Rebecca grunted to that while she swept.

"You can't go, boy," Evans said while he stroked Rock's head. "You chew up them town dogs too much. You'll get me in trouble one of these days, that's what you'll do."

"I ain't sure but what I'd say no. Of course you ain't goin', though. It's just talk."

"How's that, Becky?"

"No to Oregon."

"Now, Becky," he said, "don't be makin' up your mind independent. What if I should take it into my head to light out with the rest?"

She grunted again, and Evans knew it was because the thought of their splitting up was so outlandish. Another man, now, might not think she was much, heavy like she was and extra full-breasted, but she suited him, maybe as much for the way her mind worked as for anything else, maybe because she knew him up and down and inside out and still thought he was all right. A man got so he didn't see what other eyes saw; he got so that what he saw on the outside was what he knew lay underneath.

"Reckon Brownie wants to trail along with me?" he asked.

"You heard him say he was goin' fishin'. He's diggin' worms now."

"Good thing to do."

"There's a heap of you in him," she said, looking at him. "You used to like fishin' and such."

"And I hate work."

"I didn't say that, Lije. It ain't so."

Evans had to smile inside. Every time he made little of himself, she said it wasn't so. "Oregon," he said, letting his thoughts drift, "it would be a good thing to a man, knowin' he had helped settle the country and so joined it to America." In his mind he went back over his words; they didn't tell what it was he felt.

Becky didn't answer.

"The huntin' and fishin' ought to be good in Oregon.

2

Brownie would like that. A man wouldn't mess with rabbits and coons and possum there. Brownie wants to go."

"Last time you talked, it was the soil was so good."

"Soil, too. Everything."

"How you know?"

"It's what they say."

"Dick Summers don't think Oregon's so much, not for farmin'."

"Dick don't look on it that way, is all. He thinks about Injuns and furs and such. Farmin' don't come natural to him."

"He does all right."

"It still don't come natural. You can keep a varmint in a cage, but it don't come natural to him. Not that Dick's like a varmint."

"You ought to call round on him, Lije. Mattie looks awful poorly."

"Maybe I ought to."

She stepped over toward him. "Lije, we got Brownie to think of and all. Wouldn't do to act sudden about Oregon."

"No. But it wouldn't be so sudden."

"Well?" She strung the word out as she put the broom away.

Evans turned as the door opened and saw Brownie coming in and asked, "Want to go to town?"

The boy answered, "Don't guess so, Pa. It's a fishin' day to-day."

"It don't matter," Evans answered, still stroking the dog. "Just thought maybe you was wore out with yourself." He let his eyes travel over Brownie. "I swear, boy, if ever you get meat on them bones, you'll be a sure-God man." Brownie was, Evans thought, close to a man already, long-boned and hard-muscled, with young whiskers on his face when he let them grow. A good boy, he was, a shy and backward boy, just coming on to the time when things were hardest, when a man wanted women worse than ever in his life and didn't know how to hold himself in or let himself go, being awkward and afraid. "I hope you catch fish. I got a hunger for fish after all the salt pork and beans I've et." Evans got up. "I'll be goin'."

3

Rebecca came to the door as he let himself out. "Remember, Lije."

He nodded.

"You ain't as young as you were."

"Nobody is. But I ain't so old, neither. Thirty-five. A man's prime at thirty-five. Stay back, Rock."

She didn't say anything but closed the door slowly.

He went to the barn and saddled a mule. It was six miles to Independence. He would get there this side of midmorning if he moved right along, and some later if he let the mule laze. He let him laze.

He didn't guess he would join up for Oregon, for all that he would be proud to have a hand in it, to build up Uncle Sam and stop the British. Missouri was a good-enough country. A man could live, even if not fat, if he had a mind to work. He could live and fight fever and trade at the store and hope maybe someday to buy himself a nigger and so have more time for doing what he wanted to do. It wasn't that he wanted a passel of niggers and a big house and fancy horses, like some had in the cotton country in the south of the state. Maybe he didn't want even one nigger. He was a slave man himself, but still, come right down to the quick of it, he didn't know as one man had a right to own another, black or white. It was just that he wanted something more out of life than he had found.

It was likely a foolish business, this going to Oregon, but it was good to think about, like thinking about getting out of old ways and free of old places. Like his pa had said once, telling about coming down the Ohio in a flatboat, there wasn't any place as pretty as the one that lay ahead.

It was a time to think of moving, a time when the fields and trees, for all their raw and naked look, showed they knew spring was coming. The blood flowed quick in the body, and ideas came to a man. Once when his pa's house burned, catching fire in the stick-and-mud chimney, he had felt a little the same way, as if all the things he had been doing as a boy didn't need to be done any more, and he could strike out fresh and build his life as he wanted it. People sure would think he was crazy, knowing what was in his head.

4

The day would be warm, he thought, as the trail led out of a bunch of trees into a piece of prairie. He could feel the sun where his pants lay flat against his thigh. A woodchuck ambled in the grass and looked at him, and Evans figured he could shoot his eye out if he had his rifle with him. Mostly, now, he left the rifle at home, for it was heavy and he figured the country safe enough even if some others didn't.

The mule clomped along in the mud. A dull critter, a mule, not knowing the seasons or taking note of redbirds and thrashers fixing for nesting, or hardly knowing whether it was fair or stormy. Or maybe a mule thought about more than a man would guess and went along slow and sad under the load of ideas.

The town showed up by and by, the first cabins squatting on the wet ground, their round or squared logs dark with the night's rain, dogs sniffing at corners and running out to bark, a couple of tents shining white in the sun and three men sitting on a log near by, their rifles close to hand, probably talking about Oregon while they waited for the start. The stores were busy, with customers stepping in and out and blacks unloading goods that teams had hauled from the landing. Three Mexicans with broad peaked hats walked in front of the Noland House, looking like robbers, as the hired hands of the Santa Fe traders usually did.

Two men were standing in front of Hitchcock's store, talking earnest. One was Tadlock, the Illinois man who had come to Independence early to talk Oregon and didn't want to join any company already being formed but to set up his own. Tadlock was full of business all the time, or anyway he had been full of business, just as he was now, at the one time Evans had seen him before.

The other man was spindly-looking and had a crop of whiskers that seemed to have molted some. He just kept bobbing his head to Tadlock, as if to say yes to everything.

Evans said, "How-de-do, Mr. Tadlock."

Tadlock turned and squinted to remember and answered, "Good morning, Evans."

Evans pulled the mule over to a post and got off, feeling a

5

little stiff in the knees, and tied up. He walked over to the two men.

"This is Henry McBee," Tadlock said. "Lije Evans."

They shook hands.

"McBee's going to Oregon," Tadlock went on. "How is it with you now? Made up your mind?"

"I wouldn't say I had and I wouldn't say I hadn't. My mind kind of makes itself up if I give it some rope."

Tadlock didn't think that was funny. "Better push it along. There'll be things to do."

"Where you from, McBee?" Evans asked.

"Southern Ohio. Cincinnati, you might say."

"He's a man who knows his mind," Tadlock put in.

"Yes, sir," the man said. "All of a sudden, I sold out and put my woman and young'uns on a boat and hauled my own tail aboard, and here we come, hurrah for Oregon. Things ain't so good in Ohio nohow."

Evans nodded. "Nor here, neither. Let's have a drink."

" 'Y God it's a strong thought," McBee said, and looked at Tadlock and kind of drew in, for Tadlock was shaking his head.

Tadlock said, "I'm not a drinking man." He seemed to think twice and added as if he hardly meant it, "You two go on." He started to move off. "Got a couple of other men I want you to meet. I'll bring them around."

Evans and McBee went into the store. Hitchcock had his hands on the counter, waiting for trade. His red-veined, popped eyes swam to them. You could tell Hitchcock was a good drammer from the looks of him.

There was the smell of leather in the place, and cheese, and clothes just out of a box, and whisky that had spilled on the counter. The smells mixed with the stink of a pile of furs that lay in the back.

Evans said, "You damned old robber, how about a drink?"

"First sensible thing I heard you say since God knows when." Hitchcock drew two glasses, and thought it over and drew one for himself.

"Yes, sir," McBee said, scuffing his beard with his knuckles before he drank, "I said to myself, 'Oregon, now, there's a spot

6

for a man.' " His Adam's apple bobbed to the whisky. "No sense in workin' your guts out—and for nothin'.''

Hitchcock leaned on the counter. "It's like the hydrophoby. You get bit and you're gone. Or it's like a dog with two bones. Can't handle but one but won't let another dog have the other. Let the British have Oregon. We got bone enough.''

"You don't hold with movin' to Oregon?" McBee asked.

"Not as long as he's got a counter to lean on and whisky to drink,'' Evans answered.

Hitchcock let his big eyes slide to Evans. "What's wrong with Missouri? Same kind of people here, and more hog meat to eat, and you can sleep dainty in a sure-enough bed.''

McBee said, "I guess you don't understand. Fill 'em up, will you?" When it came time to pay, he fumbled in his breeches and finally turned to Evans and said, "I'm damned if I ain't left my money at the wagon.''

Evans paid. "You ain't the pioneer kind, Hitch. Let 'em settle, and you come after, with your bar'ls and calico and ideas of gettin' rich. Storekeepin' ain't what you'd call venturesome.''

"A hell of a lot you know about it, Lije. A store man's got to be quick on the trigger.'' He straightened his big bulk, as if to show he was ready for whatever. "And where'd you be without a store?''

" 'Y God, out of debt,'' McBee put in.

Hitchcock stared at him. "I reckon you know,'' he said, "that no wagon train's takin' a debt-skipper.''

"I was just makin' fun.''

"Take away the stores,'' Evans said, "and a man could lay by some money.''

"I get rich, I do,'' Hitchcock answered him, "tradin' for runty eggs and bad mushrat and whatever ain't good enough for you to keep. Man come in the other day and wanted to trade a goddam rock. Said it was a madstone and never known to fail and when I said why didn't he keep it then, he said he figured he was too lively to get bit and it was slow-movin' men like me needed pertection.''

"And did you trade?" Evans asked.

Hitchcock nodded. "I always trade, if a man's reasonable. I

give 'im some wooden nutmegs that a damn Yankee passed on me oncet, 'fore I was old enough to have my eyes open. I traded him all right, and the rock was so hard and slick it wouldn't pick up honey, let alone pizen, and then I threw the rock away and figured I got the best of the deal."

"How so?"

"Tradin' nothin' for nothin', I got shet of the nutmegs. It always hurt my pride, lookin' at 'em."

Evans heard the door squeaking open and turned around and saw Tadlock coming in, and with him two other men, one looking to be not much more than a boy.

Hitchcock's slow gaze went to Tadlock. "I know it ain't whisky you're wantin'," he said, as if a man that didn't drink was queer beyond knowing, maybe remembering when everybody drank and even a preacher would take a swig or two so as to be able to talk some extra fire into hell.

"Right," said Tadlock. "Evans, shake hands with Curtis Mack. And Charles Fairman. And this is Henry McBee."

They shook hands all around. Charles Fairman was the young-looking man. He had a good face, with dark eyes and a high forehead and a seriousness about him that meant he had seen more years or trouble than a man might think at first.

Curtis Mack was older, and different. Evans guessed him to be maybe thirty-five. He was the kind of man who seemed not to give all his attention to what was going on; part of him was somewhere else, looking backward or forward, fretting, maybe, over what he had to do.

"Mack and Fairman have joined my company," Tadlock said.

"Hurrah for Oregon!" It was McBee speaking up.

"With my men from Illinois," Tadlock said as if he owned them, "we have close to the makings of a train. We don't want too big a company. We want to travel light and fast."

"How many of ye?" McBee asked Fairman.

The young man answered, "My wife and boy."

"Married, eh?"

Fairman nodded.

"I was just thinkin'. Got a girl comin' seventeen myself, her and my old woman and five besides."

8

Evans wanted another drink, now that he had had a couple. Becky might scold him a little—but still he didn't drink very often or very much. He asked, "How about a drink?"

Before anybody else could answer, McBee said, "I do believe I will."

The others said they would, too, all except Tadlock.

Fairman raised his glass and said, "Here's to a place where there's no fever."

" 'Y God, yes," answered McBee. "And to soil rich as anything. Plant a nail and it'll come up a spike. I heerd you don't never have to put up hay, the grass is that good, winter and all. And lambs come twice a year. Just set by and let the grass grow and the critters birth and get fat. That's my idee of farmin'."

"Seems to me," said Evans, "that you all are ahead of yourselves. Be a month and more before you can start."

The man, Mack, nodded. "First come, best served. Best land, best damsites, best business locations." He fell silent and stood looking off, his forehead wrinkled, as if he saw Oregon and the land and the sites and the locations he had spoken of. The thumb of the hand at his side kept playing along the fingers.

"We've got plenty of work to do before we can start," Tadlock said.

The young Fairman bobbed his head. "The more I think of it, the more I think I'm doing right. No fever. New land. New chances."

"A new way of things," Evans said, reading what was in Fairman's mind and putting it all together, and Fairman gave him a little smile and nodded again.

"Of course you're doing right," Tadlock spoke up. "You ought to join, Evans, right now."

"What's the matter with Missouri?" It was Hitchcock asking, as he wiped the corner of his mouth with the back of his hand. The red eyeballs went from one to another of them for an answer.

Then his gaze slid over to the door, and Evans, following it, saw the door opening and a girl coming in. She stepped in and held the door half shut behind her and stood uncertain, like a bird about to fly, and it grew on Evans that she was such a girl

9

as a man wouldn't see every day. The curves of her gave shape to the shapeless linsey-woolsey she wore. The face above the dress was so quick and aware it almost hurt to look. The face was pale, and the planes of the cheeks long and smooth, and the mouth full as a knowing man wanted a mouth to be. The eyes were big and dark and darkly shining, except that shining wasn't exactly the word for them. Glowing, maybe, was more like it.

"Pa," she said, standing there in bare feet, the lines of her young breasts showing through her sack of a dress.

McBee looked up then. "Well?"

"Ma wants you should come to the wagon."

McBee's mouth worked in the scrubby beard. "You tell your ma I'm busy."

"She said, please, to come."

One small foot came up and slid down the instep of the other, and Evans guessed her ma had said not to come back without her pa.

"You tell her I'll come when I can, and not before. Hear?"

Evans brought his gaze away from her and looked at McBee and then at the rest and caught Mack unguarded, his eyes busy, his face marked with what might be hunger, as if for a minute, and maybe for no more than that, he had let his thoughts run away with him. The others made out not to notice anything much, maybe feeling small and out of place as Evans did himself.

"You git on!" McBee said.

The girl turned then, slowly, and went through the door and closed it and was lost to sight.

"The damn women!" McBee said. "Always wantin' you for something. That's my girl, Mercy." He reached in his pocket for a twist of tobacco.

They drank quietly for a minute, and then Tadlock changed the subject that was in their minds. "We haven't decided on a pilot. We have to find a good pilot."

"There are some who say they are," Mack said, taking his eyes from the door. "Adams for one. Or Meek."

10

McBee tongued his chew to one side. "Goddam it, I bet they couldn't follow a turnpike."

Tadlock spoke again. "Adams hasn't been beyond Fort Laramie. Any fool can get to Laramie. It's the country beyond that counts."

"What about Meek?" Mack asked.

"I understand he's already dickering, he and Adams both." Tadlock turned to Evans. "You know a good pilot?"

"I don't guess so."

"You talk as if you might."

"I was just thinkin'."

Tadlock waited.

"I reckon I do know one. Gettin' him is the question."

"Who is it?"

"I don't know as I ought to say before I can talk to him myself. Maybe he wouldn't appreciate my sayin'."

"Why would he object?"

Mack ordered drinks again, motioning to Hitchcock.

"I don't know. Maybe he wouldn't."

"How could it hurt to tell? It doesn't commit him—and we've got to know if we're going to put the proposition. There ought to be a nice piece of money in it for him. Not as much as with a big company, but the worry and work would be less."

"Well," Evans said, taking the refilled glass, "I reckon you're right. He sure-God can say no for himself. It's old Dick Summers. He's been everywhere, trappin' beaver and fightin' Indians and all. He could guide us blindfolded."

"Where does he live?"

"Neighbor to me."

"Is there a chance we could get him?"

"Hard tellin'. His woman's poorly."

"But you're sure he'd do?" Tadlock went on. "We can't have some worn-out grandpa who'll show up with a Harpers Ferry musket and a jug of whisky."

"I 'xpect," said Evans slowly, looking Tadlock in the face, "that Dick Summers is just about the best man I ever met up with."

"Would you go with us to see him?"

11

"Sometime. Tomorry or next day."

"Good. Fine. Meantime we'll figure on the pay." Tadlock figured on it in his head right then, without saying what it might add up to. When he spoke it was to ask Evans: "Now has that mind of yours made itself up?"

"I ain't sure."

"We'll have a full party before long."

Mack asked, "Why would you want to stay here when you can go to Oregon? As I said, first come, best served."

Evans didn't have an answer.

"I hope you can go," young Fairman said as if he meant it.

"Look here," said Tadlock, counting off on his fingers as he made his points. "You know the Willamette valley is fertile, pretty, too, beyond anything we know here."

"That's what they tell me."

"It's rich. It is easy to get to by water, by river and ocean."

Evans agreed.

"That Iowa committee—two years ago, wasn't it?—it knew what it was talking about."

"How's that?"

"Take climate, it said, or water power or health or timber or soil or convenience to markets, Oregon beat them all."

"That was before they got there."

"You haven't heard a different story since?"

"Don't know as I have."

"Look," Tadlock said, using his hands like a man who stood for office. "There's a better reason yet, to my mind." He paused to let the words sink in. "Is it our country or England's? You want it to be British?"

"Hitchcock does, but not me."

"Well, what's going to decide it? People, that's what. People like you and me. if we've got gumption enough to settle there."

The blood had climbed to Tadlock's face. In his temple Evans could see a vein stand out. His words had a ring to them. In spite of himself, Evans was moved.

"They say fifty-four forty or fight," Tadlock went on. "By God, we won't have to fight if enough of us are on the ground!" He let his voice fall. "It would be a proud thing, Evans, for you

12

and your children and their young ones, too, saying Pa or Grandpa helped win the country. Or do you want to sit in a chair and let others make history?"

Tadlock pulled a handkerchief out of his pocket and wiped his forehead. "That's all—except to say again we want you."

"What do you think?" Mack asked.

Evans read in Fairman's face the hope he would say yes.

"You're bunchin' up on me." Evans looked from face to face, and saw them all solemn and waiting, even McBee's. Almost before he knew it, he said, "Tell you what. If Dick Summers goes, I will."

"Good enough."

McBee said, " 'Y God, shake hands."

They had another drink—all except Tadlock and Fairman—and then Evans went and untied his mule. Riding home, he told himself he had let the whisky talk, but still he wondered what he would do and still didn't wonder, either. It was as if the course had been set all along, and he had been playing that it wasn't, acting like he could say yes or no. He would go if Dick went, and, maybe, by hell, he would anyway. Free men, brave men in a great, new nation. A new way of things. Soil good. Hunting good. Climate good. No fever. Hurrah for Oregon! He wouldn't figure too much why it was he went. The head got tired, figuring. He would just go because he wanted to, for all sorts of reasons. He would go if he felt the same as now after the fire died in him.

He unsaddled the mule and turned it loose and made for the cabin, remembering of a sudden that he hadn't eaten and was hungry. The sun was sliding down the western sky, showing through the tail of a cloud. Likely it would be fair tomorrow and he would have to dig and grub and split and bend and lift and jolt as if his life depended on it, which it did. A man didn't make history, staying close to home.

Old Rock welcomed him, as if asking what was up, and he opened the door and saw Rebecca stooping at the fireplace. "Get your breeches on, Becky," he called out. "We're goin' to Oregon."

13

Chapter - - - - - - - - - - - - - Two

AFTER EVANS had left the store, the others drifted away. Tadlock announced he had business to attend to at the Noland House, and McBee guessed he'd go see what it was his woman wanted, and Mack excused himself by saying he was figuring on buying some cattle.

As they walked out the door, leaving Hitchcock staring moodily after them, Tadlock halted and watched Evans riding away on his mule. "There's a man I'd like to have in my company," he said.

It was what Charles Fairman had been thinking. He liked this big man with the easygoing manner, liked the signs of good humor in the broad and fleshy face, the indications of physical competence in the stout hands and big frame. He was, Fairman thought a little enviously, what a man should be who contemplated a long, hard, dangerous trip. He gave promise of being a better companion than Tadlock, who would be officious, or than Mack, who would be difficult to know, or than McBee, the poor white.

"My bet is that Evans will come along, after that sermon you preached him," Mack said to Tadlock.

"It was the God's truth."

"God's truth on Tadlock's tongue," Mack said, smiling, and settled his hat on his head and began to walk away.

Fairman signaled a goodbye and set off for what he called home. It was two rooms in a ramshackle house, but better, at that, than a tent. He doubted that Tod could have survived in a tent, the way the fever raged in him. He had to have shelter and care—but more than anything he had to have the high, dry air, such as people said you found in the valley of the high Platte, in the mountains, in Oregon, where there was no fever at all.

Looking around him, seeing the cabins breasting into the mud, feeling the wetness in the air in spite of the high-riding sun, Fairman wished they could start at once. Independence was as miasmal as the lowlands of Kentucky. Sometimes he wondered why his father had left Virginia, to travel through the Gap to the canebrakes of Kentucky and, by stages, to the Ohio. Virginia was healthier country. At any rate his father had admitted as much in his later days, when the push of adventure had died in him and old, remembered things filled his mind. People didn't yawn and stretch there, he said, and stand slumped as if they couldn't move.

As Fairman approached, the woman of the house opened the door and with a split broom fanned out the dirt she had swept up. As always, the tip of her nose was red from cooking. "Oh, it's you," she said, stopping her sweeping and letting her arms hang loose from her hold on the broom handle. "They was a man here." Her glance shifted from him to a sleepy sow that had lifted herself from the mud of the yard and stood grunting, her small eyes winking with dull alarm. The woman flourished the broom. "Git, you! I declare!" The sow gave a quick, outraged grunt and lumbered away.

Fairman asked, "What?"

"They was a man here. You been saying you wanted another man."

"Oh! That's good. You mean to go with us?"

"He said he would—for the ride and victuals."

"Did he talk to my wife?"

"Wouldn't do it. Said God knows women have aplenty to say, but no say-so." The red nose sniffed.

"I see. Where did he go?"

"He traipsed off somewheres. Said he'd be back."

Fairman said, "I see," again, hoping the man would be back. With two wagons and the cattle he expected to trail, he would need two men at least. He had one, a quiet hand who chewed tobacco all day long and had spent his life working with horses and mules and oxen.

Fairman stepped into the house.

"He had a pinched-up face," the woman said over her shoulder.

He walked through a room and opened the door to the quarters he and his family occupied. He looked at Judith, letting his face ask how Tod was. She smiled and called out, "Toddie, your father's home." Tod came out of the kitchen, riding a stick for a horse.

"Pretty frisky, aren't you, boy?"

Tod unstraddled the stick. "I'm going to ride him to Oregon."

"That's a fine horse," Fairman said, touching the stick. "For a five-year-old you're a good picker."

Judith smiled at the boy and put her hand on his head. "He'll be ready. He's getting to be a stout boy."

"This is still fever country," Fairman cautioned her.

"Not like Paducah."

"Maybe not. He does look better." Fairman told himself it was true that Tod did. The boy was still thin as a twig and frail-looking, like a young bird, but his eyes were clear now and his color better.

"I'm fine," Tod said. "Why don't we go now? Why do we have to wait, Pa?"

"We'll be going soon. And remember to say Father."

Judith barely shook her head as if to say not to bother over trifles.

"I don't like 'Pa,' " he answered, knowing she was right.

"We've eaten," Judith told him. "You were so long. There's cold chicken and corn bread and milk on the table."

He went into the kitchen, or the room that passed for a kitchen, and sat down at the hand-hewn table. "Judie," he said while he tore a thigh and drumstick apart, "we're doing right." She and Tod had followed him in.

"Oh?"

"Not the fever alone. The whole thing."

"I hope so."

"It makes a man feel like something, this—this big adventure. We'll have a good company. I've been talking to some of the men."

16

He let his thoughts move ahead while he munched on the chicken, seeing the farm they would have in Oregon and the wheat waving yellow and the great ships riding the Columbia for their produce. He saw Tod strong at last, with healthy flesh covering the thin bones, saw him growing up with the country, saw him growing important with it. He felt almost gay, free of the quick irritation that forebodings aroused in him.

"It'll be rough at first," he said, "but we can stand a little roughness all right. Eh, boy?"

Tod, astride the stick again, called, "Whoa!"

"There's just one thing," Fairman said while he studied Judith. "I almost wish I had tried bringing a slave along."

"Don't worry about me. I'll get along."

"All right," he said, making his tone hearty, but his mind had slipped back to Kentucky, to country where the Tennessee and the Cumberland joined the Ohio, and one lived in a house, not a cabin, and colored folk did the drudge work, and life, except for sickness, seemed now to have flowed smoothly. For a minute he felt again a great misgiving, doubting that even Judith could bear the hardships before them. She was not a strong girl, but, God knew, not languid, either. She worked to the limit of her strength, so that night often found her near collapse, and it seemed to him then that the flesh of her cheeks and lips was almost transparent, and he would look into the gentle, pale-blue eyes with quick and secret alarm.

She often fell victim to fever, too, and went through the agonies of chill and heat, the induced vomitings, the calomel and blisterings and quinine. It was for her sake, if not as much as for Tod's, that he had sold his small plantation and placed his few slaves and taken the steamboat for St. Louis and then for Independence. A few wretched Kaws had been aboard and, for a pint of whisky offered them by some travelers themselves half drunk, had sung a rusty, discordant Indian song. The boat was dirty, the men dirty, the Indian beggars verminous. Along the shores the bare trees crowded, straining up for room and air, their lower trunks lost in a tangle of vine and bush. It seemed to Fairman he could see sickness there, could see fever breeding in the breathless overgrowth. It ran with the water under the

17

boat, too, with the yellow, sickly flow of the Ohio and the Mississippi. He felt like turning back.

But he was right, he told himself now. He knew himself to be a not very practical man, but he had to be right about Oregon. They knew—he and Judie—that Tod couldn't live in the low river country. Sickness lay deep and malignant in him, easing away only to return as regularly as time, shaking him to pieces with chills, wasting his flesh with fever. If ever he recovered from one illness—which was to be doubted—he promptly caught another. And so Fairman and Judith had come to live in dread, mostly unspoken but real as a burden on the back. He had lain at night and thought about the boy in health, with his hair like tow and his skin touched with the color of gold, and then, in spite of himself, he had turned about and dreamed about fever and seen the boy withering under it—the dread realizing itself—and had awakened in a sweat, his heart thumping in his chest, and had sat up in bed and tried to shake the picture from his head.

Tod asked, "What you thinking about?"

"I thought I might go out and look at some mules."

"Isn't it still early?" Judith said.

"Prices probably will go up later, when the real crowd gets here."

Tod asked, "Can I go, Pa? I mean Father."

Fairman looked at his wife.

"I don't think it will hurt him, if you're not gone too long. It's nice out."

"I guess you can, Son," Fairman answered, rising.

Tod came and took his hand, and they left the house and walked down toward a yard that Fairman had noted before, a pole yard built to keep sale stock in.

It was a good day, the kind of day that made a man want to start at once, while the sun was friendly and the spring wind down to a breath. Only the mud argued for waiting. No matter how wide-tired, wagons would have a hard time in the mud. Fairman picked his way through it, guiding Toddie before him.

He was having his own wagons re-tired with three-inch iron, bolted on, though most tires were two inches wide and some

18

even less. He had bought two substantial wagons, made of well-seasoned wood, with falling tongues and well-steeled skeins. He had contracted for boxes for their effects, to be built of even height so as to provide a flat surface to lie on if need be. He had laid in a good supply of horse gear and gathered some simple tools and had bought a good rifle and a pistol and a shotgun for fowling. He had purchased a sheet-iron stove with a boiler, and a Dutch oven and skillet and plates and cups of tin, since queen's ware was heavy and likely to break. He had a tent, two churns—one for sour and one for sweet milk—and two plow molds and a supply of rope for tethering animals.

The list of equipment, he estimated as he counted the items off, was almost complete. Now he had to think about supplies—flour, meal, bacon, sugar, salt, dried stuff, coffee, rice, maybe a little keg of vinegar. And books, especially schoolbooks. Books would be scarce in a new country. With two wagons he could transport more than some travelers—a cherry chest that Judie liked, the best of her dishes, buried in the flour, quilts, extra clothes, dress shoes, jams and jellies. Whimwhams they would be called by men who swore to travel light.

More important was the question of stock—oxen for the wagons, seven or eight yokes of them at least; mules to ride, milk cows and cattle to drive. Should he try to take sheep, chickens, geese? One got all manner of advice. He wished he could be sure.

And medicines. He mustn't forget an ample supply of medicines.

He had arrived at that subject when a voice called from behind him. "You lookin' for a man to go west? Be you Mr. Fairman?"

He turned and said "Yes" and waited, seeing a long splinter of a man in a hickory shirt and high-hung homespun breeches and an old piece of felt hat.

"Name's Hig," the figure announced. "Or that's what they call me. It's bobtail for Higgins. I been on your trail, as maybe the lady told you."

The lady had been right when she said his face was pinched up. He wasn't old but had lost his teeth, so that the mouth turned in and the small jaw sat snug under a thin nose. The eyes seemed crowded, too, under the close line of brow, but the forehead, Fairman noted, was good, as if nature had tried to make up for the stinginess below.

"I hanker to go," the man said. "Gimme a place to lay my head, any old place, and somep'n to feed on, and I'm your gooseberry. How-de-do there, boy."

"You're experienced?"

"A man don't live to my age without learnin'."

"I mean you can handle stock, drive a wagon, lend a hand when needed?"

"Sure, mister. Maybe I look green like a gourd, but I'm ripe inside."

"What's your purpose in going?"

"I dunno. Jest to get where I ain't."

It was, Fairman reflected, as good a reason as most. "How old are you?"

"That I wouldn't know. As my pap used to say, too young to die and too old to suck."

A grin appeared in the pinched face, a thin but merry grin which might have been wider had there been room for it.

"The man I take mustn't be afraid of work."

"Can't say I love it, but I done enough to find it won't kill you. Same time, I might as well tell you, I like fun. I got me a fiddle." The slitted eyes questioned Fairman. "You'll stand in need of fun, time you eat a bushel of dust and your critters get sore-footed and your woman's askin' how was it you lost your mind and headed for Oregon."

"Where you from?"

"Now or then?"

"Well—both."

"Now, from Pittsburgh, Wheeling, Louisville, and p'ints between. Then, from right here in Missouri."

"This is serious business. You'd have to stay sober."

"That ain't hard. Not for me. Not to say I ain't been drunk, neither."

Fairman debated, looking the man over, from the good forehead to the squeezed face to the spare figure to the feet shod in old peg boots. He did need another man.

While he debated, Hig said, "I'm a fixer, too. Used to be a pewter tinker. I can doctor sick rifle-guns and busted wheels and all. You'll see." He waited, and when Fairman's answer didn't come at once he thrust his hands out. "Lookit! These here paws didn't get that way lyin' folded in my lap. I'm skinny but strong, like a razorback hog. I ain't askin' anything but to go along and help you and eat out of your pot."

"Well—?"

Hig had bent down to Tod. "Me and you'll make a team, young'un. We'll have us fun."

Fairman felt Tod's hand tighten in his own and looked down and saw that the boy was smiling. "My name is Tod," he told the man, "and I got a horse already."

"Tod it is," Hig said. His face lifted to Fairman's. "If it's all right with you, mister, you done hired yourself a man."

Fairman said, "Well—?" again, not wanting yet to commit himself. "I was going to look at some mules."

"I'll tail along if you don't mind."

Hig reached down and took Tod's willing hand, and Fairman thought, a little helplessly, that, sure enough, he had done hired himself a man.

The mule trader was standing by the pole fence, smoking a cigar and looking through the smoke at the animals inside. He was a puffy man with a round belly and a loose mouth that squirmed around the butt of the cigar. In his belt he carried a dirk. He said, "Figurin' to buy mules?"

"I thought I might."

"I got some the likes of which ain't often found."

Hig said, "That's Scripture, I bet."

The man looked at him sharply and went on, "You take that big bastard there." He pointed with his cigar. "He'll take you there and bring you back. Broke to saddle, pack, harness, and all. Good in a team or by hisself. And sure-footed! He can turn around in a hen's nest and never crack a egg." The man puffed at the cigar as if to restore his wind. "Tolty's the name."

"Fairman, and this is Higgins."

"Strangers, ain't you?"

"I haven't been here long."

"Me, neither," Tolty said. "Jest long enough to get set up for the Oregon trade. You bound for Oregon, I reckon? Good country, Oregon is."

Tod said, "I won't have fever any more."

"Now that's good. Fever's damn mizzable, congestive, relapsin', intermittent, bilious, or plain shakes. Now about them mules—" He walked to the fence and let down the bars of the pole gate, pausing as he did so to look at a horseman who had jogged up and sat quiet for a minute and then swung out of the saddle.

"Lookin' for mules?" Tolty asked while he held a pole in his hand.

"Just easin' home," the man answered. "Neighbor asked me to see if you had some smart ones." He took off his hat and ran his hand through a thatch of silvery hair. His movements, like his talk, were deliberate and easy, as if he had lived long enough to feel at home in the world.

"Damn right I got smart ones," Tolty said. "I'll git to you directly." He turned to Fairman. "I can let you have one or a dozen. That there big mule'll pull hisself blind if you don't watch out. Man, he's a puller."

"I just want riding stock. I'll buy oxen for the wagons."

"You ain't bought 'em, eh?"

"Not yet. I'm in the market for some cattle, too."

"Now let me tell you something," Tolty said, gesturing with the cigar. "I sell mules and oxen both, even if I ain't got ary oxen right now. And if I was goin' to Oregon, I'd go by mule."

"Why?"

"A mule's faster, smarter, quicker handled, and better all around. Nicer to sit behind, too."

"More wind, maybe, but less drizzle," Hig said, smiling his thin smile.

"An ox, now, will do his best," Tolty continued, "but when he peters out he lies down, and by God you can't get him up with a hayfork."

Tod yanked at Fairman's hand. "I want the big bastard, Father."

"That's not the way to talk, Tod."

"Beats all," Tolty said, "how they pick up things. Now whare'd he hear that, you reckon?"

Fairman asked, "How much?"

"Forty dollars each, two for seventy-five, and take your pick."

"It's enough."

"Cheap. Cheap as dirt."

Hig got into the conversation again. "Where you from, that dirt's so dear?"

Tolty only looked at him.

"And you'd take mules?" Fairman asked.

"You can ride a mule or pack 'im, which same you can't do with a ox. Come a time when you wanted to circle up against Indians, whare'd you be with a slowpoke of a ox?"

"You haven't traveled the trail?"

"No, and neither did I ever drop a shoat, but I know good bacon."

"Your advice isn't what I've been getting."

"People'll tell you anything."

The man outside the fence put a foot on a stump and dangled the bridle reins in his hand. He wasn't thin or fat, but, Fairman thought, somehow fluid with muscle. His face was lined but calm, as if it knew trouble and patience both. On impulse Fairman asked, "What do you say, sir?"

"It ain't my deal."

"Deal, anyhow, will you?"

The man addressed himself to Tolty. "How do Injuns feel about mules?"

Tolty was quick to answer. "Crazy about 'em, like everybody else. Plumb crazy about 'em."

The man nodded silently, as if he had made a point, and looked down at the reins in his hand.

Tolty's mouth opened, as if suddenly he realized he had overstepped himself but couldn't figure how he had.

"What Injun love, Injun steal," Hig said, and the man looked up, his mouth impassive but his eyes grinning.

23

Tolty faced around toward the man. "You got a goddam long nose."

"Wait!" Fairman broke in. "I asked him a question, and he answered it. You mean Indians will steal mules but not oxen?"

"Could be."

Tolty tried to stare the man away. "Leave the gentleman buy what he wants. It's none of your never-mind."

The man was quiet, flicking the reins against the palm of his hand. When he spoke again, it was still mildly. "That big mule there. Seems like he used to belong to Tom Proctor. Tom allowed he was the sure-footedest critter he ever did see."

"That's just what I been tellin' 'em."

"Yes, sir," the man went on. "Tom said that mule would look close and pick out the teeth he wanted to kick out of a man's face, and then he would let fly and never miss. Not once."

Hig said, "Now that's what I call sure-footed. If I had me a tooth, I bet he would kick it out."

"Whyn't you get the hell away?" Tolty almost shouted. "Damn if I ain't a mind to run you off." He moved toward the gate, acting full of purpose.

The man stood quiet, his foot on the stump and his hands resting on his uplifted knee. Fairman wondered whether he saw the dirk at Tolty's side. All he said was, "Take it easy, hoss."

Tolty stopped, like a dog that had run out full of noisy fury and had to brake himself at the last minute to keep from biting off more than he could chew.

The tone of grievance came into Tolty's voice. "You ain't goin' to buy nothin'. You got no honest business here."

"I reckon you're right," the man said, and took his foot from the stump and stepped back toward his horse.

"What might your name be?"

Hig answered Tolty. "It might be Old Hickory. Might be Andy Jackson himself in person."

"Dick Summers."

"Dick Summers?" Fairman repeated.

"You got it right." The man swung a leg over his horse and sat still for a minute. He took them in, Tolty with his cigar,

24

Hig, Fairman, Tod clinging to Fairman's hand. Then he swung his horse around.

Fairman wanted to call to him, to ask if he was the mountain man, to ask if he'd pilot a company to Oregon, but he stood silent as the horse jogged away, knowing only that he'd seen the second man he'd like to travel with.

Chapter - - - - - - - - - - - - - - Three

Dick Summers sat on a stump and smoked his pipe. The days were longer than before, but dusk already had settled among the trees, and in the cabin the women had struck a light, maybe more for the cheer of it than to see by. He hitched himself on the stump, knowing he ought to go and find the cow and milk her, seeing as nobody had, but he still sat and smoked, thinking he would do it after a while.

Down along the creek, where the water had leaked out into a little marsh, the frogs were tuning up. There was the smell of spring in the air, of spring full-sized and growing into summer. The dogwood and redbud had put out their flowers, and leaves waved on the poplar and wild cherry. He ought to go and milk the cow.

Far off, beyond the long plain of the Platte, along Green River or the Popo Agie and north toward the Three Forks, the trappers—or those that were left of them—would be busy, setting their traps and making their lifts and counting days till rendezvous, except that there wasn't any rendezvous any more but only Jim Bridger's fort, and it was built more for movers than mountain men.

A man moved away from the cabin and Summers saw it was his neighbor, Lije Evans, who finally had made up his mind to go to Oregon and now wanted everybody else to go. Evans asked, "Mind company?" and eased his big body to the ground and got out a green bottle and handed it to Summers. He had bought it, Summers knew, for him. They drank from it and went back to their pipes, and by and by Evans said, "She makes a real purty corpse, Dick."

Summers nodded, not speaking, letting the alcohol warm his stomach while he thought about beaver country. He had said goodbye to it once, feeling old and done in. How long ago?

Eighteen thirty-seven to eighteen forty-five. Eight years, but it seemed like forever, so sometimes he wondered if the Seeds-kee-dee ran like always and the mountains lifted blue out of the plain and buffalo bulls made thunder in their rutting time.

He had said goodbye to it and had come back to Missouri to farm, and so had bought himself a team of mules and built a cabin and married a white woman and set out to grow corn and pigs and tobacco and garden stuff, and had counted the old life as something done with except as his mind remembered it—except sometimes as his inside eye saw the sun push up over the edge of the world and make its great sweep and slide in fire behind the mountains. Under the sun he would see maybe a beaver pond and hear the smack of a tail on water, and then the riffles running and dying out and the pond lying so quiet you would think nothing lived there.

Or he would see an Indian village, and squaws with red blankets, and a young one with full breasts looking his way as much as to say yes, tonight, while he told the chief the white brother's heart was good and he spoke with one voice, and the pipe made the rounds. Or he would see friends like Jed Smith or Dave Jackson or Jim Deakins, and all of them dead now and the Grand Tetons rising lonely by Jackson Lake. And then the smell of pig manure would come to his nose, or Jack, the old mule, would bray, and he would know he was nothing any more but a grayback farmer who'd better be tending to his chores.

Evans said, "You made up your mind what to do yet, Dick?"

Summers shook his head.

"Reckon I oughtn't to ask you that. It ain't a time when you'd want to figure."

"It's all right."

"I wouldn't ask, except time is pushing. We got to know before long now."

"Uh-huh." Summers took the bottle that Evans offered and drank from it again. Up the Sweetwater and over the Southern Pass and down the Sandys to the Green he was seeing the wild goats, or antelopes as people were calling them now, and the young ones running with them, light and skittery as thistle bloom. And it came on toward night, and the sun was down and the fire of its setting dead, and the coyotes were beginning to yip on the hills and the stars to light up, and there was the good smell of aspen smoke in his nose. He ought to milk the cow.

Evans drew in a breath, as if he took notice of the smoke, too, but what he said was, "Them crab trees smell nice."

A man lost one thing and thought about others lost before. Like he thought about Jackson's Hole and the Wind Mountains and the squaws he had known, a long time ago when the blood was hot in him. Like he thought about the buffalo on the Laramie plains. Jesus Christ, so many that he had fuddled himself trying to put a figure on them! Like he thought about his old friend, White Hawk, a chief of the Shoshones. Like he thought about streams running quick and clear and the stands of white-trunked quaking asp.

"Tadlock is bound and bedamned on an answer," Evans said. "Can't say I blame him too much now, Dick."

"Why you goin', Lije? You didn't leave nothin' there."

"I told you. We got to take Oregon, Dick. I feel I got to help."

"That ain't all."

"No. I ain't been there, but I been here. I ain't satisfied just to work to keep myself up so's I can work some more. There ought to be more to livin' than that."

"I never figured you for lazy."

"Maybe I'm not. There just ain't enough range in Missouri."

Summers nodded.

"It's in the air, Dick, like the fever hangs over a swamp. Brownie wants to go and so do I, and Rebecca's willin'. What the hell? I don't care much to ask myself why. I'll just go."

Summers made as if to get up. "Got to milk the cow."

"You milk the cow! Set down!" Evans' voice went out in a bawl. "Brownie! Hey, you Brownie!"

Summers could see a figure coming from the direction of the cabin. Brownie lagged up, a boy still mostly arms and legs and neck, who probably thought he was a man but wouldn't smell like one yet. "What's it, Pa?"

"We forgot about the cow. Your mother and them other women did. Get yourself a bucket and go hunt up Dick's cow and milk her."

The boy scuffed the ground with his toe.

"Let 'im be," Summers said. "Hell, a man don't like to do women's work."

"This ain't like ordinary, Brownie," Evans said. "There ain't anyone going to make light of it at a time of death. You go on."

The boy said, "All right," in the sudden, coarse voice of the calf turning bull. The unexpected sound of it seemed to rattle him. He wheeled around and made for the cabin.

"How old's he?" Summers asked.

"Long seventeen."

"Don't hardly seem that old."

"He's been slow growing up, like weedy young'uns are. Mostly stalk so far, but he's comin' along."

"Good boy."

Summers could tell Evans was pleased.

Evans said, "It's partly for his sake I'm goin'. I'd like for him to know something besides root, hog, or die."

They drank again.

Afterwards Evans asked, "Is it such a hell-buster of a trip, Dick?"

"Easy, by foot or horse, I don't know as to wagons. I used to think a wagon couldn't travel beyond the Green much, but some have."

"I oughtn't to plague you, askin' questions," Evans said, shifting his position on the ground. "Anything I can do for you?"

"Reckon not."

People wouldn't let a man with a grief do anything for himself. They brought him meat and bread and cake—more'n he could eat in a week even if he took to fancy fixin's—and they tidied up his place and built a walnut box and dug a grave and the women laid the body out. And all of them stayed around—the men smoking and chewing and talking pigs and crops and the women talking women's talk—until the body was in the ground and the earth thrown on top. And then they might build a grave house so's to close the body away from weather and varmints.

"Tadlock's a good-enough man," Evans said. "Got more

29

learning than most. Spills over with feelin' for America. He sure-God wants to be captain of the company."

"Where'd you say he's from?"

"Illinois. Illinois-river country, but I don't figure him for a farmer. Officeholder, more likely. I seen him in town this morning. Told him not to come out, but it could be he will. He's a mule-headed man."

Summers didn't let himself answer, not being sure what to make of Tadlock. Right off, though, he didn't take to him.

After a silence Evans asked, "You want to take a look?" He bent his head toward the cabin. "The women want you should have a look."

Summers said, "Sure enough," but he didn't get up. He didn't want to get up just yet.

He felt sad and, in a way, at home with sadness. It was only the young who took on over death and disappointment, maybe because they expected more than God Almighty would ever give. In time a man took losses as they came, a man going on to fifty did, anyway, remembering old goodbyes.

That was how he was saying goodbye to his woman. She hadn't been a well woman, not ever since he'd known her, but yellow and drawn out by fever and sick to death once before, when she'd slipped the young one he had planted in her. But for all that, she had been a good woman, not smart-looking or playful or gentle on the outside, but hard-working and wishful of good things for him. Was she alive now, she would follow the cow out in the morning to find where the young wild greens were growing, and so boil him a kettle of them along with a piece of fat meat. It wasn't exactly the fever that killed her; it was just as if her strength had run out. She had taken to bed and died in two days, knowing all the time she had to die and looking at him with fever-shiny eyes—and neither of them able to say anything to each other but little, piddling things like never seen a nicer spring or wonder if Lije Evans sold his place yet so's to go to Oregon. He had seen old horses die like that. He had seen them go and lie down and give up and look at you with slow eyes while life leaked away.

A plain-looking, goodhearted woman. He thought maybe he

30

ought to feel worse at losing her, as if the way he felt wasn't fitting to her. He oughtn't to be thinking of young squaws and old days in the mountains. But he had always thought about them some, even while she was alive. Her being dead didn't make the thinking worse.

Like everything else, feelings got mixed up, so that you could be sad and know you ought to be sad, and still be kind of light-spirited, too, as he was himself. Down in him, if he didn't watch against it, he felt free again. It was as if the world had opened up. He felt free, and it was spring, and the mountains stood sharp in his mind, and he could pilot a wagon train to Oregon as well as anybody. He took himself for an old fool, but maybe it didn't hurt to think he could begin fresh, or get back what had made the young years good. He was sad, sure enough, but set up, too. Already he could feel the west wind in his face and see the cactus flowering. He was glad he didn't have to explain to anyone—to God, for instance—the way it was with him.

It had grown so dark he couldn't see the people at the cabin, except when a head moved across the lighted window. He could hear their voices, though, the throaty talk of men holding themselves in while they sat around outside the cabin with a bottle and the higher voices of women coming from inside. Down toward the barn the hogs were uneasy, making a noise like growling, which some folks would say was a sign of storm.

" 'Nother thing," Evans said. "There's a preacher takin' the night at the Tuckers'. Tucker wanted I should ask you do you want him to preach the funeral."

"I left it all to him."

"But he didn't know about this preacher. The preacher just drifted in. A Methodist, Tucker said he was."

"One's as good as another, I reckon. She would want a preacher."

"Funeral in the morning," Evans said, not asking a question but telling what he knew.

Summers nodded.

"Be best."

Summers kept on nodding.

31

"Preacher might want a piece of money, Dick. 'Course, we could sing a song and Harry Barlow could read Scripture and say a prayer, and we could let it go at that?"

"Let the preacher come, Lije. I figured Tucker would get one out of Independence, a Campbellite if he could, for that's the way his mind runs."

"I'll tell Tucker. This here preacher's bound for Oregon, or so I hear."

"That so?" Summers got off the stump. "I better see how the women done." He walked with Evans to the cabin.

The men fell silent as he passed through the sitting circle, and the women hushed and stepped aside when he entered. They looked flushed and livelier than usual. He thought, without faulting them, that there was nothing like a death to bring women to life. They spoke low or just nodded to him—all except Mrs. Evans—and he knew they were uneasy with him around, remembering maybe how full of chatter they had been or wondering what he would say. There was a joint of meat on the kitchen table, and greens, and a white-flour pie and a pan of corn bread and a pile of other stuff. Through the door to the bedroom he could make out the body in the box Lije Evans had built. The box rested on two trestles that Summers had used in his carpenter work.

"After you take a look, you come and eat," Mrs. Evans said in her strong voice. "Everybody's et, and you got to eat, regardless." She walked into the bedroom with him, a hefty, big-bosomed woman who stepped light for all her weight. In one hand she carried a slut. The weak light of it made moving shadows in the room. She held it close to the box so that he could see.

They had scrubbed Mattie and combed her hair and laid her out with her arms crossed on her chest, and she looked like death-by-fever, as Summers had known she would. For a long minute he looked down at her, hearing Mrs. Evans breathe by his side and feeling the women waiting for his words. He saw the new dress they'd bought and saw the hands worn and ingrained with dirt in spite of scrubbing and the color of old fever on the brow and cheeks. The hair, now that he came to

32

look at it, was whiter than he remembered. He wouldn't see her any more, dyeing homespun with bark or copperas or indigo, or sewing, or making candles, or mashing flint corn for starch, or looking at the sun mark on the kitchen floor to tell what time it was. All that was left was the still, shrunk body, and come morning it would be gone, too, and it would be like Mattie never lived except as he remembered her.

She had been his woman. She had shared his bed and kept his house and done her full share and more of the work and been a good if not exciting wife in all ways, and he ought not to be wanting to get away from what was left of her, from the yellowed skin and sunken eyes and the sober-sided look she always wore.

He waited another minute, not touching her and not wanting to, and then he turned around, nodding slow. "I'm obliged, a heap obliged," he said to the women as he stepped back into the kitchen. "Don't see how anyone could do it nicer."

"She does look natural, don't she?" Mrs. Evans said. "We been saying how natural she looks. You come and eat now."

Lije Evans poked his head inside. "That there preacher dropped by, Dick, and Tadlock, too. You want to talk to the preacher?"

"No need for talk, I reckon," Summers said, but while he was saying it the preacher stepped in. He was tall and old and lean-looking, and hollow at the temples, and his face showed weather and worry over sinning. He had slicked himself up and put on a black coat that didn't go with the faded jeans cloth of his breeches. He held his hand out. His voice was old, too, and cracked—cracked maybe, Summers thought, from calling on sinners to come to Jesus.

"The Lord giveth and the Lord taketh away."

Summers took the hand without speaking.

"My name is Weatherby, Joseph Weatherby, Brother Summers. I come from Indiany."

"That's all right."

The cracked voice said, "I feel that the Lord has guided me here, to this house of grief."

The words rolled out of his mouth, full-shaped and extra-

33

ripe, as if being offered to the Lord. "Do not grieve. God works in mysterious ways."

At another time, Summers would have had to smile to himself. Preachers and medicine men—they were cut from the same cloth. They made out to know what nobody could. Companyeros to the Great Spirit. But he didn't smile now. He just looked into the faded blue eyes and the old face, and knew it for a fact that Weatherby believed what he said.

"Brother Tucker tells me you would like for me to conduct the service."

"That's neighborly."

"Do you have a favorite psalm or text? Or did she?"

"Not as I remember."

"I will read from Ephesians then."

"You pick it out."

The bony head bobbed, then lifted to say, "They tell me you may pilot a party to Oregon?"

"Might be."

"I want to go. I feel the Lord is calling me to the new land, perhaps to bring His blessings to the heathen."

"It's a long piece, for them as ain't young or used to it."

"I put my faith in Him."

"You won't have any trouble findin' a company. There's plenty aim to go, from Independence and St. Joe."

"What about yours?"

"It ain't mine, even if I go. Companies make their own rules. I reckon they'd be glad to have you."

Mrs. Evans tugged at Summers' arm. "Come and eat."

"Maybe I better see Tadlock," he answered. "I'll be back in a shake."

Tadlock was standing just outside the door. "We'd like to talk to you a minute, if you'll forgive us for coming at this time."

"Who is it?" Summers asked, as if he didn't know.

"Several of us, representing the society."

Mrs. Evans' voice floated out the door. "I declare! You ought to give a man time to eat."

Tadlock led the way over to the big oak that shaded the

34

cabin at noon, or that would shade it when it got its leaves out. There were four other men there, counting Lije Evans, who spoke up to say, "This ain't my idea, Dick."

Tadlock said, "Someone has to take responsibility." He stood solid on his feet. His face turned from Evans to Summers. "This isn't pleasant, let me tell you. But it was a month ago, almost, that we asked you, and you didn't quite say yes or no, and now, as we see it, you have no particular reason to stay on here. Time is running short. We have to have an answer. We want to be first on the way. Are you going to pilot us or not? If not, we must find another man."

"Maybe you better be lookin' around."

"As I said, we want to be first out, so we don't have to eat the dirt of trains ahead of us, so that we'll have grazing for our stock."

"Good idea," Summers said.

Evans put in, "We'd rather have you, Dick."

"It's just that we can't fool around," Tadlock said. There was something about him, about his stand and his talk, that put Summers a little in mind of a man daring you to spit in his face.

"Do what you please," Summers answered.

He turned and made for the cabin, thinking over what he had said, thinking it wouldn't have made any difference if he had told them now. It was just that Tadlock graveled him—and perhaps for no good reason at all except his outside manner. A man didn't like to be pushed.

Summers already knew well enough what his answer was. He wished the funeral was over. He would sell out, except for the land itself, which he might have to come back to, and except for the critters he would need. He would saw open the big log where he had cached his beaver, banks being what they were. He would saw open the log that he had bored into and put his money in and sealed with a peg sawed flush. It wouldn't take him long to get ready.

The breeze that fanned his face might have swept down out of the far mountains, across the long roll of the plains, from places realer to him still than the ground he walked on.

Chapter - - - - - - - - - - - - - Four

T HE WAGON, backed up to the back door, was nearly full, but not so full it wouldn't take what was left in the house. The pots and pans had been boxed and loaded, the bedding rolled up, the good dishes, such as they were, buried safe in the barreled flour, the clothing packed away, the few pieces of furniture they would try to take along mostly stowed beneath the wagon cover.

There wasn't much to do, not much before they closed the door and rolled away and left the Evans home to be somebody else's. Doing the last-minute things, finding a forgotten towel or stirring spoon, sweeping up so's to leave the cabin tidy, Rebecca Evans tried to match the cheerful hurry of the men. They had got the second wagon loaded, with bought food, plows and harness, the grinding stone and anvil, tools, the heavy stuff that Lije thought might be scarce in Oregon. Afterwards they'd tramped from the barn to start emptying out the house, Brownie asking, "What's next, Ma? What's next?" Lije saying, "It don't matter much now how we load. We'll straighten up at rendezvous."

It was like men, she thought, to be excited and not to feel with their excitement such a sadness as a woman did at saying goodbye to home. To a woman a house long-lived-in remembered the touch of hands and the tread of feet and the sound of voices speaking low at night. It remembered deaths and bornings and the young, gay talk of people newly married.

"You can take the walnut chest," she said and watched Lije and Brownie heave it up and saw the torn emptiness it left.

Each stick and splinter of this place was built by Lije, each little touch of prettiness put there by her or him. Everything had something of them in it. They had come here young and sure and seen the years pass and known trouble and happiness.

It was, she thought again as she worked her broom, as if the house had shared their times and feelings, as if, quiet in the walls, sad in the empty rooms, was the memory of their doings, was the dread of strangers coming.

Outside, her menfolks talked, thinking out loud how to place things in the wagon. Lije's voice came to her strong, full of a sort of forward feeling she hadn't heard in years. And so it was all right, she told herself. The moving was all right, hard as it was. Oregon was all right. What Lije needed—and what Brownie would need later—was a better chance than in Missouri. What he needed was a dare. What he needed was to find out what he amounted to. A slow-going, extra-easy-tempered man, said people, not understanding it was his self-belittlement that made him so, not knowing that, without it, there wasn't much he couldn't do. That was one thing she was sure of. Except for giving up the house she could be almost glad that Lije had got one of his rare and sudden notions and signed up for Oregon.

She swept the dirt out the door and took off her dustcloth. Everything was in the wagon. Everything. Nothing in the house but space, space and the broom and the flecks of dust she'd raised and the unspoken loneliness.

"Old Rock's ready, Ma. How about you?" Brownie's voice echoed in the dead rooms, in the room where he'd been born, where he'd lain as a baby in the cherry cradle Lije had built.

Lije walked from the wagon and came in and had a look around. "Seems you got everything, 'less you want to load up the house, too."

"Wish I could."

"Me, too, Becky," he said and patted her shoulder and went back out, asking, "Ready?" on the way.

"Soon's I get this poke bonnet on." She stepped outside, into the unbearable bright cheeriness of the early sun.

"Pa says I can herd the loose critters along, and him and you'll poke the teams," Brownie told her.

She said, "All right," and added, "Wait a shake," and turned back in, for it occurred to her, as if she had been slighting and forgetful of one who's served them well, that she hadn't taken the last long look that would be her goodbye. For a long minute or two she breathed the deserted air and in imagination put back into their places the fittings that had been torn away.

"Hurry up, Ma!"

She lifted her head and walked out, making sure the latch they'd used so many times was closed behind her.

L IJE EVANS had been to some powerful stump speakings and to revivals where people got the shakes and hollered in the unknown tongue. He was reminded of them now, here at what was called rendezvous, where officers would be elected and outfits inspected and things made ready for the march. The racket of it filled the ear, women clacking, men yelling at mules and oxen and talking in little groups, young ones shouting, dogs barking, and every once in a while a mule braying or a cow bawling. The eye couldn't rest. People were staking down tents and driving cattle out to pasture and reloading wagons, having found, driving from Independence or Westport, that their plunder wasn't arranged right. Children ran among the white-topped wagons and tripped over tent pegs and sprawled in the dusty grass, and now and then a new wagon, splash-marked by the Missouri Blue, would jolt up from town, and women and young ones would blossom out of it, and the men would get busy unyoking the critters.

Off a piece Brother Weatherby was moving among the people, stopping when he could get someone to listen, his shoulders stooped in their tow-linen shirt, his old face solemn with the weight of what he knew. Evans caught echoes of the rusty voice, which was likely setting things up for a preaching tonight, for Weatherby's Methodist argument on "One Lord, one faith, one baptism." Brother Weatherby loved to exhort, as he called it. A mule slowing the train while it stopped to lift its tail was almost enough to make him cut loose. After exhorting, he would get the hat passed. "Remember, the Lord loveth a cheerful giver." Evans imagined that was one of the reasons he preached so often; he didn't have anything. But if you put it up to him that he preached for money, just like a man farmed or traded or kept store, probably he would say he needed the

39

money to do the work of the Lord. Maybe he did. You couldn't listen to him and doubt he believed God had singled him out to spread the Word.

Evans stood with his foot on the wagon tongue and watched and listened. A bitch in heat went by, trailed by all the dogs in camp, including old Rock, and they all lifted their legs, one by one, at a little hazel bush and trotted on, each hoping, even the littlest, that the Lord had singled him out, too.

Like Brother Weatherby, Tadlock, the politician, was making the rounds, though no one stood for election against him. He was an important talker and he carried an Oregon guidebook with him to show he knew more than anybody, except maybe Dick Summers, about the way to get west.

Somewhere off where Evans couldn't see, a man was cussing a mule or an ox. Evans saw Weatherby hold up and listen and knew he was thinking about the wickedness of swearing.

While the sun sailed quiet in the sky and the little winds ran in whispers in the grass, the voices of the camp rose harsh, like the voices of excited geese. Though they were only twenty miles or so west of Independence and hadn't seen an Indian except for some Shawnees and some scabby Kaws that a Missouri man might see any day, already a few people were afraid, as if they had cut loose from all safety and faced enemies the like of which no one of them had ever known. There was Mrs. Turley, who was all holler and no heart, who kept talking and looking around as if she expected the biggest Indian ever born to show up swinging a hatchet; and Mrs. McBee, a sharp-tongued snipe of a woman who wanted to go back to Ohio; and McBee himself, talking big to hide his littleness. And there were others—Evans wouldn't know how many—with worry on their faces and fear in their stomachs while they thought ahead to the Platte and the Pawnees and the Black Hills and the Sioux.

Rebecca sat in the shade of the wagon, fanning herself with a pie plate for lack of something better, for though April wasn't gone, the sun was hot. Brownie was out watching the cattle, along with the man, Hig, that Fairman had hired, and a bunch of others, mostly young men without families. You couldn't tell when a Kaw would take it into his head to make off with

40

a horse or a cow, though they were a chicken-gutted lot and not knee-high in any way, so Dick Summers said, to tribes like the Pawnees and Snakes and Blackfeet. Still, you didn't want them stealing your stock.

Evans watched Rebecca, and by and by, just to make conversation, he said, "I don't hardly feel like we've started yet. Way most of 'em act, you'd think we was bushed in the mountains some place." Rebecca kept on fanning herself. "I could light out now afoot and be to the old place almost in time to do the chores."

It seemed strange to him, come to think of it, that he called the farm the old place. He had just left it, just shook the hand of the man who had paid him four hundred dollars cash money for his quarter section. He had just driven away, seeing the patch of flax greening and the leaves of the young tobacco fleshing out in their bed. He had taken a last look at the corn-field, where the first frail spears would soon push up, and at the cabin where he and Rebecca had come really to know each other and where Brownie was born. And now in his mind it was the old place, and he felt a little sad at leaving it, as if a part of him and Rebecca and Brownie had been left forever behind. Give him a little time, though, get him across the Kaw and up the Little Blue to the Platte, and he would be all right. Already, seeing the hills and woods opening, he could imagine how it would be along the great, free desert of the Platte. Oregon and the new way of things. Oregon for America, you damn bet! He and others would take Oregon by occupation, and what could the British do then? He felt almost like an old-time Oregon man himself.

"Feelin' better, Becky?" he asked. "About goin'?"

She let him have a little smile. Her face looked hot but not tearful now. She had cried for a minute when they left the old place, and then had set her face west and not looked back. Evans had an uneasy feeling that he couldn't realize, ever, what it was to a woman to give up her home. They were finer drawn than men, women were, mixed more in their thinking, so that you couldn't tell what went on in their heads. A woman might hate moving because of leaving her marigolds.

Yet he understood Rebecca, too, in ways; she would make the trip, and no complaining, either, and her talk cheerful and her clever hands doing what was to be done.

"I'm all right, Lije," she answered. "Hot, is all. Why you ask? Changed your mind?"

"Not me. Anyone at all gets to Oregon, it'll be you and me." Her voice was soft. "You're the biggest fool, Lije."

He knew what she meant. She meant it still struck her queer that he should bow his neck for Oregon and feel better all the time for doing it. Well, it was queer. An old plug didn't often prance.

She said, "Hello, there, Dick," and Evans saw that Dick Summers was strolling up. In the old buckskin breeches and red-checked shirt he had put on, Dick was something. Tall, silver-haired, strong-looking in arm and leg and body, he was a man to catch the eye, different from anyone Evans knew, different from those who traveled the Santa Fe trail, from the Mexicans who dressed to show off. There wasn't any show-off in Dick. He was just himself.

"I'd think you'd melt to a grease spot," Rebecca said, looking at the buckskins.

"I reckon I got ahead of myself, sure enough."

She said, "It's the sun got ahead of itself, Dick."

"Hell of a mess," Evans put in, making a wide sweep of his hand, to the wagons, tents, people, talk, horses, oxen, everything. "Some'll be turnin' back."

Summers put tobacco in his pipe. "It'll straighten out, likely."

"Tadlock's the big toad," Evans said.

"Looks so. Got such a start nobody else'll stand."

"Maybe he'll make a good-enough captain?"

Summers nodded as if he didn't quite agree. "Have to keep a tight line on him." He pulled on his pipe while his keen gray eyes went over the layout.

"Wants to kill all the dogs, down to my old Rock."

Summers went on smoking.

"That's what I hear on the quiet, anyhow. He won't come out for it open, I don't guess. Might cost him votes." Evans put his words so as to be questions. "They say dogs can't make it anyhow? Say they'd give us away to the Injuns?"

Summers looked at Rebecca, the faint tracks of a smile on his face. "They make good meat if food runs out."

"Ah-h!"

"The Sioux eat pup, and I've chewed a few. Taste like hog meat."

"Sure enough, Dick," Evans asked, "you think we ought to kill the dogs?"

"Be hell to pay."

"I know, but you think we ought?"

"Dog can go where a cow can."

"I hadn't thought of that."

"And they won't give us away any more'n they'll put us on guard." Summers was silent for a minute. "Mighty hard thing to sneak into an Injun camp, on account of the dogs."

"Tadlock wouldn't know about that. We got to ejicate him." Evans got out his own pipe. He was filling it when the horn sounded high and strong above the clatter, calling the men to the election.

Evans and Summers walked toward the center of the camp, where the men were gathering. On the way, Evans saw the file of dogs again. A little boy, cotton-topped and thin, was following them. Evans heard a voice call, "Toddie! Come here, Tod." The voice belonged to Mrs. Fairman, a long-legged, well-turned girl with light hair and eyes as pale as pond water. She walked out and got the boy by the hand.

Nearly everybody in camp collected for the election, the men standing in front, chewing and spitting, and the women behind and the young ones open-eared on the fringes. Because he had been chosen temporary captain—or commandant captain, he called it—Tadlock brought the meeting to order. He stepped up on a wooden bucket and beat a spoon against a tin plate to get silence. When the talk had toned down some, he pitched into his speech, standing square on the bucket. Everything about him was square, Evans thought—square face, square body, square way of standing. Evans wondered if he was square inside, too, while he admitted to himself that Tadlock made a

43

figure, the teeth showing white, the face tanned on the cheek-bones and blue-black at the jaw with the roots of beard, the eyes bold, the arms moving easy. He might be an all-right man. It bothered Evans to think maybe he wasn't. He didn't like to think bad of folks.

Tadlock was saying, "Our company, I have reason to believe, will be the first out anywhere. The St. Joe trains, we hear, won't roll for several days. So it appears we'll be the trail blazers—and also escape the dust of the desert, find grass for our animals, and arrive first at the Willamette."

Some of the men yelled at his words, and he closed his mouth, giving them time for their hurrahs. When they were finished, someone kept shouting, "Chairman! Mr. Chairman!"

It was Brother Weatherby, crowding through toward the bucket. The old preacher had put on his rusty coat, though he must have been hot in it. The cracked voice rose: "We had no prayer. We didn't open with prayer."

Back of Weatherby someone said, "Sit down! Christ sake!" and another voice answered, "I kin remember my pap braggin' Sunday'd never cross the Mississippi." Other men were muttering or just grinning, but the women, Evans noticed when he looked around, mostly were nodding their heads, thinking Weatherby was right.

Tadlock wasn't fazed at all. He said, "I'm sorry, Brother Weatherby. It was an oversight. Will you lead us in prayer?" He bent his head.

Weatherby bent his head, too, and by and by raised his arms. He asked God to be merciful to poor sinners. He said they knew the way was long and dangerous, but they put their trust in Him. . . . We pray Thee to protect us against the elements and against the heathen and the wild beasts, and against sickness and accidents, and to give us strength for the journey and to make our hearts stout, whatever may come to pass. . . . And make us grateful, too, O Lord, for all Thy blessings and lead us to know Thy glory and make the sinner to repent and the swearer to see his wickedness and the man and woman in adultery to understand their sin and do it no more. . . . We pray Thee to breathe the influence of Thy spirit on us and make us

44

all Christians. . . . God bless the little children whom Jesus said let come unto Him. . . . And may the storm hold back its fury as the wind is tempered to the shorn lamb, and may the earth give up its abundance. . . . Make us to fear Thee and to sing Thy eternal praise. . . . Amen. Amen.

What with one thing and another, Weatherby took a long time talking to God, time enough for an ant to crawl from the toe of Dick Summers' moccasin a distance of two ax handles, not counting the backings up and the side trips along spears of grass. Evans sneaked a look at Summers while the preaching was going on and saw his head hardly bowed and his eyes empty with distance. He wondered whether Summers believed in God at all. Not that it made any difference. Any God worth praying to would know Dick Summers for a good man, even if he didn't bow and scrape and make little of himself and beg for blessings regardless. Evans didn't guess Summers ever would beg for anything, not even from God.

When Weatherby was through, Tadlock said, "We have rules to adopt and a permanent organization to set up."

Another voice was yelling at him. Tadlock tried to drown it out and then to hush it with his hand, but it kept piping up. Finally Tadlock asked, "What is it, Turley?"

Evans moved around so as to see Turley. Turley had joined the company late, from the hill and pine country of the Meramec. The words came high-pitched from his thin mouth. " 'Pears to me the first thing is to think again, do we want to go on or wait for some that ain't quite ready? This here's a small train. Ain't enough growed men in it, to my way o' thinkin'. Where we be, meetin' the Pawnees or Sioux? There's a passel of people comin', like we all know, hunderds of 'em. Doc Welch of Indiany said we could j'in him. Told me so his-self. I say let's wait. Be a hunderd wagons along directly."

Hoots and hollers arose all around, more hoots than hollers.

"Quiet! Order!" Tadlock roared, beating on the plate. His voice sharpened as the noise died. "This has all been thrashed out. Anyone who joined this company knew we planned to start early—to get there first. Our company's big enough. Twenty-two wagons, nearly thirty armed men." His arm came out, pointing. "Ask Dick Summers there. He knows. He'll tell you a company can be too big, so big that it's slow and hard to manage." He looked at Turley. "Anyone who's afraid can wait. We're going on. That's settled."

Turley shuffled while more voices sounded out. Evans imagined it was Mrs. Turley who had egged him on.

Tadlock was all business. "Is the committee ready to report?" he asked as if he didn't know.

Mack answered, "It is," and stepped forward with the wrinkles of thinking on his face and said, "Your committee recommends that Irvine Tadlock be elected captain and Charles Fairman lieutenant, and Henry Shields captain of the livestock guard, each to serve to the end of the trail."

An Illinois German named Brewer made a motion to accept the report, and Hank McBee, speaking loud out of his mangy beard, seconded the motion.

Tadlock made as if to step down from the bucket, saying, "Will someone preside? It isn't right for me to," but the voices went up in yells of "Yes" and "Keep the stump" and "Whoa, there," and Tadlock put his foot back on the bucket and asked, "Well, if it's unanimous?" He got more yells for an answer.

"Thank you. Thank you all. I'll do my very best. Is there a further report then?"

There was. Mack read it off. Evans, listening with just half his mind, heard it in snatches. . . . Recommend the train be called the On-to-Oregon Outfit. . . . Recommend a governing council of six be elected. . . . Recommend tax to pay expenses, including two hundred dollars for the pilot. . . . Recommend no ardent spirits be taken, except for medical purposes. . . . Require wagons be capable of carrying a quarter more than their load, teams of drawing a quarter more. . . . Death for murder. . . . Thirty-nine lashes for three days for rape. . . . Thirty-nine lashes on the bare back for adultery and fornication (big-sounding words for something simple). . . . Council to fix penalty for indecent language. . . . Recommend train start at seven o'clock every morning and travel from ten to fifteen miles every day. . . .

A long list, that made Summers snort once. Evans' attention

46

strayed off, to Mack, to Fairman, to McBee, to Brewer, and off to one side, beyond the men, to the girl, Mercy McBee, who wore a red poke bonnet and stood, her eyes fluid above the pale planes of her cheeks, like a young doe that had heard a noise. Sadness in the face, or maybe only emptiness. A look to squeeze a man inside. In animals you knew what you'd get, crossing scrubs. Question was, did the scrubs cross or a good stud get in the pasture? More likely she was scrub, too, underneath. Thirty-nine lashes for fornication. That was a warning, aimed mostly by the married men at the single ones who'd been engaged to help out on the trip.

Brother Weatherby was wanting to add to the list, asking that the company go "on the moral code written by God in the breast of every man."

A little smile was on Tadlock's face. He knew better than to laugh, but he knew to smile, too, letting on it was best, if a little overdone, to give the preacher man some rope.

The man back of Evans muttered, "Make the old fool shut up. Wants to make the rules, and him without a pot to piss in."

Mack read some more. . . . Require provisions in the following amounts . . . two hundred pounds of flour per person, except for infants . . . seventy-five pounds of meal . . . fifty pounds of bacon. . . . Name three inspectors, to look over wagons and supplies. . . . Move report be adopted. . . . Aye. . . .

The voice at Evans' back said, "That'll fix the preacher."

It occurred to Evans that the rules didn't go far enough yet. Nothing had been said about cattle and how many head to a driver. Some men, like Tadlock himself, had a big bunch of loose cattle and some had no more than their teams and a milk cow or two. It wasn't fair, expecting each man to take turn about when some had more than others. He had a notion to speak up, when Tadlock said, "Many things will have to be worked out as we go along. If we have trouble, the council can settle it. The thing now is immediate organization, so that we can make a start."

The words were fair, and Evans found himself feeling a little guilty. There wasn't any cause to doubt Tadlock, once you got used to his way. He was a man who liked to take things in

47

hand—and there wasn't anything wrong with that. Like Tadlock had told Summers the night before the funeral, someone had to take responsibility. Tadlock was all right, except for his fool idea about dogs. Nobody had said anything about dogs yet.

"Any more business?"

It came then. McBee moved that the dogs be left behind or killed. Hearing him, seeing the words shaped by a mouth bushed around like a terrier's, Evans knew McBee had been put up to it. And he knew, too, of a sudden, that McBee always would side with the top dog. Let Tadlock be upset, and you'd find McBee honey-fuggling the upsetters.

Was there a second?

Again it was Brewer, the Illinois man, the German, who spoke. Dogs couldn't travel all dey vay to Oregon. Dogs vould be signal to Indians, yah. Second da motion.

Tongues all around were wagging. Yes. No. No. Yes. By God, I'd like to see anyone kill my dog! Reckon the fool German never heard of a watchdog. Who in hell wants a dog?

Tadlock beat on the pan. "Let's thrash this out."

A half dozen people spoke, one after another, trying to lift their voices above the arguments that were going on all around —McBee, Fairman, Brewer again, a Yankee named Patch, Evans himself. McBee said, 'y God yes, shoot the dogs. They weren't no real good to nobody. Just made more mess to step in. Fairman said let each man do as he pleased, it wasn't a thing for company action.

Evans shouted, "Ask Dick Summers! Ask Dick! He knows more'n anyone."

More beating on the pan. "All right, Summers. Speak up!"

Summers seemed a little uneasy, talking to a crowd. He hitched his leather breeches. "It don't make a heap of difference. Some dogs'll get through; some maybe won't. Anyhow, a dead dog's no loss but to the man that owns him."

By grab, that was so, Evans thought. People argued a dog couldn't make the trip and everyone took that as a good reason, like they took other talk, until a man like Dick showed it didn't hold water.

48

Summers went on, "Dogs'll tell the camp about Injuns just as quick, and maybe quicker, than they'll give us away. Me, I don't look for Injun trouble anyhow, except for beggin' and a little stealin'. Injuns ain't likely to light into a party as big as this one, not the Injuns we'll come up against."

Tadlock ran his hand along his jaw while the talk broke out again. After a little while he tapped on the plate. "I'm thinking more just of the bother of dogs," he said. "They're a nuisance. They'll slow up the train. They'll be underfoot in the mornings, and they'll get hurt and lost and cause delay, I'm afraid. At any rate, let's vote."

You couldn't be sure, by voices, which side had won, but after Tadlock had called for a show of hands and counted them careful, he said the motion had carried. He didn't push it further, though. He didn't say who was to do the killing and when. Evans figured he would have some business with the man who came to shoot Rock. The prospect troubled him. He liked things peaceful.

While he was thinking about it, Tadlock went on with the election of a council and the naming of inspectors. It was a little to Evans' surprise that he found himself on both lists. The crowd elected him to the council, and Tadlock named him an inspector. When he had had time to reckon, though, it was natural enough. What Tadlock aimed at was to work everyone over to his side. By one thing and another, he figured to get the most of them in the same bed with him.

Well, anyhow, the business was about done. Evans looked around and saw that Brownie had ridden up on his mule, and then he glanced back to the stretch of prairie where the animals grazed and saw the mules and horses hobbled or pinned out and the oxen resting safe, and he knew, as he knew all along, that Brownie could be depended on.

His gaze came back to Brownie. The boy was sitting his mule quiet, his eyes fixed, on his young face an unhidden, troubled, hankering look, as if he stood alone and saw now and for the first time all it was a man might hope for. Before he turned his head, Evans knew what Brownie saw. It was the girl, Mercy McBee, with her sad, watching face and her red poke bonnet

49

and the two little hills of her breasts showing against her linsey-woolsey.

For a long minute Evans stared at her, and then back at his boy. They were about of an age, the only two, as luck would have it, who looked like seventeen. The look on Brownie's face was like the look on the man Mack's, when first he'd seen the girl. It was like it, and still far different, being gentle and young and unknowing, not thinking of bed alone and maybe not at all, but of tenderness and beauty and happiness, so much of it the heart flowed over.

Evans turned away. Damned if he wasn't building things in his mind, out of nothing, you might say, out of his own feelings of long ago. But good God! Scrub stock. Marry into scrub stock, and it was all right! Call Hank McBee pappy and Mrs. McBee ma and have 'em on your hands all your life and everything was fine. But they whipped you for fornication. Thirty-nine lashes.

Chapter - - - - - - - - - - - - - *Six*

Dick Summers thought lazily that these were different from mountain men. These couldn't enjoy life as it rolled by; they wanted to make something out of it, as if they could take it and shape it to their way if only they worked and figured hard enough. They didn't talk beaver and whisky and squaws or let themselves soak in the weather; they talked crops and water power and business and maybe didn't even notice the sun or the pale green of new leaves except as something along the way to whatever it was they wanted to be and to have. Later they might look back, some of them might, and wonder how it happened that things had slid by them. They would remember, maybe, a morning and the camp smoke rising and the sun rolling up in the early mist and the air sharp and heady as a drink, and they would hanker back for the day and wish they had got the good out of it. But, hell, a man looking back felt the same, regardless. There wasn't any way to whip time.

Off a piece from camp, where there wasn't so much racket, Summers sat cross-legged on the ground and fiddled in the dust with a stick. If he looked, he caught sight now and then of Evans and the other inspectors making their rounds, seeing everything was proper and according to rule. Some of the women already were getting supper. Those that didn't have stoves had made their fires too big and kept wiping smoke tears from their eyes while they tried to settle their cookalls in the flames. The heat had gone out of the sun now, and the critters had got up and were grazing on the slope. The camp was quieter, the young ones being hungry and played-out and the men busy for the morning start and the women separated at their fires. Off toward the trees a whippoorwill cried.

Somehow the whippoorwill brought Mattie to mind, Mattie lying cold under the dirt, the last goodbye said and nothing before her but the long sleep, though Brother Weatherby thought different. In his funeral sermon Weatherby had opened the gates of heaven and got the soul inside, safe in God's love, and it was pretty to think so, seeing rest ahead and the quiet heart forever. What was it Weatherby had read? "Grace be to you, and peace, from God our Father, and from the Lord Jesus Christ." Weatherby said the words came from Ephesians. He was a great one for Ephesians.

For Mattie's sake Summers hoped Weatherby knew what he was talking about. She had a right to rest and to be shut of fevers and torments. But things dying jarred against prettiness. Things died ugly, seeping blood and matter, as gut-shot Indians died, or they shrank down to nothing but skull and ribs, as Mattie had. Let not your heart be troubled.

Summers didn't guess his heart was as troubled as some. There wasn't any bur under his tail. He was a mountain man, or he had been, and traveled with hunters who never gave thought to soil and timber and tricks to pile up money but went along day by day taking what came, each morning being good in itself, and tomorrow was time enough to think about tomorrow. That was how Summers felt yet, but the movers were different. They traveled to get some place, as they lived life. Chances were they couldn't enjoy a woman and a bed for thinking what they had to do next. They argued. Would prairie grow a crop? Hell, land that won't grow a tree won't grow nothin'. Thing to do is to make deadenin's, like always, and cut your trees and plant among the stumps. In his mind's eye Summers could see them, ahead along the Bear or the Boise, pinching the soil, smelling it, tasting it, while the young ones played around them. They were family men, settled with their women and easy with their children, the hard edges worn smooth, the wildness in them broke to harness. They looked ahead to farms and schools and government, to an ordered round of living.

Like Lije Evans, who was coming up to Summers now, his feet setting themselves sure in the dusty grass, a half-smile on his face, and Rock, his old dog, following at his heels. Like Lije talking about the country, the United States of America, spreading from one ocean to the other. The thought had grown big in Lije. No reason, he said, just to give Oregon to the British. His pappy had fought the British, while the damn Yankees were tucking their tails and making as if to pull off from the other states, and he would fight them himself if he had to.

Not that Lije was such a fighting man, being too friendly, too self-littling, as big and powerful men sometimes were, as if feeling guilty because they had the best of it in size. What he aimed at was to get the country settled by Americans and so make it American. And not that Lije was like the others, either. He didn't fret or wish for time to pass so as to get him to a place that, after all, was just that much closer to the grave. As much as for anything, Summers imagined, as much even as for what they called patriotism, Lije was going west for the fun of it, as Summers was himself. The tameness in Lije had still proved wild enough to make him breach a fence and head for other pastures. That was the best reason of all. It was a slim chance that people would find themselves better off once they'd staked off land in Oregon.

Evans was looking at Summers' little pile of plunder. There wasn't much there, not near enough by the rules—a blanket and an old buffalo robe that covered just a teensy keg of whisky, a little bit of meal, about a shirttail full of it, and salt meat and coffee and tobacco and a kettle and a couple of knives and two rifles, his Hawken and an over-and-under double barrel with one bore big enough for bird shot. He had a little of Indian goods, too, blue and white beads and fishhooks and tobacco and a roll of scarlet strouding and some vermilion. All of his plunder put together wasn't more than a couple of pack horses could carry easy. Even so, it was more than he needed. He could travel from hell to breakfast with no more than a gun and a horse, and would get there in time for dinner without the horse.

"It ain't much, Lije," he said.

"No?"

"Don't need much."

"Not you, I reckon."

"Never saw folks with so much plunder. It ain't the way we used to travel."

"Things are different."

"I traveled many a mile, and nothin' to eat except what powder and ball would catch."

Summers could see that Evans was bothered a little underneath, caught between friendliness and plain sense on one side and the rules he was supposed to see to on the other. That was a thing Summers liked about Evans—what he felt was worth doing he wanted to do right. He was a man to tie to. This was a fool thing now, though.

Evans lifted the robe, bringing the keg of whisky to sight.

Summers said, "Rules are all right, only I don't guess they fit me. Can't you just forget me, Lije?"

Evans nodded, his mind of a sudden made up, and gave Summers a slow grin. "I ain't going to torment myself about you, Dick. You're plumb growed up. There's a sight of vinegar in that there keg, though. Here, Rock, damn you. Don't sneak off."

"I'm a vinegar man. Might be you'll be needing some."

"Might be. Good vinegar?"

"Better'n apple. I always say corn's better'n apple."

A rifle shot sounded from the other side of the camp, where they couldn't see.

Evans looked down at Rock. "It's that damn McBee startin' out, likely," he said. "He's the dog killer. Feels big about it."

"What you aim to do?"

"All I know is, he ain't goin' to shoot Rock. Lie down, boy!" He rubbed his jaw with his knuckles. "Them McBees didn't have nigh enough food and such."

"Then McBee ain't a proper one of the party."

Evans shook his head. "Tadlock filled in, and Mack a little, so they wouldn't have to turn back. Didn't have any money, either, Dick. Couldn't pay the tax. That'll cost you, I reckon."

"It don't matter. What for did Mack and Tadlock help out?"

Evans shrugged. "McBee, I bet he's a sloper, and we got a rule against slopers. Bet he owes more'n you could count."

"No way of findin' out, short of sending a man to Ohio."

"No. He says he's all clear."

"Smart-lookin' girl he's got."

"Too damn smart."

"Botherin' you?"

54

"Naw. Women don't bother me."

The rifle sounded again, and now they could see McBee, the smoking gun in his hand and out from him, away from camp, a black dog broken in the back. The dog began to howl, the high, steady howl of deadly hurt. He scrambled in the grass, trying to get up, trying to ease himself, while the howl thinned high like a whistle. McBee strode toward the dog, picking up a club as he went, and the dog turned, as if expecting help, and got the butt of the club on his skull. A boy ran out, crying, and a woman after him. The woman cried out at McBee while the boy bent over his dog, and McBee said something and turned away, toward Evans and Summers, as if his business was too important for him to listen.

Rock rose on his forelegs. "Lie down, boy!"

McBee stopped to charge his rifle and saw them and walked over, his face solemn as an owl in its beard. "You got to get rid of that there dog," he said to Evans, "else I'll have to shoot 'im."

"You ain't goin' to shoot my dog, McBee."

"It's rules."

"Rules be damned!"

"I'm app'inted to carry 'em out. Get shet of the dog or I'll have to kill 'im."

Evans was a slow man to act. He hadn't angered often enough, Summers thought, to know how to answer to anger. He hunted around for words. "You kill my dog, McBee, and you'll pay for it."

McBee spit in the grass. "There ain't any gettin' around the rules."

"I'll draw off from this here company and take them that have dogs with me. Tell Tadlock that."

Give some men a rifle and a piece of power, Summers thought, and they got too studdish to put up with. "Tell him yourself," McBee answered. "I got a job to do."

"I told you. Not Rock."

Evans stood big beside McBee, though he let himself sag a little, as if ashamed he had more height and heft. An oversized, mild, troubled man, who feared he might do wrong.

"Lije," Summers asked, "whyn't you cut him down to size?"

"I ought to, I guess."

What Evans didn't understand was that McBee might be dangerous now he had a rifle in his hand and importance in his chest.

Summers got off the ground. "I swear, McBee," he said, "I don't know why someone ain't kilt you!"

McBee hitched his rifle up, his eyes rounder than before. "It's rules. 'Y God, I got my duty to do."

"Tell Tadlock," Evans said.

Summers caught a twitch in McBee's face. He saw the muzzle of the rifle, not quite pointed at him, begin to make a little nervous circle. Scared, McBee was, but trapped in his pride, the mind whirling and the finger shaky on the trigger.

Summers made his voice soft. "Lookit, now, McBee," he said. "We ain't huntin' trouble." He pointed to Rock. "Look at this old dog—"

It was easy. As McBee's gaze turned, Summers jumped ahead and made a sweep with his hand and wrenched the rifle away. McBee half fell, trying to hold on to it, and then got his feet under him and backed up a step. Summers could see the inside of his mouth through the mat of whiskers.

"You ain't gonna get away with this!" McBee's voice came out high and womanish.

"Like Evans said, you go tell Tadlock."

"I'll tell him all right." McBee shuffled off, toward the center of the camp, looking back at them once over his shoulder.

"We'll have to watch him now," Evans said.

"Yep."

"There wasn't any reason for you to bust in," Evans said. "I would've made out—but not so fast."

"Sure. I just acted sudden. Rememberin' that black dog got me riled, I reckon."

Evans fell silent, and Summers thought he didn't want to talk more about McBee, maybe figuring he had made a poor out of it. To change the subject Summers said, "What about old Ephesians?"

"Who?"

"Weatherby."

"What about him?"

"He make out all right, with his plunder?"

Evans shook his big head. "He ain't got nothin', Dick. Couple of poor horses and maybe a thunder-mug o' meal. I got to report him."

"You talk to him?"

"Said he'd go it alone if he couldn't trail along. Just him and God. I got to report."

"Leave McBee time to talk to Tadlock." Summers let his eyes travel over the spread-out camp. He saw a group of men and McBee making for it.

"All right." Evans looked at the sun. "Time enough, I guess."

They smoked a pipe and then got up and started for the group.

"Becky says come take supper with us," Evans told Summers.

"I can make out."

"Not accordin' to Becky. She says you won't get the proper victuals. Says you're to come now and regular, from here on."

"That's good of her, you and her both. I'll see there's meat in the pot."

"Shot with McBee's gun?" Evans grinned, looking down at the two rifles Summers carried.

"That preacher," Summers said while he thought back, "damn if he would take money for Mattie's funeral!"

"Here, Rock! I thought he always had his hat out."

"He preached his head off and wouldn't take pay. Said preachin' was one thing and funeralizin' another."

"I be damned!"

They walked past the cook fires, among the tents, between the wagons, Evans being careful to see his dog followed at his heels. Later, camp would be pitched according to plan, with one wagon close behind another and joined to it with ox chains and the whole of them forming a circle so people could fort up in case of Indians; but now all was sprawled out every which way.

Tadlock was holding court, you might say, calling on the inspectors for reports and nodding or frowning to them and marking on a piece of paper as he heard the figures. Fairman and Mack were with him, and other men had gathered around —Brother Weatherby, Brewer, Higgins, and some whose names Summers was just learning—Gorham, Carpenter, Byrd, Daugherty, Patch, Holdridge, Martin. They were a good-enough looking lot, saving one or two like McBee. Summers stepped over to McBee and handed him his rifle and stepped back.

The sun had grown to a red ball in the sky-line haze. With its setting a wind came out of the west, fanning the fires that Summers saw as he looked around and making the women circle about to get out of the smoke. He could hear the first sounds of bugs, not the steady chirp and whir of crickets and katydids and grasshoppers that would come later, but just now and then the buzz of a new pair of wings. The tree frogs, though, sang a steady song, sounding thin and far off, and the whippoorwill called again.

Tadlock looked up from his paper and saw Evans and Summers and said, "I'm glad you came. We didn't mean to have trouble over the dogs."

Summers said, "Wasn't no real trouble."

"With the consent of everyone here, I'm going to suspend the rule against dogs until we can have another general meeting, along the trail some place. Is that satisfactory?"

"It will be," Evans answered, "if you change the rule."

"That will be up to the company." Tadlock paused a minute. "But I think we will. No one wants the train to split up over such a little matter."

The men were nodding or agreeing with words to what Tadlock said.

McBee spoke loud, "That'ud suit me. I don't prize the job nohow."

What Tadlock was saying, Summers thought, was that dogs would be allowed after all. It wasn't likely the subject ever would come up again.

Tadlock said to Evans, "Have you finished your inspection?"

"All done."

"Well?"

"Everything's all right, I reckon. I got the figures. Except—well—it's this way, Brother Weatherby's short. Beggin' your

58

pardon, Brother Weatherby, but you know you're way short."

Weatherby turned his seamed face to Tadlock. Tadlock asked, "That right, Weatherby?"

"Materially, yes."

"You know the rules."

"I'm going, short or not, with you or alone."

"I wouldn't be stiff-necked."

"The Lord will provide."

Fairman's man, Hig, interrupted. "While you're gettin' stuff from Him, get me a new pair of pants, will you?" He hitched the worn pair he wore.

Tadlock frowned, as if this was no time for fun. "It's all right to put your trust in the Lord, but trust alone won't pass, not with this company." Tadlock's voice was sharp, as if he was tired of figures and reports and wanted to get the chore finished and be on the way and no arguments about it.

Weatherby's faded eyes argued with Tadlock's black ones. At last he said, "I haven't lived to my sixty-fourth year without learning that the Lord will provide."

The other men were quiet. Summers thought most of them felt kindly toward the preacher but knew at the same time how foolish was his talk.

"Don't you see, Brother Weatherby—" Tadlock spoke now as if to a child, trying to show him reason—"we can't allow you to take that chance, for your sake or for ours? I believe in the Lord, too, but I don't believe He approves of recklessness. He wants men to help themselves."

The men nodded to this, they spit and nodded and let their glances run from Weatherby to Tadlock and back.

"I wouldn't be any kind of captain," Tadlock went on, "if I permitted you to go. I would just be inviting trouble."

Weatherby's gaze still was steady on Tadlock's face. "The Lord Jesus said, 'O ye of little faith.' "

The edge came back into Tadlock's words. "It isn't a matter of faith. It's a matter of common sense."

"I'll be running the risk, not you."

"We can't travel every man for himself. We couldn't let you starve. We'd have to divide, no matter how slender our stores.

59

And if you got weak or sick, we couldn't desert you." Tadlock held up, giving time for words to form in his mind. "We'd have to be our brother's keeper."

Weatherby said, "I'm going."

"Goddam it! Not with us. You won't listen to reason, so I'll just have to tell you. Not with us. You understand!"

Weatherby looked around, searching the faces of the other men, his own troubled but hard with purpose, the shadow of Tadlock's goddam on it. As if he had got his answer, he bowed his head and said quietly, "I feel the Lord is calling me. I'll go alone."

"We can't keep you from doing that. But, understand, we refuse to take any responsibility."

Off in the shadow of the woods the whippoorwill cried.

Summers heard himself saying, "Hold on, Tadlock! I'll take him on."

"What do you mean?"

"I'll see he's all right. You ne'en to worry."

Tadlock looked at Evans. "You're the inspector for that section. Has Summers enough for two?"

"If Dick says he'll take him, he'll take him, and no skin off anybody's tail."

"That wasn't the question."

"I said I'd take him on," Summers broke in. "Ain't that enough?"

"It's enough for me," Fairman said.

Weatherby turned on Summers, the trouble on his face gone, as if he had just seen the hand of the Lord. "God bless you, Brother Summers." His voice rose. "I said the Lord would provide."

Hig was grinning his close-lipped grin. "Where's my pants?"

Afterwards, Summers wondered at himself. He sat quiet at the Evanses' board and wondered. Vouching for a preacher! A preacher who thought God was an old man with whiskers and rode the closest cloud, a thunderbolt in one hand and a sugar-tit in the other.

"No tellin' what people'll do," he said out loud.

60

DRIVE, plod, push, tug, turn the wheels. Eat dust, damn you! Eat mud. Swim in sweat and freeze at night. Work the sun up. Work it down. Keep rolling.

Watch the stock. Fix the wagons. Unload, load, unload. Sleep dead like a brute while the wheels keep turning in your head, and then get up and go. Drive, plod, push, tug. Damn the dorbugs. Damn distance. Damn gullies, streams, trees. Keep going. Three cheers for Oregon.

Fall into bed at night and feel your wife's warmth and know her back is turned. Know it and not care, except deep in you where you keep your hates. Let the knotted muscles melt. Let your mind drift. Let women come into it, like the girl, Mercy McBee. As a man thinketh in his heart, so is he. All right, so is he. Let sleep flow over you, if you can.

Curtis Mack didn't talk to Amanda, not as man to wife, or encourage her to talk to him. Not these days. Not, he hoped, ever again. They said what had to be said. And sometimes she tried the idle things, weather or mud or dust, and he answered shortly and saw the hurt in her face and was glad of it, and that was all.

It would be all, he told himself as the train rolled on toward the Little Blue and the tension built up in him. He wouldn't bemean himself again. Let her save it, and to hell with it! He wouldn't beg as he had begged that night after they had crossed the Kaw.

Spring had been in the air, and a night bird cried outside the tent, and a breeze played along the canvas, and he wanted her, as so many times before.

"No, Curt," she said. "Please!"

"It's been a long time."

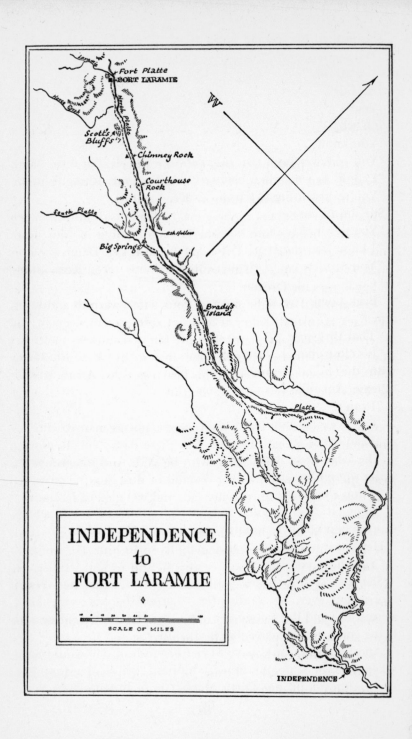

INDEPENDENCE
to
FORT LARAMIE

◆

SCALE OF MILES

She pushed his seeking hand away. "Please."

"Why not?"

"I'm afraid."

"Afraid?"

"Yes."

"Of what?"

"You know."

"You've never been that way yet."

"I could be—and then having no doctor or anything."

"You're just using that as an excuse."

She didn't answer.

"You never have really wanted to."

"I know you think that."

"You think it isn't ladylike, I guess. A lady isn't interested."

"Curt!"

"Back home you never wanted to. It's always been a case of rape."

"That isn't true."

"It's close enough." He was silent for a long minute and then, with the urgency mounting in him, he let himself plead. "Please, Amanda. I'm sorry. Now please."

"I can't."

"I've been patient, but I can't go on forever. Please."

"I can't. I'm afraid."

The edge came back into his voice. "You mean not ever, while we're traveling?"

"I don't know."

"My God! You're going to quit being the half a wife which was the best you ever were. Is that it?"

Her voice was small. "I can't help it, Curt."

"You mean you won't."

She was crying, crying softly, the sobs shaking her. Now, more than ever, he wanted her, wanted the hot, wet cheek against his, and the wounded mouth, and the body yielding and being comforted—except that it wouldn't be.

Another man would have forced her to him. He would have taken her, yes or no. A wife without desire still had a duty. But he wouldn't do it, not Curtis Mack, late of Buffalo, New York,

who was built of soft stuff, who had to recognize, beyond his
fury, that something stood in her way that he couldn't understand. The recognizing made him madder. Why would God put
beauty in a woman's face and give her full breasts and fine
thighs and then withhold warmth?

"If you had been a real wife," he said, "we'd have stayed in
Buffalo."

She didn't try to answer.

"Why do you think I quit business and started west?"

She kept silent.

"To quit stewing, that's why. To get things off my mind."

"You exaggerate so."

"That was at the bottom of it."

Her answer was more crying.

"What you want for a husband is a damn monk."

She cried out, "Why do you say those things? We love each
other. We have so much to live for."

"I'll never ask you again," he said, and hated himself, not for
the lie he had spoken but for the weakness in him that made it
a lie. He had said the same thing before, and then she had come
to him, and he had forgotten resentment and lost his fury and,
relaxed in the warm and rumpled bed, had spoken his love for
her. He had asked forgiveness and laid the blame on himself for
times like tonight's. Soft stuff, Curtis Mack, weak, unstable and
—all right—sensual. Was anything wrong with sensuality? What
was wrong was her tyranny over him. What was wrong was that
he couldn't help himself and was light-spirited or surly, depending on the grant or refusal of so small a favor.

He said, "You drive me to other women."

"I don't mean to, Curt."

"I can't help looking at them and thinking. I'll find another
woman, too."

"If that's what you want."

"What do you care? You don't want me."

"If that's what you want."

"Want, hell!" He lurched over in bed. "You ought to have
married a steer."

Lying there, hearing her soft weeping, feeling with a fierce

64

pleasure the spasms of her body, he told himself he would find another woman. He wanted to be faithful, and she made it impossible, and so he would throw his restraints aside. He would get out of the mold he'd been cast in. People like his parents, lecturing him about sin! People like preachers, like old Brother Weatherby, preaching against evil! People like these emigrants, fixing lashes as punishment for fornication and adultery! All the men lustful and all fearful, one of another, wanting to save what they had for themselves but maybe to sneak a little on the side. But suppose a man had nothing, or next to nothing?

He would find himself a woman, he would wrench loose from the morality that had been ground into him. He swore it to himself, resisting, while he swore, the doubt that he could, pushing aside the forethought of a conscience so guilty it might unman him.

The night bird still called outside, and the breeze still played along the tent. He heard the sneeze of a horse and the distant mooing of a cow. And steady to his ears came the sweep and mutter of the Kaw.

They had crossed the river that day and moved upstream to a piece of open prairie that lay along the bank. He made the scenes pass in his mind, like a gloss over his fury. They had decided against the ferry because so many of the train were poor, and had had Dick Summers lead them to a crossing. He saw Dick Summers now, riding boldly into the river, exploring it for the best passage. He saw the wagons rolling into it, the oxen blowing water, and the tight wagons like his own riding easy. Summers and a crew snaked up logs for some of the others, like McBee's, and lashed them to the boxes, making houseboats of a kind. A band of Kaw Indians, curious and intrusive as goats, ran on the bank and splashed in the water, their blankets and feathers and odds and ends of calico shirts showing vivid against the new green of the land. Others paddled back and forth in rough dugouts, ferrying women and children across and the supplies that had been unloaded to lighten the wagons. Their pay was tobacco and beads and pieces of old clothing and, it developed later, whatever they could get their hands on and make away with.

Now, as then, Mack let himself look at the women and speculate about them—at Judith Fairman, a pale, tall, pretty girl, long-legged and graceful but a little flat in the bosom; at the little New Englander, Mrs. Patch, who might hide something behind that matter-of-factness; at Mrs. Tadlock, who was quiet and, in a quiet way, comely; at Rebecca Evans, a sociable and good-humored woman with a front like a butt of hay; at Mrs. Brewer, who had borne ten children and looked it. He saved the best until last. Then he let Mercy McBee come to his sight. Dark hair and white skin. Young breasts. Mouth young. Eyes eloquent of something, of sadness like hunger, or hunger like sadness. She wouldn't know about things, but she could be taught.

He couldn't look at Amanda as another man might. He could describe her. He could say she was fair and medium tall, that she had a good form, that her face was oval and her eyes wide apart and more green than brown when you looked close—but he couldn't see her as another man might. Would another man see her differently if he knew she was cold?

Were the others cold? Did the other men have their troubles and go to sleep hungry and sore? Were women like Mrs. Brewer just more obliging or really more ardent? Thou shalt not covet —but he let himself play with the idea of having one of them, of having one who yielded eagerly and tenderly in a secret bed or along a green bank in a screen of willows. Tenderly. That was the word. Maybe what a man wanted, more than anything else, was just tenderness. Amanda couldn't be tender, not outwardly. It wasn't in her. You knew she loved you because of things unsaid, of gestures half completed, of feelings indirectly shown, of favors given with restraint. And, damn it, it wasn't enough.

He wrenched the thought of her out of his mind and went back to the river to watch the crossing. The women and wagons and supplies had gone over, and the cattle and loose work stock were footing down the bank, led by Dick Summers and pushed and kept in line by horsemen white and red. The leaders took

66

to the water and the others followed, and now they were swimming, making a long, eyed line in the sweeping current.

It was an easy crossing. Not an animal lost, or a barrel or a box or a sack, except for small things that the Kaws sneaked away. It was a crossing to make a man jubilant, to make him playful, to make him want his wife.

Mack reared up in bed, pulling the cover from Amanda. "No use to snivel," he said, and got up and pulled on his pants. He couldn't sleep tonight.

He walked around the tents that ringed the corral made by the wagons. He could feel rather than see the horses hobbled or picketed inside the corral. The camp was quiet, except now and then for a mutter, or the hard breath of a man lying on his back, or the sudden, frightened cry of a dreaming child. The fires had died down. Overhead the stars seemed few but big. In their light the wagon tops swam against the dark. A wolf howled somewhere. Or it might have been an Indian. He had heard that Indians imitated wolves sometimes, or wore the hides of elk, while they stole in to make away with stock. He brought his rifle into the crook of his arm.

Someone said, "Hello, hoss," and he knew it was Summers. He made him out by the ghost-white of his buckskins and saw he was seated in the clear, where he could watch.

"Don't you ever sleep?"

"Slept enough, farmin', to last me the rest of my life. I reckon."

"I thought farmers were up early and late."

"Nothin' like followin' a mule to rest the mind."

Mack imagined Summers wasn't resting much tonight. While he talked, he still kept listening, still kept looking, as if conversation didn't any more than touch his surface.

"Expecting trouble?" Mack asked.

"Maybe not. Those pore Kaws, though, they get hungry and cold. And stealin's fun to an Injun."

Mack said, "Damn nuisances," and felt a little surprise when Summers answered, "They got their ways, like we got ours. I reckon we're a heap big nuisance to them."

67

"I can't see it," Mack answered, though he did. He put an edge in his tone. "They'll have to learn."

He waited, but Summers answered only, "Reckon so."

"I'm going to have a look at the cattle."

The grass was new and soft underfoot, so that, even in factory shoes, he could walk as quietly as an Indian himself. The cattle would be to the north, away from the river. He took his bearings and confirmed them, idly, by lining up the side of the Dipper with the North Star. After a while he saw movement ahead and called out and walked on up and found the movement to be the boy, Brownie Evans, whom he had hired to help with the cattle. "All quiet?"

"Critters are kind of scary."

Mack narrowed his eyes and saw the cattle, a darker patch against the dark slope. "Wonder why?"

"Injun smell, I figger."

"Any sign of Indians?"

"Not unless it's them wolves."

"Nearly time for the next watch, isn't it?"

"Be a spell yet."

"Who's out, besides you?"

"Holdridge and McBee and Patch, with the cattle. Summers wanted a strong guard tonight."

"Right."

"Summers says sometimes thievin' Injuns make out to be wolves."

"You'll have to watch out."

"Says he's seen 'em do it, but maybe the Kaws won't. Not much grit in their gizzards."

"You watch, just the same."

"Sure. Dick says any time you get over the Kaw you better look out. This here's Delaware country."

"Delaware?"

"But it's the Pawnees you have to keep your eyes skinned for."

"Does Summers know everything?"

"Why," the boy said, "I s'pose not, but he knows a store of things."

68

Mack liked Summers and he liked Brownie, but still he was prompted to say, "You'd think from the talk that no one had any sense but Summers."

Brownie didn't answer. With a boy's deference to his elders he kept quiet, but Mack knew he was resentful, as he wanted him to be.

A star streamed down the western sky, and, as if glad for its excuse, Brownie asked, "You reckon that star hit in Oregon, Mr. Mack?"

Before Mack could answer, a rifle cracked at the far side of the herd. The sound of it died into a sharp, thinking silence. Brownie jerked his rifle up. "Injuns! Injuns!"

"Listen!"

What Mack heard was the camp shouting, shouting out across the darkness. He heard the clank of ox chains and the sound of running.

Off beyond the dark blob of the cattle another rifle spurted fire and boomed above the shouting. The cattle were climbing to their feet. Mack could see the close ones struggling up. They stood dark in the night, the breath loud in their nostrils. Farther on, the edges of the blob began to flux.

Lije Evans' voice was bellowing, "Brownie? Where you, Brownie?"

"Here. Here, Pa."

Evans came pounding up, and behind him a straggle of men. A rifle cracked again.

Mack heard the gun, and then the sound of hoofs. The dark patch was flowing into a string, and the head of the string was running, drawing the rest after it.

Someone yelled, "Goddam! There they go."

"Horses! Get horses!"

"No. Can't head 'em." Mack knew Summers' voice.

"Get horses, I told you."

The head of the string was lost to the eye.

"No! Wait!"

Summers stood before Mack. "Injuns? You see Injuns?"

Mack said, "No."

"Critters was uneasy," Brownie put in.

69

Mack couldn't see the cattle now. The sound of their hoofs was a far drumming. Above it he heard the sudden voices of the other sentinels.

Summers asked them, "Injuns?"

" 'Y God, yes," McBee answered.

"Sure?"

"No," Patch said.

"I seen one. One, or a wolf," Holdridge added.

Tadlock shouldered ahead. "Get horses, damn it!"

"Hold up!"

"What's wrong with you, Summers? You want to hold a meeting?"

Summers didn't answer, but Lije Evans spoke out, "Leave it to Dick."

"Summers isn't captain. Get your horses!"

Summers spoke then, spoke with something in his voice that Mack liked but still resisted. "Don't forgit yourself, hoss."

"I'm not forgetting those cattle."

Patch's tone was mild. "Most of them are yours."

"Goddam it! What's that got to do with it? You want to lose yours?"

The men had crowded into a close bunch. A half dozen of them were trying to talk. Summers' words rose above the rest. "Rules say it's up to me to call a war party."

Tadlock faced up to him. "Call it then!"

Mack spoke without thinking, spoke, he knew later, out of temper and hunger for a fight. "Rules be damned, I say, if they don't work."

Summers stepped up to him. "Mack," he said quietly, so quietly that everybody listened, "these here could be Pawnees, and, besides, I don't aim to send green men out at night, even against Kaws." He paused as if to let his words sink in. "You'll get more cattle back, come daylight, than you can now."

Summers faced around to address the others. "I'll be the war party. You all watch the wagons." He didn't say any more. He faded out like a shadow. One minute Mack saw him, ghost-like in his buckskins, and then he caught the glimmer of him mov-

70

ing off, and then he was lost, lost in darkness, lost in the sudden pressing emptiness, lost on the brooding land.

After a minute the talk picked up, but Mack didn't wait to hear it. He would be a war party himself, a one-man, green-man war party, riding with his anger, riding like a fool to dull the edge of it, and maybe meeting Indians and fighting them and so spending himself in another way than with a woman. A man got so he found his pleasure in being crazy and perverse—but he never could explain to Amanda how it was. If he could, it wouldn't make any difference, not with Amanda.

Some of the women ran out to meet him, a squall of alarm, of questions, of entreaties. They pulled at his sleeves and ran around to face him again after he had passed them. "Everything's all right. I said everything's all right." Others waited at the corral, wanting to know, too, and he said, "It's all right," and went on, hardly looking at them, hating them, all of them, because they were women. Mrs. Turley was crying, "I knowed we shouldn't've come. I knowed it." He stepped over a wagon tongue and got away.

The fires outside the corral had been replenished, and the flames licked in the big eyes of the horses, which were standing high-headed, uneasy with the general uneasiness. He caught his saddle horse and led it over and tied it to the wheel of his wagon and threw a saddle on it. Then he loosened the ox chains between his two wagons and pulled the tongue aside and led the horse out, putting the tongue and chains back afterwards.

When he turned around, he saw Amanda. "What are you going to do, Curt?"

"Hunt Indians."

Her face looked pale and drawn in the firelight, and shadowed with sorrow. "Alone?"

When he didn't answer, she said, "You don't know Indians, Curt."

He put his foot in the stirrup. "Know one when I see one."

"I wouldn't go."

"Wouldn't, eh?"

"Please!"

71

Please. Please hell! For her please she would get what he got for his.

He turned his horse and heard her "Please be careful," and realized that it was partly, maybe mainly, to distress her that he went out on this crazy business. He didn't care about that, either. And he couldn't help it. The horse stumbled as he kicked him into the darkness.

Unguided, the horse rounded the corral and made for the river and lowered his head and drank and raised it, savoring the water, and let the breath rattle in his nostrils.

It was darker here in the growth. Mack felt the trees shouldering him. Even the river ran dark, dark to the black band of the far shore. A bright star shone on its moving bosom. Looking up, he saw the same star in the sky. The words of Scripture went through his head: "When they saw the star, they rejoiced with exceeding great joy." He could remember reading them as a child and being moved by them, back in the church that had left its scars on him.

He reined his horse out from the water and walked him clear of the trees and struck west, riding hard in the direction he remembered the cattle had taken.

Nothing happened. The Great Dipper wheeled in the sky and a star dropped and wolves howled and the horse stumbled and got his head jerked back for it, and nothing happened, except that the horse began to wheeze. Let him wheeze! Let him labor! Let him run his heart out and his lungs! Getup! Amanda would have protested; she believed in kindness to dumb animals. Getup!

He was far out when, faint as something imagined, he heard rifle fire downstream, from the direction of camp. He pulled his horse up, alarm leaping in him, thinking, before he had time to regulate his thoughts, of Indians and the camp and Amanda without him to protect her; and then it occurred to him that it must be four o'clock and the sentinels would be firing to rouse the camp for the day's journey. He kicked his horse into a lope.

Nothing happened. He rode on another mile and turned and began crisscrossing back toward camp, and a flush came into the

72

sky, and light, and he saw he was on a low bald ridge above the river. The camp was lost somewhere down the stream. He started for it.

He was close enough to hear the echo of voices, sounding thin in the chill of morning, when he saw the Indian in the tree. At first he took him for a big coon, or maybe a bear, and then, coming closer, he made out the shaved head with its comb of hair and the blanket gathered around the shoulders. From his vantage point above the lower growth the Indian was watching the camp. He was holding to his perch and watching.

Mack stopped his horse. The Indian had no gun and no bow that Mack could see. He would have a bow though, if not a musket, hidden by his body or the folds of his blanket.

Mack dismounted and tied his horse and walked ahead, stepping soft. He began to feel the blood beating in him, and the breath light and quick in his throat.

At this range he couldn't miss. He had only to raise his rifle and line up the sights and squeeze the trigger. He couldn't miss, not if he chose to shoot.

He looked around for other Indians and saw none, and listened and heard, far off from pulse and breath, the voices of women cooking breakfast and the deeper tones of men catching up their teams.

Even with the blood thumping in him and his lungs working, he couldn't miss, not if he fired. There was the barrel lifting and the sights lining up and the finger waiting on the trigger.

The Indian turned, his sharp face composed but watchful, and his eyes ran over the back country. Mack saw them nearing, saw them widen and fix in the shocked instant of finding him. They cried out. The eyes, the wordless mouth, the whole face cried, "Please! Please!"

The Indian dropped as the rifle cracked. He didn't shout or fling out. He hung for a bare instant, the please fading from his face, and then he dropped.

Mack ran up. The Indian was dead all right, dead as a damn doornail. He lay crumpled in the bushes with his old blanket and his proud wisp of hair, face turned up, mouth loose—a runty, thin man with scars on him and the marks of hunger, a

73

Kaw who had asked please and got his answer, and now wouldn't have to ask any more or go without, either.

Mack stood for a long minute, hearing the camp hushed and then noisy with the alarm his shot had raised. A louse worked in the tuft of hair, and a small breeze fanned it. Watching, Mack felt fatigue dragging at him, felt loneliness and regret creeping on him and bearing him down. Now, unaccountably, he wanted to talk to Amanda.

Drive, plod, push, tug, turn the wheels. Eat dust, damn you! Eat mud. Swim in sweat and freeze at night. Work the sun up. Work it down. Wear the body limp. Keep moving.

Chapter - - - - - - - - - - - - *Eight*

THE KAW lay behind them, the Wakarusa and the Kaw and the Little and Big Vermilions and the Big Blue, each standing out in memory as the train wormed up and down the hills and sidewise through the trees, each costing something —time and sweat and breath, a broken tongue or piece of harness, and maybe a wetting if the wagon boxes weren't tight.

Once passed, they stood lonely and somehow dear in the mind. They were landmarks where there were no others, and so they were remembered, and the thought of them brought up remembered things, for often they camped at crossings and, for that little while, had a home again. Thinking back, while the raw breeze streamed at her, Rebecca Evans heard the children's cries again and smelled camp smoke and coffee and saw the wagons standing white in the late sun.

It was only then, after the wagons had been drawn up and the teams unyoked and the ox chains fastened wagon to wagon, that she had a real chance to talk to Lije or Brownie. They would let down then for a little and speak about their new home or maybe about their old one, and Lije would wonder how things were going back in Missouri.

She would wonder, too, though not so much about crops and critters, but about the well and its water sweeter than river water, and had the new people fixed the door and did their young ones call from the trees that Brownie used to climb. Or she would think about her sister, living at New Madrid, her little sister whom her mind couldn't picture grown up but still small and fetching as in the old years. She always wore the new dress, of boughten goods, that Ma dressed her in on her sixth birthday, and had her pigtails tied with the red ribbon Rebecca had given her.

The camping places of last night and the night before somehow went with home. The wagon train hadn't much more than pulled out than the spot they'd stayed at joined with the old thoughts, something known that wouldn't be known again, so that a body felt lost and a little homesick, wanting the time back again, the friendly fire, the still evening, the sound of the water, the easy talk. Nothing ahead of them was known; none of it was warmed by memories.

Rebecca said "Haw" to the oxen and pulled her old coat closer about her neck. She was walking at the side of the wagon, being so tired and sore she didn't want to ride. If a person had flesh on her, she got stitches and aches from the jolting, and spots on the flesh sore to the touch.

Ahead of her Lije turned and smiled and turned back again to his team, tucking his chin into the breeze that made a mourning sound along the canvas of the wagons. Rock moved along behind him. That was the way with that dog. Most of the time he followed Lije or Brownie as if on a lead rope.

Rebecca tried to push the backward thoughts from her mind. Her man and her boy were happy, and that was enough. A happy family was all a person could ask for. It wasn't in the right nature of things for her to allow herself the miseries when she had that much.

Everything was going as well as a body could hope. They were making fair time, even Dick Summers said, and they hadn't had any trouble to speak of. Just the stampede was all, and the Indian Mack had shot for some reason and, later on, the Kaws that came to call about the shooting and had got shooed off by Tadlock. The men had found the cattle, all but one. Dick didn't lay the stampede to Indians, except that maybe the critters were spooky from the smell of them there along the Kaw. A green animal, he said, always scared at Indian scent.

Rebecca drove the second wagon mostly, though Brownie spelled her sometimes, and sometimes where the way was open the oxen could be trusted to follow along, trailed by Summers' pack horses tied behind. Riding or walking, she kept her eye out for Lije and Brownie, and for Dick Summers, too, though he was mostly out of sight, scouting for Indians or deciding the way or hunting. He kept the pot full. At first, close to the set-

76

tlements, he had come in with ducks and snipe and pigeons, but now he hunted bigger game. Last night he brought back two turkeys and a strange thing that he called a wild goat but others said was an antelope. He kept the pots full, their pot and Brother Weatherby's, too. She reckoned it was a long time since Brother Weatherby had fed so well. There was power in the sermon he preached against traveling on the Sabbath Day—but they traveled just the same.

Dick was a good man, and her Lije was, too, as people were coming to know. Lije was strong in his body and good in his mind, but it was his spirit that was best of all, being calm and kind and not set up.

She would see him, ahead with the heavy wagon and its double yoke, and him likely walking and popping his whip now and then. Or the train would have to stop, and he would go to the head of it and help others across a wash or up a bank, his clothes muddy or dusty afterwards and damp with sweat. He didn't talk too much, and never loud and bossy like Tadlock, but he did his share and more of the work.

Most of the time Brownie was back with the cows. She saw him sometimes when the train was climbing a rise and waved at him, and he would give just a little wave back, being a boy yet and bashful about showing his feelings. For all that he was only a boy, he was doing a man's work. He didn't need to be back with the stock so much, not with just the fifteen head that Lije was bringing along; but he had hired out to Mack, who had forty or more, so's to earn something. Rebecca thought that Mack couldn't have got a faithfuller man.

Rebecca punched the near ox with the stick she carried. She wanted to keep close to Lije. Sometimes she let the team lag a little, but, with the wind blowing sad and her body sore and her mind low in spite of her, she wanted to keep up today. Here along the Little Blue they would have had dust in their faces except that it had showered the night before. Wagons at the tail had to bear a sight of dust, and so it was they traded places day by day, the back ones moving up and the fore ones coming back.

She made herself look around and take note of the land. They

77

had been through changing country, the woods and hills first and then prairies such as she imagined must lie on the near side of the Rocky Mountains; then woods again and limestone and big hills along the Big Vermilion. Here the country seemed to be reopening. The eye could travel farther, and the trees were more separated into groves. You couldn't tell for sure, though; tomorrow things might close in again.

The wind that blew was not like the winds of home. It was steadier and more devilish, streaming out of the west as if there was no end to it. It bent the trees or whistled over a bald hill and ran down the hollows as if just to push at the train. People said, though, that it wasn't anything; wait until farther on. But it was enough. It was more than enough.

She was glad when the train had to stop. She took a breath and rubbed her sore behind with one hand, not caring much who saw her, and then walked up to Lije before he took it into his head to go see what was the matter. He said, "Watch the critters, will you, Becky?"

"Wait, Lije! You don't have to do all the work. Can't we talk a minute?"

He started to object, she knew, and then he looked at her and said, "Why, sure thing. What's wrong?"

"I just wanted to talk, is all."

"About what?"

"Just talk."

"You ain't like yourself, Becky. Wore out, I bet."

"I'm all right."

"Whyn't you ride, 'stead of walkin'?"

"I'm all right. It's just the wind and all."

"Down in your mind?"

"A little."

"No cause to be down. Things is fine. You just make yourself think things is fine and, sure enough, you'll see they are."

"That forever-blowin' wind."

"I was just sayin' to myself it's a nice day for travel."

She didn't answer but stepped up and turned around so as to talk to Lije with her back to the breeze.

She knew herself for a strong-enough woman, but now she

78

needed his strength. "You think things will be all right, sure enough, Lije?"

"Slicker'n grease, honey," he said, using the rare name for her as if he understood her need. "Don't you fret yourself. Hear?"

She heard sounds behind her and turned and saw Tadlock coming on a horse. He spoke while he was two jumps away. "We'll corral."

"All right," Lije answered.

"Summers says this is the last chance to get timber for axletrees and tongues. I'll have to assume he's right, I guess."

"Dick knows."

"Some of the women want to stop, too," Tadlock said as if faulting them. "They say they just have to get some washing done."

"So?"

"I dislike these endless halts."

"We'll need axles and tongues before we're through."

Tadlock said, "I suppose so—but it's annoying."

When he had ridden on, Lije said, "That there Tadlock!"

"High and mighty, ain't he?"

"Galls me."

"You been on his side."

Lije nodded a slow yes. "I don't guess I'm for cuttin' him down. Not yet."

"Some are. Patch and Gorham and Daugherty, I hear. Is that so, Lije?"

Lije kept on nodding. "It ain't bossiness altogether, neither. They say he talks hurry, but it's his critters that slows us up. He ain't got enough hands. Just Martin and McBee part of the time."

"Ain't they right?"

"Yep." Lije spoke without heat, weighing things in his mind. "Longer he's captain the mightier he gets. He's got his p'ints, though. He tries hard. It ain't an easy place, with some wantin' to hurry and some to hold back and some scared of Indians and some sorry they set out and some just naturally ornery."

"He won't last the trip, Lije."

"Question is, who'd be better?"

"You would."

"Me!" His big face spread in a grin. "You crazy?"

"You never did give yourself credit for what you could do."

Before he gave her an answer, the train began to move. Up ahead she heard the whine of axles. The wagon tops were swaying.

"You all right now?" he asked.

"Crazy, you said." She walked back and faced around into the wind and spoke to her team.

She knew she wasn't crazy. She knew what Lije could do, with a little pushing. She wouldn't think about it now, though. She would think about camp. After she got the washing done and supper fixed, she could rest. She could let herself rest, and Lije and Brownie would talk, and for a little while in this homeless land they would have a home again, walled off from the wind.

She folded her arms across her chest and brought them up snug, making a rest. A woman with breasts like hers had no business jouncing over the Oregon road.

Chapter - - - - - - - - - - - - - *Nine*

"TIME WE GET to the Platte, we can figure we've made a start," Dick Summers said.

Lije Evans answered, "Uh-huh," thinking that in Dick's eyes already was the look of the Platte, the look of distance, the look of far-off things brought close in memory.

Evans squinted ahead, searching for the hills that people spoke of as the coasts of Nebraska. "It's the on'y trip I ever made that it took the best part of a month to get started on," he said.

He knew what Dick meant, though. He meant that once they reached the Platte they'd be sure enough in a different country, sure enough on the real start to the mountains and to Oregon. He felt that way himself even though he never had been on the trail before and never seen the Platte except as his mind saw it from what people said. It would be a shallow, spread-out, sandy river with flat banks and no trees except on the islands, and it would run muddy from the feet of more buffalo than any man could count.

Patch rode along with him and Dick, Patch and Daugherty and Martin. Together they were scouting for Indians and picking out the way for the wagons that followed after. Dick carried a big rag with him and sometimes tore pieces from it and posted little flags across breaks and washes to show the lead teamster where to head. Now Patch said to Evans, "This would seem like more than a start if you had started from Massachusetts."

"A man wouldn't think Oregon fever would carry so far," Evans answered.

A little questioning smile came on Patch's face. "Ever hear of Hall Kelley or Captain Wyeth?"

"Can't say as I did."

Summers was nodding. "I knowed Wyeth. Creek back there a ways is named for him." Evans expected Dick to say more, but

81

all Dick added was, "Good man." Looking at him, seeing the face marked by thought, Evans imagined his mind was far back, remembering Wyeth and the days that had gone before.

Patch said, "Kelley and Wyeth puffed Oregon as much as anybody, especially Kelley. We had a touch of Oregon fever before others even knew about it." Patch, too, fell silent, his thin and sharp-nosed face wearing its usual look of quiet wide-awakeness. It was a Yankee face he had, Evans thought, but not a bad face even so.

Evans turned in his saddle. Old Rock had just finished a scout into the bushes after some varmint or other and now trotted at the heels of the horses. A steady, quiet old dog, Rock was, who carried himself wise and dignified. Farther back of them, maybe a mile down the gradual slope they had climbed, he could see the wagon train winding, the gray-white train squirming in its haze of dust. The time was coming on toward noon and the train had straggled out. Behind the wagons came the loose horses and behind the horses the cattle, with riders back of them and to the sides, keeping them in line and pushing them along. Out from the wagon, to the windward side so as to be out of the dust, women and children were walking, walking and probably laughing and chattering and looking for wild flowers tough enough to grow on this dry ridge between the Little Blue and the Platte. It was cactus they'd find, and thistle and low sage standing silverish in the sun. The only flowers they were likely to see were the little yellow-hearted daisies that could sprout from a stone—daisies and now and then one of the wild roses that were just beginning to bloom.

In the high sun the colors made flashes through the dust—the white of the wagon covers, the red and white and black of the critters, the blue of a dress a woman had on. Evans saw a man walking along the line. It probably was Tadlock, trying to get the train to bunch up. He was a great one for order, a great one for orders, as far as that went, though he wasn't much horseman and so didn't ride ahead as often as a captain might. Evans wondered if he ever thought about the dogs he had wanted killed. A dog trailed him now, and a half dozen others paced along with the women and children and now and then made dashes to the side. Dogs traveled more miles than any horse or ox, but still they kept on.

Evans could see his own two wagons, he thought, and a figure by one of them that he took for Rebecca. Brownie must be inside the second wagon, riding. He knew, with a little welling of secret pride, that Rebecca would be searching ahead for him, wanting him to be all right, just as he was searching back for her.

This was one day, he thought, when Brownie wouldn't have to breathe so much dust. Mack had talked Shields into helping him once in a while, and today Shields was back with the cows. Evans never thought of Mack but he thought of the night of the stampede and the Indian Mack had shot. The shooting seemed like a cruel and useless thing from what he could make out of it, though some of the men laughed and said the Indian had got a case of falling sickness. You would think from listening to them that an Indian was no different from a varmint. Still, Mack seemed like a pretty good man, if a strange one.

Evans turned back in the saddle. "Tadlock don't think we're doing so good," he said.

"Tadlock eats too many beans," Patch said. He spoke as if he had turned things over in his mind and come to an answer no one could outtalk.

Martin had come with Tadlock from Illinois. He said, "Tadlock's all right," and looked at Patch out of his dull eyes. He had a face that looked as if it knew it hadn't got any special favors when faces were divvied out. He walked and rode hunched over like a man on a cold day.

Patch wasn't one to start a fight, though Evans imagined he could take care of himself if he had to. He didn't answer Martin.

Evans said, "Maybe it ain't such a bad thing to have someone like him pushin'."

"That's what I say," Martin put in. "Like he says, someone has to take charge."

The grin took the bite out of Dick's words. "He don't have to take it like God hisself had give it to him. Eh, Daugherty?"

Daugherty didn't join in the talk. He never did talk much, though Irish was written plain on his face. He went along silent,

83

a blue-eyed, fair-complected man whose cheeks burned under the sun and wind and then peeled off like a snake skin and then burned again. He wore an old red hunting shirt and carried a flintlock his daddy must have hunted with as a boy in western Virginia.

"Long time ago," Dick said, "I pulled loose from the notion that what galled me or puked me was good for me, body or soul."

"Best not let Brother Weatherby hear you," Evans told him.

"What cured me," Dick said, just making talk, "was Injun physic."

Patch asked, "Injun physic?"

"It was brewed from a root, and it would gag a hog. My ma would grab me by the nose, and when I opened my mouth to breathe, she would pour it down, a tin cup to a dose. She figured it must be good because it tasted so bad."

"And was it?" Patch asked.

"Like doctors," Dick went on. "They figure the less life in you the less disease, never stoppin' to think the less life you got the less misery you can stand."

"You're talking about bleeders?"

"Bleeders and physickers and all. Trouble with gettin' sick is can you live through the cure."

Patch smiled as if he didn't think Dick believed what he was saying. "Did the Indian physic help?"

"It done what it was aimed to do. It overdone it. Take a dose of it, and there better be a bush close."

"So maybe it was good."

"Not to my way of thinkin'. Oncet I swallowed a piece of money, and money was skeerce with us, so Ma dug her up a root and b'iled it and got the tea inside me, and don't you know that money came out so sick it wouldn't spend!"

Patch asked, "Well?"

"The store man said it was counterfeit. Said it rang hollow. I knowed it would. That Injun physic would take the insides out of anything."

Daugherty laughed for once, and Patch grinned while he sized up Dick, as if he'd never come across the likes of Dick

84

before. After a while he said, "So you mean Tadlock's like Indian physic?"

"The talk just put me in mind of the physic was all."

"Take away Tadlock," Evans said, "and we'd have nary a thing to chew on."

He hadn't meant to stop the conversation, but it stopped, nobody bothering to say they could still talk about Indians or about turning back or about waiting up until another train joined theirs. In camp there were always people wanting to do this or that, wanting to do anything except to go on in the way they had decided in the first place.

The five of them rode along quiet, and the only sounds under all the bright sky were the little sounds of the horses walking and the saddles squeaking.

Dick picked out the nooning place. It would be a dry camp, here on the dividing ridge, and what water was used would have to come from the kegs they had filled that morning. There wasn't supposed to be any water all the way from the head of the Little Blue to the Platte, but Dick had known where a trickle of it was, a couple of miles off the trail, and had taken them to it for a camping place last night. It occurred to Evans again how lucky they were to have Dick. Without him they would have had to travel dry for the whole twenty-five miles.

The wagons rolled in by and by, pulling up in columns four abreast as they did at noon, and the oxen were unloosened but not unyoked, and the women got busy with the victuals.

Rebecca looked tired, and Evans asked while she cleared up after the meal, "Why'n't you rest this evenin'? I'll drive."

"You go ahead, Lije. You want to see the Platte soon's you can, and Brownie don't have to trail them cows today."

He smiled at her, not answering but wondering again how it was she knew what was in him. He hadn't let on to her he was anxious to get a look at the Platte.

Everybody ate fast, and what talk there was was mostly about the river, and then the bugle sounded and the train began to roll, and no one seemed to be sleepy with food and heat as they usually were after noon, but all a little excited.

Before the wagons started, Evans had climbed his horse,

going to join with Dick and Patch and the other outriders. Rock had got up, slow but dutiful, and followed him. On the way Evans saw Brother Weatherby, talking earnest to a couple of women. Even the Platte couldn't get Weatherby off the road to salvation. Tadlock stood by his wagon, his bull whip in his hand, as if ready to rouse up anyone who lazed.

The way lay level and long ahead of them, with nothing on it to catch the eye except now and then for an antelope that stood with its head high while it watched. It would turn and run, showing its white rump, and then wheel around to watch some more. Patch wanted to shoot one, but Dick told him they'd find plenty along the river bottom; no need to pack one all that piece.

They rode without talking much. Daugherty had stayed back with the train, and so there were just the four of them, and Martin's slow horse dropped back after a while, taking him out of earshot except when he pounded it to a run and so caught up for a minute.

Dick's eyes were never quiet. They ran to right and left and looked ahead and back, and what they missed, Evans imagined, wasn't much. When they crossed a trail that ran north and south, Dick gave it just a glance, but Evans had a notion that Dick knew from the one quick look just about when it had been traveled last.

"Pawnee road. To the Arkansas," Dick said.

"We ain't seen a Pawnee."

"Not likely to, yet. They'll be west with the buffler."

The sun swung over and by and by got under Evans' hat brim and struck his cheek. Some of the heat had gone out of it so that it lay restful on the skin. It made Evans drowsy. He slumped down in the saddle, letting Dick do the watching while his mind fooled with one thing and then another, none of them important.

Dick brought him to, Dick standing in his stirrups and saying, "There's the coast, I'm thinking."

What Evans saw looked like a range of high and broken hills, standing sharp and blue against the northwest sky.

"Mountains!" Patch said.

86

"Sand hills, and not as high as you'd think from here."

It turned out Dick was right. As they drew closer, weaving among a long set of badger holes, the hills shrank, until at last they were just piles of sand forty to sixty feet high, blown up by the wind and held together by cactus and thistle and, Evans saw as he rode into them, by fine grasses that his horse kept tugging for. A powderlike salt patched the ground with white.

Evans had heard about the Platte. He had pictured it in his mind. He thought he knew what he was going to see, but now that his horse stood on the summit, he couldn't believe. He couldn't believe that flat could be so flat or that distance ran so far or that the sky lifted so dizzy-deep or that the world stood so empty. He saw old Rock chase a badger into a hole, saw a bunch of antelope drifting, saw the river sluiced and the woods rising on its islands and the sand in a great gray waste, but it was something he couldn't put a name to that held him. He thought he never had seen the world before. He never had known distance until now. He had lived shut off by trees and hills and had thought the world was a doll's world and distance just three hollers away and the sky no higher than a rifle shot.

He said, "By God, Dick! By God!" and Dick nodded, knowing how it was with him, and silence stronger than any sound closed in on the words as if he had broken the rules by speaking.

He held his horse up, Dick on one side of him, Patch on the other, and Martin riding up from the rear. Feeling rose in him, a shudder of feeling that left the skin cold and grained. "I never knew it would be like this," he said aloud but still to himself. He was humbled and set up at the same time and proud now with a fierce, unworded pride that he had put out for Oregon. It wouldn't be easy. It wouldn't be what people called fun. Great was the name for it, the only name he could find in his mind.

He felt greatness coming into himself, greatness coming from greatness, and he renounced it, thinking of Tadlock and his self-importance, but still he felt greatness.

Dick clucked to his horse, and together the four of them rode down the rough slope, and Dick set a flag at a swale, and they crossed the level plain and came to the river.

Chapter - - - - - - - - - - - - - - *Ten*

H IGGINS had to smile to himself. People tickled him, especially maybe men when it came to women. Like now when the wagon train had been corralled. Like here on the Platte bank where the men had drawn off so's to be able to take up the subject of what Byrd kept calling manure. Manure, that was it, or buffalo chips or dung. To most of them, even to some of them that used the word regular, it wouldn't be fittin' to give it the name it was known by best, since women, although absent, figured in the argument. In something like the same way people talked nice in the presence of a corpse.

The question was, with wood getting scarce was it right and proper for the women to cook over fires made of buffalo chips? A tomfool like himself might think the women ought to have some say in the answer. But no. The husbands would decide and go back to their wives, serious and wise, and tell them what was right. How would they say it? Higgins wondered. How would Mr. Byrd inform his lady? "Ma'am, for want of wood we'll have to use the waste of buffaloes"?

This wasn't a called meeting. It just came on by itself. The men were standing mostly. A little to one side Dick Summers leaned on his rifle and listened and looked, looked at them and away from them to the sun sinking across a million miles of prairie. Higgins tried to guess what was in his mind. Maybe he thought there were rules out there, too, rules of making out with what there was to make out with, of cooking over buffalo chips if no wood was handy.

Byrd was speaking, saying, "I for one don't like it."

Byrd was a man Higgins hadn't come to know, except as he had seen him, plump and fair, and crack-lipped now from the wind, sitting proper at his fire or urging his team along in the way of a man not used to animals. He was an in-between-sized man, from the East somewhere, who carried himself straight and had solemn manners with the ladies and said amen to Brother Weatherby's prayers. It was natural, Higgins thought, that on this subject, if not on any others, he should have ideas.

"None of us like it," Tadlock said, speaking, as always, as if what he said left nothing over. He said to Summers, "Are you sure?"

Summers just nodded. He was still looking across the million miles of plain. Higgins guessed he was a little put out and a little amused by what must seem silly talk to him.

Higgins followed Tadlock's gaze down to the river. There was a little flanking of bushes there and some ragged stumps and three dead trees, and Botter and Brownie Evans and some others were working with axes, trying to get enough fuel for fires. Tadlock's eyes traveled upstream where the Platte, except for one wooded island, ran bare in its great wrinkles of sand.

"No wood," Tadlock said, not as a question, while he looked for it upriver. "No wood at all."

"Not enough," Summers answered.

"How about buffalo chips?"

"Plenty. We're comin' into buffler country."

"Mightn't they be scarce, too? Mightn't they have been used up?"

"They grow fast."

It was a keen answer, Higgins thought, but Tadlock didn't smile. "I can't understand it. Why are there trees on the islands?"

Fairman—who was a nice boy and good to work for—stooped and picked up a pinch of soil and rubbed it between his thumb and fingers. "This stuff won't grow anything except grass and cactus. It's straight sand."

Tadlock spoke slowly, as if coming to a deep answer. "It must be that the island soil is richer."

The men thought it over, nodding thoughtfully, until Summers said, "Injuns fire the prairies. Fire don't reach to the islands."

Tadlock looked as if he didn't care much for the answer. "At

89

any rate," he said, "that isn't the question. Could we pick up enough fuel while traveling—bushes and drift and such?"

As if to touch him up Summers answered, "It would slow us."

A cloud came on Tadlock's face. "We have to make time."

"If there's nothing else for it, there's nothing else for it," Lije Evans put in. He stood close to Tadlock. Measuring the two of them, Higgins figured there wasn't much difference in the size. Evans was taller, Tadlock thicker through the chest.

"I think we ought to give the question due consideration," Byrd said, solemn as a barn owl. "It's not something to be decided offhand. What do you say, Brother Weatherby?"

Weatherby stood gaunt and stooped in a piece of blue shirt and a pair of knee-sprung pants with a tear in them. He didn't answer right away but turned his eyes up and beyond them, as if drawing off to talk to God.

"I don't want to do all the talking here," Byrd said, licking his sore lip, "but it seems to me not appropriate. We shouldn't ask the ladies to do it if we can avoid it. It's not a ladylike thing."

Evans said, "Shoo!" and Byrd started a little, studying Evans as if surprised that anyone could feel different from himself. "My woman'll use it and think no more to it."

"Still," Byrd said, sounding less sure of himself, "the idea is offensive."

Higgins eased himself down on the ground. It struck him that Byrd and some of the others, for all that they knew better, stuck to queer ideas of women, not liking to think of them as flesh and blood and stomach and guts but as something different, something a cut above earthy things, so that no one should let on to them that critters had hind ends. Higgins didn't set himself up as a judge of women, though a pewter tinker like he used to be did learn some things, but still he bet they'd think all this palaver funny. Women had harder heads than men liked to believe. Even Mrs. Byrd did, probably.

McBee had been quiet, which was unusual for him. He spit now and spoke the awful word. "A little shit ain't going to hurt anyone. Dried out, it ain't. Let 'em cook over buffalo shit."

Patch sided with Byrd then. He spoke quietly out of his

sharp face. "It is precisely language like that and sentiments like that that make the thing objectionable."

McBee glanced at Tadlock and, getting no sign from him, let himself bristle like a feist. "I guess your woman knows enough not to step in it."

"No doubt, though gentlewomen wouldn't know it by that name."

McBee started to answer, but Tadlock turned on him and said, "Shut up!" and McBee just grinned through his whiskers and spit again and after a little pause answered, "That was all I had to allow."

Tadlock spoke both as if to warn McBee and give comfort to the others. "At any rate we can call it chips."

Higgins might not have put his oar in if he hadn't seen Byrd nodding. He asked, "Why don't you call it puddin', or cake?"

"How's that?"

"If a name makes it different from what it is, a sweet name ought to make it sure-enough tasty."

Tadlock thought about that, while Summers and Evans exchanged grins. Then he said, "This isn't a time for foolishness." He stared down at Higgins as if, by sitting, Higgins didn't show the case the right respect. "You don't seem much concerned."

"When I work I work hard, but when I set I set loose," Higgins answered.

"And you don't have to think about the protection of a wife."

"Last wife I had, I was the one needed pertection."

Brother Weatherby had pulled away from heaven long enough to give McBee a look. It wasn't his hardest look, though, and Higgins guessed it was the goddams and holy jesuses that really got his dander up.

"What do you say, Mack?" Tadlock asked.

"Nothing," Mack answered. He was looking down toward the river, where the women were doing around.

"Well," Tadlock said as if explaining to children, "let's examine the possibilities." He counted the points off on his fingers. "One, we can try to scrape up enough wood as we go along. Two, maybe enough food can be cooked tonight to enable us to get along without fires for a few days. Three—"

"Or us men can cook," Evans put in. "I don't see the use of talk."

"We want the general sentiment."

"I don't want to cook," Evans answered.

Mack had left the group, left it without speaking, like a man tired of talk. He wasn't, though. Higgins saw him down by the corral talking to the girl, Mercy McBee, and smiling while he talked.

It was Evans who kept the men pointed to the question. "You want to do your own cooking?" he asked them all.

Byrd and Patch didn't like to face up to the choice, Byrd especially. They looked at the ground and scuffed it and shook their heads slow, like a drammer being told he would have to quit or die. Higgins figured Patch had a heap more head on him than Byrd, though they were on the same side now. Patch had his proper Yankee ways but he had thought in his face, too, while all Byrd had along with his politeness was helplessness with animals, a big family, and a cracked lip.

Brother Weatherby came back to earth. "What the Lord wills, the Lord wills," he said.

"Meaning what?" asked Tadlock.

"If He has left us nothing to cook with except buffalo dung, He means us to cook with buffalo dung."

"Us?"

"Those who cook regularly."

"Suits me," McBee said, forgetting Tadlock had silenced him.

"What is not offensive in His sight should not be so in ours."

The men were nodding again, even Byrd, feeling better since God had taken sides.

Holdridge spoke for the first time then. He had been at the edge of the crowd, listening and watching out of a face made black as a kettle by beard and weather. Higgins took him for a shy man, though he didn't look it. "Who's goin' to pick the cow chips?" he asked.

"The younger ones can bring them in," Tadlock told him.

Sure, Higgins thought, the little ones and the boys not quite grown up would pick the chips and the women would cook over them and the men would make out not to notice. All but the pups could keep their put-on. All this palaver was just a bow to manners. From the first they knew they'd have to vote for chips.

Returning to the wagons, Higgins heard Evans say to Summers, "Well?"

"Heap of doin's over a cow dab," Summers answered.

Chapter - - - - - - - - - - - - Eleven

H IS NAME was Brownie Evans, and he was seventeen
. . . and the dust rose under the slow feet of the
cattle and powdered a man's skin and filled his nose, and the
sun bore through it, hot as a near fire, though summer was
just coming on, until his neck and cheeks and hands turned
dark as the saddle he rode on. The dust phlegmed the throat
and gritted between the teeth. It settled in the ears, feeling like
meal under the finger that tried to clear it out. Keep footin' it,
critters. Stay with the bunch, you. Git along! Far off, on sky
lines clear as water, heat waves ran.

His name was Brownie Evans and he was seventeen and
bound for Oregon, and this hand that held the reins was his,
this fixing of bone and joint and broken nails, made to answer
his orders; and the feet in the peg boots were his, and the arms
in the shirt and the legs in the homespun pants; and he lived
inside himself, under the ribs or beneath the skull, thinking
thoughts and feeling feelings like maybe hadn't been thought
or felt before, they were so kind of crazy . . . or it would rain,
out of a sky gray as ashes, and a wind would rise, pushing the
clouds along, and the skin inside the clothes would bunch up
against the cold, as the herd itself bunched up, looking sad and
scraggly. Giddup, and damn the loose horses! A horse wanted
to eat his head off.

The day would drag by, the long day would drag by—getting-
up time, nooning time, camping time, while the mind ran
loose and the eye looked right and left, for Indians and buffalo
and varmints like the prairie dogs the wagon train had come
on to lately and the owls that sat by the holes, or like the thing
called a porcupine that one of the men had shot. Dick Summers
said it was a prickly beaver, and the children had plucked it
clean of quills.

Ahead the eye would see the train winding, the men walking by their teams and the women and children tagging alongside if the day was fair, and the arched covers of the wagons, more gray than white now, swaying to the road. Farther on, sometimes, the outriders would come into view—Summers and Pa and Mr. Patch or Mr. Fairman and Mr. Tadlock or others, depending, and one of the rifle barrels would catch the sun and flash it back, across the long flat, over the wagons, through the dust, to where a man poked the loose stock along. Come on to noon, the riders ahead would get off their horses and begin digging holes along the shore of the river so as to get water that didn't run so thick with mud. Hig said the trouble with the Platte was it flowed bottom side up.

Hig's name was Higgins and Martin's was Martin and Botter's was Botter and Mr. McBee's was Henry McBee, and they rode often at the tail of the cow line, along with others who changed day by day. Hig talked to himself, out of a mouth that barely had room between nose and chin, or reined over when he thought of something good and told you about it and grinned afterwards, his mouth looking like a knife cut in his withered face. Martin rode stoop-shouldered and chewed tobacco and hardly ever smiled or talked, acting as if life was sorry and no help for it. People called Botter a steady man. When he spoke it was about horses or mules or cattle.

Those were their names, the names they were known by, but to know a name wasn't to know a man. The man lay deep, inside his name, underneath his talk and acts, as he did himself who went by the name of Brownie Evans and spoke and moved like everybody else but still lived secret and alone. People would say he was skinny and big-jointed and had too much of him turned under for feet, or they might say he was friendly and good-turned but bashful, but they wouldn't know him. He couldn't let them know him, for it would be the same as standing naked and maybe not looking like other folks but looking outlandish and shameful. What a person wondered was, were other people like him underneath or, more likely, solider and properer and not moved by crazy notions?

He wouldn't want to tell about how it was with him, not

even about the way his chest filled sometimes when he came to a rise and looked over the country or how his heart turned just at the smell of camp smoke or the lonely voices of the wild geese that had nested along the river. He would know then that good things awaited him, great things that he couldn't put a word to or set out in thought. He could trail cattle in the hot sun or in the winds that sprang up fierce. Or he could trail them in the rain, while storm clouds trailed over him and the feet of the stock sucked and slipped in the mud. With him would be the knowing—while he ran the work stock in and helped yoke up or went for water or poked a team or greased the axles from the tar bucket that swung underneath the wagon. It was his secret, this knowing that good things lay ahead, and probably people would smile, but sometimes at night he would wake up to the crying of wolves or the rustle of the breeze, and the goodness would lie with him like something he could squeeze to himself.

Just tomorrow they might meet Indians—Pawnees with roached hair, or Cheyennes or Arapahoes or Sioux, war-party Indians painted red and black. They came streaming on to the prairie and held up and looked while the wagons jolted into a circle and women cried and the men examined their rifles. They came on then, the Indians did, their head feathers bent to the wind of the charge, their war whoops breaking hoarse on the ear.

"Steady," Dick Summers said. He lay underneath a wagon, his rifle resting on a spoke of the wheel, and Brownie lay with him. Around the circle other men had posted themselves, and inside it the women and children peeked, white-faced, from behind the boxes and gear they had yanked from the wagons.

"They can't come it," Dick said, his cool gray eyes looking along the barrel. "They'll circle."

"Course not," Brownie said, and Dick switched his gaze over and gave him a half-smile, seeing Brownie's eye cool, too, and his hands easy on his rifle.

The Indians were all shining shields and yelling mouths and pounding hoofs, and then the two steady guns spoke and knocked two Indians from their horses, and the others broke then, flaring out like a covey of birds. They ran a bigger circle around the circle of wagons, just the tops of their heads showing or an arm or a leg, or a bow bent sharp and then the arrow streaking.

"Rifle!" Brownie pitched his empty gun back of him. His voice sounded keen as a shot.

"Here." Someone shoved a loaded piece into his reached-back hand. "Here." He let himself take one quick look behind him, and saw it was Mercy McBee, already charging the rifle he had emptied.

"Down! Down, Mercy!" But she just went on loading while the arrows pattered around her like hail.

"Two," Dick counted.

"Two for me, too. Rifle!"

"Three."

"Three. Rifle!"

It was too much for the Indians. It wasn't likely they had seen shooting like that before. They drew off, howling, and began fading into distance, and Dick Summers was saying, "Hang me, hoss, but you're a smart shot."

So it came to be that he was more like Dick Summers all the time. He had the same easy slouch in the saddle, the same seeing eye, the half-sad smile that showed just a little of what he might be thinking. He came to be like Dick Summers, except younger, and men and women looked at him as he rode by and listened to him while he leaned on his rifle, thinking how much he was and him just a boy, too, and they said to one another, "That Brownie Evans takes after Dick Summers like one pea to another."

Or a herd of buffalo might show up. They made a great, brown, rolling shadow on the slope north of the river, and men's eyes kindled while they counted balls and measured powder, but Dick Summers said, "Best leave this to me'n Brownie Evans. You all'll get a heap of shootin' later. Right now we're froze for meat." He turned, "Git your bow and arrers, Brownie."

"Bow and arrows." It was Mr. Tadlock, who didn't know beans about buffalo hunting.

"Sure."

"Bow and arrows!"

"Bow loads faster'n an iron."

"One rifle shot," Brownie said to Mr. Tadlock, "and you're done. Time you load up, them critters'll be four days gone."

They rode away, leaving Mr. Tadlock mouthing, "Bow and arrows?" They splashed across the Platte and came upwind toward the herd, riding slow. There was a mist of dust over the buffalo, raised by the stepping feet and the pawings of bulls. Underneath the mist the humps ran like waves as far as a man could see, and now on the near edge the waves heaved around, and hot eyes showed and low-held horns.

Dick said, "Ready?"

The horses sprang to full speed, the hunters silent yet, and the waves washed one way and another, and came to be parts of one great wave that flowed away as if a dam had broken.

The old bulls were the last to get going. They watched out of their dull and angry eyes and turned and broke into a clumsy gallop and turned again as if they had a mind to charge.

A yell broke out of Dick's throat, wild and strange as any war whoop, and Brownie matched it and drummed the ribs of his horse with his heels and came among the bulls and saw an opening and raced through it while the bulls hooked at him, too late. The horns clattered like a canebrake in a wind. The ground rolled up in a thick dust, hiding Dick, hiding the herd except for the bobbing rumps of the cows right ahead. The hoofs made a thunder in the head.

Brownie dropped his looped reins and took the arrow that he had popped into his teeth and notched it to his bow. His arm pulled it back to the head and let it go, and it sank out of sight in a fat cow. The cow slowed and stumbled and was lost behind.

Five cows he killed, five fat cows while the herd fanned out. He pulled up, his horse in a lather of sweat, and squinted through the dust for Dick.

He saw him at last, saw him hard after a cow that ran with two others and a bull and a calf, and then he saw the horse stumble and pitch over and Dick slammed hard on the ground.

98

Dick lay there, not moving, and the bull stopped and glared and pawed the ground and started for him.

There wasn't time to think. Brownie kicked his horse and felt him lunge and reached for an arrow while he stuck to the saddle like a bur. It was close, close as a crack, the bull right on Dick and the arrow drawn its full length, aimed dead at the heart. The bowstring hummed like a string on Hig's fiddle.

The bull fell a foot from Dick, the blood foaming from his mouth. Dick looked up. He wasn't hurt bad from the fall but only weak and winded. He said, "Half of stayin' alive is pickin' your pardner."

They rode into camp, while the men and women looked at them wide-eyed. One of the pair of eyes belonged to Mercy McBee, who stood a little to one side. They had been dancing, that was it. Mercy and the Patches and the Byrds and Mr. Mack and Botter and some of the rest had been dancing while Hig sawed on his fiddle and the music of it rose thin but brave in the empty land. Now they all stopped and looked, and one of the lookers was Mercy McBee, who dropped Mr. Mack's hand while the hunters rode by. A little smile touched her mouth, of wonderment and pride. He didn't smile back. He rode sober-faced, which was fitting to a man in such a case. All the same he guessed she knew how it was beginning to be with him.

"We'll need buffalo chips, Brownie, and if you could milk it would help your ma."

"Don't be askin' him to milk," Ma said, shaking her head at Pa.

"I don't aim for you to take it so hard."

"Milkin's nothing. It's the jolts and all."

Brownie said, "All right," and pulled the saddle from old Nellie and laid it by the wagon. Rock came over and took a sniff of the damp horse blanket and looked up as if asking what was doing next.

The wagons had drawn their night circle, and most of the oxen had been unyoked and driven out to graze. Around the wagons men and women were working, pulling out boxes and fixing to set up tents and to make fires.

99

Pa came over to where Brownie stood. "I wouldn't get morti-fied. It's the same fix with everybody."

"I milked before."

"It ain't milkin'. I'm talkin' about the chips."

"I said all right, Pa."

"It's just that it's new that bothers you. Do it awhile and you'll think nothing to it." Pa put his big hand on Brownie's shoulder. It felt warm and solid. The smile on his face was in-quiring, as if trying to see through to the Brownie that lived inside.

"It don't trouble me," Brownie said, but he didn't look at Pa. He looked at Ma, who was digging kettles out of a box.

"If you mind, I'll do it, and you can set up the tent."

Brownie shook his head. There wasn't any way out of it but to gather up buffalo chips. It shamed him to do it, but it would shame him more to show his shame to Pa. He had a lead rope on Nellie. He would take her over to where the herd was graz-ing and pick up some chips on the way back and maybe not be seen but by a few.

It was troublesome, to be ashamed of shame but to be ashamed just the same, and not just about buffalo chips, either. Here on the naked Platte there wasn't a bush to stand or squat behind. People couldn't build a brush arbor as they did at camp meetings. And, for fear of Indians, they couldn't walk out of sight. They did the best they could. Some of the women had chamber pots inside the wagons. Some hadn't and sometimes were caught sudden along the way. Or a rider would get off his horse and stand on the off side and make out to be idling or sizing up the country, but the cant of his head and the slope of his shoulders would give him away.

They thought up a system, the women did, and morning, noon, and night a bunch of them would trail off a piece, and the up-standing ones would make a shield for the others while the menfolks around the wagons made out to be so busy they didn't know what was going on.

Brownie took the rope and set off with Nellie. Maybe there wasn't anyone, he thought, as mortified as he was, and not just when it came to himself and his business, either. It struck him as ugly—the women making their shield, the men standing behind horses, the young ones squatting almost anywhere. When he thought about it, the feeling of goodness in him drew off.

He untied the rope from Nellie and turned her with the rest and wound the rope around his waist and knotted the ends, so's to have his arms free for gathering.

The chips ripped up, pulling loose from the whitened grass beneath. There were bugs under the chips, little scuttlers of gray and black that ran seeking among the stems when the roof was lifted from over their heads. He would have watched them, except that he would be seen watching. He cuffed old Rock, who made a show of himself by coming close and looking, curious as a chicken, whenever a chip was raised.

Other people were working, too, young ones, like the straw-haired Brewer girl and her two brothers, and Joe Turley and Jeff Byrd and John Shields and Harry Gorham and two or three of the Daughertys. Some of the men didn't have a family and so had to do for themselves, like old Brother Weatherby, who said people shouldn't complain but praise God that, anyhow, there were chips to make fires with. Brother Weatherby gathered up the chips slow and sober, maybe saying a prayer to himself while he did it.

The land lay quiet. The only sound Brownie could hear, except for the ring of distance and the little commotions of camp, was the tearing sound of chips being pulled from the grass. The sun was half sunk, as if just letting itself peek at what was going on. Then the children got to playing, throwing chunks of manure at one another and yelling shrill until the old folks called from the wagons and told them to get busy.

Brownie picked up one chip and another and another. They were thick here. Buffalo chips meant buffalo—and not so far away now, Dick Summers said. For two days the train had kept crossing trails from the bluffs down to the river, trails as wide as the span of two hands and worn deep as a fist and as smooth as a spade could cut. Bones lay around, too, skulls and leg bones and ribs, some of them set in circles or half-moons and splashed with paint, by the Pawnees, Dick said.

He picked up more chips, looking at nobody, and after a

101

while had an armful and stood straight, and there was Mercy McBee not five steps away, and she hadn't seen him, either, and so stood surprised, holding half an armful. Underneath the pile, Brownie could see the small fingers bent around.

She didn't speak, or turn her eyes down, either, but the blood climbed slow in her cheeks.

He couldn't think of anything to say. He felt heat in his own face and knew it was red, too, but still he looked at her, seeing the dark eyes and the face framed with hair that the wind had blown wild. He had a sudden, crazy wanting to reach out and touch her as a person might touch a small, scared thing, making up to it with the gentle hand. It was as if at the touch the two of them would melt into understanding that wiped away shame, into tenderness that went without words.

He said, "I reckon I got a load."

She looked down and bent a little and a crumb of the dried manure fell from under her hand and caught on her faded dress and stuck there.

The words he had said beat back on him, the empty, clumsy words, and he saw himself as if he stood outside, saw himself gawky, big-handed and big-footed, with the pale fine sprouts of new whiskers on his face, saw himself unproved and likely cowardly, lost in fool dreams.

He took two steps and wrenched around and said, "I could do it for you."

Her glance came up in a quick, liquid look that he couldn't understand.

"I'd be pleasured to."

"I can do it all right." She turned without thanking him. She walked away and stopped and stooped, somehow pitiful and somehow dignified, and fingered for a cow dab.

Of a sudden, while he dared to watch, he understood something about her, seeing in his mind's eye old Hank McBee and his dirty whiskers and the thin oxen, hitched along with an old roan horse, that pulled the McBee wagon, and with the wagon Mrs. McBee and her loud brood and a coop of messy chickens.

He could imagine now that a snake had been by her, a rattle-snake that someway didn't rattle, and he had seen the ugly head rise from the grass, unseen by her, and the dirty coil of it close by her ankle, and, without thought for himself, he had leaped forward and smashed the head under his heel.

He jumped and came to himself and found he was on the way to the wagon, the heel of one big foot ground into the dirt and old Rock looking queerly at him, but still he talked to her saying, "Mercy! Mercy!"

In his dream she came to him, came tenderly, with the shimmer of tears in her eyes, and put her mouth on his and rested soft in his arms—and he felt the animal rising in him, eager and pushful, and was ashamed of his coarseness.

Chapter - - - - - - - - - - - - - Twelve

TADLOCK STOOD at the side of his second wagon. "Martin," he said sharply, looking underneath. "You, Martin!"

He straightened, waiting for an answer, suspecting already that something was wrong. Not once, in more than a month on the road, had Martin lain abed after the sentinels had fired their four-o'clock volley.

"Martin!"

Dawn was firing the east, far down the shallow valley of the Platte, and here and there the waters of the river glowed to it, like puddles under the moon, but here the night lay dusky, licked by the little fires people had commenced to make. The smell of camp smoke, of dung or wood igniting to punk and powder struck by flint and steel, came sharp to his nostrils.

"Martin!" He couldn't make out the man, but only the gray hump of him under the piece of wagon sheet that Martin used for cover or tent, depending on whether the night looked fair or stormy.

Tadlock stooped and caught the corner of the sheet and pulled it, calling out again. "What's wrong here?"

The hump moved then. It lurched and settled back and a voice came out of it. "I'm sick. Jesus!"

"Get out from there, then. We'll have to make you a bed in one of the wagons."

Tadlock got no answer to that. He imagined Martin thinking it over, asking himself weakly, in the manner of an indisposed woman, whether he was strong enough for the day. In sharp annoyance he said, "You were all right last night. You stood your turn at guard."

He flicked the ground with the whip he carried. Damn the luck! Here they were at Brady's Island, within striking distance of the forks of the Platte, and the road was good and buffalo were plenty and the weather fair enough, and now a man had to get sick. The suspicion came to him again, while the dawn drew on and the itch to get going grew in him, that Martin was pretending to be sicker than he was. Some people would exaggerate a mere indisposition, especially if they wanted to turn back, especially if they had listened too long to weak talk about Indians and hardships. The train never camped but that someone, like Turley or his wife or one of the Byrds, began crying about dangers.

Dangers! They'd hardly met a one. They had had a stampede, and Mack, like the fool Tadlock told him that he was, had shot a scrawny Indian. Later a delegation from the Kaws had called about the killing, but he as captain had handled them all right. He had outfaced the bunch and sent them packing, without so much as one twist of tobacco to soothe their scurvy feelings. For the rest, they hadn't seen a Pawnee, a Cheyenne, or a Sioux. They'd made all the crossings safely. And, until now, no one had been sick, barring a mild flux or a stomach-ache.

"We'll get a bed fixed. You crawl out of there." Tadlock turned and walked part way round the circle, raising his whip when people spoke to him. His own wagons were so laden that he couldn't spread a decent bed without transferring part of the contents. He would consult Mack about that. He came first, though, to the Evans fire and on impulse stopped there, nodding to Evans and his wife and Dick Summers. The Evans boy, Tadlock guessed, had gone out to help gather up the stock.

"Little nippy this morning," Evans said, hitching his shoulders.

"We've got a sick man."

"Who?"

"Martin."

"What ails him?"

Tadlock shrugged.

"How sick?" Evans asked.

Tadlock shrugged again. "I'm going to rig a bed."

Summers took the pipe from his mouth and held it in front

of him and blew a cloud of smoke around it. The action irritated Tadlock. It was typical of the man, as if the train had all of time to consider one case of sickness. He searched for words to describe Summers. Undisciplined. Unsystematic. Accustomed to living without purpose, like a savage. "We'll roll out on time," he told Summers pointedly. "We can't hold up for one man."

Mrs. Evans was scraping out the pans they'd eaten from. "Lije," she said, "you better have a look."

Summers' gray eyes, appearing almost white against the backdrop of dawn, slid to her in an expression of approval and regard.

"Well, you can see for yourselves," Tadlock said.

"Uh-huh," Evans answered mildly. He stood up, looming big, a close, solid shadow among the shadows that were lifting to the west. Tadlock felt for him the impatience that he might have felt for a child. A slow-going, slow-witted man, Evans was, competent but without force. Tadlock found himself wondering whether the man ever lost his temper, ever came to a decision without guidance from his wife or Summers. "Come on then."

Summers knocked the heel from his pipe and got up, too.

"Don't you reckon you'd best take some medicine, Lije?" Mrs. Evans asked, and Evans nodded and went to the tail of his wagon and, after what seemed a long time to Tadlock, came back with a box.

Martin lay as before, except that now he could be seen, the hair untidy on his head, the whiskers gray and stubbled on his lank face.

The three of them bent over, like three hens, Tadlock thought, at the sight of a strange bug.

"What's the matter, hoss?" Summers asked.

"Come on out, Martin!" Tadlock ordered. "We can't doctor you there, or get you in a wagon bed, either." He tugged at the wagon cover.

Martin opened his eyes and lay staring up at the underside of the wagon. He licked his mouth and said, "Jesus!"

"Come on!" Tadlock saw that Martin's face was flushed and

his eyes feverish, but still it was in him to say, "You can't be that sick, man."

Summers said, "Reckon he knows better'n you."

"I'll handle this." While Tadlock spoke Martin moved. He got himself over on his belly and raised to all fours and came crawling out, stumbling on the wagon sheet that trailed with him. When he was out, he let himself go flat again.

"Acts bad off," Evans said.

"He won't feel any worse in a wagon," Tadlock told him.

Summers knelt and helped Martin over on his back and felt his forehead. "Easy, hoss," he said, and then, to Tadlock and Evans, "Could be camp fever."

"What's that?"

"Camp fever. No other name to it."

Martin said, "Jesus!" and closed his eyes, and Summers looked up and shook his head.

Some of the others of the camp had started to come up, attracted by the sight of the three of them standing and the man on the ground. "What's wrong?"

Tadlock felt them behind him, but he didn't turn or answer. He wished they would clear out. They would all have ideas. Some might want to go on, but some would want to wait and some wouldn't know what to do. And some would want to physic the man and some to bleed and some to blister him. The result would be an endless dillydallying, when the part of good sense was to load Martin in a wagon and start rolling.

It was like Evans to answer the question. "Camp fever," he said.

A woman's voice asked, "Is it catchin'?"

Tadlock snapped back, "No!"

Martin opened his eyes and rolled them up from face to face as if hoping to find in one of them the answer to his trouble.

Tadlock swung around. "Go and get ready. We'll move in a few minutes. Evans, if you'll take just a little of my load, I can make a bed. We'll doctor him and roll."

"I do' know, Tadlock," Evans said.

"Don't know what?"

"Do' know as we ought to."

"I'm the captain. I'll assume the responsibility."

Behind Tadlock a dry voice spoke up that he recognized as Patch's. "We're all together, you know, Tadlock, including your hired hand."

"Who said we weren't? We'll still be all together when he's in a wagon."

"That ain't what Patch means," Evans put in.

Tadlock bit back the words that came to his lips. The fools! The damn fools, acting as if this were a time and place for leisurely solicitude! He looked at them one by one—Evans, Summers, Patch—trying to stare them down. In their eyes he read a stupid stubbornness.

It came to him, slowly, that the thing had come to be an issue. A position taken, a sensible position taken, a few words said—and then the lines drawn! Now, here, authority was at stake, prestige, the leadership that forced the train along. To give in to them would be to acknowledge his defeat.

He felt movement at his side and turned and saw Mrs. McBee, a small, ragged witch of a woman. "We got some Jew David's Plaster," she said. "It's good for most anything."

He waved her away. "All right, Evans. Doctor him!"

"What I want to do," Evans said—and Tadlock felt a pulse of astonishment at his tone—"is to see everybody's took care of proper. We got to tend to Martin. I ain't for joltin' him along in a wagon."

"You want to bring up the rear, I guess!"

"I want to see Martin's took care of, or anybody else that gets sick."

Tadlock held on to himself. "Grass is already short because of the buffalo. It'll be a damn sight shorter if we let other companies get ahead."

"We ain't first anyhow," Summers answered. "There's some beyond."

"A handful if any. Light outfits with little stock. But because they're ahead you think we can let everybody pass!"

Summers was gnawing on his pipestem. He spoke almost idly. "Camp fever makes the bones ache bad."

Patch said, "I'm in favor of staying here until we know Martin's better."

Tadlock heard a mutter of approval from the crowd that had grown while they stood arguing. Their eyes were all fixed on him, it seemed, fixed accusingly when all he had sought was the welfare of the company. System was the thing, a time to get up, a time to travel, a time to bed down, a set distance to make daily, each man performing his appointed duties, each answering to the call of authority. That way, they'd get to Oregon, get there safely, speedily, ahead of the rest. But these men didn't appreciate system, organization, discipline. They didn't deserve the leadership he had given them.

His temper flared up at the thought. "We'll roll. Hear? I say we'll roll."

They didn't move. They stood quiet, regarding him with that stupid stubbornness, until Evans said, "Do' know as we will, Tadlock. Seems to me this is a thing for the council."

"Council!"

"Let the council decide, seein' as we don't agree."

"Good God!"

"Meantime, I ain't movin'."

Patch added, "I, either," and again there came the mutter of approval.

Tadlock would have cursed them except that it occurred to him that he could handle the council. Brewer was on it, and Mack and Fairman. They would stand by him. The train would lose the time the meeting took, which was to be regretted, but hereafter these muttonheads might not be so ready to dispute his orders. "Stay then!" he said and laughed at them. "We'll talk our way to Oregon."

Evans stooped at the sick man's side.

"Take your time," Tadlock told him. "No hurry. We're only going as far as Oregon City." He added, "The council will meet in an hour."

For a time he watched the self-appointed doctors while they got Martin in a good bed under a tent and talked themselves into believing calomel was the proper medicine. Not that, alone, he wouldn't have cared for Martin and done it just as well. It was just that there were too many wanting to take a hand, too many holding out for Sarsaparilla Blood Pills and Balsam of Life and emetics and calomel and bloodletting.

Leaving, he debated the question of talking to Mack and Fairman before the council met. He decided not to. On this open plain a private conference was impossible. Seeing them, Patch or someone would suspect a conspiracy. He would ask McBee to serve notice of the meeting.

Having asked him, he strode about the camp, confident but still sore, now and then flicking his whip at a grass stem and feeling something gratified when the popper snapped off a blade. The women, he saw with approval, were making the most of this idle time. Five or six of them were at the river's edge, washing clothes in the sandy water. A couple had washboards. The others scuffed the washing between their hands and slapped the heavier things on rocks dug out of the sand from God knew where. For the most part the men not tending to Martin just stood around talking while children ran squealing among them. They were talking, Tadlock had no doubt, about him and about Martin and what was the thing to do. Well, he could tell them.

Later, at the upper end of the camp, away from the tents and the talk, Tadlock saw Summers by himself, standing still as some old bull while he looked to the West that had molded him. Tadlock walked up to him. "I can't understand you, Summers," he began.

Summers half turned, his two hands clasped on his rifle, the butt of which rested on the ground. "Countin' buffler, is all."

"I don't mean that," Tadlock answered, knowing Summers knew that he didn't. "We ought to be traveling."

Summers looked at the sun, now well above the eastern horizon. "Could've made three or four miles, I reckon," he said, his face grave. In his eyes, though, Tadlock caught a gleam that exasperated him.

"Goddam it! This isn't a thing for fun."

"Not sayin' it is," Summers answered, the gleam in his eyes fading, "nor for thinkin' miles instead of Martin."

"One man isn't a train."

"I didn't figure you knew that."

"What do you mean?"

"Ain't you the whole shebang?"

"You're the pilot, Summers. That's all." Tadlock spoke deliberately, wanting to irritate the man, wanting almost to bait him to a fight that would relieve the feelings in himself. He waited, the butt of his whip held tight in his hand.

Summers turned and looked across at the river and the island that stood wooded in it. "That there's Brady's Island," he said so casually that Tadlock was unprepared for the rest. "A man named Brady got himself rubbed out. That was back in 'thirty-three."

Summers' gaze came back to rest on Tadlock. In it, Tadlock thought, was the cool, the deadly expression of an animal waiting for a kill. Not until then had he known how dangerous the guide could be. He wasn't afraid but still he felt relief when Summers lifted his rifle and moved off. Tadlock watched him go. Summers' gait was the soft and easy gait of an Indian. His hair was beginning to hang long in back, Indian-fashion, too.

Well, to hell with him, Tadlock thought, and to hell with his parting look of contempt or hostility or whatever it was! Looks didn't hurt. A man could afford to ignore a half-savage pilot.

The restlessness in him made him want to move. He stepped on westward, letting his gaze roam over the sunlit country while his mind worked. Ahead of him were wagon tracks, the tracks of the emigrants of 1844 and before. They would have had their troubles, too. No doubt there were fools aplenty in those trains, men who couldn't lead but balked at being led and, by the balking, showed the need of the very thing that they resisted.

Across the river he saw buffalo and tried to guess how far away they were. Here in the fine air of the Platte one underestimated. A bluff or a turn of the river that looked but an hour away might be a day or more. A crow a half mile off appeared within good rifle range. Details stood out—the swags and rises of the sand hills, the bars of the river and the water frothy in an eddy, the beards of the distant buffalo, even the very blades of grass. This clear air, he thought, made the world at once smaller and bigger, smaller because the eye saw, bigger because it saw so far. Sound mixed one's impressions, too. By night every noise was intimate and distinct; by day the report of a rifle was a faint pop in a silence that rang the head like quinine. It was a strange and awesome world. It required decision and management.

He had shown the qualities it took. He had kept the train in motion. He'd managed. They owed a debt to him—and paid in criticism! Take the day Mack shot the Indian, the day that followed the stampede. When daylight came, Summers had led a mere handful of riders out to hunt the scattered cattle. With him away—and with him his precious right to name and organize war parties—Tadlock had appointed other riders, until nearly every last manjack was gone. But still the train went on, the ox teams poked by women and the bigger children.

A storm came up that morning—a wretched, all-day rain that greased the ground and later soaked it, so that the rearward wagons floundered half-stuck in the mire. The rain was cold, slanted by a chilly breeze. The drivers climbed up in the wagons to escape it and got colder yet for want of exercise and climbed back down and stumped along, their feet heavy and misshapen with the clinging mud. But they went on. That was the point. Women driving, children driving, they went on.

Tadlock had shown the way, since Summers was scouting with the men, but often he turned back to give his people help and heart. One thing he could do, he'd have to say for himself, was to get an ox to pull. Give him his whip and he could lift a piece of hide. More than once that day he'd taught a team a thing or two.

He taught the Indians something, also, taught the six-man delegation that caught up with the train two hours or so after it had started out. Byrd, who rode so poorly that Tadlock hadn't sent him with the men, had seen them first and managed to get himself aboard an extra horse and bounced ahead to give the news to Tadlock.

The train wasn't in position to corral. It had spread out in the mud. The going was too heavy for a quick maneuver. A hill rose to the right. Trees grew to left.

All these considerations came to Tadlock while Byrd panted

out his message. On the instant he saw them clear and knew what he would have to do.

"Get the women armed!" he barked. "You and Willie Brewer and the preacher come to the rear, with rifles." He jammed a fresh cap on his own. "How many Indians?"

"I just caught a glimpse."

"How far away?"

"Close."

"Do what I tell you!" Tadlock dug his heels into his horse and galloped toward the line, leaving Byrd to follow. He held up his hand for a halt. He couldn't see the Indians yet. They were lost in a strip of woods, lost in the mist.

Charging by the wagons, Tadlock saw the white faces of the women, the suddenly frightened faces of children, the face of his wife written over with anxiety. He hoped that, beholding him, they were finding courage.

A hundred yards below the tail-end wagon he spied the Indians riding from a brake. He slowed his horse and walked it toward them. Six Indians. That was all he saw. Six Kaws, he guessed they were, with roached hair mussed by rain, with odds and tatters of attire glued wet against their skins. The leader had a soggy blanket draped around him. Tadlock caught the black-wet shimmer of gun steel, the tight arch of a bow. A mangy set but maybe mean, he thought, and rode straight at them until they pulled their horses up.

He stared at them, making his face as tight and blank as theirs. It stirred his pride to think, as he went from gaze to gaze, that he felt, not fear, but challenge, the heady, hard conflict of wills. He asked, "What you want?"

They were a long time answering. Never, he imagined, had they been received like this. They expected the pipe, the oratory, the soft courtesies that were the custom.

The Kaw with the blanket spoke. "Kill Injun." He pointed back, toward where Mack had dropped the Indian from the tree.

"Kill Injun, yes," Tadlock answered. "Injun steal, so kill Injun."

"Injun no steal."

113

"Injun steal. Heap dead."

"Injun love presents."

"No presents."

Tadlock saw thought working in their eyes. He saw what he supposed was disappointment rising from his refusal to make amends with gifts. Now was the time, he knew. Now was the danger. But still he felt no fear. Looking at this ill-fed, scrap-clothed crew, he felt power surging in him, power to bend them, power to treat them as he chose. It was as if, with one sweep of the hand, he could wipe them from the earth.

He caught the leader's gaze and stared it down. In the flush of certitude he said, "Get!" and hitched his rifle closer. He said, "Now get!" and touched his horse a step ahead.

He was the master of them. One by one they turned. The eyes sliding off from his had a look of craven injury. They filed back as they had come. He sat straight and still, by his power and presence willing them away, until the last of them was gone from sight.

He had reassured the women afterwards, had got the train to moving, had met the riders coming in and told them no, it wasn't time to camp. Rain, mud, Indians, scattered cattle—and still the train had rolled a decent distance. Eight miles, maybe ten, he estimated. Which showed what management could do. Which showed what a little spunk could do. He didn't exaggerate his deed, though he heard the women talking of it to their men. It was no more than the duty of a captain to his company. He'd do the same again in spite of Summers, who said, "It worked this time, but don't never try it on a Pawnee or a Sioux."

That night he let it be known the cattle guards would have to show some sense. The idea, firing at imaginary Indians and so causing a stampede! Of course the Indians were imaginary. Hadn't the riders found all the animals but one? Had they spied a single thief? He didn't hide his sentiments about Mack and his behavior, either. Not that one Indian mattered much. It was the consequences possible. The men took it well enough then. They knew they had it coming.

But now, because he said a sick man didn't justify delay, because he said Martin would be as well off in a wagon, they acted up! Tadlock popped another blade of grass.

He reminded himself it was about time for the council to meet, but for a minute longer he stood where he was, pecking at the ground with his whip. He saw, again with approval, that other women had joined the group at the river's edge. One of the men had built a fire for them, and water was heating in a tub and a couple of buckets, sending up wisps of steam into air still a little chill from the night. To the south the animals grazed, herded loosely. Three horsemen were splashing across the river, hurrying to keep from miring in the quicksand that formed the bed. He identified them one by one—Summers and Gorham and the boy, Brownie Evans. He supposed they were going to hunt the buffalo that grazed northward.

It irritated him that they should set out, for buffalo grazing at a distance, away from where the road led. It was as if they assumed already, prior to the action of the council, that the train wouldn't move. Under good discipline the act would have been recognized as an act of impudence, if these people understood that word.

He blamed Summers most of all—and not for this small offense alone. He had the feeling that Summers contaminated the company with his casual independence, his backwoodsman's uncertain respect for authority. Summers knew the trail. He was a good guide, an expert hunter, a watchful scout, a never-sleeping sentinel. He was all of these, Tadlock had to admit to himself, but he was also a man hard to manage or impress, a man admired for his Indian graces and rude skills and so imitated in attitudes.

Walking to the council meeting, Tadlock found himself wishing resentfully that he had Summers' frontier lore to go along with his own impulse for order. It was Summers who suggested, along the Little Blue, that horses be tied to the branches, not the trunks, of trees. That way, he said, they wouldn't break the bridle reins. Summers could lure buffalo cows to him by imitating the call of a calf. He could put an arrow or a ball into a cow and leave life enough in her to drive her close to camp, thus eliminating the chore of packing in the meat. And who but Summers would think of tying his horse to the horns of a killed buffalo while he butchered? Summers could handle oxen, mules, horses. He could, it seemed, smell game and water and Indians. He was deadly with rifle and bow. He struck the quickest fire. The manner in which he rounded the wagons into a corral at night was simple and effective, though it did lack military style. For himself, Tadlock would have preferred a method he had been told about, by which the train divided into equal sections, with an officer for each, and made smart right-angle turns and formed a square. Still, he had to admit, Summers' way was good. Damn the man, anyhow! He was competent—though outwardly modest if somehow insolent—and independent as a hog on ice! Why couldn't a man of wider view, of greater education, possess that wilderness wisdom? Small a qualification as it was, it still would promote the recognition of leadership.

The other councilmen, out fifty yards or so from the wagons, were waiting. Tadlock checked them off—Evans, Fairman, Mack, Brewer, Daugherty. He sat down by them. "How's Martin?"

"No good," Brewer answered in his thick German. "He vill die, you bet."

"He's tough."

Evans said, "My woman's watchin' him, along with Brother Weatherby and some others."

Tadlock nodded, thinking not so much about Martin as about the council, as about an issue that had grown beyond its true importance because it was a challenge to authority. He wished, almost, that he had proposed the delay. Still, it was all right. Brewer he could count on, and Mack and Fairman. They and he would compose a majority. "Still could make ten miles or so," he said, squinting at the sun. "Every mile counts."

They didn't answer. Only Brewer, sitting cross-legged, his paunch spilling over into his lap, so much as nodded.

"Martin's out of his head," Daugherty said in what might have been reproach.

Tadlock sized him up, wondering now as he had wondered

116

before why this hillside Irishman opposed him. Could he have overheard some incautious criticism of popishness?

"Just yells Jesus," Evans added. "Yells Jesus and follers with 'To Thee I pray.' "

"That doesn't show he's out of his head."

"He was niver a great one for prayin'," Daugherty said.

Tadlock had the feeling that in their faces was the look of something withheld. He studied them, then let his gaze stray off to the camp where the wagons stood idle and the new-done wash stirred on lines the women had run from wagon to wagon. He saw the tent that had been put up to shelter Martin and Weatherby standing by it, his rusty coat donned out of respect to sickness. Women and children moved among the wagons and the fires that were being allowed to die. Women always managed to improve the movement, Tadlock reflected while his eyes went from them to four men who lay by Patch's wagon. One of them was stabbing idly at the ground with a knife. He thought he could hear Martin's voice, maybe crying to Jesus.

"Well," he said, "we have a decision to make."

They didn't answer him. They sat waiting, their lids narrowed against the sun. It would be warm today and dazzlingly bright, the sun striking back from the sand and the saltlike patches that lay on it.

He caught Evans' eye. "You're willing to abide by the decision of the council?"

"Are you?"

"Naturally." Tadlock gave his attention to the others. "We need to remember that the trick is to keep moving. It will be late fall before we reach Oregon in any case."

Evans brought his hand to his face and rubbed his broad cheek as if rubbing helped him to think. "I ain't denyin' what you say, Tadlock, but we been makin' good time. It ain't as if we couldn't spare a day or two."

"We'll meet other delays, you know."

"Maybe so."

"Delays we can't avoid."

Evans changed his position on the ground. When he spoke he looked at the others. "It don't seem to me we have to be so

117

hellbent to beat everybody. Way I figure, we'll pass and be passed before this jig is over."

Mack said, "You're half racehorse, Irvine. You're bred to run in front."

"Ya. Better to keep ahead, you bet," Brewer said.

In his astonishment at Mack, in his rising vexation, Tadlock spoke sharply. "If someone didn't push, the whole company would sit on its tail."

"If one of us was sick, I think we'd want the train to wait," Fairman put in.

So they were all against him, Tadlock thought incredulously, all but the thickheaded German. He had led them, he had worked, organized, directed, pushed—and they were all against him. Or were they? When it came finally to decision, wouldn't Mack and Fairman side with him? "Let's vote," he said. "Mack, Fairman, I assume you'll support my recommendation."

Mack answered, "No." The smile was gone from his face. Fairman was shaking his head.

"No!"

"No," Mack said again. Fairman kept shaking his head.

Evans tossed a piece of buffalo dung at his old gray-whiskered dog, which was digging in a hole near by. "Reckon you'll have to wait, Tadlock," he said.

Tadlock felt the blood hot in his face. "All I have to say is that it's a goddam-fool decision."

Mack spoke quietly. "I have to tell you something else."

"What?"

"There's a meeting tonight."

"Meeting?"

"Whole company."

"For what?"

"Can't you guess?"

"This is a guessing game, is it?"

"They're going to unseat you, Irvine."

"You're a goddam liar!"

"I'll wait for your apology."

The meaning of Mack's words, the full import, came to Tadlock slowly. He clenched words back while he considered it. They meant to kick him out. They meant to elect a new captain. He could see how the thing had come about. Patch, the little, stiff-necked New Englander, Daugherty, Gorham, Carpenter—these men, he had known, opposed him, and now they had politicked around, trading on the unpopularity of leadership, making big this little issue of the sick man. "We'll see about that," he said to Mack. "I'll stand on my position about Martin."

"Can't you see it's not just that?" Mack asked.

"I see. I called you a fool, and that's what you were."

"The world is all a fool to you," the Irishman put in.

"I was a fool all right," Mack said, the color climbing in his face, "but it's not that either, Irvine. It's the airs you have. It's overbearance."

"And it is your animals and not enough men for them that slow the train—and you foriver cryin' for speed," Daugherty added. "And it is you and your pushiness that sour us, and that's the God's truth."

"You say you're not sore," Tadlock said to Mack. "Then where do you stand?"

"I've got to vote for harmony."

"What about you, Fairman?"

Fairman said, "Same here."

"You can't get away with it."

"You tell him, Brewer," Daugherty said.

"I be for you," the German explained. "McBee, too. But ve not be enough."

So it was true. So they had conspired against him. So he had to resign or suffer the humiliation of being voted out. Brewer wouldn't lie to him. "That's the thanks a man gets. I've worked, figured, risked my neck."

Evans said—and Mack nodded to the words—"That's what makes it hard, Tadlock."

"I can split this train in two. I have a few friends."

"You're losin' 'em by the minute," Evans said with what for him was heat.

Tadlock lurched to his feet. "To hell with all of you!" Not

119

until he had taken a half a dozen steps away could he bring himself to throw back, "I resign."

Tadlock walked to his lead wagon. "I just quit," he told his wife.

She was seated on a box, mending a pair of trousers that he had ripped in loading the wagon. She gazed at him without speaking.

"It was resign or get kicked out," he went on, getting a kind of perverse satisfaction out of the admission.

Still she didn't speak. In ten years of married life, he thought with a stir of pleasure, she had learned better than to inquire into his business. What he wanted her to know, he would tell her. He waited, almost hoping she would put a question so that he could spend his outrage on her.

When he didn't go on, she said, "Martin's worse."

"I guess that's my fault!"

"I didn't mean it was anybody's fault."

"If we'd been traveling, everyone would have said it was mine. They'd have been glad to say that."

"I'm glad you resigned."

"So you're glad, are you!"

"You take it so hard."

He grunted, disarmed. She was one, anyhow, who knew how much he gave.

She stitched quietly for a minute as if thinking about him and his resignation, but when she spoke it was to say, "Martin depended on you. I think you were the only friend he had."

"I don't know anything to do for him."

"I know, but—"

He walked around to Martin's tent. Brother Weatherby was outside, holding an old Bible.

Tadlock asked, "Well?"

"I have been praying. The Lord's will be done."

"Out of his head?"

"Now. Yes."

Tadlock stuck his head inside the tent. Martin lay on his back, his mouth open and his eyeballs showing white through lids not quite closed. Listening, Tadlock heard the light, fast breath of fever. He stepped back, repelled by the sight and sound and smell of sickness. There was nothing he could do, he told himself. What did they think he was? A doctor?

Weatherby said, "I think he saw the light."

"Calomel work?"

Weatherby nodded, and Tadlock went back to his wagon.

He spent a bitter, fiddley day. He kept going over what had happened and experienced each time a renewed injury and anger. He examined and repaired wagons and equipment and went back twice to Martin's tent. On his second trip he found Martin alone and soiled and senseless. Here was something he could do. Here was something, by God, he would do. No one could say he was indifferent or neglectful or heedless of the discipline he asked of others. Washing Martin off, he wondered fiercely who would do as much. As he finished, Byrd came in. Byrd had a lancet and thought, like others, that bleeding would be good for Martin. Tadlock helped bleed him.

The meeting of the men at night was what might have been expected—a common hurly-burly made more orderless by the women and children who were allowed to press around. Thinking about it afterwards, Tadlock was still surprised that Evans and not Patch was elected to succeed him. He would have sworn that Patch was agitating in the interests of himself. Evans himself had acted honestly astonished when Mack put his name in nomination. He had turned and looked at his wife and then stumbled ahead. "Nope, Mr. Chairman. I ain't cut out for it."

Seated at a little distance where he could hear and see enough but still not dignify the meeting with his presence, Tadlock had caught the look on Mrs. Evans' face. It was an expression he couldn't describe, of motherliness, concern, pride, assurance, ambition—he didn't know what. But for an instant, before he thrust it aside, he had the feeling it would be good to be looked at that way. His second thought was that only big, dull, forceless men ever could be so regarded.

Another thing stuck in his memory as he sat by his wagon in the gathering dark after the meeting had adjourned. It was the parliamentary disorder that was allowed to prevail, the promise of the general disorder to come. While Evans' name was still in nomination, Turley piped up, irrelevant to the subject, and Patch let him proceed. "We're a-turnin' back." Turley's voice was a high whine. "Me and my woman and young-'uns, we're a-turnin' back, by Moses!"

Mrs. Turley shouted from among the women, "Amen! Amen!" Tadlock heard her crying hysterically afterwards, as he had heard overwrought women cry at revivals.

"We're headin' backwards for the Meramec," Turley went on, "seein's this company won't wait for others and seein's everybody is at outs besides. Who wants to turn back with us, welcome."

Patch asked, "What about it, Summers?"

Summers stood off to Patch's right. He said one word: "Dangerous."

A little silence followed—except for Mrs. Turley's crying—that Patch broke by asking, "Anyone else want to turn back?" He waited. "Byrd?"

That, Tadlock had thought through his bitterness, was good management, was one accidental stroke of good management. Let Byrd say yes or no. Get him committed and hold him to it.

Byrd said he'd stick.

Patch went on, "If anyone plans to split off from the train, we'd like to know it now." He didn't look toward Tadlock but others turned to do so. Tadlock stared back, silent and unmoving. Split off? How could he split off? It was an impulsive threat he'd made. Who would go with him? Brewer and McBee and Martin, maybe, if he lived. A sorry lot, without oxen enough and some of those already sore of foot. He sat stiff and wordless, but he wanted to jump up and cry out, calling them the ingrates that they were. He felt like rising with his whip and lashing them one and all until they saw the truth of things. Cattle? Drivers? The charge was just a cheap excuse. Hadn't he brought Martin along and scoured Independence for a man and finally made a deal with Hank McBee to help out with the hundred and ten head of stock he had? Hadn't he done the best he could—and not because they forced him to it, either?

For a long time after the session was over Tadlock sat still, seeing but still not seeing the people who passed gingerly, knowing his wife had gone somewhere and wondering how she could mix with those who had mistreated him.

The camp quieted to low, good-night tones and by and by they quieted, too, and of human voices there was just a murmur from Martin's tent, which had been pitched at the other side of the corral where water was close. One by one the fires winked out. The stars came on, cold-bright as faraway suns. Southward Tadlock could see the horizon rolling against the sky. A child cried in one of the tents, cried a frail cry that silence closed around.

Tadlock, he thought, trying to see the name apart from himself. Irvine Tadlock, who'd left a paying business in Peoria to try his talents in a bigger field and had been undone by ragtag emigrants. Tadlock, who liked discipline and method and knew how to organize, who, but for the stories this crowd would take along, might in time have been the territorial governor, the governor of the eventual state.

What now? he asked. What, since these chuckleheads could blight him? Texas? Could he get to Texas? Just this past spring it had been asked into the Union. It would need leaders—a governor, senators, representatives. California? Some said California was a better place than Oregon. It would offer opportunities. It would stand in need of able men.

He felt his wife's hand on his shoulder. "You'd better come to bed, Irvine."

"I know when it's bedtime. You don't need to tell me when to go to bed."

"It's late, Irvine."

"What of it? I've got to look at Martin yet."

"I've been there. There's nothing more you can do. They're trying mustard."

"You go on to bed."

He waited a few minutes, just to assert himself, and then got up and went into the tent and took off his coat and hat and shoes. Texas? California? They needed men all right. They needed leaders.

He stepped outside in his bare feet and picked up the whip

that he had forgotten on the ground and put it in his wagon and went back into the tent and lay down by his wife.

He was just getting to sleep, after what seemed a lifetime of sleeplessness, when Weatherby came by to tell him Martin had died.

Chapter - - - - - - - - - - - Thirteen

EVANS LAID the yoke on one of his oxen and pinned the bow and spoke to the teammate, holding the yoke up while the second animal stepped into place, its ankles creaking. It was a satisfaction to a man to have well-trained stock, he told himself while he worked. Saved time and trouble.

When he had his teams yoked and ready to hitch, he looked at the watch Mack had lent him. Six-forty. He would be ready in good time, as befitted the captain. Not all the tents were struck yet, nor the wagons loaded. Inside the corral where he stood some of the other men were beginning to get busy with oxen just driven in, and outside it others were pulling tent pegs and lowering poles and folding the tents afterwards and then lifting their plunder into the wagons. They worked fast, grunting to their chores as men did with sleep still in them and the muscles stiff from the night. The women had scraped and scoured the breakfast things and stood inside the wagons, helping arrange the loads. Or they had wandered off, some with their young ones in tow, to empty themselves and so be ready for the morning drive.

Morning, Evans thought, was a time of fret, before the circle broke and the train got strung out on the trail. When the men quit their grunting it was to speak sharp, and to be answered sharp by women who were tired, too, and felt the load of the day too heavy. The young ones cried or yelled, being cranky or frisky, one. The boxes made a clatter as they were pitched into wagon beds. Now and then one of the oxen driven in for yoking would line out neck and head and let out a long bawl. Underneath the louder noises was the steady hum of mosquitoes that made a little cloud around every head.

Evans stooped and gave Rock a pat on the head and straightened and stretched, pulling in a deep breath through his mouth.

The air had a taste to it here, a taste light and sharp as high-spirit drink. For all the fret he felt good.

"Be a nice day, Becky," he said, looking between the wagons to where she worked outside. She had just closed and latched with its leather hasp the box that held pots and kettles and tools to eat with.

"I almost wish it would blow and clear out the mosquitoes," she said.

"They won't be so bad oncet we roll. Ain't hardly a stir of air."

It was cool enough, but the sun was beginning to work. In the direction of it he saw Courthouse Rock, looming big yet, its near side purple with shadow. Off to his right apiece Chimney Rock rose slim and rusty. In a land that was all pretty much the same a man wouldn't think to see so much color—purple and rust, the gray of the sandbars, the sun slanted yellow as butter on the long flats, the sky so blue it hurt the eye. In all the sky there wasn't a cloud.

He said, "I never feel so sure as on a good morning."

"Sure?"

"About everything." He stepped across and lifted the cook-box and put it in the wagon and brought the cover snug with its drawstring. "Nothing left but to hitch."

He stepped back into the corral and angled through the oxen, looking to see if anyone needed help, and came to where Hig and Fairman were wrestling with an ornery steer. They had a rope over its horns that Hig was trying to hold while Fairman lifted the yoke. They held up when they saw him.

Hig gave Evans his thin smile while he bent back with the rope. "I'd as lief yoke a buffalo as this damn ox."

"Whyn't you take a hitch on a spoke?"

"Comin' to that," Hig answered. "On'y I hate to. I got a bet up with this critter, by God, that I'll hold him or bust." Keeping the rope tight with one hand, he took the loose end of it with the other and looped it over a wheel spoke and drew it up. "I'm busted."

Evans clapped the ox on the rump. It stepped ahead balkily while Hig snubbed it.

"I'm shy of good work stock," Fairman said, his forehead wrinkled with the thought of it. He rubbed the mosquitoes off the back of one hand. "Sore feet. The sand wears the hoofs down to nothing."

"Same with all of us. By and by the hoofs'll get tougher, they tell me. I been cleanin' 'em off and puttin' hot tar in the cracks."

Evans walked on. Dick Summers was throwing packs on a couple of horses, packs that held his little plunder and that of Brother Weatherby. Weatherby stood by, as always, looking as if he'd like to help if only he knew how. Evans spoke to them and got Dick's quiet grin and a solemn nod from Weatherby.

"Ready," Dick said, tying one horse to the pack saddle of the other. He took the lead rope. "Reckon they'd foller all right, but maybe I better tie on to your wagon again. Might scour off."

"I'll be along."

It seemed everybody was about ready, even the McBees, who couldn't ever seem to be on time. Until lately they couldn't, that was. "Mornin'." His idea was working all right, Evans thought, feeling again part proud and part guilty that it was. He hadn't been captain long until he called the men together one night, to find what was on their minds and to hear any grumbles and especially to cure the fault of late and ragged starting. He had told Mack his idea, and Mack had helped him, asking the men how about it: if a man was late he lost his place in line and had to bring up the rear? They had thought it was Mack's plan and had voted yes and now no one was late; but still Evans felt a little guilty. It struck him as somehow sneaky, this trick of rigging a meeting. It was better, though, than laying down the law on his own, better than cracking an ox whip.

McBee said, "How be you?" and Mrs. McBee stuck her head from the tail of the wagon and gave him a pleasant good morning. Three McBee boys were chasing each other. They circled around and stopped, looking at Evans from under hair that didn't know a comb. Evans didn't see Mercy around.

"What we waitin' fer?" McBee asked, set up over being ready. His whiskers moved to a smile.

Evans consulted his watch. "'Bout time." Looking between the wagons, he saw the horse herd, out for its quick morning graze, and the loose cattle that Brownie and the other drivers had brought close.

"Been meanin' to talk to you," McBee told him as if he had something important on his mind.

"About what?"

"I'll be seein' you. It's personal-like."

So it was personal. Evans didn't like the thought. "Any time."

He went over to his own wagons and hitched the teams and saw Rebecca to her perch and took out his watch again. It was time, lacking a minute or so. Summers sat a horse at the wagon that would break the circle. It was already pulled out a little, ready for the start. Mounted near Summers were Shields and Carpenter and Brewer, who would ride ahead today. Evans could see Tadlock standing alongside Summers, holding his silver trumpet. Evans had asked Tadlock if he wouldn't keep on sounding the horn, just as he did while captain. Out of a kind of sympathy he'd asked him, thinking maybe Tadlock prized the task. Besides, the trumpet was Tadlock's. Evans had to grin at himself, wondering which was the real reason. Anyhow, Tadlock had agreed, in that new and hard-eyed way of his.

Tadlock looked across at him, and Evans raised his arm, and the trumpet sounded. Teamsters spoke. Whips popped. Oxen pushed into the yokes. Axles whined. Dust puffed up. With commands and pops, with whines and dust the circle unwound. The On-to-Oregon train was rolling.

Evans' place was near the tail of the line. Walking out a little from his team, he could see Summers and the horsemen and the wagons lurching along behind them, the distance from wagon to wagon growing as the train settled to the drive. They would be farther spread before the morning was over. It was a thing he must watch, he reminded himself. They could be too far spread for safety against Indians. Back of him the loose stock was ambling into line.

Indians could raise the devil if they wanted to, though he didn't look for them to do it, not since a bunch of mounted soldiers had passed by. Dragoons, they called themselves, the

128

First Dragoons, led by a Colonel Kearny, who said their purpose was to awe the Indians and to warn them they'd better leave the emigrants alone. Three hundred men or thereabouts were in the bunch, not to mention wagons drawn by mules and two wheeled cannons and butcher beef and sheep that came along behind. They were in a hurry, bound for Laramie and onward to the Southern Pass, where they'd turn back. Watching them press on, their blues and golds proud in the rising dust, Evans had felt easier in his captaincy.

Other things were right enough. People were in good spirit and in good health except for the diarrhea that Platte water or too much fresh meat brought on. They had got across the South Platte, double-yoking every wagon on the advice of Summers and stringing ropes between some and splashing through the quicksand fast. For a while they had followed along the north shore and then angled across and come to Ash Hollow and the North Fork. It was a good place to remember, Ash Hollow was. There was shade there and cool-water springs and good grass, and the wagons had got down the hills that ringed it with no more damage than one tip-over.

So, in time, they had reached Courthouse Rock and the tower that stood close by and had camped on a creek there, and people had felt like celebrating, as if, coming to a known name, they could be sure they were on the right track. Or more as if they were nearing home and had caught sight of a thing to mark it by. The celebration was quiet, though. Weatherby had held services, and nobody had made light of him, thinking of Martin and the Turleys.

For a long time the Turleys had been in sight after the train pulled out. They had squatted there with their old wagon and their few head of stock, refusing to go with the company but still not starting the other way, as if quitting the bunch had taken all their get-up and now they would just wait for whatever. They had squatted, Turley and Mrs. Turley and their two thin children, watching out of stubborn eyes, saying thanks and no more for the sweetening and flour and bacon that Rebecca and Mrs. Mack and Mrs. Tadlock had left with them against the time that buffalo and antelope ran out. To watch them, to hear their noisy mouths now held to a bare word or two, a man would think that the company was treating them wrong. It wasn't so, but still no one felt quite easy.

Like the others, Evans kept turning his head as the train went on, realizing as the distance grew how small the Turleys were—a man and his woman and his young ones and a ramshackle outfit pressed on all sides by the great emptiness, or not pressed but loose and lost on the long flats, among the bald sand hills.

After what seemed a long time the Turleys had got moving, pulling a little tail of dust and shrinking with distance until at last distance swallowed them. Trying to spot them, Evans couldn't be sure but what he saw was just a fleck in the eye. He wasn't extra religious, but he felt better because Weatherby had prayed for them, begging God to keep the Indians off, and the storms and the accidents, and please, God, guard Thy sheep.

Just before, Weatherby had given Martin into God's keeping. Evans and Summers and Tadlock himself had dug the grave, dug it in silence while each man thought his own thoughts, and when it was ready they laid Martin by it, and Weatherby came and read out of the Book, taking Ephesians again. Not having a coffin or wood for one, they wrapped Martin in the blanket he laid on and lowered him and shoveled the sand in. Then Dick burned gunpowder over the grave and had them trail the stock across. That way, he said, wolves or Indians weren't likely to find the body. Neither, Evans figured, was anyone else, or anything. It was a lost grave as soon as left, and Martin's bones would lie in it till kingdom come, and buffalo would gallop over the spot and wolves trot across and wagon trains track it, and none would know that here lay what was left of a man—a dull-eyed man with bowed shoulders but with hankerings and troubles and rights of his own, who had set out for Oregon and got sick and cried out to Jesus and died.

Evans thought with a little turn about shaving Martin. Rebecca said he ought to do that. A man should go to his grave looking decent, she said. And so he had scraped off the wiry whiskers, and they had dressed Martin up in the best clothes he had, which weren't much, though Martin made a nice-enough looking corpse, considering.

The train had got under way then, Evans feeling low in his mind and small in his new place as captain, as if he couldn't come it, and Dick had ridden up and unforked his horse and walked along with him.

He was glad for Dick's friendship. He leaned on Dick. He was stronger inside because of him. Maybe that showed he wasn't fit for captain. Maybe a captain ought to be stout enough to stand alone, wanting no help from anyone except the help that would be expected of any pilot, like advice on crossings and routes and watch-outs for Indians. Well, that wasn't how he was cut. Never, anywhere, had he wanted to be boss. So he would lean on Dick, and when hard questions came up he would call the council together. They would have solid ideas. But there would still be times, he realized uncomfortably, when he would have to act. A captain had to be more than a leaner and a caller of meetings. He had to give confidence to people, and encouragement. He had to see, one way or another, that the train kept together and kept going. He had to lead, no matter if he didn't want to, else the train would fail. He wished he had just his own family to watch out for.

Evans blew the dust out of his nose and brought a hand up and wiped his eyes. The valley was deeper here and narrower, and a traveler saw new kinds of plants, like the spiny clumps that Summers called Spanish bayonet and Weatherby said was Adam's needle. Flowers he didn't have a name for waved along the way, some coned and some daisied, colored purple and white and yellow. The women and children were forever picking posies if the day was fair. Here they would have to be careful. Rattlesnakes were getting thick. It would be just luck if someone didn't get bit. The thought troubled him. It added itself to his feeling of burden.

In a way it was as if all hands had entrusted their future to him, expecting him to have the sense and force to see them through. And some of them he hardly knew, except to pass a good morning! There was Fairman's man, Botter, and Mack's hand, Moss, and Shields and Carpenter and Insko and Davis-

131

worth. They had voted for him, he reckoned, or anyhow not against him. He made a note to himself to get better acquainted. Because they were not forward men or easy met, he had let himself stand off. A captain ought to know his company down to the last pup.

He looked back and saw that Rebecca had climbed from the wagon and was walking alongside. He winked at her. She had thinned some on the road, but she didn't seem so worn as before or to get so tired and sore. He didn't know when he had seen more life in her face.

He cleaned his nose again, holding one nostril closed with his finger and then the other. He figured he would arrive in Oregon with some of the Platte sand on him. Sandy water didn't wash off sand.

Anyhow the wind wasn't pushing at them today. The dust puffed straight up and powdered him and settled back slow, so that, turning again, he saw the hanging trail of it far beyond the cattle. The sun rode friendly, just warm enough for comfort. A few white clouds had come into the sky. The mosquitoes had thinned out, likely resting for the night siege.

The Tadlock wagons rolled ahead of him, Tadlock walking by the side, still wearing the many-pocketed coat he had put on in the chill of early morning. He walked straight and square, with his head up. Tadlock had taken his upset fairly well, Evans said to himself, feeling easier at the thought. He had stuck mostly to himself, not marching around with his eye out for fault, but he stood his turn at guard and spoke civil enough, though spare-worded and unsmiling; and he had made a deal with Brewer, now that Martin was dead, for Brewer's twelve-year-old to help with the stock and spell Mrs. Tadlock at his second wagon.

Evans hawed his team, following the swing-out of the line. The wagons creaked and jolted and in some places ground in the sand. Now and then he could hear the rattle of a loose tire that Hig, the handyman, would have to fix. He had a system better than driving wedges between tire and felloe. He took the tire off and shaved a thin hoop and tacked it to the felloe and heated the tire and put it back on. Made something extra doing it, too, though he would rather play his fiddle for a reel.

At Laramie there would be a bellows and other tools, probably, and they could cut and weld the tires and fit them snug. Until then Hig's system was all right. They would buy supplies at Laramie, too, if they could, stuff like flour and smoked buffalo tongues. And some were talking about buying oxen or trading their sore-footed ones. How far to Laramie? How far did Dick say from Chimney Rock? Sixty miles or so? With good going they would be there in four days, five anyhow. Ahead and to the left the hills were beginning to run high and ragged, leading, Evans supposed, to Scott's Bluffs. Closer at hand he saw a half dozen wild horses gazing down from the ridge, their heads held high.

While Evans watched, McBee came riding up from the cow column, his whiskers gray with dust. He spit and smiled. "Critters are gettin' along all right. I'll keep my eye back."

It was the report, Evans understood, of a man to his captain, the report unasked and needless, said to show the sayer knew the due of leadership. He didn't like it or the manner of its saying.

McBee got off his horse and walked along with Evans. "'Y God, she's a fair day."

"Good enough for anyone." Without thinking why until afterwards, Evans turned and saw old Rock following at his heels. He wondered then if the only reason he didn't take to McBee was that McBee had wanted to kill his dog. No, he decided. He wouldn't go for McBee regardless. He was dirty and shiftless, and there was nothing to him anyhow. Not to him or his wife, either—and how they got a pretty thing like Mercy beat him. He had to admit she was not only pretty but seemed to be a good-enough girl. She couldn't be much underneath, though, not with that breeding. Give her a few years and a few young ones and she'd be just like Ma and Pa, he guessed, and then brought himself up. He reckoned the Lord had the right to visit the sins of the father—but not Lije Evans. He owed her a chance, just as a man owed anyone a chance, but still he was relieved that Brownie wasn't following after her.

"I said to my woman today, 'y God, we're a-goin' to make it. Fer a time I didn't know, fer a fact."

Evans tried to imagine what McBee's face was like under the mat of whiskers. Slack-jawed, probably, and loose-lipped. Weak. And yet there was something tough about him, as there was often about ornery people, something that kept him going, something tougher than the stuff of Turleys.

"Yes, sir, we're a-goin' to make it." McBee grinned, showing teeth broken and dirty beyond believing, and bobbed his head.

Watching him, hearing him, Evans knew. This was it, plain in the words, the smiles, the bobs of the head. McBee meant them to be admiring. McBee was courting the captain. He was honey-fuggling, wanting the importance of the shadow of importance. He would have something especial to say; he would have something to bring up—but this was it.

"We always were going to make it," Evans said.

"That is as may be. Anyhow, we are now."

Evans didn't give him an answer. He knew what he ought to do. He ought to tell McBee to go to hell; but it was a hard thing. Somehow a man balked at slapping the compliment out of another's mouth. Not that it was the compliment, either. Compliments didn't fool him. He just hated to speak blunt to friendliness, even if the friendliness was only a show.

McBee said, "I been meanin' to tell you, I don't hold no hard feelin's. About the dog and all. Nary one."

"All right. None here, either. Over that."

"Like my woman was sayin' today, you was bound to work up to captain."

"I didn't work for it."

"Course not."

Evans turned on him then and spoke with more than the needed stress because he disliked what he had to say. "McBee, you better stick with Tadlock."

McBee's loose mouth closed. Deep in his puddled brown eyes Evans saw the sudden, skulky glint of hatred. "Oh, sure. I aim to do that." He walked along in silence for a while, leading his horse, and then said, "Reckon I better be gettin' back." He climbed the horse and rode away.

Evans watched him and then shortened his gaze, seeing Rebecca smiling the twisted smile of knowing and old Rock padding between them.

Now, more than ever, he told himself, he would have to watch the man, not for any open act but for some sly and miserable trick. He would ask Brownie to keep close watch on their stock, as he would himself. It was hard to believe anyone was underhanded, though, until the proof came out.

Chapter - - - - - - - - - - - - *Fourteen*

FROM THE SLOPE to the southeast the forts shone white in afternoon sun except where the long shadows of the trees fell across. Spotted on the bottom were the tepees that the Sioux had pitched, looking white, too, or tan, depending on their age. There was movement below, men and women coming and going, children dodging among the lodges, the thin Indian dogs limping, nosing low for scraps, and, farther out, the horses beginning to graze as the afternoon cooled.

Summers sat his horse and watched, thinking how things had changed. This country was young, like himself, when he saw it first, young and wild like himself, without the thought of age. There wasn't a post on it then, nor any tame squaw begging calico, but only buffalo and beaver and the long grass waving in the Laramie bottoms. The wind had blown lonesome, the sound of emptiness in it, the breath of far-off places where no white foot had stepped. A man snuggling in his robe had felt alone and strong and good, telling himself he would see where the wind came from.

Now there wasn't a buffalo within fifty miles or beaver either —the few that were left of them—and the wind brought words and the hammer of hammers and the bray of mules and the smells of living under roof. The far post near the neck of the Laramie and the Platte would be Fort Platte, built after Summers had left the mountains; the near one Fort Laramie, or William, as some had called it, but even it had changed. Change coming on change, he thought. He remembered it from 'thirty-six—or was it 'thirty-seven?—when it was a cottonwood post like any other. Now it was 'dobe and white and spiked at the top like a castle might be, and the trade was in buffalo skins that a true mountain man wouldn't mess with.

Beyond, the Black Hills climbed away, dark with their scrub

cedar and pine, with Laramie Peak rising oversized among them. Farther on, out of sight, there were the Red Buttes and the Sweetwater and the Southern Pass and the Green, where he had spent his young years like a trapper spent his beaver, thinking there was always more where that came from. On the near side of the pass, to the north, the Popo Agie. The Popo Agie. He formed the words with his lips, remembering how a Crow girl had got the sound of running water in them. Ashia, the Crow word for stream. Popo Ashia. The liquid sound, the girl warm at his side and both of them fulfilled for the time and easy, and she laughing while he practiced the tongue. Even her name was lost to him now, and she was dead or old, one, and the laughter gone from her, and did she remember at all the Long Knife who had bedded with her? He couldn't bring her face back. What he remembered was the warmness and swell of her and the young-skinned thighs. They went along with the Popo Agie, with water running white and blue and the green trees rising and the Wind Mountains higher still and the rich lift from the dam that never had seen a trap before.

He ought to be getting back to the train, but he stayed a minute longer while memory wakened to things seen. Laramie. It was the gate to the mountains once and before that a part of the mountains themselves, and a man traveling had to keep his eye out and his hand ready, watching the way of his horse for Indian sign, watching the way of buffalo while he hung to his Hawken rifle. There was danger still, from Pawnees and Sioux and maybe Blackfeet farther on, but it struck him as different, as somehow piddling. A cornfield, even like the sorry patch by the fort, didn't belong with war whoops and scalping knives. It belonged with cabins and women and children playing safe in the sun. It belonged with the dull pleasures, with the fat belly and the dim eye of safety.

He hadn't let himself think, back there in Missouri, how much of the old mountains there was still in him. He had butchered hogs and tended crops and dickered for oxen or mules and laid down at night by Mattie, shutting out the thought of beaver streams and canyons opening sweet to the eye and squaws who had comforted him and gone on, joining with the lost and wanted things. Popo Ashia, like running water.

He was a mountain man underneath, and always would be, even if he went to plowing and hoeing and slopping hogs again —and there was no place in the world these days for a mountain man, and less and less of it all the time. A few years more and a man fool enough to trap like as not would stumble on to a picnic. The buffalo were thinning, for all that greenhorns said that three calves were dropped for every cow killed. In not so long a time now people in the mountains would be living on hog meat, unknowing the flavor and strength of fleece fat and hump ribs. Unknowing, either, how keen an enemy the Rees and the Blackfeet were. He almost wished for the old Rees, for the old Blackfeet that the white man's pox had undone. They had given spirit to life; every day lived was a day won.

Well, he had set out, hunting old things remembered as new, and he would go on hunting, finding a kind of pleasure in awakening memory, feeling the heart turn at the proof in mountain or park or river that, sure enough, once he had played here, once he had set traps and counted beaver and spreed at rendezvous and seen the wild moon rise. At the nub of it did he just want his youth back? Beaver, streams, squaws, danger—were they just names for his young time?

Summers shook himself. Christ, a man could moon his life away! Better to make the most of what was left. There wasn't anything in feeling sorry for yourself.

He reined around and rode back to the train.

Rebecca Evans said, "I can't hardly wait to get to the fort." She had stepped ahead, so as to walk beside Lije, letting the single yoke of oxen hitched to her wagon follow by itself.

"That much farther along," Lije said as if he knew what she meant. "Be there pretty soon."

"How long will we be stayin'?"

"No longer'n need be. Day and a half. Maybe two days. We got to get on."

"Ain't Laramie halfway, Lije?"

"Now, Becky, hopin' it's so won't make it so."

"How far?"

"Dick says somep'n over six hundred mile."

"And from there on?"

"Maybe thirteen hundred."

"An' it's the worst?"

He didn't answer to that but walked along pulling on a dead pipe, his face cheery, watching the wagons ahead and now and then looking back, making sure all was right. They had slanted out a piece from the river, to upland where the grass ran crisp under the wagon tires. With the thought of Laramie in their heads the teamsters were popping their whips or punching the oxen with sticks. The oxen didn't pay much notice. A sore-footed or worn-out ox never did.

"We might have to stay longer, the way the critters limp," Rebecca said, but Lije just got a bite on his pipe and shook his head.

She sighed inside, thinking it would be good to stay at the fort the rest of her life and so be done with dirt and hard travel and eyes teary with camp smoke and the back sore from stooping over a fire and the legs cramped from sitting on the ground. There she wouldn't have the grainy feel of sand forever in her shoes.

"We're comin' along fine."

"Yes," she said. "Fine." Men were queer, she thought. Even Lije was queer, taking such a real and simple pleasure in the work of his muscles and the roll of wheels. The more miles they made the better-spirited he was, as if there wasn't any aim in life but to leave tracks, no time in it but for go. He didn't mind eating mush with blown sand in it.

She knew they had to get to Oregon all right. She knew they had to travel, but she couldn't be so all-fired pleased, come night, that they were far gone from the morning. At night she felt tired and a little sad with tiredness and didn't like to think about tomorrow; and she got to wondering then if Oregon was what it was cracked up to be.

Lije liked the sun and even the wind and walked through the dust as if he had put it out of his mind, since he couldn't still it. She found the sun cruel sometimes, lonely-cruel for all its brightness, and the wind sad-rough, and she hated the grind of sand between shoe and foot.

"There's Dick."

Ahead she saw Summers in his buckskins, waving the train on. She had to squint to see him, for the sun shone straight in her face unless she kept it tucked down under the shade of her poke bonnet. Her face, she knew, was a sight, reddened by the sun and coarsened by the wind until it was more man's face than woman's. For all that God had made her big and stout and not dainty, she wanted to feel womanlike, to be clean and smooth-skinned and sometimes nice-dressed, not for Lije alone but for herself, for herself as a woman, so's to feel she was a rightful being and had a rightful place. She thought ahead to the fort, to clear, hot water and time to wash up and maybe to ease the long ache of her bones; and she thought backwards, too, to Missouri and the old springhouse and the fresh coolness of it and the milk creaming there in its pans. She thought of oak shade and trees fruiting and cupboards for dishes and victuals and chests for clothes and cookies baking and the smell of them following her around as the smell of camp smoke followed her now. She had had a home in Missouri, a place that stayed fixed, and, looking out door or window, she had known what she would see. She had been cozy there, seeing the hills and trees close and the sky bent down. And when she was tired, she had had a place to rest.

It was the time of the month, she knew, for she had been doing better lately in body and mind both, but now she felt she couldn't go on. Lije or no Lije, Brownie or no Brownie, she couldn't go beyond Laramie. She wanted to slack down right here on the prairie and let the train roll on while the wind blew and the sun burned and the dog-tiredness eased away and the disquiet died and dust went back to dust.

She stood still, not wanting Lije to catch sight of her face, and watched him push ahead while her own team came up. She fell into step alongside, saying to herself Lije was so gone on to Oregon he wouldn't think there was anything in her mind but to see to her wagon.

She bent her head from the sun, watching one foot step out

140

and then the other and wondering that they did so, the way it was with her. Rock trotted up from somewhere and brushed her side and slowed and gazed into her face as if he could scent the trouble inside her. While she patted Rock, she head Summers' voice. Summers had ridden up and turned about and was riding half around in the saddle while he talked to Lije. "Laramie Fork ain't so high. We can ford, I'm thinking."

"Good."

"Best camp is west of the fort, on the bank."

Lije nodded.

"You'd best be callin' on the bourgeois, too, Lije."

"Sure. Who is he?"

"Culbertson, Alexander Culbertson, used to be. Somewhere I heerd that Jim Bordeau was now."

"All right."

"How you, Mrs. Evans? Rock ain't dead yet, I see."

"He just this minute come up. I'm tolerable."

"That's slick. I'll be gettin' along, Lije."

The lead wagons were sinking from sight down a slope that Rebecca figured led to the Laramie. It was as if the wheels were sinking into the earth pair by pair, and then the beds and then the swaying tops.

Lije whoaed his oxen when he came to the top of the hill. Rebecca walked up to him and saw the train winding down and, below it, Fort Laramie, white as fresh wash, with trees waving and shade dark on the grass and the river fringed with woods. More to herself than to Lije she said, "I never thought to be so glad just to see a building."

"It's Fort Laramie. Sure."

"Not because it's a fort. Just because it's a building."

"It's Fort Laramie all the same."

"You reckon they've got chairs there, Lije? Real chairs."

There was a light in his eyes. He said, "Sure," and cut a little caper with his feet and sang out:

> "To the far-off Pacific sea,
>   Will you go, will you go, old girl, with me?"

She said, "I just want to set in a chair."

She thought she never had been so happy as now. The music had wings to it, and the night was wishful, and the big stars watched from overhead, looked down smiling and promising, just on Mercy McBee, so that, for this minute, she knew Pa was right. In Oregon everything would be different. Do-se-do. And how are you, Mr. Mack, with your white shirt and sleeves held up with their holders and the look of trouble gone from your forehead? And did you know how often I thought of you, knowing I shouldn't, and looked for you along the dusty line of travel: Did you bump a-purpose, sir, doing do-se-do?

Music outside her. Music inside, singing talk she was too shy to say, singing talk outlandish that forever was her secret. The soft night around, lightened by the big fire that made little fires in the eyes of the Indians ringed about. Music's got a time to it, Brownie Evans. 'Bout time you learned it's got a time. Let music move your feet.

Swing, Mercy. Step out and swing, arm bent to arm. Saw, Hig, saw your fiddle, you and the dark part-Indian sawing with you. Saw in the night. Saw to the stars. Saw for little Mercy McBee who's joined the grownups now and's scared to speak a word.

Watch, eyes. Watch, stars. Watch, wishful night. Mercy's got a dress with a flouncy collar and her feet are in shoes, and who's to know that once they fit old Mrs. Brewer, who needed help with her chirren? Mercy can dance. Mercy's good turned. I declare, I never saw the beat of her!

Arm tight in arm, tighter'n need be. Hand pressing hand. Men noticing. Important men with clean-shaved faces and solid ways and stout teams and cattle following behind the column. Men noticing, not boys, though boys took notice, too, the young fear showing in them and the young questions.

Howdy, Mr. Byrd. You dance mighty pretty. Howdy, Botter, with your jaw of tobacco. Howdy, Mr. Fairman. You got a clever woman. No, I ain't. I just wisht I could be as clever as her. Howdy, Mr. Gorham. Well, Mr. Mack, if it ain't you again, and where's your wife at? Don't she like to dance?

Bow to your partner and do-se-do and swing. The stars smiling, the night crowded in, the music with the high beat of the heart in it, the feet moving of themselves, the body moving, and things a-shine in Oregon. Mercy McBee! Sixteen and dancing and happy, but scared almost to smile. Not knowing what to say. Not knowing how to answer to arms or pressing hands. So used to being biddable that words and wishes said and shown by older folks were still like orders to her. Hard tellin', Mr. Mack, hard tellin' how to act when you're sixteen and all your life long you've done as told. It ain't I don't like you. I do. I do. You're clever and rich, and the likes of you's never looked at the likes of me before, and I got a wanting to brush the black curl of hair back from your forehead. It's just I don't know. Growed up in body and not in knowing. That's Mercy, Mr. Mack, and beg your pardon. Must be, sometime, you had to learn yourself.

The music stopped. Hig laid his fiddle across his knees and put the bow with it and smiled his toothless smile. She let herself smile back, feeling at home with him for Hig was no-account like folks she'd always known and full of jokes besides and wouldn't take too serious whatever she said or did.

Mr. Mack's voice spoke in her ear, spoke soft while people moved around. Would she like to take a walk? Would she care to meet him out from the fire towards where the camp was pitched? On his face when she turned was a half-smile that made him look like a boy, like a boy timid but with some unsaid notion in him. It was a nice night, he said, still talking low among the voices raised around them. The music wouldn't start up for a while, the fiddlers being tired. Would she care for a little walk?

She reckoned, inside, that she would, while for the moment her heart stood still, waiting her answer, afeard of yes and more afeard of no. She reckoned she'd best as long as growed-up Mr. Mack had asked her to. Mr. Mack, with his dark eyes and lean face and the handsome look of trouble. She would walk proper and talk proper and not think about the ring of hair that needed pushing back.

Her head nodded to him, and she watched him lose himself among the others. Now she'd made up her mind, it was as if she couldn't wait. She felt the blood tapping in her and the breath high in her throat, and all of her saying I'll come, I'll come. I said I'd be there, Mr. Mack. Please, I'll come.

Brownie Evans stopped her on the edge of the crowd as if she had time for him. "If you're goin' back to camp, maybe I better go along so's to see you're all right." His boy's face was awkward with the words, as if they came hard to him. Looking at him, of a sudden she knew how he was. She knew and was roiled by knowing and a little pleasured, too, and would have dodged around except that in his gaze she saw the naked, humble owning-up of his feeling for her. She was brushed by sadness, and she said gently, "I'll be all right, Brownie," and slipped into the welcoming dark, remembering, until she met Mr. Mack, how his face had lighted at her tone.

"You came," Mr. Mack said softly, as if not quite believing that she would. His hand cupped itself on her elbow, guiding her away from the camp, upstream from it, where people didn't pass on their way from tents to fort and back. "Beautiful night."

She said a bare "Yes," her throat full with beating blood and breath. "Ain't it dangerous out here?"

"Not so close to the fort. I have a pistol besides."

They walked along and the hand on her elbow slid on her arm and found her hand, and she let him have it, feeling the fingers work against her palm and the thumb warm on her knuckles.

"I guess you think I'm a million years old, Mercy."

"No."

"I feel young, anyhow. Tonight. As young, maybe, as you."

"I don't know nothin', Mr. Mack."

"Nobody does."

A tree stood black at the edge of the river, and he stopped her there and said with what seemed to her an in-held anger, "Nobody wants to."

The river made a murmuring by them, and a breeze joined with it, stirring the leaves of the trees. The music took up, far off, and far-off voices sounded. The distant fire was one of the big stars, burning on the ground.

"Nobody wants to," he said again and let go her hand and

144

turned and brought her to him. She cried out silently while his mouth came hungry to hers. Is it right, Mr. Mack? Is it all right? You're older. You know. I got a feeling it ain't right. It ain't right, but you said nobody knows. Her hand laid back the curl from his forehead.

Ground under her, and hands seeking, older, wiser, dear hands; and the music and the dance calls fading in the roar of blood and stars misty with the heat of breath, and pain in her like a blade and pain and pain and eager pain, and the music lost and the sky lost and all lost but this but this but this. The stars wheeled back and burst and lit the sky with trailing fire.

Afterwards she wanted nothing but to cry, nothing but to lie and cry while the night and the music and the voices came again. She felt his hand on her, urging her to sit up.

"I'm sorry, Mercy." There was such a misery in his voice that the weight of it bowed her over. "A man's a fool."

"Don't you be sorry," she whispered. "It makes it worse if I know you're sorry."

"You're a dear girl."

She bent her head against him, wanting gentleness, wanting comfort. "I knowed it wasn't right."

"I'm to blame."

"It's bold to say, but it was liking for you done it."

His arm tightened on her, but he answered, "It can't be love, Mercy. Don't you see, it mustn't be love?"

"I know."

She sat for what seemed a long time leaning against him, circling the question that lay fearsome ahead. Her voice was small with fear when she asked it. "Will anything come of it, Mr. Mack?"

He answered quick. "I don't think so. I'm sure it won't."

"Sure?"

"Sure."

"I haven't anyone to hold to but you."

"You'll be all right. I'm sure." He drew his arm from around her shoulders. "We better be getting back."

"I don't care to dance no more."

"I'll follow along and see you're safe to your tent then."

145

"Seems like I don't want to do nothin' except set here by you."

His hand came back and lay kind on her shoulder. "We better not stay any longer."

She got up and straightened the dress with the flouncy collar and went to him and bent her head against his chest, holding to his shirt with her hands.

"Mercy!" he said, while his arms came around. "Little Mercy!" There was misery in his voice still but also a beginning of something else again, together making a kind of wild torment that she found assurance in. "I'm crazy. I'm not good for you, Mercy. Say no! Say no for your sake! But we could see each other tomorrow night?"

There was a sort of power in the Indian drums that oppressed Brother Weatherby. The devil, he thought, watching the dancers, forever was at his wicked work, so that the beat of a stick on a dried skin became more than a measured thump and a grunted song more than a chant. They became an invitation to violence, to the dark passions, to sin. To the idolatry suggested by the dancers' expert imitation of the buffalo.

The light hadn't gone from the sky yet, though the sun was down, and he could make out every turn, every buck and jump and headshaking of the young Indians. They had draped themselves in buffalo robes, to which the horns were still attached, and they leaped and pawed and bellowed to the rhythm of the drums. Standing back with members of his company and watchers from the fort, Weatherby despaired of bringing to these simple savages the wonders of the Word.

He had felt better earlier, after he had held services for the Sioux in the shade of a cottonwood grove. To be sure, the place was not God's house, where he would have been more effective and at home, supported by the close, familiar appurtenances of the ministry. Out under the vast sky, with no pulpit or Bible stand or walls around him, he felt a little like a prophet of old crying in the wilderness. Still, it had been a good meeting. The Indians, men and women, had been decorous and attentive and had listened with what he took to be interest to his prayers and

146

exhortation and to his singing of "Watchman, Tell Us of the Night," though, of course, they could not understand the import of his words.

Dick Summers had attended, on request, to interpret the questions and answers that Weatherby anticipated. He had listened, grave as any Indian, except that, now and then, an inward smile seemed to lie in his gray eyes. A godless man was Summers, good in his way but godless, with the suggestion about him of a superior knowledge and of private reservations caused by it. Weatherby resented the suggestion—there was only one knowledge, and it was love of God—while admitting in fairness that there was nothing of the disputer or the braggart about Summers. He was companionable, kind, even overly generous, and capable as any company could wish, and Weatherby remembered often to thank God for sending this sinner among them. It almost seemed to him that if he could make Summers see, he would have done his work for the Kingdom of Heaven.

He finished his final prayer and motioned Summers up and had him put the questions: Did the Sioux want to learn the ways of God? Did they want to be saved?

Summers spoke in Indian gutturals, filling in with what he called sign language, and the Sioux nodded, all of them, men and women alike, and an old chief rose and spoke at length, using signs, too, standing so controlled and dignified that Weatherby would have envied him had not envy been unworthy.

"What did he say, Brother Summers?"

"It's a go. They want to learn the big medicine of the white man."

Medicine, Weatherby thought. Medicine? For an instant he had a notion to speak out, to scold the chief for this low misunderstanding of the high and holy, and then it struck him that the chief was right. The way of God was medicine, medicine for the suffering soul. He made an inward note to use the illustration with white congregations.

"What else, Brother Summers?"

"He says they figure the Book of God will keep meat in their lodges and help 'em against their enemies."

"It will save their immortal souls. Tell them that."

"Ain't any word or sign for soul that I know of, unless it's spirit or maybe shadow."

"No word for soul!" Looking at the earnest, unenlightened faces, seeing the rough garments and the poor gewgaws that passed for pretties, Weatherby thought both souls and bodies were rude and graceless. He felt a sudden, overflowing sadness for these simple folk, a compassion that bent him over, a loving-kindness such as God Himself must feel at sight of the wretched creatures of earth. Be long-suffering, please, O God, he asked. Remember, I pray Thee, they have not had opportunity to know Thee. Breathe the influence of Thy spirit on them and make them Christians. Let judgment be passed on the worldly and on the deists and the swearers, if Thou wilt, but not yet on these, Thy simple children.

It filled him with a wondering love sometimes and sometimes with a wrong impatience that God should be so long-suffering with whites who had the choice of righteousness or sin and chose to drink and to blaspheme and to commit, he supposed, outrages of the flesh. Let them have their reward, he asked, while he studied the grave faces before him. And then he reconsidered and asked: Let me be not hasty in judgment, Lord, remembering it is for Thee in Thy love and righteous anger to dispose. Let me recall my own time of temptation and of sin and thank Thee that it has passed and Thine own spirit is strong in me. Let me do Thy work with humility and understanding. Let me be long-suffering, too.

After the questions and answers the Indians had come to him solemnly, one by one, and wrung his hand, and never had he been so sure that the field was right for the tilling.

Now, while the young warriors pranced and bellowed, doubt entered his mind. Grown men imitating beasts! Others chanting to the devilish tap of the drum! And all encouraged by the white people standing around! Behind him someone said, "Them Injuns are pretty goddam good at it."

A miserable business, he thought, while discouragement washed over him. With the glories of God all around, with the wonder of the night firmament coming into sight overhead, with death and judgment waiting, the Indians could find nothing better to do than to ape brutes, and the whites nothing better than to watch and enjoy. He had heard that the American Fur Company now frowned on the use of spirits in trade, but he smelled the ugly smell of whisky.

The dance stopped and another one started, the dog dance this time, and Weatherby watched for a little while, only half seeing, and then turned and walked away, tightening his arm against the Bible that was his comfort and assurance.

Night had fallen finally. Away from the firelighted dancing place it lay thick and soft, tempting in itself, he thought despairingly, recalling the days of his weakness. It was in God and only in God that the soul found mastery over the flesh; and it was the mark of God's infinite wisdom that the greater the heat of blood the greater the saving and triumphant righteousness. If only he could open the blind eyes of white men and red! He knew the way of salvation, but now, for this moment, he was depressed by the knowledge of sin and the magnitude of his task. God had called him to go afar, and he was obeying, but with the present feeling of being weak and unworthy. Let the Lord forgive him for faltering. Let the Lord give fire to his words so that the wicked could see the living light.

He was thankful, as he read in the stars the proof of the divine power and omnipresence, that his God—that the true God—was not distant and unapproachable, to be propitiated by a Romanish counting of beads, to be communicated with through the dubious intermediaries that Daugherty professed to believe in. God was close and attentive, ever ready to hear the prayers of the penitent. If the good man searched in his heart he felt Him there.

To Weatherby's right, off the line of travel from camp to dance, a figure moved and stopped, almost as if to avoid the meeting, and Weatherby halted and called out, "Who is it?"

"Mack," the figure answered, walking up. "Good evening, Brother Weatherby."

"Good evening."

"Been watching the dances?"

"I find them offensive."

"Doesn't the Lord approve?"

"You joke about God!"

"No. I only wonder."

"Have faith. It is the answer to doubts."

"But not to living." The words and the tone of them added to Weatherby's depression.

"We must believe that it is."

"No matter what?"

"No matter what. We cannot always understand God, for His greatness is beyond understanding."

"I was taught that, back in the Methodist Church."

"I didn't know you are a Methodist."

"Was."

Weatherby shook his head, sorrow deep in him, and the sense of inadequacy, and irritation at this rejection of the eternal truth. "Have faith. Sorrow, difficulties, temptations—they are only to test us."

Mack laughed a short, mirthless laugh. "Everything bad is our fault; everything good we owe to God."

"You talk like a deist."

"A light word for me."

Weatherby was too tired to argue, too down in spirit to answer as he should. He said, "You will come back to Methodism. I pray it will be so."

"You'd better pray for all the train, Brother Weatherby. They tell me the country ahead swarms so with buffalo that even travel by company is risky. There'll be Indians, too."

"I always pray for all, but I will pray especially for you. You will come back."

"Once a believer always a believer," Mack said. "Or once a believer never a successful unbeliever. Maybe you're right."

"Good evening, Mack."

In his tent Weatherby said another prayer. "I put myself in Thy hands, O God. Give me the strength and wisdom to do Thy bidding, I pray Thee. Help me with the sinners and the savages and the doubters like Brother Mack that they may see the

150

greatness of Thy works and fall down and worship Thee. Let me remember that all is right that the Lord doeth. And bless our little train, I pray Thee, and see us safely on to Oregon. Amen."

Through the soft and breathing night there came to his ears the beat of drums for the dog dance.

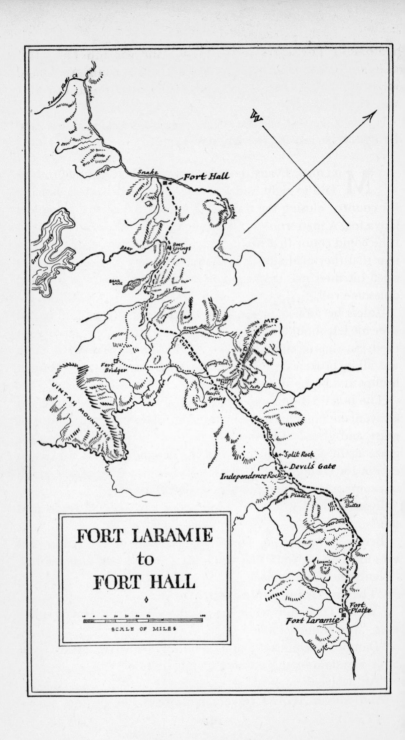

FORT LARAMIE
to
FORT HALL

SCALE OF MILES

Millions, Evans thought, a meemillion of buffalo, buffalo to right and left and ahead and behind, hairing the country, closing the train in, hoofing up dust that hung low like a fog. A man wouldn't live long enough to count them even if he could count that high. And he couldn't parcel out the uproar that they made. Bulls bellowed and cows bawled and calves cried for their mas, and the voices joined in what was one big, dolesome roll.

Unless he looked to the Red Buttes, rising bare and naked over his left shoulder, or to the lonesome drying-up ponds with their crusting of salt, Evans could almost believe that the earth was alive, broken out of a sudden like a setting of eggs, but in humps and horns and shaggy hair.

The buffalo didn't run from the train, not much, but lagged away, made mulish maybe by their numbers or sore for want of grass, and glared after the wagons, and then went hunting for graze again, for they had picked the ground clean as a chicken except for clumps of high-growing sage that gave off the smell of camphor, or turpentine, where they'd trampled it.

Evans said, "I would've called you a liar, Dick, if you'd told me."

Before he answered, Dick slued around in the saddle, his eyes fixed on the train that was jolting along a half mile behind. "Plenty meat, all right."

"The grass is just pinfeathers."

"Well," Dick said, while for a minute the light played in his eyes, "you wanted buffler."

"Damnedest country! Don't do nothin' by halves. Either there ain't a buffalo or there's nothin' but buffalo."

"An' wolves."

And wolves. Wolves traveling in packs like he-dogs after a

she, bringing up the tail of the bands of buffalo, their eyes yellow and their tongues wet while they watched for a stray calf or a cripple or one too old to keep up. Off to the right a bunch of them swarmed over a cow that had mired in a salt sinkhole, feeding on her while she still tried to pull free. A couple of buzzards slanted down and slid to the ground close by.

Buffalo and wolves, Evans thought, and grasshoppers with no grass to hop on and rib bones and skulls lying around, picked clean as a clean platter, and, here and there where the rocks broke through, a rattlesnake looped, his tail aquiver.

Evans never had thought to set his eyes on such a sight as this. It was a wild, strong sight, a rich and powerful sight that awed a man and lifted him inside—the plains climbing into ridges where, once in a long while, trees stood spare and tough, the sky curved across, so blue it pained the eye, far things brought close and sharp as through a glass, and buffalo on all the land and the roll of their bellowings in all the air.

Again he felt greatness, smallness and greatness both among such wild riches. And, seeing the train winding behind him, he thought with pride of it, of the onwardness of its people, of their stubborn, unthought-out yondering. It wasn't a thing for reason, this yondering, but for the heart, where secrets lay deep and mixed. Money? Land? New chances? Patriotism? All together they weren't enough. In the beginning, that is, they weren't enough, but as a man went on it came to him how wide and wealthy was his country, and the pride he had talked about at first became so real he lost the words for it.

It was good, he thought, that they'd laid by two days at Laramie and fixed wagons and traded teams and bought supplies, though the trading was one-sided and the food high as a scared cat's back. Flour at forty dollars a barrel, and not so damn superfine at that! Still, they were better off, even mangy Hank McBee, whom Mack had trusted for the price of coffee and sugar and flour and the boot it took to make a trade of teams. Evans liked Mack for being generous, but still he knew he was foolish. The money was as good as lost.

The train was a top train now, victualed and repaired and leaned down for travel. Stoves lay along the line from Laramie, and anvils and grindstones and pieces of furniture, thrown out as the wagons climbed the thick-dusted ridges or circled gullies cut by heavy water. This, Dick had said as if not saying much, was the roughest part of the trail east of the great pass.

The train was better ordered other ways, more regular about time and the round of work, more knowing about stock. Wiser, too. Like with rifles. The men carried them loaded still, but not capped or primed, not since Botter by accident had shot a hole in Hig's pants and plowed a furrow in him. Hig had taken it good-natured, telling the men he could spare something behind but not a bit in front. Afterwards Evans had asked that the caps be left off and the priming undone until the need came, and everybody said it was a good idea, seeing as accidents could happen.

Even Indians didn't affright the people too much any more, or find them unprepared. Out from Laramie they'd met a bunch of ingoing Cheyennes, loaded with buffalo hides, and the company had rounded brisk into a fort while Dick went on to make palaver. A little tobacco and some beads and a red shirt and powder and ball had fixed things up, though afterwards the women got uneasy because squaws and their broods and some of the bucks kept peeking under the wagon covers, wanting to see and to finger the white plunder. Some of it they stole —a few knives and Davisworth's ax and an old rifle that belonged to Shields. Dick said any train would lose that much.

Evans didn't take to himself much of the credit for the betterment, knowing the people would have learned no matter who was captain, but still he felt good about it, and pleased because the general spirit seemed so stout. Even Tadlock had got some of his brashness back, acting at the fort almost too much like his old self.

Dick broke into Evans' thought, saying, "Fixin' to storm, west."

Not till then had Evans paid any mind to the cloud that had risen low over the hills. "That the way storms come from here?"

"Can't always tell. They used to say at Laramie that an east wind brought rain."

In the silence that followed, Evans was aware again of the long bawling of the buffalo.

"It ain't so far to good-enough water, if I remember right."

"Meanin' we ought to camp early?"

"I seen buffler thisaway clear to Laramie and to hell and gone beyond."

"You don't like it, Dick?"

"Puts me in mind of old times."

"But you don't like it?"

"One winter on the Powder the buffler was so thick we had to build fires to keep 'em off from camp. Lucky, I'm thinking, they didn't take it into their heads to run."

"I get it. It's come to my mind, too, but mostly I been thinkin' about no grass and Indians bound to be about somewheres with the critters so many."

"You never seen a buffler stampede, Lije."

No, Evans thought, with the pinch of fear in him now that Dick had put words to what had been just a stray flutter. He never had seen a stampede, but with a storm making up and the levels and slopes dark with animals he could imagine it. He could feel himself waking at night to thunder in the ground. In his mind he could leap up, terror in him and the thought of Rebecca and Brownie and the rest, and he helpless as in a bad dream while the thunder rolled up and he saw the first low-held heads and the pounding feet of it before it ran them over. "I don't like the notion of it."

"But for the women and young'uns I wouldn't think anything of it," Dick said.

"Wouldn't they shy off even from a train?"

Dick waggled his head, not saying yes and not saying no, while he squinted to the west where the sun was maybe three-quarters down from overhead. He twisted half around again. "Cows look all right, and the horses."

"Funny about them buffalo calves," Evans said, speaking what was second in his thoughts. "You wouldn't think they'd j'in up with us and foller tame cows."

"Sometimes. Like I said, what you got to watch for is your own critters don't chase off with the buffler."

"I got every man we can spare back there. Reckon I ought to be back myself, 'stead of scoutin' with you."

"If we got salt enough, we could salt tonight to keep the cattle close."

"Don't know as that would do it, they're so ganted up. Anyhow, looks like they'd get enough of this wild salt, the way it's patched around."

"Pizens 'em. You know that."

They didn't say more until they came to what the sun had left of a lake, each thinking the same thing, Evans supposed, while their eyes took in the herds and the west cloud swelling slow. The lake was just a skim of water, ringed wide around by the white crust, in which some old bones were half sunk. Dick got off his horse, anyhow, and crunched through the salt and dipped a finger in and tasted it and shook his head. "Pure pizen."

"We'd best put out a flag then so's the train don't come too close," Evans said. "Them thirsty critters might make a break."

They rode out from the water and tied a rag to a high clump of sage and watched to see that the lead teamster took notice. "I figured that lake was no good, but still maybe good enough in a pinch," Dick told Evans then. "Wasn't any wood for fires even so. Lake that won't grow anything but sage and greasewood, an' no willows or cotton trees, is always bad water."

They rode for an hour longer, pushing buffalo out to the sides of the line of travel almost as a farmer might push his pastured stock. There was no end to them, just no by-God end to them, no end to cows and calves and fighting bulls and dust that gritted in the teeth and noise that tired the ear. Once Evans asked, "What's this place we're headed to?"

Dick answered, "Hell, Lije, I do' know. The mountain men didn't put names to ought but beaver streams and the Tetons and a hole or two."

Evans shut his mouth, deciding Dick didn't want to talk, and watched the cloud ahead. It was full and ugly, but it seemed to have held up, as if uncertain where to go. While he looked, a bolt of lightning tore it.

Dick rose in his stirrups and pointed. "I'm thinkin' that's it."

Through the dust, beyond a white sinkhole, over the backs of buffalo, Evans could make out a winding fringe of growth.

Riding to it, he thought: a no-name place, seen now and soon to be camped by and soon after left behind, if they were lucky; a place like dozens of others—campsites and crossings and hills and hollows—all the way back to Independence. It was hard for him to put them in order, hard even to remember where they had camped night before last and the night before that. The spots were lost in a stream of days that stretched back to forever. They were scrambled in the miles, mixed on the long plain of the Platte, confused in the hills west of Laramie. Kaw, Big Blue, Little Blue, Platte, Ash Hollow, Courthouse Rock, Horse Creek, Laramie, Big Spring, Deer Creek, North Platte crossing—and what were the places in between? Scott's Bluffs, Brady's Island, the Wakarusa where, a lifetime ago, he already had the feeling he was getting far from home. The no-name points, the nameless miles along the river, the cut where an axletree broke, the campgrounds bare as a bone. He could dig them out of memory, one and then another, but what filled this back part of his mind was the day-after-day roll of wheels, the dust, the heat and wind and rain and mud and chill, and the Turleys turning back and Martin crying for grace. His life before seemed like another life. All he ever had done was poke a team or explore the trail or push cattle along. The only way he ever faced was west.

And it was good. It was all fine and dandy, except that uneasiness lay on him now.

A few buffalo stood in the spring water or around it, stragglers from the bands that had come to drink and cool off and had cropped the banks down to the quick and now were moving off, on the hunt for grass. If bawling would find it, or pawing, they'd have full bellies before morning.

Dick let go of his looped reins and looked to the cap on the nipple of his rifle. "Might as well drop a cow or two, while they're close." He rode slowly, giving Evans time to cap his own gun, then kicked his horse into a gallop.

The buffalo stood quiet for a minute, dim-witted and waiting, and turned and broke into their clumsy run, the ones in the water wrenching out of it and getting away last. Dick broke his cow down not ten yards from the spring. Evans was slower, but his shot was good. The cow hunched up as if drawn together from the middle and tried to get lined out again and fell on her side kicking. They had hardly fallen before a couple of wolves showed up, winking hungry from over a little rise.

Evans bled the cows, and he and Dick stepped back to have a look at the spring, trailing their horses after them. Dick set to work charging his rifle, watching the wolves meantime to see they didn't make bold with the meat. The herds of buffalo coming and going had churned the water and so fouled it that Evans said, "It ain't fit to drink, Dick."

"It's wet."

"Might as well drink from a cow."

"It'll clear some. There's a fair amount of water runnin'."

"I bet it'll grow hair on a man, if it don't kill him."

"Shoo," Dick said, sliding his wiping stick in place, "I drunk out of wallows so thick they wouldn't pour."

"I ain't sayin' you ain't right, but it pret' near makes me wish we'd took the left-hand road by the river."

"Same thing there. With such a galore of buffler about you can't get away from mud and sand and buffler doin's. This here's sweet water. There's no pizen in a buffler, Lije."

Dick studied the lay of the land, so's to know how to draw his circle, and as the train came up he mounted his horse and led the lead wagon around, ending up, as always, with a perfect ring.

Evans had stepped back by the cows so the wolves wouldn't come to them. It would be a broody night, he thought, black and broody, sounding to wolf howls and buffalo bawls if to nothing more. The sun was sliding into the swollen edge of cloud, making a dark fire there.

Dick came up, saying, "I got help with the butchering," and Evans nodded and led his horse to where his own teams had stopped and tied it to a wheel. He said, "Howya, boy?" to Brownie. Before and behind him, and all around the circle, people were busy with their oxen, some of the women and older children doing the unhitching since so many of the men were bringing up the loose stock. It struck Evans that this was an uncommonly quiet camp, sobered, as he was himself, by the sense of being lost in distance, by the red light on the land and by the brutes about.

"Where's Rock?" he asked.

"Somehow he lamed himself a little and so I boosted him into the wagon," Brownie answered.

Rebecca got down stiff from her perch in the second wagon. "I declare, Lije, such a sight of critters!"

Brownie said, "I had to laugh. Ma was scared to walk."

"Not afeard exactly," she answered, "but offish. I'll allow to being offish, And, besides, this here wild salt eats your shoes away." She breathed deep, easier now, Evans knew with the pride that wouldn't stand words, because she stood by him again. "I don't never hope to get rid of that bull-roarin' in my ears."

"I got so I don't notice it, hardly," Evans said while he went to unhitching.

"So! You don't hear it now, I reckon?"

"Not with people talkin' so much," he answered, and looked up and winked at her.

He worked fast, hoping others did, too, feeling on him the push of coming darkness and the weight of the cloud at his back. "You water 'em," he said to Brownie, "and take 'em out to graze. That way looks best." He motioned with his thumb. "Come about dark, we'll put as many oxen in with the horses as the corral will hold. We'll forgit about milkin'. Cow doesn't give but a cupful, anyhow."

"I'll take the horse, Pa," Brownie said and untied and got on, driving the three teams before him.

"You're anxious, Lije." Rebecca didn't put the words as a question.

"Just a mite. I'll be back in a shake." He left her and made the rounds of the wagons, talking to what men he saw. Hobble every horse before turning them out for their hour or so of grazing! Keep the best oxen close, to shove in the corral with the horses! Best grass was that way, what there was of it. Then come and cut wood for fires! Buffalo might run. The men nodded, not questioning him, though the thought came to him, and was pushed away, that he spoke like Tadlock. The horse herd came up in a bunch and narrowed into a line and flowed into the corral through the gap left for them. He told the drivers what he had told the rest. "Botter, ask the cow guards to take 'em south, but not too far. We'll herd separate from the oxen." He sized up the meanderings of the flow from the spring. "There'll be enough water there, I reckon."

The directions given, he went back and gathered some loose wood and struck fire for Rebecca, and then took his ax and made for the brush, where other men joined him when they'd tended to their animals. They spread out along the fringe that followed the water, pulling out what dead wood there was and chopping up the big pieces.

Holdridge had gone to work close to Evans. "Hell of a storm makin' up," he said, resting for a minute on his ax. Coming out of the dark face, the words seemed dark.

"Maybe not. That cloud ain't hardly moved for an hour or more."

"No wood to speak of. The green stuff don't burn for nothin'." Holdridge went back to swinging his ax. Together they had quite a little pile pitched up when Dick came by, a smear of blood on his buckskins from the butchering. Evans thought Dick probably had skinned out the buffaloes; he always said the hides might come in handy later.

"I figured to set fires north, south, east and west, not a quarter of a mile out," Evans said.

Dick scuffed his jaw with his knuckles.

"All right."

"Seems so."

"Which way are they like to run, Dick?"

"No tellin'. Maybe north. They're driftin' north."

"I got the cattle south, beyond where I figured to put the fire."

"Don't know as it makes any difference. No matter where they're at, they'll likely run if the buffler do."

"We'll set the biggest fire south then. And if we got time,

161

we'll cut some sage, I thought, so's to be sure this wood catches good enough."

"Need a wagon for haulin'," Holdridge put in. "I got one as has some room in it with the cook stuff out."

"Find a team then and bring it on."

Dick said, "I'll see can I beg some salt."

Evans began chopping again. When Holdridge came up with the wagon, Evans helped load it and went to the next pile and helped with it and afterwards led the way, showing where the fires would be. They cut sage at each place, and at each one Evans put a man in charge, taking the south post himself. "Get what help you can. An' take rifles. Shootin' might turn 'em if they run." He studied the sky and the land lying red under it and the herds still to be made out from the light of long streamers slanting above the cloud. "I don't guess you need to fire up yet. We got time to eat."

Evans went to his wagon, joining Dick there for the supper Rebecca had ready. "Brownie et?" he asked.

"Come in and gobbled a mouthful and went back to the cattle. That boy works too hard, Lije."

"No helpin' it tonight. Everybody works. I got to get out there and tell the guards not to stick if the buffalo start runnin'. We'll set the tent later." He put his plate aside and got up, telling himself he'd best get more powder and ball while he thought of it, and also the Colt's six-shoot pistol that he never had bothered to carry. It was loaded but not capped.

When he came back, Dick said, "I raised some salt here and there." He sat cross-legged on the ground near the pot. "Not that I know it'll do any good." As he spoke, a little gust of wind worried at them.

"That wind!" Rebecca passed biscuits she'd cooked in the Dutch oven. Evans knew it wasn't the wind she was thinking of, but of the storm maybe a-coming and such a sea of buffalo around and Brownie out with the cattle. Still, he couldn't baby Brownie. Brownie was a grown man, almost, and as a man had to take his chances with the rest.

The gust whipped at them again, and Dick said, with the look in his face of expecting something, "She's comin', Lije."

162

Evans got up, a sudden anxiety on him. "I'll round up the men." The wind took the words from his mouth. Mixed with the whine of it he could hear the restless bellowing of the buffalo, now sounding far off and now close. The red light still lay on the land, grown to a kind of dark fire like that shed by a camp blaze. A bolt of lightning jagged down the western sky, and thunder rumbled.

He saw as he passed a curve of the circle that Weatherby was holding services, though not a handful listened. Some of the words came to him. "Let us put our trust in God. He rules the earth and the seas and the mountains and the savage tribes and the wild beasts and the storms . . ."

"Patch! Brewer! Tadlock! Insko! All of you! To the fires!"

Of a sudden the world was all wind, all fierce and driving wind that choked the words back and scoured his throat with sand. "Mack! Gorham!" The cloud reared up, closing off the dark fire, and let loose a bolt that stunned the eye. In the dark that followed it, all Evans could see was a stream of sparks blown from a campfire. "Fairman!" He didn't know when it was he had begun to run. "Patch! Come on!"

He ran south, feeling his shot pouch beat on his middle and his pistol bulky in his belt. A small rain drilled at the side of his face, and lightning blinded him again and thunder boxed his ears.

He grabbed wood from the pile, and sage, and shielded it with his body and poured powder out and reached for flint and steel, until he felt someone at his side and, in the glare of a bolt, saw that it was Patch stooping with his firemaker. The powder flashed and went out. Patch pulled a rag from his pocket and rubbed a hand of powder in it and tried the spark again. The fire started slow, nibbling at the edges of sage while the wind tried to tear it away, but at last it was going, blowing low to the east.

"Keep feedin' it! I got to see the herders." Evans ran again, heading still to the south, bowed into the wind that tried to slant him off, crying to himself, "Come on, Brownie!" as if the wish could reach him.

He ought to have had sense enough to bring a saddle horse,

he told himself, and then the night exploded. Lightning tore the sky and broke the earth and left after its crack and boom a sudden, breathy silence in which he thought he heard the thin howling of wolves. He thought he heard it and then it went from his mind, for under it, under the high whine of the wind, another sound came on, deep like a far drum. He slowed. He had to tell himself this was it, this was a million buffalo gone crazy, the pound of their hoofs beginning to shake the world so that not even thunder sounded.

He ran again, crying, "Brownie!" into the wind, into the swelling drum of hoofs, crying, "Guards! Run!"

Closer, he heard the newer rumble and a bolt split the sky, and he saw the cattle sweeping to him, pushed, he took it, by the buffalo beyond. He stumbled ahead and fell and drew himself up and fired into the black memory of them, hearing the poor pop of the rifle, seeing the little fire jet from the muzzle. The end had come, the end to Brownie and Rebecca and all his good knowing of them, but he ran on, tearing the pistol from his belt and firing while he ran until there was nothing to do but wait for the charging heads and the outflung hoofs and the long trample over him. No need to run for the fire. No time to reload. Stand straight and go down and call it quits. Hurrah for Oregon!

Noise drowned out thought and feeling. The swell and beat of it drowned them. There was no feeling but noise, thunder shaking out of the earth, rolling to the shaken land, unseen and awful thunder, all the brutes of God gone mad while God hid beyond the night. He thought it queer that he should notice now the camphor smell of broken sage.

He felt the first beasts pounding by. He could make out the black blur of their flight. He breathed the breath of them and knew their heat and waited, all of him caught up and held in the moment.

Lightning flashed again. He saw the cattle heaving by on his right and the humped buffalo hard on their heels, hump beyond hump to the end of sight, and he thought without feeling that the stampede might miss the corral.

He knew he had a chance now. He might make it back to the

fire. But he stood still, he didn't know for how long, fronting up to his time, if this was it, while his body shook to the shake of the world and the face of Brownie kept forming in his mind.

After a while he realized it was all over. The drag of the herd had beaten by and was gone and the drum of feet was drawing off, and the wind had gentled and a softer rain was falling. Back of him he saw Patch's fire and back of it the fires of camp.

Feeling flooded back on him then, relief and misery both, so that his voice broke as he ran, "Brownie! You there, Brownie?"

No one answered. He heard Patch call to him, but he ran on, tripping on the battered sage and calling out. A hump would show him, a hump that had been a horse, or a flat, thin shadow. "You here, Brownie?"

He didn't know Patch was with him until Patch took him by the arm. "Better come on, Evans. If he isn't at camp, we'll get all the men out."

He pulled away, resentful and afraid to speak, and Patch came to him again, gently, saying, "He may be at camp, you know."

Evans let himself be led, noticing but hardly noticing the rain and the lightning flashing fitful to the east, thinking how could he face Rebecca.

Hoofs, soft in the muddy ground, sounded ahead. Patch called out, "Who is it?"

"That you, Patch!" It was Dick's voice.

"Right."

"Seen Evans?"

"He's here."

"Pa! Are you all right, Pa?"

The young voice sounding in the night, the boy's face with a boy's high hopefulness, the voice bending him down, bursting his chest. "All right. I was afeard for you, Son."

"I told Ma you'd make out. Dick come and stayed with us herders, and when the storm broke, and the stampede, we rode wild as could be. I swear, it was fun."

The letdown from worry left Evans suddenly tired and sore. He said, "Fun, was it!" So it was Dick again, Dick always Johnny-on-the-spot while he himself was stumbling around in the dark like a fool. A man would think Dick couldn't make a mistake.

Patch spoke up quietly. "If it hadn't been for Evans that herd would have overrun the train. He ran out into it, firing."

"You can always count on Lije," Dick said.

Evans found only a grunt for that, while the notion came and grew in him that he ought to apologize for words thought if not said. A right man couldn't prize Dick enough.

"Take us half a day, at the least, to gather up them cattle," Dick went on, "and then like as not we won't find 'em all."

Chapter - - - - - - - - - - - - *Sixteen*

JUDITH FAIRMAN straightened slowly and pressed her two hands at her sides, easing the ache in her back. "Toddie, you stay close." She sighed while she looked up at Independence Rock where some of the men were climbing, hunting good places to chisel their names. Washing was a hard chore, even on a balmy day on the bank of a good stream. And riding and walking were hard, and mornings were hard, though she hadn't been bothered much by nausea but only by a feeling of discomfort and distention that sometimes at night brought her bolt upright in bed. She would belch then, from deep in her, and Charles would stir and ask, "You all right, Judie?" and she would sink back, relieved but burdened by the unloveliness of the act while she reassured him.

She wasn't the only one, and she found courage in that. There was Mrs. Brewer, who accepted her condition as she might have accepted the coming of a season, and Mrs. Patch, who hadn't much to say, and Mrs. Byrd, who made a kind of meek to-do, hoping again and again that she'd have a roof over her head and a decent place to lie when her time came. Maybe there were others, keeping the secret in them along with the seed. If there weren't, how did they manage? Mrs. Mack, for instance, with her wide-set, green eyes and her good shape?

The question came and went, leaving the thought that today was a day of relaxation and play for all except the women. The men and boys climbed the rock, and children romped, and even the oxen, lying in the eastward bottom, had a chance to rest their feet. Charles had ridden out with Dick Summers and Lije Evans. They would make a scout, they said, and bring in meat, returning in plenty of time for the Fourth of July oration that Tadlock was to deliver, prematurely, for today was the first.

Work or no, she welcomed this one day in camp. What did it really matter, except in men's imaginations, if the backward trains caught up? What did it matter if they passed, as one—the first so far—had done today? It was a little company with little stock that overtook them and waved and shouted and went on, too bent on leadership to waste time with a visit. Their captain informed Evans, though, that four of his command had died. Well, let them go. Let them race. Let them put the eager miles between them and the graves behind.

Standing while the pain in her back lessened, Judith thought that the whole train needed a rest, even though it had made poor time since the crossing of the Platte. One whole day and part of another had been given to a hunt for the cattle that the stampede had scattered. Most of the men, delegated by Evans, had ridden hard while the rest watched camp and fiddled with repairs and chafed at inaction and wished that the sun would go down, for it cast a breathless heat. The women had cooked and sewed and longed for a patch of shade and clean, cold water and had acted fretfully with the fretful children hanging to their skirts. The riders found parts of the herd here and parts of it there and came trailing them in, one after another, sitting their saddles as if too cramped to change positions, their hats pulled low over burned faces. Some of the cattle had mired in the sinkholes and some had crippled themselves and some just weren't to be found. Three of the twenty left behind had belonged to Charles.

"Don't get too close to the water, Toddie."

Yes, she said to herself, the sight of idleness was good, though she was not a part of it—the wagons halted tongue to tail along the green banks of the Sweetwater, the casual breeze stirring the loosened covers, the cattle and horses farther out under the lazy guard of men who had dismounted and sat half reclining in the grass, letting ground and breeze renew them; and westward the rock, the bald, gray lift of rock waiting the ages out. Cool water. Shade. Rest. Only around her, only here where the women worked was there the purposeful fret of living. Only here were the little, draining businesses of rubbing and scuffing and wringing out and hanging on a line. Did the other women feel the load of things, the day-by-day doing of chores that would just have to be done again? Mrs. Tadlock? Mrs. Daugherty? Mrs. Gorham? Mrs. McBee? Rebecca Evans? Any of these with wet, red hands that the dry air would chap worse still? Did they feel the load? And, beyond it, did they share the dark disquiet that afflicted her, the wordless apprehension that made all troubles big?

She knew she was feeling sorry for herself, but for the moment she didn't care. She bent over and soaped a shirt and began rubbing it on the board that slanted from the tub and asked Tod again to stay close to her. Charles had set blocks under the tub, but still she had to stoop and, stooping, bring back the ache in her back. Underclothes, shirts, Tod's things, dresses, a pair of woolen breeches she felt sure would shrink despite all pains. Wash them and wear them and wash again, week on week to Oregon, to the end of life. For a little while she let herself think she suffered more than others because her life had been gentler. She knew what it was to have black help, to find time for the pianoforte and for needlework and to care for her hands. A tear slid from her eye and fell on the washboard and disappeared in suds.

She pinched other tears off, impatient with herself and touched by guilt. Work was work for anybody, and she always had worked if not at such long drudgery. She always wanted to work; it was just that she was tired now and filled with forebodings.

"Tod, please don't wander off. Come back. Mother's busy."

He lifted his face to hers, his eyes light blue like her own, his cheeks and mouth still marked by babyhood. "Can't I wade, Mother?"

"Afterwhile. You stay close now."

While she spoke to him, Rebecca Evans came from the line she had strung. "I got my things all done," she said. "Lemme help you. You look tuckered." Her strong hands went to work with the rinsing and wringing. It occurred to Judith that she was the type of woman for the trail. She was stout and assured and able and unafraid. If ever a cloud hung over her, no one knew it. If ever the thought of miles depressed her, she didn't let on.

Miles. Distance. Distance was the enemy, not Indians or

crossings or weather or thirst or plains or mountains, but distance, the empty, awesome face of distance, the miles on wrinkled miles of it, the levels and hills and hollows and bluffs, unconquerable by the slow turn of wheels or the creaking step of oxen. There was no end to it, not even any shortening. Morning and night it was there unchanged, hill and cloud and sky line beyond reach or reckoning. Sometimes she wondered at the stubborn, crazy courage of men who thought that day on day would add to Oregon.

"It seems so far," she said to Rebecca.

"Don't it, though?" Rebecca tossed a twist of clothes into a basket. "Tell you what helps, though. Don't think how far. Just think one day at a time."

"And one piece of underwear at a time, and one shirt?"

"I declare, Judie, you are wore out!"

Judith felt the quick, inner spasm of tears and wrestled it down, ashamed but close to crying still at this excitement of self-pity. She turned her face away, to Toddie who was punching at the ground with a stick. "I wish I was more like you, Rebecca."

"Like me?"

"Things don't seem to bother you."

"An' I never feel broke down or sad or anything?"

"Do you?"

"Sometimes I walk on my lip, it's drawed so low."

"No one would know."

Rebecca's breath came out in a little explosion. "Don't ever think that what you feel ain't felt by all at one time or another. I get down in my mind, and then I think I got a good boy and a good man, and I ought to be praisin' the Lord. You got a good man yourself, Judie."

Judith agreed by nodding. A kind and thoughtful man, Charles was, earnest and well intentioned if not forceful even in the quiet way in which Lije Evans was forceful. Give him time, she thought, give him Evans' years, and he might be so. "I don't know why I get so gloomy."

"Same with all of us, more or less," Rebecca answered while she kept busy with her hands. "Less with me, now. I'm pretty perky mostly. Course, with you it's different. Maybe a woman's got to feel sick and low and go through birthin' so's to set a proper store by her baby."

"Maybe."

"A woman ain't cut like a man, not so adventuresome or rangin' and likin' more to stay put—but still we foller 'em around, and glad to do it, too." Rebecca laughed a throaty, half-rueful laugh as she pitched another twist into the basket. She was, thought Judith, more masculine than most women. She had a broad face, like her husband, and the suggestion of a mustache on her sun-darkened lip. Rebecca went on, "Your boy there's chipper as a squirrel."

"We think he's cured of the fever." She ought to be over-joyed at that. She ought to be singing thanks to this high, raw country and the sharp smell of sage that Dick Summers said was medicine itself. She ought to be happy at the tanned glow of health in the delicate, still-baby face bent now to the ground and the stick that stirred it. But old misgivings rode her, the weeks-long sense of overhanging misfortune. In her was the heavy impulse to retreat, to flee to the plantation in Kentucky, to go to her mother, who lived graciously in Lexington, to visit her sister, safe and happy at Vicksburg. She hoped the letters she had written and left at Fort Laramie to be carried by the first eastbound travelers seemed as cheerful as she had tried to make them.

"Yes," Rebecca said. "He's in good case all right."

Tod lifted his head. "Can't I go and play with the other chil-dren, Mother? They're all playing."

So they were. One group was down the river, splashing in the shallows, only half watched by their elders. Another kept streaming around and out from the corral, frisky, like pups, at release from the grind of travel, the young voices raised in shouts and screams and laughter. But still Judith said, "We'll go wading soon."

"I want to play now."

"I know, Son. It does get tiresome."

Rebecca's face asked why she didn't let him run along.

"I'm too careful, I guess," she answered, "but he was so sick.

So sick. So long." To Tod she said, "How about mud pies?"

"I'm tired of nothing to do, Mother."

"How about mud pies?" she asked again, thinking how time bore on a child, remembering from her girlhood how long an hour could be. She put herself in his place, imagining the never-never-ending roll of wheels, the hot sun unmoving in the blank sky, the slow and deadly daily round, and all the bursting energies pent up, confined to fidgets and complainings. How much farther to the Southern Pass, Mother? How long before we stop? How far is it now to Oregon? Nothing to do. Nothing to do except to wait on time that wouldn't pass. And now, when he could play, she feared unreasonably for him to leave her side.

"I'll get the water, Toddie." She took her hands from the tub and picked up a piggin and walked to the stream and filled it and brought it to him. "You'll have fun, playing mud pies. I'm almost through." She bent to kiss the small, protesting face.

They finished the washing, all but the hanging, and she said to Rebecca, "That was a big help. You go now."

"Things'll be all right with you. We'll get to the Willamette long before your time."

"I'm not worried about that. It's just—I don't know—I'm just foolish."

"What comes usually ain't near so bad as feared. You remember that." Rebecca smiled and flicked the water from her hands and went to gather up her things, walking straight and sure and strong. The other women were dumping tubs and collecting the tools of their work and one by one trailing back toward their tents.

Judith was lifting the basket when Hig came by. He said, "Mornin'," and let his lean limbs down by Toddie, favoring the wound that Botter's accidental shot had made. "How you, boy?"

"Mother won't let me play."

"Why sure, now, she will. Me and you'll build us a fort. Get that dead branch over there."

Judith set the basket down, wanting the dry, queer cheer of Hig. "I thought you'd be on the rock."

"Fer what?"

"To carve your name, of course."

"Not me," he answered, breaking the branch and setting the sticks while Tod looked on.

"Why?"

He grinned. "I could say I don't know writin'."

"Oh."

"But that ain't it."

"What is it?"

Thought lighted his narrowed eyes. "This here country puts its mark on a man, and the mark is that he ain't sure who he is, being littled by the size of it."

"I don't see—"

"So he puts his mark on the country, like they're doin' on that rock, and then he can say to hisself, 'By Godfrey, this is me, all right. There's my name writ right there in the stone.'"

"Well?"

"Shoo, boy, we forgot to leave us a gate." Then, "What I'm tryin' to tell your ma is I'm too simple-minded fer it. I wouldn't any more'n cut my name than I'd wonder was it really me that cut it and, besides, was that sure enough my name anyhow."

"I thought they cut them for other people to see."

"Men puts me in mind of a horse that j'ined us today. Been lost, I reckon, from a train last year, and wanderin' over this God-big country ever since, wonderin' about hisself, thinkin' was he a horse sure enough, an' if so just what horse was he, Shorty or Pete or Blue or what. Or was he just a stray thought blowed by the wind? When he seen us, he really cut a caper. You never seen a horse so glad, an' all just because he could kind of put hisself together again. Now, boy, we'll set a cannon inside to keep the Injuns off."

"Don't they write their names for other people to see?"

"People as knows me knows my name, an' them as don't don't keer, or maybe would be tormented tryin' to place me."

"You think funny things, Hig."

"Who don't, ma'am?"

Who didn't? Was this long uneasiness of hers any odder, was it as sensible as Hig's whimsies? "Anyhow, we're glad you're with us, Hig."

"Same here. Now, Tod, there's a dandy fort for you. Keep them redskins scared away. Hear? I got a job of tire fixin' to do."

He drew his long legs under him and got to his feet and ambled off, a scarecrow, Judith thought, a scarecrow with a mind.

She picked up the basket. "You play fort, Tod, while I finish, and then we can wade." She went to the rope she had lined between two trees and put the basket down and began shaking out and hanging up the wash.

A scarecrow with a mind. A personality behind a face like a forgotten apple. And more than that. A spirit that kept itself good-natured and whimsical, that found fun in a fiddle and rewards in the moment, undaunted by hardship or travel or distance or the dark disasters the brooding mind made up.

She would be more like that, she told herself. She would cast off anxiety. She would meet trouble when it came, and not before. She would be cheerful and strong and so make a better wife and mother. She made herself hum a snatch of song and felt a kind of fierce cheer and a kind of fierce strength rising in her, put there by her will. She let herself enjoy it, let herself exult with it while she hung the clothes, her mind passive, knowing only the high comfort of courage. She hung the last garment and turned to speak, and saw that Tod was gone.

He didn't mean to run away. He just meant to move around a little, being so tired of forts and mud pies and staying in one place that he couldn't hold still any longer. He walked out from the washtub, stepping through a patch of dry grass, and a great, gray grasshopper with blind eyes looked at him and jumped up with a flutter of red wings and a whirring clatter. He ran after it, watching its crazy flight in the breeze, and saw it settle. He came up with his hand lifted and cupped, a little fearful of clapping it down. The eyes stared and the legs hitched and the stone-gray body rose, turning red again, and clattered ahead.

He stooped and grabbed two finger stones, thinking he would kill the grasshopper with them, and set off after it, running toward a grass clump where it had lighted. It winged up just as he thought he had lost it, and he ran again, holding a rock in each hand. He threw and missed, and the grasshopper rose and he followed, and it rose and he followed, hot and eager with the chase of it.

After a while he did lose it. It wouldn't rise from the dust or the curled grass where he thought it had landed though he scuffed the place and scuffed it again, feeling let down because fun should have been taken from him so soon.

Giving up, he looked around and saw that Mother was out of sight, over a swell of land, beyond a wagon itself half hidden by the swell. He couldn't see any person, not a man or a woman, and not even any children, though their shouting voices came to him.

A sudden emptiness came on him, and he started trotting back, wanting the safe arms of his mother and the soft bosom and the mouth scolding while it kissed him.

Then he heard the grasshopper again, the nervous, whirring rattle of it coming from somewhere in a ragged pile of rocks. The known sound reassured him. He stopped trotting and angled off toward the pile.

Low on the ground, hard to see against the broken stone, among the sun-browned grasses, a little-man's face looked at him, pinch-mouthed and hard-eyed, with two holes for a nose. A tongue licked red and quick from the tight mouth.

Little-man's face! Snake's face! Rattlesnake's face, the coil behind showing dusty on the dusty rock, the tail blurred with shaking!

In the shock of first knowing, he couldn't run. He stood there with fear washing in him while his eyes blurred with the blurring tail and lost the face in the fast, red licking of the tongue.

"Toddie! Oh, Toddie!"

He swung around and started off and felt the bite of needles in his leg and the drag of the coil before it pulled free.

Lije Evans pulled up when he and the others had rounded Independence Rock and could get a good view of the camp. "There she is, safe as sassafras."

Dick Summers and Charles Fairman had reined in, too, and

175

sat easy in their saddles, gazing down the tilting plain to the covered wagons a half mile away. Back of them the four meat-laden pack horses nosed up and melted into the positions of rest. "We got a fair load on them critters," Evans said, sizing up the two that trailed him.

"We been fools for luck—so far."

Fairman asked, "What do you mean, Dick? So little sickness?"

"Injuns. We ain't hardly seed an Injun."

"Plenty of time yet," Evans said.

"Acrost the mountains is friendlies."

"But no buffalo."

"Few. Ought to dry meat tomorrow or next day, Lije, I'm thinkin'. Seemed today like the buffler'd run out soon now." While he spoke, Dick kept his gaze on the camp.

Evans glanced at it and then up at the sun and said, "We come back in good time to hear Tadlock on independence, like we promised." Thinking about Tadlock, he was a little soured —Tadlock, who kept saying they ought to have a Fourth of July speech at the rock and then had acted as if he didn't want to make it when they asked him why he didn't speak himself then. Said that wasn't the idea, but all right, then, he would, since they asked. He was a man so hungry for importance he kept chasing it away.

Tadlock went out of Evans' mind when he glanced at Dick again. "What's wrong?" He followed Dick's gaze to the camp. The wagons sat safe in the sun and around them the tents; eastward the herd straggled along the river, where he could make out a guard or two.

"Maybe nothin'," Dick answered. "Don't see nobody this side of the corral."

"They're by the river."

Dick grunted, and Evans found himself wondering, as he had before, at the way of Dick, who could look off and see things that others wouldn't and add them up to a solid guess.

Dick said, "There's doin's on yonder side."

Squinting, Evans now and then caught sight of figures through the gaps that the cluster of tents and wagons left. "Probably Weatherby's exhortin'."

"Could be."

"My wagons are over there." The shadow of misgiving showed on Fairman's face.

"Let's git on," Dick said, and jerked the lead rope on his two-horse pack string.

Evans jerked, too, and kicked his mount and felt his right arm strain at the socket as the near horse pulled back. He reckoned he'd never learn to handle a rope and a rifle and reins as Dick could. "Getup!" The horses came to a trot and then to a slow lope, the meat thunking against their sides as they hit the end of stride. Fairman, without a pack string to pull, had gone galloping ahead.

Dick was right, Evans thought, as they pulled to a stop on the near side of the ring where Fairman's horse stood hip-shot and untied. There wasn't a soul here. Everybody was yonder. They slid off and tied up to wheel spokes and stepped over a wagon tongue and crossed the enclosure now empty of stock and stepped over another tongue and came to the company grouped outside Fairman's tent.

Evans grabbed the first man he came to. It happened to be Hig. "What is it?"

Hig's squeezed face seemed squeezed more than ever. The words came thin from his mouth. "The boy got snake-bit."

"Tod!"

"Rattlesnake-bit."

"For God's sake! When?"

"Been a spell back. Middle of the morning."

"Dick!"

Hig's voice wasn't much more than a whisper. "Looks like a goner."

"Dick! You hear!"

"I heerd," Dick said and shook his head.

They pushed on to the flap of the tent where Brother Weatherby stood old and stooped. Evans brushed by him and bent to clear the canvas and went in. He saw Rebecca first, sitting on the ground by the side of the bed, a pan in her hand. She didn't speak, except with her eyes.

Evans said, "I—we just heerd."

The boy lay in his bed on the ground, covered so that nothing could be seen of him except his shape under the blanket and, at the head of the bed, his face pale on the fresh pillow and his eyes half closed.

Evans' gaze ran from the boy to Judith Fairman, who sat across from Rebecca, holding the boy's hand in both of hers. "How is he?"

Fairman swung around. He had been kneeling by his wife's side, staring at Tod as if a spell had been put on him. "In the name of God, do we just have to stand and gawk?"

The boy stirred weakly and murmured something that his mother bent to hear. She took a towel from a little pile by her side and touched his forehead and mouth with it. "Do you want another drink, Toddie? Want another drink?"

Evans called, "Dick!"

Dick had stayed just outside. He crowded into the tent and nodded and rested his eyes on the bed.

"We'd best look, too, Charlie," Evans said.

"He was cold. He told his mother he was cold," Fairman said, low-voiced, as if asking pardon for being impolite before. He laid back the cover, watching their faces while they looked.

Inside himself Evans shrank from what he saw—the leg swollen double-size clear to the thigh already, and the skin drawn bursting tight and the shank lumped and polkadotted with the black and blue of poisoned blood.

Fairman took the heel of the foot, gently, and, while the boy whimpered, turned it so as to show the bite. Someone had cut at the fang marks, and the cuts leaked a black ooze that had washed little rivers in a black dust.

All of them, Evans thought, were silenced by the evil of the thing, until Rebecca said, "Mr. Byrd lanced him and rubbed salt and gunpowder in. It was all we knew to do."

"Don't you know something?" Judith Fairman's voice wasn't much more than a whisper. She hadn't spoken before, and now he looked at her face, and there was such trouble there and so much of prayer in her voice that he couldn't say the truth. While he hunted for a lie, Dick asked, "Did you suck him?"

She shook her head slowly, as if under a gathering load of guilt for not thinking of sucking.

Evans couldn't look at her longer. He couldn't stand to see hope trembling against despair, and her so young and comely and deserving. His eyes went to Rebecca, sitting silent, giving in silence of her strength. It came to him that women suffered deeper and endured longer and understood better than any man. In grief and death men were only children, as he was himself, and had to lean on the motherness of the Rebeccas of the world.

The boy moved, and his half-shut eyes flickered, and a spasm wrenched him, ending in vomit that Rebecca tried to catch in her pan. Judith leaned over and wiped him with a towel.

The boy cried weakly, "It hurts, Mother."

"Plainest words he's spoke," Evans said, trying to find the tone of hope.

"I know, dear. I know. Do you want a drink?" Judith's face didn't cry; nothing but the pale-blue eyes cried, putting the shine of tears on her cheeks.

The boy didn't answer. He sank back, and his lids lowered, and Evans feared he saw the blue of death under the eyes and on the temples. He listened for Tod's breathing.

Fairman cried out again, as if they were all at fault, "Do we just stand and wait?"

"Easy, Charlie," Evans said. He walked stooping to the door of the tent. "One of you women bile some milk, will you?" Then, to the ones in the tent, "Keep 'im quiet as can be. Dick!"

Brother Weatherby still stood at the entrance. "I'll be around if you need me."

"Obliged. Come on, Dick."

He led Dick over to the side, away from the people who had divided into knots and were talking in the tones of the sick-room.

Dick said, his voice hard with helplessness, "There ain't a thing to do, goddam it, Lije."

"Except to make Judith think every God's thing was done."

Dick studied a minute and answered softer. "You're a good

hoss, Lije. There's a root the Sioux swear by, though it's no account. I'll dig some."

As Evans started back through the waiting ones, he felt a hand on his arm and heard the pipe of Mrs. McBee. "If we could git a warty toad, now, that 'ud be the thing."

"Toad?"

"You lay it on the bite, and if'n it lives, it draws the pizen out, and if it dies, you git another."

"Go find a toad," he said, and pulled loose from the claw of her hand and re-entered the tent. "Dick's gone for wild medicine, an' he 'lows suckin' still might help."

Fairman's eyes met his. Fairman said, "All right," and laid the blanket back.

"I'll do it, Charlie."

"He's my boy." Fairman bent his head.

The boy didn't move as the foot was turned. He lay there quiet, he and his little leg and the big, black leg that would kill him.

"We'll put on a root-and-milk poultice," Evans said. "That might fotch it."

Judith was stroking the hand she had brought back into hers. "He hasn't had any fun," she said, not to anyone, as if speaking a faraway wish for a new chance with him. The tears kept spilling from her eyes and sliding down the uncrying face. "He's been sick so much."

Fairman raised his head and spit and bent it again.

Judith went on as if she was all alone: "I should have played with him this morning. I should have known how tired he was of doing nothing."

"Don't fault yourself, Judie," Rebecca asked. "Please don't fault yourself any more. You ain't to blame."

Evans wished Judith would break down, wished she would begin to whoop and holler and take on as some women did and so ease herself and all the rest of them.

Dick came in with a kettle of hot milk in one hand and some straggly roots in the other and sat down at the door of the tent and put a root in his mouth. When he had chewed it up, he spit it into his hand and took another bite. "All right, Charlie."

Fairman brought his head up and cleared his mouth. Some grains of powder showed around it. "What is it?"

"A root the Sioux use." Dick moved up with his handful of chewings and plastered it on.

"Got a rag?" Evans asked.

Judith took a towel from the pile by her side and leaned across to hand it to him. He went to the kettle and dipped the towel in the hot milk and folded it and came back and laid it over. Fairman spread the blanket again.

"Would whisky help?" Fairman asked.

Dick just shook his head while he sat cross-legged, his face showing nothing but the hard patience to wait.

Evans let himself down and put his hand to his neck that was stiff with stooping, and for what seemed a long time they sat there, out of talk, while Dick chewed fresh root and Evans dipped the rag in the heated milk that Mrs. Mack kept bringing back. From outside came the wordless murmur of voices.

Judith's far-off voice picked up by and by. "He was what we were going to Oregon for."

Fairman broke in sharply, "Was!"

"I mean is, Charles. Is."

Evans stared at his hands, and then Judith cried out, cried the breaking cry that he had been wishing for and couldn't stand now, and he saw the thick and sickly matter bleeding from the boy's closed lids and knew that he was dying.

He scrambled up and ducked outside, spitting "Bad," to all the questions asked him, and found Brother Weatherby and asked him to come. Sometimes he felt like thanking God for preachers.

IT WOULD be a dry, raw day, windy-warm, and a man would go along licking his roughening lips while the juices in him parched away. Already, with the sun no more than a hand above the eastern sky line, Evans felt the touch of it on his back. It would burn later and hurt the eye with its glitter, and the wind out of the west would draw up the skin of the face. The thought dodged into his head that Byrd's cracked lip wouldn't get any better today.

He stood with the rest, waiting on Brother Weatherby to start. Weatherby had his coat on and his hat off and his Bible under his arm. By him was the dirt piled on canvas and the hole left from it and the walnut box that held Tod Fairman. Evans didn't know what Weatherby was waiting for, unless for a go-ahead from above.

When, finally, the rusty voice sounded, Evans was back in yesterday, making the box again out of the chest that Rebecca swore she wouldn't need anyhow. It was a good coffin, better even than most made in Missouri, and he had found rest for his mind in the building of it. For the time, he almost had forgotten sadness in measuring and sawing and hammering. He had eased it by the movements of his hands and the sight of the box taking shape under them, its joints tight and smooth and its lid close-fitting. He reckoned it was the same with Dick, who had gone with Patch and Fairman and picked a spot for a grave and, so Patch said, cut the sod and peeled it back as if skinning a fine fur. He and Patch had dug the grave, deep so as to be beyond wolves, and had pitched every grain of dirt on a cover.

Evans lifted his head, for Brother Weatherby was done with praying for the time being and was saying that God worked in mysterious ways—which was the plain truth. He tried to stay on the track of Weatherby's words, but his mind kept straying off, asking itself questions, bringing back the pictures of things seen. Rebecca and Mrs. Brewer had washed the little body and laid it out and wrapped it in its winding sheet and put it in the box along with the leg that fouled it and afterwards had sat most of the night through, kept company and later spelled by Evans and Patch and men and women who came and went, bringing meat and bread and sweetening, stammering old comforts for the Fairmans, who sat up, too, quiet for the most part and dulled by grief. Rebecca finally had talked Judith into going off for a nap, but Judith didn't stay long and Evans doubted that she'd slept.

It was a long, hard night. Outside, things were quiet except for wolf howls far off and now and then a breeze that found the tent and whispered death and slid away, but the breath of time seemed to sound, of time and distance and things that had been and things to come. Hearing Judith sob as her loss came alive in her, feeling the press of misery on him, Evans was struck by the littleness of grief here. It had to be walled in, it had to be kept close in a tent, else it would blow like dust and be gone and never a sign of it remain in the high sky or on the long land.

" 'Let not your heart be troubled: ye believe in God, believe also in me. In my Father's house are many mansions . . .' "

Mansions! What would a little boy care about a mansion? His mother was the best mansion he had. But God worked in mysterious ways. Leave it to God! There wasn't any choice anyhow. Leave it to God!

Evans felt the tired sadness and the strength of Rebecca, who stood by him, her arms crossed loose under her breasts, her eyes big with misery and too-little sleep, and he guessed her thoughts were on their second-born, who had sickened and died in a year and so left all their hopes on Brownie, for Rebecca couldn't catch again.

Brownie stood on his other side, in his face a boy's wonder at the hard way of things. How could a man explain it to his young one, who expected goodness and fun not just all the days of his life but all the days of his life forever and ever? He could say it was the will of God, which probably it was, but that was like saying he didn't understand, which he didn't. So saying, he felt ignorant and poor-suited as a father and had to catch what comfort he could in knowing that death was an acident in the minds of the young. It came and was done with and wouldn't come again except maybe far off, at a time too distant to worry about.

Bring comfort to the bereaved, Brother Weatherby was praying. Let them accept Thy will. Let them find comfort in Thee and be strengthened by Thy loving strength.

Ahead of Evans, closer to the box, the Fairmans bowed to the prayer. They were a little apart from the rest, for people had drawn back to leave them with their grief. While Evans watched, Judith's shoulders hunched to a choked crying.

The prayer would be the end of it, except for a song and ashes-to-ashes, Evans thought, and then Weatherby lifted his head and pointed his bony arm and put power in his voice as if of a sudden his feelings had got the best of him. "God created everything and it was good; save thou, alone, snake, are cursed; cursed shalt thou be and thy poison."

Scripture? Was Adam's curse Scripture, or just a saying that some people believed would make a snake crawl off and die? Not that it mattered, and anyway the snake was dead. Brownie had chopped it up, or one just like it. In quick revengefulness he had grabbed the hoe when he heard the news about Tod and had gone off as if to square accounts and had come back with rattles in his palm. Evans had nodded at him, letting him feel that in killing the snake he had done the prime thing.

More praying after the curse. More bowing down. More asking of comfort. For the Lord knoweth the way of the righteous: but the way of the ungodly shall perish. Even in a funeral preachment Weatherby couldn't keep from taking a lick or two at the swearers and the Sabbath breakers.

A song then. "The Day Is Past and Gone." A kind of queer song for a burying. Weatherby lined it out and pitched it with a voice that showed its age when he tried to sing, and the other voices joined in, frail beside the rock, frail over the lost tumble of country and the wild buffalo grazing and the breeze blowing out of nowhere into nowhere.

The day is past and gone;
The evening shades appear:
O may we all remember well
The night of death draws near.

We lay our garments by,
Upon our beds to rest;
So death shall soon disrobe us all
Of what is here possessed.

Lord, keep us safe this night,
Secure from all our fears;
May angels guard us while we sleep,
Till morning light appears.

Evans walked up, along with Summers and Patch and Mack, and lowered the box with ropes, and Weatherby took a pinch of earth and recited ashes and dust while Judith broke down again.

The crowd drifted off, going back to their wagons to ready for the start. Evans and Dick filled in the grave and carried what dirt was left and dumped it in the river. "If God's so goddam loving-kind," Dick said while he shook the dust out of the canvas, "He's got a queer way of showin' it."

"I reckon you got to take God or leave Him, whole hog or none."

"You can have Him. This child wouldn't care for none."

Hearing Dick, Evans knew something about him he hadn't quite known before. Dick was tender and tough, both, and the one explained the other when you came to think about it.

Dick stuffed the canvas under his arm. "You go on. Give me a little time, and I'll fix the grave so no Injun eye can spot it."

"All right. Might as well let me take the canvas." Evans headed for camp. Halfway there, he saw Brownie coming to meet him.

"Pa?" Brownie said while still a half a dozen steps away.

"What is it, boy?"

"I got the tent down and the wagons loaded and the oxen hitched and all."

"So?"

"And it ain't my turn with the cattle."

"What you workin' up to?"

"So could I stay back and chisel my name on the rock?"

"You had all yesterday, Brownie."

"Not all. I stood guard and killed the snake and things."

"It ain't safe."

"Please, Pa. It's safe enough. You'll be in sight for a long ways."

"Why you so took of a sudden to cut your name?"

"I just am, Pa."

Evans noticed that Brownie's eye wouldn't quite meet his. The boy was holding something back, some foolish notion, likely, that was still his notion and his secret and not to be pried at by grownups who thought themselves so wise. He smiled into Brownie's waiting face. "You're doin' a man's work, boy. I reckon you can decide for yourself. Only hurry up, I don't care much to leave you alone."

"Thank you, Pa," Brownie said, showing a quick and thankful gladness. "I'll wait'll you roll."

"Watch for Injuns."

"Sure."

Evans walked to the Fairman tent. It was the only tent not struck yet, and Fairman's teams were the only ones not yoked. He stooped and went inside and saw Judith seated on the bed, her face in her hands, and Fairman standing motionless.

"Ain't Becky here?"

Fairman didn't answer.

"Can I help, Charlie?"

It was another minute before Fairman spoke. "She's coming back. I'll get to it."

"I could yoke your teams now. My outfit's ready."

In the waiting silence Evans heard Judith's held-in sobbing.

"I'll get to it."

"We got to roll, Charlie. You know we got to roll."

"I know."

"Not yet, please!" The words cried at Evans, coming out of the wet, torn mouth that the hands had left, coming out of a face past bearing to behold. "We can't leave him yet. Don't you see! We can't leave him."

"And not know where he lies!" Fairman burst out. "Never again to know where he lies!"

"Toddie," Judith said, talking to the grave. "Poor Toddie."

Fairman's voice was rough. "Don't you see? Can't you see?"

Evans saw all right, and wrenched with the seeing, and he saw Dick Summers, too, poking his head in the tent and coming in silently and standing stooped, his face solemn and the twinkle gone from his eyes. "I kin always find it for you, ma'am, any time," he said.

S UMMERS LED OFF, and the wagons rolled into line, the Fairmans' outfit right after the lead team though it wasn't their turn to be shut of the dust. The herders behind shouted and whistled, riding among the animals to the flick of reins and rope ends, and the horses and mules started frisky, snatching for last bites of the bottom grass before they ran. The cattle got going slow, stopping to bawl and spatter the ground, and crowded into the strip between Independence Rock and the Sweetwater.

Brownie sat his horse and watched the train file away and fell in at the tail and helped push the cow column through. He held up then and waved at the riders and reined right and came to the even-steep western face of the rock. A man could climb here, though he had to watch for a slip that might crack a bone.

He slid off his horse and tied it to some high-growing sage, wishing while he did it that the flies weren't so bad. Already, with the sun hardly more than two hours high, they were warmed up for the day's business. There were little, yellow ones that bit like bees and gray ones with bulging eyes and shiny-black ones with white wings that drove a critter crazy. They had followed up, out of the damp of the river growth, against a wind that still must have blown some of them away. He rested his rifle against the rock and laid his hammer and chisel down and went over Nellie, especially the tender, un-haired skin of her tits. His hand came away smeared with sucked-out blood. He wiped it on his pants and picked up his chisel and hammer. He wouldn't need the rifle, he figured. It would just clutter him up. He'd leave it right here.

The climb was stiff, though more dangerous-looking than dangerous, up the slanting face of rock flecked with grays and browns. Part way up, he stopped to blow, remembering too late that Dick Summers had said the way to mount a hard rise was to step slow, one step and afterwhile another, so as not to wind yourself. He faced around and sat, holding to the chisel and hammer that might clatter down if he let go.

The train was stretching out as it settled to the day's pull, heading for the gap to the left of Devil's Gate, which from here wasn't a gate but just a niche in a sudden pitch of mountain. Dick Summers rode in the lead, as always, trotting his horse to put a proper distance between himself and the first wagon. Dick was easy to make out. His buckskins marked him, and the rifle carried crosswise, and his way of riding, which was as if he'd been born with a saddle between his legs. The riders with him were harder to fix, but they would be Botter and Davisworth and Insko, who usually herded but were going to have fun today, scouting ahead for buffalo, finding out for the train whether to stop and kill and dry meat against the climb over the pass. Brownie saw buffalo far beyond them, a small herd that seemed to swim in the shimmer of the morning sun.

Closer, the wagons inched away across the reach of plain, tilting right and left as the wheels hit the clumps of sage, Daugherty and his red-painted wagon cover in the lead and then the Fairmans and then Pa and Ma and then Holdridge or Gorham and Tadlock. Brownie ran his eye along the line, seeing could he make out every outfit. Some he guessed at by the dogs that trailed along, or by the children. There wasn't any way to miss Brewer and his crowd, or maybe there was. Byrd and Daugherty drew a tail of young ones, too, and McBee.

With his eyes closed, he thought, he would know the McBee wagon, for Mercy was driving. At this distance, with her no more than a flutter of dress and a shadow that marched before, he could see her, the straight, strong little body and the face above it that didn't smile often but spoke with the eyes. He remembered the voice of her that night at Laramie, not the words so much, not the "I'll be all right, Brownie," but the tone she used, the gentle tone. He wondered if others saw her for as pretty as she was, for as touching on the heart. Davisworth? Hig? Botter? Moss? Any of the single men? Or the married ones like Mack that he felt thankful to for being nice to her family that the rest made small of? No, it was his feeling and his alone, for no one else could feel the same, and he would hold it to him while he waited for the time to speak.

The horses and mules followed close on the wagons, driven by Hig and Willie Brewer, and after them lagged the cattle, hating to face up to distance, moving balky while Gorham and McBee and Shields and Patch worked at them. They all had crossed the river, which meandered toward the Gate, its banks sprouting bushes close-pressed by the sage.

Last of all came the dust, streaming the other way, driven hard by the wind. It was a strange sort of country, where the wind blew with hardly so much as a cloud in the sky.

Down in the shadow of the rock Nellie stomped against the flies. Up here there weren't any flies, or any dust-shot in the face, and the shadowed stone was still cool from the night, and a man could hear distance singing with the wind, from the mountains ridged far off to left and right, from the great pass and Dick's Green River and from Oregon, where Pa said wheat was growing rich and stock fattened and fish swam solid in the rivers.

A woman, tired already but not tired enough to ride, was hanging to the tail of a wagon, letting the oxen pull her feet along. It was Mercy's wagon, and the woman would be Mrs. McBee, who couldn't be very strong and so talked about miseries and cures while weller people smiled behind their hands. Maybe they would act different if they really knew. Maybe the McBees never had had a chance and would show up good if given one. So they all got to Oregon, and he, known now as Mr. George Brown Evans, made a heap of money, being rich in land and grain and animals, and he set up his in-laws, saying, "Don't think nothin' to it," and they did just fine, and McBee shaved and tidied up, and a nicer bunch of people you'd never want to meet.

The dream didn't come sharp or stay long, being dulled and cut off by the underthought of death, of Tod Fairman and the life gone out of him and his mother choking at the burying, and, farther back, of Martin with no one to grieve over him except a nephew in Illinois who would get the money that his little plunder earned when auctioned off at Laramie. Were they part of the sky now? Was it their voices sounding in the wind, mourning at being gone? Did they look down and see and know from under the wing of God?

He couldn't imagine himself dying, but he could see himself dead, lying pale and cold while Ma cried over him and Pa said, "Boy! Boy!" and Mercy sobbed open and unashamed, owning up now to the feeling she had had for him. How he came to die was that he stood off an Indian war party while the train corralled. He had stood between them, steady behind his horse, his aim true on the chief, and had brought him down; and when his own horse had fallen, he had forted up behind it and drawn the pistols at his belt—he happened to be wearing Dick's pistols—and done for two more before an arrow found him. People had said, after they had got his body and pulled the arrow out, that he was the bravest thing they ever saw.

The bravest but also the deadest! He shook the fool picture out of his head. He had to laugh at himself, making out to be so brave when like as not he'd fill his pants if ever he met up with an Indian alone. Maybe he'd turn tail and run. No telling what he would do. When he brought himself honest against the face of danger, he felt the cold turn of fear and so, except when he let dreams drift in his head, went around with doubt in him. He wasn't stout inside but weak and watery. And what he did that might seem bold, like staying here at the rock, wasn't bold at all, for there wasn't any felt risk in it.

He was about to get up and climb some more when he saw a dog loping back from the train. It was Rock, leaping high-headed through the sage, coming to see were things all right with him. "Here, Rock!" he shouted into the wind. "Here, boy!"

He scrambled down the slant. "Here I am, boy. I come to meet you, like you come to meet me." Rock trotted up to him, wet from the river, and wagged his tail and held his head to be scratched and touched Brownie's palm with his cold nose. "You got no business to be runnin' so, you that was lame just a shake ago. Don't you know that? But I reckon you knew I was struck with lone and so come to cheer me up." The words sounded thin against the windy distance. "Now I got to do all that climbin' over again. Kin you make it, boy?"

He took a dozen steps up and called to Rock. Rock held his head to one side, his whitish-blue eyes full of thought, and then, as if he had done with figuring and come to an answer, he stepped up to the face of the stone, took one great bound and found his footing and bent low to the climb, traveling faster than a man could go.

"Easy, Rock. You think I'm a bird? An' you got nothin' to carry—remember that!—no hammer or chisel or nothin' but you."

Brownie climbed by Dick's advice, while Rock followed by little dashes, catching up and stopping, feet braced, while his face asked why so slow. After a while he went ahead, as if sure of the way now or put out by the pace.

Toward the top Brownie met the sun, floating lazy in a sky bluer than he could find a word for. This way, he thought as the curve of it came in sight over the rock, it was as if it lay still, waiting for him to rise out of the west. He could be the sun, opening his eye on river and plain and hill while the world thought Brownie's come up, Brownie's shining, see, on yonder butte.

By Dick's system it didn't take much time or too much wind to get to where the rock leveled off, running then in dips and bumps not to be seen from below. Here the names were fewer, cut or scratched in the stone or painted red or black, for most men chose the footings of the rock to north and south, where they could stand on the ground or on boxes or kegs while they worked.

He found a spot he liked, the lip of a cup unmarked by brush or chisel, but before he sat down to his task he stood with his head up, letting the wind blow him while he looked around. Only the tops and edges of the world showed here, far off, the rest hidden, all ways, under the spread of rock. He couldn't see old Nellie fighting flies or the train crawling for the gap or last night's camping place or Tod's grave. There was just the flowing stone and the wind and himself and Rock and distance and the voice of distance.

He ran his thumb over the edge of the chisel. He would put her name first. That was the proper thing. He would put her name and then his own and then the day of the month and the year and maybe box them all in, so as to close forever in the stone the oneness of the two of them.

A long time from now she was teasing him. Care for her so far ago? Ah, it was a dream, Brownie, a made-up thing, and you can't josh me. And so they came back, man and wife, by stage and turnpike, and climbed the slant and were here again, and he pointed, saying, "There she is, just like I cut 'er back there in 'forty-five." She kissed him, tenderness in her eyes and laughter, and said, "I knew you did, Brownie. I always knew you did. Don't you know I just like to be told how you care for me?"

It took longer than a man would think to cut a letter. The tap of the hammer on the chisel left just a whitish scar that had to be deepened by tapping and more tapping, until the hammer arm tired and the chisel hand cramped. By and by he found it better to hit harder, to set the chisel careful and hit harder, squinting against the bits of stone that shattered out.

Rock loped after some little birds—ground sparrows or rock wrens or something kin to them—and came back and lay down, his head on his paws, his big mouth leaking a little at one corner.

"Just you wait, boy. It won't be so long."

He got her first name spelled out, and it was pretty, and set to work on the last after flexing his arm and hand to get new strength in them, thinking what would the people in the train be saying if they knew what his secret business was. They would smile at each other, probably, and make little jokes, as if his feeling was no more than a boy's notion and not to be taken serious. He couldn't let them know, he couldn't let even Ma or Pa know, not till later, not till things turned out. Then it would be different. Then they could see they would have been making fun where fun wasn't fitting.

"Just me and you," he said to the old dog. "Just me and you's all that'll know, Rock, and you think it's all right, don't you?"

Rock gave a slow wag of his tail for an answer.

Just himself and Rock and the little birds and the watching

193

sun and maybe Mercy herself, knowing with a woman's knowing as she urged the team along that he had held back to set their secret in the stone. Just them and the wind, which spoke but didn't tell.

Should he chisel the name he went by or the full and proper name of George Brown Evans? The short one matched the length of hers better, so let it be Brownie. Mercy McBee. Brownie Evans. July 2, 1845. Set chisel. Swing hammer. Set chisel. Swing hammer. The sun was pretty high.

Before he finished, Rock rose on his forelegs, facing south, and growled deep in his throat, holding back the bark while he kept sampling the wind.

"What do you smell, boy? A b'ar or something?" There was nothing in sight except what had been there before. Whatever Rock had smelled he couldn't smell again. He let himself down as if not sure yet that his nose was right.

Set chisel. Swing hammer. He had it now, all but the box to close it in. Set. Swing. Set. After he was through, he sat for a while, letting the wind dry up his sweat. Sweat was different here from in Missouri. It came and went. Didn't keep pouring out, sopping the clothes and dripping from the chin and smarting in the eye.

He got up, stiff from sitting, and spoke to Rock. It was pretty chiseling, he told himself before he turned, and all the prettier because of what it stood for. "All right, boy. Let's go down."

The chiseling had taken longer than expected. When he came to the brow of the butte, he saw that the train was somewhere out of sight beyond the Gate, maybe pulled up already for its nooning, for the sun was sailing high. He would climb on Nellie and gallop to it. He would hurry, since a kind of emptiness, like homesickness, was on him now that he had done his work and had nothing to take his thought. It wasn't fear. It wasn't the dread of anything he could put a name to. It was just emptiness. There came to mind a mole that he had pitched out of its tunnel once. Sun and space had scared it witless, and it had run crazy on the open ground, wanting the close, blind walls of home.

Rock stopped and growled again, his shoulder hair rising

while he sorted the air, his eyes searching for what his nose suspected.

"What ails you, Rock? Tryin' to scare me? You got to be a fraidy-cat?"

Only by the quick dipping of an ear did the dog show he had heard.

Brownie freed his arms for the down climb by putting the chisel and hammer in his pocket. He stepped short, so as to keep his heels under him, ready to catch himself with his hands if he slipped. "You comin', you old fool?"

Rock looked down on him and back to where his nose had pointed and then, like a guard leaving his post, began to sidle down, his throat still rumbling.

There was Nellie, fighting flies. There was his rifle, standing as he'd left it. There was the trail leading away to the gap. In a minute he would be mounted. Not so far off in time he would catch up with the train, and men would be saying, "How-de-do, Brownie. What kep' you? Break your leg in a badger hole?"

Quartering down ahead, Rock halted, stiff-legged on the slant, and the growl in his throat boiled into his hoarse bay.

He saw the reason then, saw the mounted Indians rounding the turn from the Sweetwater, their hides shining dull in the sun, their faces lifting to him from the wind-shelter of hunched shoulders. He saw them and froze, a wild sickness turning in him, while Rock jumped ahead, baying.

He could turn and scramble for the top while their mouths worked at seeing him and their arms waved him down and a hand lifted a bow. He could run and be outrun or get an arrow in the back. Or he could jump. It wasn't much more than a long jump to Nellie, a long jump and a long slide, and then maybe a leg broken and the skin ground off his backside and the Indians on him before he could mount. Beyond his thinking his voice sounded, "Back, Rock! Back!"

He tried to lift his arm, as he would have to Hig or Botter. He stepped downwards, fighting the rottenness of fear inside, fighting the show of it on his face, willing his hands to be steady, his feet to be sure. Easy was the way, if there was a way, poky and easy and assured. His mouth said a cracked "Hello."

One slid from his horse and ran and grabbed the slanted rifle, waving it as a prize, and the rest came on after the little startlement of seeing him and sat their horses by Nellie, their dark faces upturned, their eyes narrowed under ratty hair. The wind brought him the smell of them, the rank, smoke-grease-body smell. Nellie was trying to pull free of the sage. She reared up, smelling them, too, and fought the air with her forefeet. A young Indian with a long blister of scar along his cheek dropped from his horse and stepped to her and knocked her quiet with a stone he had picked up. She stood trembling, beaten by the blow on the head, while he stripped the saddle from her.

One shouted and another, and they all were shouting, and motioning him to come down the dozen steps between. They pranced around, waving bows and raising spears, coming at him as if to run him through and then turning and yelling while the wind bent the feathers in their hair. The scar-faced Indian was throwing Nellie's saddle on his horse.

There was no choice but to come on, against the bows and lances and a battered carbine that another young Indian kept aiming, hollering fit to kill as others brushed it off its bead.

His mind and body felt far away, and fear was a thing reaching through a dream, and all below him came quick and sharp to his eyes—the Indians numbering upwards of twenty, the bare hides and crotch covers and leather breeches and one man with nothing on at all except a pair of moccasins and shells hanging from his ears, the sorry horses behind them and their sorry fittings, the mule rigged with white man's gear, the lean dogs looking up, barking back at Rock.

Then he was down, and hands were poking at him and arms pulling and voices yelling and eyes looking for the look of fear in his. "Here, now! Here!" He tried to make his tone strong. "Me, friend."

His hat lifted from his head, and his shirt tore to a yank— and it wasn't any use to fight. He could only push back, trying to act man-size and unafraid while they pried and tugged and drew bows and made as if to spear him.

Above their crazy yelling he heard Rock's big voice and with it snarlings and the yelps of hurt, and he wrenched clear and saw Rock swarming with the wolf-dogs of the Indians. Rock went down and rolled up, set upon from front and rear and sides by the half dozen of them, his teeth flashing, his gray muzzle already red-scarred. His old head ducked, and a dog cried high, like a whistle, and stood aside, one leg hanging while the fight heaved away from him.

Rock sank under the pack and came up again, like a block out of churned water, and leaped free and could have run but stood fierce and proud and met the new charge and was carried over by it.

He would die. The teeth were too many for him, the weight too great. He would die unwhimpering, not running or begging mercy or even asking for the help he had a claim to. He would die forgiving while the rightful help looked on, scared by Indians who had stopped their fun to watch.

Brownie felt weight in his pocket and knew of a sudden it was the hammer, not taken from him yet, and he jerked it free and lunged through the Indians, crying out without words. He swung, hammer head on dog head, and swung again while the fight surged around him and teeth ripped his shank.

It didn't take them long, not him and Rock together. The two Indian dogs that weren't killed or crippled ran off growling. He knelt down and felt of Rock and saw he wasn't hurt bad and got up, telling Rock to stay to heel, for the Indians were coming up.

He held the hammer tight, thinking they would want to kill Rock, but they pointed at him while he growled his dare at them and shook their heads and made noises in their throats as if they prized bravery, too. For a minute in this quieter time Brownie felt the touch of cheer.

It was just a touch, for they turned on him then, twisting the hammer from his hands and wrestling him down on his tail while he cried to Rock to keep out of it. Two of them took places behind him, poking him with spear or arrow points when he so much as shifted on the ground. The others began to talk again, quieter than before, arguing for one thing or another. They mixed in front of him and waved their weapons around while they spoke, all except the scar-faced one, who'd gone to beat the brains out of the crippled dogs.

When he came back, he joined in, louder than the rest and violenter, and the young Indian with the carbine and the one with Brownie's rifle sided with him. They dashed at him, turn and turn about, one with a spear outheld, the others with the carbine and the rifle, as if to put an end to him instanter, and faced around and yelled their thought and came at him again. If he flinched, he saw the jeering in their eyes and felt the points prick him from behind, and he made himself sit quiet, holding his fear in, holding it down so it wouldn't race the heart or shake the face or show up in his gaze.

The three set the rest to shouting, as at first. They were all shouting, shouting and prancing and pointing and swinging weapons, so that the eyes swam and the head rang while the held-in fear beat deep with the heartbeat. Temper showed in the slant-eyed faces and hunger for blood and the marks of scheming and the stain of old war paint not washed off clean. An older Indian with a hawk's nose and hawk's eyes and deep-pocked skin talked most against the three. He yelled at them and tried to wave them back and shouted at the shouting others, as if to make them see.

But still there was no kindness in his face, none there and none anywhere, and no way to make them know he didn't wish them ill. He thought he couldn't listen more, or watch, or hold his load of fear. A man could hold only so long, and then he broke out, wild for an end to things, good or bad. It was hours they'd yelled and swung their arms and made their dashes at him. It was last year he'd climbed down from the rock. Better to be dead quick. Better to fight and die than sit like a chicken while they argued whether to spear him or shoot him or wring his neck and did they do it now or later.

The sun was swinging down from overhead, making for the west and home. Somewhere the train was lurching along, its people thinking of camp and supper and rest while Dick rode out looking for wood and water. Ma and Pa would be anxious by now, for they didn't look for him to be gone so long. Inside him tears welled up to be shed and an unsaid cry wrenched at his throat. Let the wanting legs jump and the wanting arms strike out and the chest get its spear.

While he teetered between sitting and acting, the shouting died away and heads turned, and he strained for a look, not prodded by the points now, and it was Dick Summers like an answer to prayer, old Dick Summers galloping his horse across the flat, riding straight as a drawn line, his uncovered hair silvery in the sun, Dick Summers not scared of one Indian or a nation, coming to save him from his fix. The rising murmur of the Indians drowned out a cry that was half sob.

Dick broke his horse to a jog and then to a walk as he rode closer. He clinched his rifle under one arm and got his pipe out and made as if to be pounding tobacco in it. He held it up and came on. Twenty feet from them he reined in. He wasn't in a hurry to talk. His eyes ran over the Indians and took in the side of rock that flanked him on the right. His voice came big and rough out of his throat, Indian-fashion, and his hands and arms began making motions. He had just a glance at Brownie, but at the tail end of his Indian talk he said, "Easy, hoss. I'm makin' medicine."

The hawk-faced Indian answered him, talking loud and gesturing as Dick had done.

The carbine was itchy in the young Indian's hands. It kept waggling as if about to come up and go off. Brownie slid over, unnoticed by his guards.

Dick talked again, for what seemed a long time, making shapes with hands and arms and turning in his saddle and pointing back to where the train would be. Brownie thought it was in the nature of him, in his looks and carriage, in the straight, gray eye and the unafraid face, that the carbine should dangle in the restless hand and the young, wild mouths be silent.

Hawk Face answered, shorter this time, and Dick spoke in turn, and for a minute there was silence, until the scarred Indian broke it, nerved somehow to argue in spite of Dick. He gave courage to the two he teamed with. They shouldered up to Hawk Face, their mouths running with words.

Dick spoke short and, when he had their eyes, came up easy with his rifle, aimed toward the side of the rock, as if just pointing with it. The rifle cracked, and where one of the little birds had been was now just a pinch of feathers, glued to the stone by a spatter of blood.

The Indians brought their hands over their open mouths, and their eyes hunted one another's and went back to Dick.

Dick spoke Indian again and got a quieter answer and said to Brownie, "Come on, hoss. This here spree's over. Git Nellie."

"They got my gun and saddle."

"Best dicker for 'em later. Your hair's still on."

Not an Indian raised a hand as he untied Nellie and climbed on, bareback, and called to Rock. They watched him silently and went to their own horses that had strayed toward the river for graze.

Brownie rode alongside Dick, and Hawk Face and two others rode up, and the rest trailed behind, quiet except for what might be self-talk, slow-spoken.

"Sioux, these niggers are," Dick said. "Teton, or some cut of Sioux."

"Dick?"

"Got a camp somewheres pretty close. They was just hellin' around."

"Dick?"

"Speak out. They don't savvy."

"I'm much obliged, I reckon you know."

"It wasn't nothin'."

"Dick?"

"This child's listenin'."

"I made a poor out of it, Dick."

"How so?"

"I'll feel better for tellin' you, I'm that shamed. I was scared puky."

Dick put a hand on Brownie's knee. "Shoo, boy! Every hoss is scared in a fix."

"Not as bad as me."

"I seen you slide over to knock that Injun off his aim if need be."

Dick looked around, not as if to see that none was fixing to settle them from behind. "It's these young niggers you got to watch. The Sioux ain't much for mindin' their chiefs."

"How'd you do it, Dick?"

Before Dick answered, he and Hawk Face traded words. "First, I asked 'em if they'd seen the great, white war party, meanin' Kearny and his men."

"Did they?"

Dick shook his head. "Then I told 'em we spoke with one tongue and was headed for the big water and would kill any of their enemies we saw, specially Blackfeet. Said we had some red earth for their faces and beads and awls and such and maybe a little of the red firewater from the hollow wood, meanin' whisky from a keg. That's why they're trailin' along—for presents."

Dick talked to the other two Indians fronting up with him, speaking sure and comfortable as if to old friends. They came to the river and let their horses drink and forded it and lined out for the gap that the sun was turning golden brown. Not till then did Brownie notice the wind was dying down to nothing. It was, he thought, like the wind that had blown mad in him and now was eased off, leaving him tired but good-spirited. Dick had said he hadn't done bad. Everyone was scared in a fix, the first time, anyway.

"I didn't look for you to shoot," he said.

"Kearny and presents didn't gentle 'em enough. So I said we had thirty men who would black their faces if you was hurt, an' everyone could shoot as good as me. That's when I fired."

"What if you'd missed that there dickey-bird?"

Dick's face creased to a slow grin. "Next I'd've said, 'Pleased to meet you, Jesus. Shake hands with my friend, name of Brownie Evans.' " The smile faded, leaving just the marks of good humor. "I reckon you ain't looked at this gun, Brownie. It's my second one, an' double bar'l, an' I was readied up for fowl. The bar'l I fired had bird shot in it."

E VANS WOKE UP early, before the camp was astir. He lay quiet, feeling done in but relaxed, done in from yesterday's long worrying, relaxed from knowing that Brownie was safe in camp again and none the worse for his mix-up with the Sioux. If he listened, he thought he could hear Brownie's breathing, from the bed laid near the tent under the sky.

While he cocked his ears, there came to them a soft padding that he guessed was made by Rock, up early to see what the day had brought.

It was dark inside the tent, so dark he knew Rebecca slept by him only by the soft breath-heave of her body. Outside it would be dark, too, and the juttings of land would rise strange and misshapen, the secrets of the night still on them, yielding slow to the weak forecoming of the sun.

He let his muscles melt into rest, let run in him the returned confidence in the trip and Oregon and all. They would meet more trouble. The hardest travel, the steepest climbs, the biggest rivers, the greatest calls on strength and purpose still lay before them; but he was equal to it. Now, resting, knowing all was well, he was equal to it.

A person could change in a day, or even an hour, from low spirits to hope. Yesterday, while anxiousness weighed on him, he had wanted to give up, to turn around and head back for the tame life of Missouri. He hadn't been able to keep himself from looking behind for Brownie, though he knew Rebecca was watching him from her seat in the second wagon, building up fears in her mind as he was in his own. Independence Rock was out of sight now that they had passed the Gate. There wasn't anything to be seen eastward except the rise they had come over in rounding the spur of mountain through which the Sweetwater cut. Only ahead could the gaze travel, running along the high, flat, sagebrushed valley, picking up Split Rock in the distance.

It was, he had thought, as if all that lay behind them was forever gone, as if there was no return, as if the one hard choice was to go on. It never had struck him so strong before that he couldn't change his mind. They were cut off behind and closed in, far but fast, at the sides, by bald and stony mountains on the right, by green, high-rising ridges to the left. Where could that boy be? Blowed away by the tarnal wind that just now was falling off?

"He'll be all right, Becky," he called back, setting his face in a smile. "You know how boys are. They got to have a look at everything, and time don't mean nothin' to 'em. Don't be gettin' in a flutter."

He was in a flutter himself. What could have happened? What could be happening? Here it was drawing on toward camptime. and no Brownie. By now he could have chiseled out the names of all the company, alive and dead.

He shut off the horrors that kept coming up—the rattlesnake lying on a ledge ready to bite the groping hand, the horse falling on its rider, the Indians sneaking up with drawn bows and scalping knives ready. He told himself it was just Tod's death that made him nervous, but still the fears arose. He should have gone back with Summers. He should have taken a party and gone back, though Summers waved the idea away. What good was Summers, good as he was, against a bunch of Sioux? He should have put aside the push, push, push to Oregon. Oregon didn't mean anything without Brownie, just like it didn't mean anything to the Fairmans without Tod.

The shapes that rose ahead, like Split Rock, seemed queer and dangerous, standing hard and bare, standing purple and red under the tiring sun. They might be warnings, he thought, warnings not to go farther, to keep off wild, outlandish land untouched by the feet of the likes of him. Where was that boy?

He shook himself for thinking womanish. He was half sore at himself, at Brownie, at the train, at the country, at the whole damn business. Missouri was better, Missouri and boresomeness and drudge work unmixed with anxiousness.

He dropped back and spoke to Becky on her perch. "I'm goin' back, bein' as you're nervous."

"You're nervous yourself."

"Account of you," he answered, for once nettled because she could see through him.

"Don't lie, Lije."

"Ain't lyin'. He's bound to be all right."

"I pray God so. You take some men with you."

"Ah-h!"

"You do that, Lije."

"On account of bein' so helpless, I reckon? I'll tie this here team to the tail an' you drive the lead. The goin's good enough. Git down."

He walked ahead and whoaed his team and tied her oxen to his wagon and saw her down and up again. Before he spoke to the steers, he got his rifle out.

"You take someone with you, Lije."

"Don't worry about that. You just watch the teams."

He walked back along the oncoming line, expecting to borrow a horse from one of the drivers. He was about halfway to the horse herd when, beyond it, beyond the straggled line of cattle, upcoming from the far rise, he saw heads lifting, and shoulders, growing into horsemen that he took for Indians. He couldn't be sure. He waited, squinting, with dread sharpening in him, and saw two figures unlike the rest and one of them like Summers. His eyes filmed with straining.

He knew what he had to do. He knew what a captain had to do, regardless. He shouted, "Botter! Bring your horse! Quick!"

He jumped on, throwing out, "Injuns! Git the men to push the horses up! We'll corral."

He galloped to the head of the line, crying, "Injuns! Come on!" as he galloped, waving the train on toward the stream where it would be sure of water come a siege. He curved it around on the bank. "Cap your pieces, all of you! And stay inside. I'll look."

He wrenched the horse around to his own wagons. "Becky, I seen Dick, and Brownie, I think. Looked all right."

He didn't wait for her answer. He kicked the horse, hearing

her protest at his riding alone, and reined out to meet the party. The drivers had brought the horses close and headed the cattle for the river and were making for the corral, racing to see who got there first. He shouted angrily, "Davisworth! Git the horses inside! You and the rest! You got time for that."

It was Indians all right, Indians and Dick and one that had to be Brownie, one that was Brownie. Goddam, he thought—and no disrespect intended—it was sure enough Brownie, and Rock trotting by the side.

He rode for the bunch, and they for him, until thirty feet apart, when Summers reined in and held up his arm for the rest to do so. "Company, captain," he said. "Nabobs from the Sioux."

Of the words that crowded Evans' mouth only a few came out. "You two all right? They peaceable?"

"They won't rub you out, 'cept in fun."

"What do I do, Dick?"

"Git your pipe out and act to be loadin' it. That's peace sign."

"All right."

"I'll camp 'em off a piece and fix for palaver soon's they can fancy up. I'd just as lief hold 'em the night, for there's a village around somewheres. Can't take on the whole damn tribe."

"Kin Brownie come on?"

"Let 'im stay. He's beaver, sort of, that they aim to trade. I'll bring him directly."

Looking into the dark faces of the Sioux, seeing the bows and spears they carried and their eyes mean under the feathered hair, Evans couldn't keep from saying, "I told you it was dangerous, boy."

"Pick some men for these niggers to smoke with," Dick said. "We'll keep 'em out of camp. They're touchy sons-of-bitches."

"All right."

"Ain't much risk now, Lije, long as we're careful. Keep some shooters inside. Ain't nothin' whets an Injun's appetite like scalps to be took safe."

Dick spoke to the Indians, and they talked among themselves, turning their eyes on Evans as if to see was he really friend or

205

foe. They slanted for the river, toward a spot a holler and a half downstream from camp.

Evans didn't wait to see them get there. He rode to the corral. "Everything's good," he told Rebecca before he began to give directions. "I'll trade a bead for Brownie by and by. Now set easy. I ain't got time for talk."

For smokers he named Patch, Byrd, Carpenter, Mack, Gorham, and himself and on second thought added Tadlock, who could do more harm with a rifle in his hand than a pipe. It was a good selection, he figured, that left in the corral some of the better shots, like Daugherty and Hig and Shields.

The Indians showed up soon, led by Dick, their faces red- and black-smeared for the party. Dick stopped them fifty yards from camp, where Evans and the other smokers met him. Dick said, "Set in a half circle," to the white smokers and the same, seemingly, to the Indians, for they slid from their horses and let themselves down, grunting, all except one young one who'd been named to tend the stock.

While they were seating themselves, Evans chose a spot by Brownie. "How's it, young'un?"

"They got my rifle and saddle."

"I knowed I shouldn't've left you at the rock for a tomfool thing." There was still the edge of soreness in Evans' voice. He added, "It's all right, though, long as you come out on top."

"All set, Lije." It was Dick, speaking at his side.

" 'Pears to me now's the time to get the saddle and rifle back, before we treat 'em."

Dick said, "Right. It went plumb out of my mind." He spoke then to an older Indian, the chief by the looks of him and the manner of the others, and the Indian spoke back, and turned and said something to a young one with a scar on his face. The young one got up, his eyes sulky, and made for the Sioux camp.

They waited for him, the whites sitting silent and unarmed, glancing now and then to the corral as if to make sure the riflemen were ready, the Sioux grunting once in a while, their bows and spears laid by, as Summers had directed.

The young Indian came back, carrying the saddle and rifle, and pitched them in front of the chief and went and sat down, his face still surly. The chief pointed while he spoke. Dick picked up the stolen things and set them before Brownie. The saddle had been slashed with a knife, out of spite, Evans guessed.

The chief was speaking. His voice came out, loud and measured, and his hands worked to it. There was a kind of force in him, a kind of practiced enjoyment like in a white politician holding a crowd. It seemed he spoke for a long time, though Dick wasn't so long in putting the words into English. The Indians' hearts were good, Dick said. The country belonged to them, but still they let the white brother pass. They let him kill meat and scare it away, so that they had to hunt far for it and their young ones cried hungry in their lodges. It was the way of white men to make presents, of powder and lead and beads and red earth for the face. That was good. Let the white man pass in peace, though he frightened the game.

Evans knew it was his turn then. As captain he had to speak for the whites. While thought circled in his head, Dick said, 'Tell 'em anything, Lije. I'll fix it in Indian talk. Tell 'em your heart's friendly, but your arm strong if need be, and you got some presents for 'em to show what a heap you love 'em. Tell 'em we're just passin' through and don't aim to settle. Spread it out, and kind of make a show. Brownie, fetch that pack I got my Injun plunder in."

Evans made his voice roll out and his arms work. The white men were going to the big waters of the west, where their great father owned land. They came as friends, as the Sioux must know, for they brought their women and children with them. Men did not take their wives and babies to war. They were friendly folks, the train was, but powerful and ready to fight if they had to. Every man had a rifle and knew how to use it. They had brought presents for the Indians and pretties for their squaws, and they were glad to smoke with their friends, the Sioux.

Dick put the one tongue into the other and afterwards said to Brownie, "You kin pass them awls around now, one to each, and then the tobacco the same way. I promised 'em a little whisky, Lije, fer the fix was tight."

He went to the corral and came back with a burning stick and a bucket and tin cup. "Won't be enough to put the devil in 'em. I watered 'er down. Now, Brownie, them beads to the chief, and the vermilion."

Tadlock spoke the first word spoken by the other white men, saying, "I think whisky's bad business."

" 'Tis so."

"You think a promise has to be kept—with savages?"

All Dick answered was, "Mostly, I keep 'em." He passed the bucket among the Indians himself. The Indians drank, noisy as horses, and eyed the bucket after it was emptied.

Dick got out a pipe, an Indian stone pipe with a long stem, and lighted it with the brand, pointing the stem north, south, east, west and up and down before he handed it to Evans. "Start 'er around, Lije."

It all went off easy enough. The Indians got up and went to their horses after burning up three or four pipes of Dick's tobacco, taking along as a final present a big chunk of meat that the train's hunters had killed. Later, downriver, their fire made just a spark in the dark, put out now and then by a moving body.

So here he was, Evans thought, lying melted in his bed. Grayback farmer. Captain. Speechmaker. Speechmaker and show-off. Him, Lije Evans, that didn't like speeches and didn't like shows, leaving them to the Tadlocks of the world. And to hear and see him were just half a dozen white men and the rest red, haunched down with their knees up and not enough clothes on, hardly, to patch a bullet with, their ears not understanding, their eyes dark and demanding on him, the bared skin of their shoulders and bellies looking like leather in the low-lying sun. It made him want to laugh that he had found a kind of pleasure in the speech, feeling sureness in him and strength while the words sounded out. Things drove a man away from his wishing.

Things changed the train, too. Like with rules. Nobody had said anything about Dick's whisky. Rules? You hardly thought of them but made out as best you could according to the time. You voted them and let them lie. No whisky. No swearing. Whippings for rape and adultery and fornication. The moral law. The train was moral enough. Wasn't a woman inviting anything, as far as he could tell, nor any man behaving bold. Still, the way it was with men, maybe the rule served a purpose, especially with unmarried ones about. Just because a rule wasn't broken was no sign it wasn't needed. Maybe just the fact of it kept it from being broken. He was amused a little, though. There wouldn't any whip get him, nor any man get to Rebecca. Gently, in order not to wake her, he put his hand upon her.

The sentinel's rifle brought him out of bed. "Time to shine," he said as Rebecca stirred. In the lightening dark of the tent he pulled on his breeches and shirt, and then a jacket against the chill that night brought to this high country. Brownie already was up, about to go out, along with others, to round up the animals. "Mornin'," Evans said. "You dream b'ars last night, boy?"

Brownie grinned. "Injuns."

Evans collected a few sticks and whittled shavings and got a fire started. When Rebecca came out, he rolled up the beds and struck the tent and began packing the wagons. It took time to get started in the morning—critters to drive up, oxen to hitch, a horse to saddle, beds to roll, tents to stow away, breakfast to cook and eat and clean up after. Around him while he worked he heard and saw and felt the bustle of the other wagons. Later a man would just wish for miles to pass.

The sun was bulging up like a punkin. He could see where the Indians had camped downriver, but he couldn't see any Indians. Already they had lit out. And good riddance, he thought.

While he was thinking it, Tadlock walked up. "Those red devils stole two of my horses."

"No!"

"The horses were down to skin and bones. I hobbled them and picketed them close, outside the corral, so they could get some grass."

"An' they stole 'em?"

"I'd have sworn I'd hear them. Why, the mare had a bell on her."

"I be damned! Hello, Dick."

Dick had come up so quiet that Evans didn't know he was there until his eye caught him.

"Tadlock here's lost two horses to the Injuns."

Dick asked of Tadlock, "Them two?"

"Of course."

"I 'lowed it was risky."

"I couldn't starve them to death."

"Bones is better'n tracks."

"What do you propose to do?" Tadlock asked Evans.

"Eat and roll."

"You won't help me get them back?"

"It ain't worth the gamble, Tadlock."

"Particularly when the horses weren't yours."

Evans said, "Damn it, man! You was for rollin' when Martin was dyin'."

"That was different. We couldn't help him. We can teach these red devils a lesson."

"Be out of Sioux country in a shake," Dick put in.

"You wouldn't stop to think, Evans, that your boy caused the loss!"

"How's that?"

"He got us in the mess."

The words brought Evans up. He hadn't figured things that way, and no one would but Tadlock and maybe lawyers. Still it troubled him that he might be partly in the wrong. "I don't go along with you on that," he said, "but I'm willin' to leave it to the council. If they decide against me, I'll make the loss up to you."

Tadlock snorted.

Dick said, "To hell with him then, Lije."

"I aim to do what's right."

"Right!" Tadlock's voice had a sudden fury in it, as if all that had happened against him was brought to point now. "But you won't track those Indians down?"

"No."

"I'll kill an Indian or two before this trip's over."

"No sense in killin' one that didn't do you wrong," Evans told him.

"One's like another."

"You faulted Mack for killin' that Kaw."

"I wouldn't expect you to acknowledge that the circumstances are different."

"Tadlock," Evans said, "I'm peaceable, but, by God, it's hard to keep from twistin' your neck!"

"It's the truth that roils you."

"That's as may be, but we ain't chasin' Injuns today, an' if you want to roll with us you best be gettin' ready."

Tadlock spit out, "You're the captain."

"That's what they tell me."

Tadlock ground around on his heel and walked away.

Evans saw Rebecca watching him from the fire she had fed some sticks to, and he wondered how much she had heard. Not much, likely, at this distance.

"That was the way, Lije," Dick said. "Stand up to that mouthy nigger—but still it takes a heap to set you off."

"Does it?"

"A heap."

"I kep' thinkin' maybe Brownie's part to blame."

"So you held in. Christ, it weren't the horses! Not them alone. That staggy stud horse can't get over bein' set down. One day you'll have to geld him, Lije."

"I keep sayin' I won't."

THE HIGH SWEETWATER, flowered along its banks. The Southern Pass. The buttes now named for Oregon. The Sandys, Big and Little. The Green that trappers knew as the Prairie Hen or Seeds-kee-dee and, before that, as the Spanish River, winding wooded in the tableland of sage. High country, chill by night with the snow that patched the Winds, lonesome and good as when Dick Summers first had seen it but with the scar of wear on it, the scar of wheels that later wheels would deepen. The Winds rising, naked and bright in the sun, broody in the dusk, hiding the high valleys where he had set his traps, hiding the shame of no-beaver where beaver once were plenty.

If he sniffed, he smelled the smoke of quaking asp, and, looking, saw the little fire and him and Jim Deakins and Boone Caudill seated around it while meat cooked on roasting sticks. If he listened, he heard the old voices raised at rendezvous, the hearty, young, old voices that laughed at age and change, the voices rich with strength and whisky, shouting over horse races or the Indian game of hand, the full and easy voices good-tempered by the squaws. Smoke of campfires lifting slow, hi-ya, Bill, and hi-ya, Buck, tepees white against the green, horse herds frisky in the mornings, coyotes singing in the nights, bright blankets on soft shoulders, held around young breasts, and young country all about, high valleys, beavered streams, good hunting, youth on the land, youth in the loins, and youth and youth and youth to youth, and who'd have thought then it would pass?

Deakins was dead and Caudill disappeared, and of the mountain men who had hunted and spreed and squawed with him, was there a handful left? He didn't want much to see them, with years in their faces and aches in their bones and the past in their heads so that all they could talk about, while whisky stirred dead fires, was this and that of long ago. Like with Joe Walker, a mountain man if ever one lived, whom the train had met on the pass, and he so changed that Summers hardly knew him, strong yet and able but with a half-sore sadness because his world was gone. Like with Tom Fitzpatrick, whom they'd met still earlier, guiding Colonel Kearny's Dragoons back from the divide. Tom wasn't one to hang his feelings out, but in his face were old rememberings. It would be the same with Jim Bridger and Old Vaskiss at their fort down on the fork.

He had given the fort the go-by, taking a short cut, hard as it was, to the Green and on toward the Bear, for the train had food enough and the oxen were harder-footed than before and the wagons mostly in fair shape, though shrunk and shaken some by the long, dry, sandy miles between Pacific Springs and the Little Sandy.

Still, he had been uneasy, for the desert of the Green was rough going even for hard-case hunters and horses lightly packed. Could wagons and oxen make it, and farmers and town-livers and women and their young? He had dragged the short cut back to memory, had hoofed again the forty-odd dry miles of it, over thirsty sagebrush and rifted gravel and down the harsh fall to the Green, the wind fierce in his face, the day sun-stroke-hot or snow-cold, for desert weather seemed always one or other. But it was water that mattered most, or the want of it. Not any place was there a drink for man or brute.

"I do' know," he said to the council that Evans had called to-gether. "I'm thinkin' we can come it, but it's hard and chancey."

Mack asked, "And if we do?"

"Save two days, at the least."

"And if we don't?"

"No don't to it. There can't be any don't."

"It's worse, I reckon, than anything before?" Evans said.

"A heap."

"Worse'n what we're bound to meet?"

"There's a lot of hell ahead, Lije, beyond Fort Hall."

" 'Bout time we were gettin' a taste of hell then."

Tadlock agreed to that, saying, "We're not traveling for

213

pleasure. Maybe we can cut ahead of that company that passed us."

"If'n it's hot, we'll have to roll by night."

"We ain't scared of the dark, Dick," Evans said.

And so they had decided on the short cut, partly maybe because it was a dare, partly, Summers thought a little uneasily, because they didn't know how fierce the trip could be.

They had cut right at the Little Sandy and headed across the divide and rolled down to the Big and filled buckets there and kegs and barrels eaten empty and had waited until the day cooled, for the sun was hot as a blister. At four o'clock by the watch that Evans carried, Summers had led them out.

They traveled all night, bumping over the sagebrush, grinding by the beds of old lakes, crunching in the rifts of gravel, dusting through the sand, while the moon came up and watched and tired of watching and went to bed, leaving the land so black Summers wondered if his sense of direction would guide him right.

As the desert lightened with the coming of the sun, they stopped and doled out water for the critters and turned them loose for what little bait that grew and breakfasted on dried meat and bread baked day before and yoked up again and went on, the venturesomeness of the night worn off, strain in the faces now, droop in the bodies, lag in the legs that pushed feet through the sand. And this was just the easier part of it! Behind them the sun fired up, making distance dance ahead.

There never was such a day in his remembering, Summers thought as noon scorched close, none so hot or breathless, none that made a reach of miles appear so far. He rode ahead and back and back and ahead, hunting in old memories for the way, seeing could he help with team or teamster when the course was set. There never was such a day. None in which a trust had weighed so heavy on him.

Roll! he urged from inside. Roll, goddam it, roll! Roll, you graybacks! Roll or die, while heat smothers you and your hearts pound in your heads! Roll for the Green! Roll coughing in the dust! Poke the goddam oxen! Roll!

Think, Summers! Think hard! Left or right or straight

214

ahead? How was it long ago? You can't be wrong. How was it now? Left, it's left it was, left by the bulge of hill. Point the party left!

The McBee girl looking sick, sweating pale beside the wagon. Up, young'un, and ride. You want to catch a stroke? Sand and beard cobwebbed on the face of Hank McBee. Sand rivered on the sweating other faces. The beat of blood in the cheeks. Emptiness in the women's eyes, the look of seeking for a piece of shade. One ox down, and it unanswering to goad or whip, its eyes big and sad. Kill it! Kill it out of kindness while the ravens wait and bring up another and go on. One ox don't count, Brewer. Not in this fix. Roll for the Green!

Fairman done in and laid out in his wagon and his woman crying, and the sick heat-flush in the fair-skinned faces of Daugherty and Byrd, and what's a cracked lip now? Go it, you hosses! Poke up the oxen that walk low-headed, bawling hoarse for water. Come on, you women with your crosspatch pups! You wanted Oregon, didn't you? Pray, Weatherby, pray but plod, and no knucklin' under to the will of God!

By Jesus, Summers thought, these folks were strong, strong in purpose even when weak in body. Rebecca Evans walking stout, mettled like a good mare; Lije helping those he could, encouraging all, his broad cheeks grayed by sand; Patch, Mack, Brewer, Shields, and Tadlock—damn him!—and their women, and the herders clouded by the dust. Judith Fairman driving while a tear washed down her face, Mack's woman stepping squinch-eyed, her chin hard to the west, and Daugherty unheeding the thumping sickness in him.

Strong folks, and strong for what? For Oregon and fish and farms, for wheat and sheep and nation. And now it came to him, while his own skull tapped to the heat, that that was what had ailed the mountain man—he didn't hanker after things; he had all that he wanted.

It was push now, pull and push and strain at spokes, for some teams couldn't climb a rise alone. Push or double-team. Push to the whistle of breath and the shower of sweat and the hammer in the skull. Push, Lije! You're a bull for work, I'm thinkin'. Push, Mack and Tadlock, Brewer and Patch and

215

Shields! Stout hosses, you all. Push! It ain't so far now. Less'n I thought. Lead team needs some pushin', Lije. By God, there she is!

There it was, the Green and shade and rest for all and pasture for the ganted stock. It was still half a dozen miles away, down a long pitch too steep to drive and then across a humpy bottom, but the sight of it was like a double drink of whisky, and flushed faces broke into smiles and grainy voices joked, saying, "What was it you said, Summers? Chancey? The word ain't knee-high to it. We made it, though, good as ary mountain man." Women and children came from the line of wagons and stood chattering, the strain gone and the fret.

The men unyoked the teams and let the wagons down with ropes, made serious again by work under the punishing sun, grunting to the pull of lines against arm sockets while the sweat ran out of them.

When they were down and the teams brought up and hitched, Summers said to Evans, "Lije, these critters'll be a handful when they smell water. Run away, that's what they'll do, and dive in, wagons an' all."

"What you tellin' me, Dick?"

"I'm thinkin' we best drive on a piece and turn 'em loose and herd 'em forwards till they smell it. Plenty of time to get the wagons later."

"Thanks, Dick. Wasn't for you, I'd be a prize captain now, wouldn't I?"

"I don't see no flies on you."

"Cold water on hot stummicks ain't so good."

"No helpin' it."

"I'll get the oxen and horses and loose cattle scattered out some, so's they don't run over each other. What about Injuns?"

"No need to worry much."

It came out as Summers knew it would. Once they winded water, the critters wouldn't be held. They galloped crazy for it and plunged in. One ox he saw had just his snoot above the surface. Afterwards, with some of the sizzle gone out of the day, the men with strength left in them brought the wagons up. The cutoff hadn't been too bad but only close to bad. One ox dead of thirst and one of water and quite a few thrown off their feed. No wagons lost. No people dead. Of the sick ones all recovered quick, even Charlie Fairman.

Now that the cutoff was behind them, Summers thought, he could torment himself some more by going back to days that had been. He tried to shy his mind away from them by making talk with Brother Weatherby, who rode ahead with him, "It ain't so far now to the Bear. Barrin' a breakdown, we'll git there a spell afore dark."

Weatherby turned his gaunt face on Summers. "I marvel at your memory. You remember every hill and turn."

"Ought to. I been over most of it, time and ag'in."

"I still marvel. There's so much of it."

"Looks just like it did." While he answered, Summers thought it was only the earth that didn't change. It was just the mountains, watching others flower and seed, watching men come and go, the Indian first and after him the trapper, pushing up the unspoiled rivers, pleased with risk and loneliness, and now the wanters of new homes, the hunters of fortune, the would-be makers of a bigger nation, spelling the end to a time that was ended anyway.

He didn't blame the Oregoners as he had known old mountain men to do. Everybody had his life to make, and every time its way, one different from another. The fur hunter didn't have title to the mountains no matter if he did say finders' keepers. By that system the country belonged to the Indians, or maybe someone before them or someone before them. No use to stand against the stream of change and time.

Time, he asked, what was it that you couldn't bring it back? Where did it go to? It wasn't in reason that everything should pass and nothing remain to mark it by except old men gumming pipestems while memory worked in them. A man could think, almost, there was a great journal somewhere, like the journals he had known travelers to keep. Turn it back and there you were again, high-spirited and stout, fresh again and free, and the earth fresh.

Like on the Popo Agie, as he remembered. Like with the

217

Crow girl. Ashia, running water, back in running time. It struck him queer again that he should think so often of her, who was just one of quite a few, and of the Popo Agie, which was just one of many. They had come, somehow, to stand for all the squaws and all the hunted streams, for fun and frolic, campfires at dusk, fires in the keen mornings, rich lifts, high passes, big doings, for the everlasting young time that was gone so quick.

There on the Sweetwater he had wanted to cross over to the Popo Agie, which wasn't but a run and jump away. He had wanted to see the singing waters of it and the trees that had known him and the place where he had camped and the ground where they had lain, marked still, maybe, by the press of bodies though too little for the eye to see.

Weatherby said, while his gaze ranged ahead, "I keep thinking how different this land is from Indiany."

"Or Missouri."

"Or Missouri."

Not often did Missouri enter Summers' mind as he came again to places deep-set in memory—the pass, the first water west that emigrants had named Pacific Springs, the Sandys, the Green, the glimpsed peaks of the Uintahs, like snowy clouds, where Brown's Hole would be. It was as if Missouri never was, nor farming, nor Mattie and her fever. Those were the days of his giving up, of growing old before his time because his world was old. Hell, he wasn't old now except in mind, except by mountain reckoning. Forty-nine. And his limbs were strong and his eye keen yet, and he could answer to a woman. It was the way of thinking that made him old, the knowing that he had outlived his time. He could farm in Oregon and grow with the country, as Lije had put it, if only the thing seemed worth the try. If only he hadn't known the Popo Agie.

Day by day and night by night bits of the old years had come back to him, flashes out of the long-unremembered, out of the pushed-aside, out of the clutter of mind, brought to him by sight of hill and water, by doing what he'd done before. Drying meat—and he was with Jim and Boone again, fresh-crossed from

218

the Powder to the Wind, eating old bull blue with winter while they talked about spring hunting. Topping the pass—and it was a soft day and the cactus was blooming red and yellow, and he had said, "Them's pretty now," and old Etienne Provot had spit and answered, "Pretty goddam prickly, I'm thinkin'." Seeing the Wind Mountains, harsh-rising on his right—and he green then, unbelieving he rode on top of the world, asking, "Is this it, sure enough?" The Green again—and his first sight of it, and beaver so thick you could shoot them in the eye, and everybody gay like in a child's dream of finding pretties.

He lived in the now time and in the then time, passing talk with people like old Weatherby, guiding, advising, hunting, joshing with Brownie or with Lije, while gone days and gone folks filled his mind. "Summers! Oh, Summers! You goddam old coon! Ain't seen you since we stood off the Rees. How be you? Fat, I'm thinkin'." Voices calling across the years, mouths laughing, hands slapping him on the back. "Worth a pack of beaver to see you, you ol' bastard, and if you got a dry, here's whisky."

Weatherby pulled up, for below them, far below, down one ridge and another, ran Muddy Fork and, beyond it, the rich, green valley of the Bear. "God in His goodness," Weatherby half whispered as his gaze took it in. "In His might."

"It's mighty, sure enough."

Weatherby wagged his head slow. "I couldn't have believed it. I can hardly believe it now, seeing it."

"It's some."

Bear River. The wooded, berried Bear, smooth-running through the roughed-up land. It hadn't been named for nothing, for Weatherby's God had put bears there, black and brown and, king of all, the great white bear, feeder on ants and fish and berries, unknower of the feel of fear. There was the time Summers had lifted a trap, heavy with beaver, and stepped out and parted the willows and looked Old Ephraim in the face, and it was one or the other right then, the world too small for both of them. Summers' shot had struck fair in the chest, where a hand could have felt the beat of blood, and the bear whoofed it away and came on and knocked Summers over and

219

fell on him. Summers wrestled for the knife at his belt, fur in his mouth and musk and blood in his nose and weight on him like a fallen horse, and then he realized the bear was dead. With a hole in his heart as big as a hoe handle he had charged. Old Ephraim, the mighty, the unafraid, the unforgiving, stouthearted with his heart shot out.

"Best wait for the train," Summers told Weatherby. "Got to angle down the slope and push the critters by some springs that it seems like I remember to be pizen. They're God's doin's, too, I reckon."

A cloud came on Weatherby's face. "They're there for a purpose, Brother Summers. You may be sure of that."

"Fer the purpose of killin' stock?"

"Doubt not the wisdom of God."

"What I'm doubtin' is these here springs."

Weatherby bent his head. "I wish you would see, Summers. You're too good a man to be lost."

"Past savin', parson. Best keep your wind for the Injuns. There's a heap of 'em in need of grace."

"But you think that's no use?"

"Don't recollect sayin' so. They're strong for medicine."

"Medicine. I keep hearing medicine, as if God and the way of salvation were just superstition."

"Maybe you can learn 'em that a cross has more power to it than a medicine bag."

Weatherby sighed. "Your lightness makes me sad. It saddens God, too."

"I didn't aim to damp you. You're all right, parson. As fer God, He don't have to stand between us."

Before Weatherby spoke again, the train rolled up, McBee in the lead. " 'Y God," McBee said, stepping up to them and looking down on the sweep of valley while his hand worried his beard, "she's fair."

Summers saw the wagons down, slanting them one way and another so the pitch wouldn't be too steep, and rode back to the herders and helped with the stock, thinking about Weatherby and his notions as he rode. Was there a scheme to things after all, and the present just a little part of it, and a man so small he couldn't see it whole? Indians. Fur hunters. Farm hunters. What next? Was it all a stream that went somewhere, that had a sense too big to understand? Aw, the hell with it. He was getting like Jim Deakins, who was dead now and maybe savvied how it was but, living, always wondered. If there was a scheme, it was messed up mighty sorry.

The bottoms were shank-deep in grass, and flowers waved, and chokecherries were ripening, and the women and children that weren't already down from the wagons got down, a sudden frolic in them, smiles on their faces and little cries on their lips, and the men studied the grass and kicked up the soil and followed the rimmed valley with their eyes and allowed this would be fine farming country if only it wasn't so far from things.

Far from things, from markets and stores and churches and soldiers and law and safety and all. Far from the way that was their way. Summers put himself in that time of first seeing again —the river and its branches swimming with beaver, and berries ripe, and Old Ephraim bloody-mouthed from the eating of them, and not a sound except the sounds of nature and no white face, and the sun great and the moon great, and the world his and no one to say him nay.

"There's trout in the river," he said to Brownie. "Trout big as rails."

He rode ahead and came to Evans. Evans raised his broad face, which was lighted as if by good news. "Now I can believe in Oregon, Dick."

"Good, ain't it?"

"Best ever I see, but I could do without these here mosquitoes. Becky's goin' to make a gooseberry pie and maybe find some greens."

"That's slick. An' there's wild onions if you like 'em. Figure we can go on a few miles, to Smith's Fork of the Bear, though there's a hill between."

Evans bobbed his head. "I swear, Dick, I thought I was tired of plowin', but a man wants to stick a plow in this country."

"Yep."

221

Summers passed McBee and led out, traveling alone, for Weatherby had slid his old bones from his horse and was walking with the train.

The day was cooling off, or maybe it was just that the valley was cooler than the sagy ridges. Or maybe it was the feel of fall, with August just around the bend. Along the Big Horn, on the upper reaches of the Gallatin and Madison, a man could be thinking about the fall hunt, if there were any beaver to hunt and anything in hunting them. The sun swam golden as it westered, touched already by the moons to come.

He climbed the hill and rode down it and came into the proper valley of the Bear and rode on toward Smith's Fork and saw an Indian village ahead. They would be Snakes, he thought. They would be the friendly Shoshones that he'd lived and traded with in his long ago. The Shoshones, paled by pale and unnamed blood, and their squaws fair to mountain eyes.

He reined into the brush and found a game trail and followed it, wanting to make sure the village was Snake and not Bannock or maybe Crow or Blackfoot, who used to be far travelers. It was Snake all right. He turned into the open, his pipe in his hand, and dogs began to bark and faces turned, and a man got up from the ground and stepped out, waiting, and it came to Summers that this was White Hawk, White Hawk and years and weather, squinting to make out a face as altered as his own.

"It is good to see my brother."

A shout came out of White Hawk, a sudden, childish shout, and he ran up while Summers dismounted and held out his hand like a white man, saying, "Big Hunter! I thought you had gone to the spirit land."

Summers had to hunt for the words that used to come so easy. "I have been too many moons away." Of all the Indians he had known, the Shoshones were the friendliest, friendly in a simple, trustful way, though they would steal you blind like any others. They were the friendliest and the gayest-spirited, and they gathered round him now, young men and old in pieces of leather and children bare as new-hatched birds, curious about the looks and manner and getup of the man that called them brother. Squaws eyed him from the lodges, and lean dogs came sniffing, as if agreeable to peace.

"There is meat in my lodge and a robe to sleep on," White Hawk said.

"White Hawk is good. I lead many white men and their squaws, to the big water."

"Your squaw, too?"

"My squaw is dead."

"It is bad. It is bad for a man to have no squaw."

"It is bad. Do you hunt the Green still and the Lewis River?"

"And we cross the mountains for the buffalo. The Blackfeet used to fight. They do not fight much now. They are fewer."

Summers nodded. "The big sickness."

"I have meat and a robe," White Hawk said again.

"You are my brother."

"I will give you a squaw." Before Summers answered, White Hawk called out, and a young woman with deer eyes came from a lodge, her body upstanding and rounded under the leather dress. "You will be Big Hunter's squaw as long as he smokes with us."

She didn't speak or nod her head, but the look of willingness was in her face, as if he, old Dick Summers, was something under a robe. Maybe he was, he thought, maybe he would be after the long no-having, but it was still the mark of age that he should doubt himself. It struck him, in the little time before he answered, that doubts were age. Doubts of self, of the worth-whileness of living, of the purpose of things—they were age. The young didn't doubt.

He said, "You are good. I do not know. It is many moons since I lived with the Shoshones. I have been a long time away, and I do not know. My medicine is weak."

"Come and smoke."

"I must lead the white party to camp, and then we will all smoke. Does it please you if we camp upstream?"

"Tell the white brothers to come, and we will smoke and give presents and trade."

The sun slid behind the westward hills, leaving high in the sky the blaze of its going, while wagons were set and tents pitched and Indian met white and the pipe passed and goods changed hands. Against the noise and movement of the meeting, the night fell gentle, dimming the sunset, drifting into groves and gullies to wait its time to claim the land. And then the moon swelled up, the red fires whirling in it, and whitened in its climb. In the still silver of it, Summers could see things plain—the faces of the smoking men, the clean lines of tree trunks rising, the Indian lodges pointing up, the caught moonglimmer of a blade of grass.

The men smoked quiet, Indian and white alike, speaking only stray words that Summers put into one tongue or the other, for the solemn talking was over and the solemn smoking. Evans sat with him, and Patch and Gorham and Carpenter and Daugherty, and White Hawk and half a dozen of his men. Yes, the hunting was good, for sheep and deer and elk, and the fish were big and many. White Hawk would see that the Shoshones did not steal from their friends. He had posted soldiers to watch. How many miles to Fort Hall? How many sleeps to the British house, White Hawk?

No air stirred, not a breath. The fire they had built grayed with ash, just the heart of it alive. And no noise sounded except the tiny hum of mosquito wings and the lazy words they spoke. The children were abed, and the women waited their men, and the dogs were quiet, and the wolves and coyotes not yet tuning up. It was as if the earth and sky listened while the question turned in Summers.

Why did he ask instead of act? He didn't believe in the sin the preacher did. Men and women were made different for a purpose, like hes and shes of any breed, and mostly he had done what he wanted and got up and forgotten, except now and then for a thought of the half-breeds he might have left behind. But they would fare as well as Indians and better than a heap of whites. The Indians never shamed a bastard, nor called it wrong to let a brother have a woman. They had a right to their ideas, like Weatherby to his; and mountain men took what they found and let the questions go.

But still he asked and, asking, knew it was the age in him that asked, for young Dick Summers would have gone ahead. Age asking not what was right and proper but was he an old fool who thought to catch the past by lying with a squaw, who thought to find the lost, high spirit under cover of a robe, in the body of a woman who would be lousy but also young and tender and warm for him. He knew the answer. He would cover her and lie back and realize it was no use except for the minute's now-dead fever, and thought would circle in his head so that he couldn't rest full and easy as of old. But still . . . But still . . .

Overhead he heard the whistle of wings, and of a sudden the name came to him, the name of her who'd been with him there on the Popo Agie's banks. Broken Wing, it was, as near as he had been able to make out from the Crow. The One with the Broken Wing.

A breeze fanned the graying fire, reddening the ash, and all at once the Indian dogs woke up, baying to the sky.

He guessed old fires had a right to shine, if they still could, and dogs to holler for the moon.

He got up.

"What you smilin' at, Dick?" Evans asked.

"Was I smilin'? Just feelin' good, I reckon."

LIJE EVANS had only part of his mind on hunting. Another part of it roamed around, thinking what he had seen and done and felt since leaving Independence far back in the spring. And still another part had stayed at Big Timber, where the train had camped early so the stock could rest, feed and get ready for the leaner miles ahead. It seemed he couldn't ever wrench all his thought away from the train. Try as he might, worry would come sneaking on him—about the state of the wagons and the stoutness of the oxen, about the Fairmans with their grief, about the hard going that lay before, about the great Columbia and the wicked rapids he had heard about. Whenever he was away from the train, like now, he had the feeling maybe he was needed. Maybe something had come up. Being captain put a duty on a man he couldn't take leave of even for a little while without the feel of guilt.

He rode Nellie along the bottom, looking to the prairie and the brush and to the ridges on the side for sign of antelope or elk or mountain sheep. It wasn't that the company was short of meat especially, not with Summers to hunt it out, not with game plenty and trout hungry in the Bear. It was just that he wanted to get away for a while, to slide out from under the weight of the captaincy and get his breath and refresh himself. Most of the things he had thought to do while back in Independence he hadn't done except in piddles if at all. He had shot two buffalo on the Platte and one of them a tough old bull that wouldn't even boil tender. He had brought in one antelope. That was all. He hadn't wet a fishline in the Bear. He had had time for fun, he reckoned, but not the notion for it. Duty fretted him too much—and for no good reason now.

Everything was fine. There wasn't a case of sickness in camp. No fevers. No bowel troubles. No one wounded by Indians or hurt by accident. The train was just lazing along the Bear, but for a purpose—to strengthen horses and cattle and especially oxen for what Dick said were stone deserts high above the Snake. They had crossed the Bear twice, to round a mountain that jagged in from the east, and had saved a hard climb by it, though adding to the miles. But the fords were safe enough. The Bear was a slow and peaceful river, with trees growing on it to float the leaky wagons with if need be. He wished the Snake would be as easy, knowing that it wouldn't.

Yes, he told himself for the tenth or twentieth time, the train was in good case. He had a right to hunt, though it seemed he'd go back empty-handed. The people had got along fair with the Indians, though the Snakes were quick and sneaky-handed and had made off with pots and kettles and knives and a rifle and some pieces of clothing, including the many-pocketed coat that Tadlock liked to wear. Tadlock had got sore as a sore-tailed bear and grew even sorer when old White Hawk couldn't get his men to give their plunder back. Said White Hawk could make them if he set himself to it. Said like as not White Hawk had the coat himself, which Evans didn't believe. He figured White Hawk had tried, both to stop the stealing and find the stolen things. It was just that a word wouldn't stay a thief or make a thief fork over, in red or white crowds either one. But it wasn't any use to argue so with Tadlock, who thought a head man wasn't head unless the rest obeyed.

Some of the others of the party were ill-natured from their losses, too—Daugherty, who missed his old flintlock, and Hold-ridge, who lost a knife and bridle, and Brewer, who wanted back his cookall, and Shields, who said his woman turned up shy a skirt. McBee hadn't lost a thing but talked mad just the same.

Well, Evans thought while his eye ranged, they would get over it. This was too good a country to stay mad in. Soreness didn't team with the wild oats and barley and rye that softened Nellie's steps, nor with the flax that waved blue in the grasses, nor with a kind sun. He pulled Nellie up and let her reach for a bite of feed and sat quiet while she savored it and the green juices slobbered from her mouth. It was too good a country, where the children ran safe, chewing balsam gum and rolling rocks down hillsides, where the women tinkered happy over food seasoned with wild yarbs and talked about the sermon preached by Weatherby last Sabbath. That was one day, anyhow, the train had given up to worship. Weatherby had gone again to Ephesians for his subject, exhorting on the verse, "Awake, thou that sleepest." In a thieving country, Evans thought, it was good advice in a way that Weatherby didn't mean.

He let Nellie foot along aimless while she cropped at the grass. Of all the land that he had seen this seemed the richest and the peacefulest—woods, water, pasture, soil laid down for a plow, all closed in, all protected by hills high-rising in the quiet sky. It was better than the Green, better than the Sweetwater and, God knew, better than the Platte. Maybe it was better than Oregon, except a man would feel he lived upon an island. This place was Oregon by the reckoning of Summers, who set the line between the waters of the east and west. And it would be settled one day. It was bound to be settled, he knew now. No keeping it from being. People would come west and more people would come west, as he had himself, not thinking exactly why but knowing just the push of feeling, as if God Himself had willed it. He could see them, wagon after wagon, train on train, winding up the Platte, toiling up the mountains, fording the protesting rivers. Some of them would sicken and some of them would die, but the great company would come on, for the thing was greater than any grief. The pictured line caught a man's imagination. It made him wonder. It made him somehow big.

Evans touched Nellie with his heel and she lifted her head as if to see did he mean it and fell to cropping again, and he didn't care. He didn't guess it was for hunting that he had come out.

A new time, he thought. History written on the land by the turn of wagon wheels. A new, good time to all but men like Summers, who couldn't feel the deep excitement of it. They had been turned different, these men, shaped past changing by tools now wearing out, by beaver and Indians and danger and lone-

228

ness. They were like deep drammers; what they thirsted after was more of what they'd had.

Still, maybe not with Dick. Maybe he would come to see, maybe settle in Oregon as Evans hoped and be the important man he could be. There wasn't anything beyond him if he set his head to it, governor or Congress or whatever. And he could still hunt some and sometimes pitch a camp and so lead a balanced life.

Now that Dick had come to mind, he knew one reason why he kept saying things were all right with the train. It was because Dick had drawn off from him somehow, leaving him, he felt, to manage almost all alone. Dick would come if called; he would help if help was asked; but still he'd quit the old close teaming that kept the spirit stout. He was different from before, different in a way that Evans couldn't quite explain, as if the sight of things known long ago had won him off from interest in the train. Dick was, Evans thought while he wondered if it was just a kind of jealousy that made him think so, a little like a man who saw an old sweetheart and up and left his marriage bed for her. He snorted inside when the thought was formed. Be damned if he wasn't womanish, womanish and weak! He would handle the train by himself then. It was about time he learned to stand alone.

But still he couldn't keep his head off Dick. Below Big Timber the train had met up with four of Bridger's men, four dark and weathered men who talked spare in front of strangers and, by themselves, spoke language strange to settled ears, saying "this child's thinkin' " and " 'pears to this coon" and "we was froze for meat, we was," and "wagh."

Evans had sat around their fire with Dick at night while Dick's whisky got drunk up and memories worked and tongues loosened, and he had felt like an outsider even with Dick, for here was a side of Dick he didn't know. Here, glimpsed in the talk, was a strange, wild life that Dick had been a part of and a big part, too. 'Member the time the goddam Crows lifted our cache, Summers, and it was you went to make medicine and came back with the furs and a smart-looking squaw to boot? Never could figure the way of that, Summers, 'less you catched the squaw in a berry patch and showed her what a mink you was and got her help in stealin' back our plews. She was gone on you. She was now. Purty as paint and a gone beaver on you. An' damn if you didn't traipse off with her. You was allus kind of a loner, I'm thinkin'. . . . 'Member that nigger you had to rub out on the Siskadee, back in 'twenty-six or 'twenty-eight or sometime? Took so much of him, you did, and dast him to irons and give him the best of it and kilt him afore his finger could bend. Wagh and Jesus Christ! Them was fat days. . . . Savin' that cheerwater for kingdom come? This hoss is terrible dry. . . . Ain't so poor a bull hisself, this child ain't. Got two calves with the Nepercies and a purty Shoshone heifer that's camped with that there preacher-doctor, Whitman, by Walla Walla, and's gettin' manners rubbed off on her.

Hearing them, seeing the side of Dick he didn't know, Evans said to himself that Summers was just shaking hands with the man he had been. And over the meals at camp, where Dick sat silenter than usual, not making fun with Brownie or teasing Rebecca, he said Dick was only reliving old times and would come out of it. But still he felt the touch of loss.

He pulled up Nellie's head, thinking he would never get meat if he just sat on his tail and let his head spin, and then, against the scant-grown hillside, he saw movement. It was an elk, a young bull by the looks of him, too distant for a shot.

He reined Nellie over to some brush and circled around under cover and came to the ridge and tied Nellie in a patch of trees where thieving eyes wouldn't find her easy and went ahead on foot, wishing while he stepped that he could hunt like Dick. Let a critter show itself and Dick became part of the land, noiseless and unseeable, like a fawn in the grass or a snake sunning in the sand.

He slid under some branches that wept over the game trail he followed and saw the young bull standing in an open place ahead. He pulled one foot even with the other but didn't raise his rifle. It was as if he waited for the notion to shoot, for the arms to want to lift and the eye to want to sight. Waiting, he thought how much the grown mind ranged. Take a boy or a young man, now, and he would think but of the killing, and his breath would breathe eager in his chest and his hand tighten on his rifle. He wouldn't parcel out his brain, to the bull and Dick Summers and the camp and maybe troubles ahead, and wasn't this a fine day, though, in a fine land. He wouldn't see the blue flax waving nor the sun patterned on the grass. The bull would blind him to all else, the bull and the brown hide and the young horns and the liquid eye. Sometimes it seemed too bad that life had to live on life.

The elk leaped with the ball and fell thrashing in the brush, and Evans went to him and bled and rough-gutted him and then walked back for Nellie.

Later he led Nellie toward camp, turning now and then to see that the elk was riding all right slung across the saddle. She didn't like the looks or smell of it and kept snorting as it shifted to her step. "Whoa, now, Nellie, that there bull won't bite you." It was a fair load for her even if there had been room for him besides.

It wasn't suppertime yet, though the mountains had shut the sun off, when camp came into view. It was a good sight, he thought as he neared it—the wagons squatted into rest, the stock grazing easy to eastward, the tents light against the green of woods and turf, a feather of smoke rising, untouched by any breeze. It would be a pretty evening—pretty, too, for the mosquitoes that swarmed out as the cool came on. Looked like there was always something to make you wish it different. The sight of camp reminded him he was hungry. He hoped Becky had made a stew like she promised, with wild onions cut up in it and maybe dumplings floating. You couldn't beat her for stews.

He was within a yell of camp before he noticed the men gathered nearer by the river. He thought, while a little uneasiness turned in him, how poor a mountain man he was. Dick would have spotted the men first thing.

There were eight or ten of them, close-grouped by a tree that held a branch above their heads. Tadlock he made out as he walked closer, and Brother Weatherby, then Brewer and McBee. He didn't try to single out more, for now he saw an Indian with them, hands behind him, naked from the crotch strap up.

Brewer held a rifle on him. **Weatherby and Tadlock** were arguing. Tadlock had a rope.

The fact came slow to Evans, and then he hardly believed. He looked to the wagons for signs of every-day. No one moved there except for Mrs. Brewer, shooing her young ones out of sight. He couldn't see another soul until his eye fixed on the tents and saw the heads of women poking. He dropped Nellie's reins.

The men didn't notice him until he spoke. "What you all aimin' to do?"

Tadlock turned around, the rope tight-held in his hand, and a quick displeasure showed on his face. "You've got eyes, haven't you?"

Weatherby turned, too. "They're going to hang a man." His long finger poked at Tadlock. "I warn you, Brother Tadlock, you'll be breaking the Commandments. The sin will be on you."

"If it's a sin it will be on all of us."

"We kin stand it," McBee said. "What you want us to do, say thankee to a thief?"

"Thou shalt not kill."

"Do we argue foriver with this preacher?" It was Daugherty asking, the heat in him giving an extra Irish to his words.

"Go away!" Tadlock waved at Weatherby. "You've done your duty. Now go away!"

While they yammered at one another, the Indian stood quiet except for his eyes. They went from face to face. He wasn't much more than a boy, Evans thought, an Indian boy no older much than Brownie, standing naked except for a tag of leather, standing dignified with a molty feather in his hair, hiding the fear of death if fear was in him while old palefaces fixed to string him up.

"What'id he steal?" Evans asked.

"Enough."

"What'id he steal?"

"Damn it, he was wearing my coat for one thing. For another, Shields caught him chasing off a horse."

"That ain't hangin' business."

232

"It is to us. You find it mighty easy to be lenient when your things aren't stolen."

"I told you I'd make them horses up to you if the council said so."

"The council!"

"How was it Shields didn't shoot him?"

Daugherty spit. "Ah-h, he is a trader, that Shields. He has two lousy buffalo robes and some fish, but no rifle innymore."

"I catched him all the same," Shields said.

"It's better this way," Tadlock told Evans. "We're going by law. We'll string him up and let him swing, and these thieves will know what white man's law is."

"Law?"

"Let's git on with it," McBee put in.

"We sat on the case," Tadlock answered. "We voted."

"Who?"

"Those we could find. Some were fishing and some hunting."

"Didn't put yourself out to find them as would disagree, did you?"

"We found whom we could. Would you mind stepping out of the way? This will help later trains, you know."

Evans said, "You don't care about them."

"Or about the Commandments," Weatherby added, working his long finger.

"We care about justice. There were just two votes, besides Weatherby's, against it. Byrd's and Fairman's." Tadlock had made a careful loop in the rope. "If you haven't got the stomach for justice, go away like they did." He held the loop in one hand and the coil in the other. "Make way!"

The Indian stood quiet and straight-eyed as before, his hands behind him. They were tied behind him, Evans realized suddenly.

Before he stopped to think, Evans asked, "Where's Summers?"

Tadlock answered, "Out with his mountain friends, I imagine. What difference does that make?"

Holdridge hadn't spoken before. Now he said, "We figgered maybe we could limp along without 'im."

"Yah," said Brewer, speaking for the first time. "Ve could do it. Yah."

For a minute they all looked at Evans. In their eyes he read his weakness. In them he heard himself again, bleating out, "Where's Summers?"

His gaze fell below theirs and traveled on the ground and came to Weatherby, who stood at the side as if praying, and went from him to the feet of the Indian and climbed up and saw the boy, dirty and thin and sturdy and unflinching, facing death because he had done what it had been born and drilled in him to do; and a sudden fury took him over, rising out of shame and outrage. "No," he cried out, "by God, you don't do it!"

There was blood-hunger in the faces, blood-hunger such as he had seen in the faces of the Sioux, hunger and vexations and itching disappointments like Tadlock's and envious no-goodness like McBee's and fret and strain and worry and boredom, all now to be spent, all to be eased in the killing of a boy.

"Drop the rope, Tadlock!"

Tadlock took a tighter hold on it.

"I said drop it!" Evans took a step and then another and shoved at Daugherty when he tried to come between. "Rest of you ain't really in this, 'less you're bound to be. This is between me and Tadlock, and long a-comin'."

Tadlock threw the rope aside and squared away.

Evans never had hit a man before. Never in his grown life had he struck out. Now, seeing Tadlock's hands lift and rage darken his square face, it was as if it wasn't him that swung but someone kin to him and far off in his feelings.

The swing missed and left him open, and Tadlock struck twice, the short and heavy blows of one who knew the use of fists. Evans swung and missed again and felt the double hammer of the practiced hands.

The blows shook him. They jarred his brain and struck lights in his skull and dizzied his aim and step, and he knew he fought clumsily, flaying out at air while his feet staggered under him. His strength was no good to him. The slow strength that could lift an end of log that two men couldn't hold was no good; it worked wild and awkward, leaving face and belly open for the stunning fists.

A lick landed high on his cheek and nearly knocked him over, and when he found his balance he stood rattled and let Tadlock work on his face before he could think to go after him again. He heard cries like little echoes around him and in the wheel of sight saw the men ringed about and the Indian watching, his hands rope-held behind him, and, farther out, the women pushing up and Becky at the front of them.

Blow and blow and lick on lick, and the brain stunned and the eye dimmed and his fists forever off the mark, and in his mouth the salty leak of blood. He was strong and he was right and he was beaten. But bore in! Bore in and swing and meet the swings and stand as long as could be! Stand for Becky! Stand for Brownie! Stand for what he knew was right!

He was standing yet. He could stand some more. It came to him as Tadlock's fists battered at mouth and jaw that he could stand a long time. He could stand forever. There wasn't power enough in Tadlock's arms to lay him out, or wind enough in his belly. Here was Tadlock backing off, mouth working like a landed fish's, blood in his unbruised face and sweat on it, and in his eyes the peaked owning-up of doubt.

The wild fist found its mark, and Tadlock spun half around and tried to get an elbow up before the next lick hit. He lunged for footing and set himself and got his two blows in and staggered at the answer to them. With all his power Evans swung at the boned line of his jaw.

Tadlock didn't falter and then melt. He slammed backwards all at once, head and shoulders and butt and heels, and moved a little and lay quiet with blank, half-opened eyes.

Evans pulled in a breath and looked around the circle, at Brewer and Holdridge and Daugherty and the rest, and then he walked to the Indian and untied him.

He didn't see the Indian slide into the brush, for Rebecca tugged at his arm as the rope came loose. "Come on, Lije."

"What?"

"Your face is a sight."

"That don't matter."

"I'll doctor it. Come on."

He stood uncertain while the world steadied around him, the trees getting fixed again by the river, and the people singling themselves out, and Rebecca's face not just a blur but a face with eyes that held pride and pleading both. He saw Mrs. Tadlock was bending over her man, and Weatherby bending with her, and the men watching out of questioning and guarded faces. Nellie grazed beyond them, grown used to the elk across her back.

Rage died in him, and the pride of rage that had made him glare his dare at the men, and he said, "We best see to Tadlock first. I didn't aim to hurt him bad."

Afterwards he felt cast down but somehow wholer than he had been. It wasn't fun to beat a strong man down. It left a wound upon the winner deeper than blackened eyes and broken lips. But still he had had to take his choice, and he had taken it and stood by it, and the taking and the standing made him a wholer man.

When Dick came into camp, he said, with the quiet grin in his gray eyes, "I hear you done the needful, Lije." But Evans didn't have to have Dick's words to feel solid in the right.

Chapter - - - - - - - - - - Twenty-Two

WHILE THE CHILDREN shouted around her, Mercy McBee dipped up a cup of bubbling water and stirred a spoon of sugar in it and handed it to Tom Byrd. His young, soft lips sucking at the rim of the cup reminded her of a catfish's mouth.

"I'm next," Dolly Brewer was yelling above the rest. "I'm next, ain't I, Mercy?"

"You aren't. I am. I am."

"I said fourth."

"Didn't, either."

"Did so."

"Hurry up, Tom."

They were all crying at her and at one another, crying and pushing and shoving up, the Byrds' children and the Brewers' and the Daughertys' and Harry Gorham and her own brothers and sisters, each of them wanting next on the soda water that boiled out of a low, white mound. Stirred with the sugar that Mrs. Tadlock and Mrs. Mack had given, it made a sweet and fizzy drink.

"Land's sake!" Mercy said. "Just wait now. You'll all get some." She cupped it up without letting herself think about the taste of it, for the thought troubled her stomach as the smell of frying bacon did or of onion-seasoned stews. "I'm goin' from the littlest to the biggest. That's fair."

They quieted for a minute, and she heard again the regular sh-h-h of another spring, closer to the river, that surged in its closing of rock, making a sound like one of the steamboats she had seen on the Ohio. All night she had listened to it, the puff of it like a hard-blown breath above the murmur of the river and the voice of the wind in the trees. "Sh-h-h," it said and breathed in. "Sh-h-h," as if it knew.

"Here, Dolly."

The train was camped out a piece from the river and the spring she dipped the water from. She could see the women stirring around it, poking fires and readying Dutch ovens for the bread dough they had mixed, using water from the springs in place of yeast or saleratus. This country was all springs. It was all a kind of giving birth, the water pushing up and out of the sodaed lips that held it.

"All right, Billy."

"And then I'm next."

"I'm after you."

The men were hunting, or fishing upriver, or watching the stock across the Bear, where the graze was better. Only Brownie Evans was in sight, wandering among the tents and wagons as if lost for company.

"Now me. Now me, Mercy!"

She was glad for the children, glad for their shouts and shovings. They kept the mind filled and the hand busy. She said, "I'm all right," when Mrs. Brewer came from camp, waddling with the child she carried underneath her apron.

"Nah," Mrs. Brewer answered. "Too much time you couldn't giff. Not good, it is not. De mudders take de young vones now."

"Wait till the sugar's used up."

Mrs. Brewer stood solid and silent, a mild cow of a woman with the little calf lumped in her, not wanting to sit, Mercy guessed, because of the work of getting up. She marched the children back to camp when the last grain of sugar was gone.

Mercy watched them traipse away and listened to the young voices complain. She sat dangling the cup from a finger, thinking as the voices faded that the earth might be coming to an end, and this here, this now, was the last of it, the river flowing into nothing, the sun going forever home, the high hills darkening, the spouting water saying its last, "Sh-h-h. Sh-h-h." The sh-h-h that others would be saying if the world went on. Sh-h-h! Mercy McBee! Do tell! It could be the end and she wouldn't care. The end was rest and peace in the mind and nothing mattering any more.

She bowed her head with the sick weight of thought in it,

telling herself maybe it wasn't so. It didn't have to be so. It could be it wasn't. A body couldn't tell for sure so soon. Later she would look back and think how foolish was her misery, and she would laugh then because her fear was a child's fear and there was no cause for it. She tried to put herself forward in that time, tried to gaze back on herself, sitting here with shame and sadness, and it was as if she was two persons, the cheerful one ahead and the fearful one by the spring. Why, she had studied herself a dozen times, when the brush offered a place or the tent was empty. She had looked and she had felt, and there wasn't anything wrong. She was flat and slim as ever. There couldn't be anything wrong. For a minute she felt the spurt of comfort and of courage. Things would turn out right. No need to cross a bridge before you got to it. Plenty of bridges never came to be except in the mind that built them. Then her stomach turned with sickness.

The cup trembled from her finger, and she set it down and locked her hands in her lap, trying to catch hold of fear, trying to bring it in from hands and legs and head and lay it deep inside the chest. Ma would throw up her hands and take on terrible, crying, "I tolt you to stay clear of men, didn't I? But, no, you knowed better, and this is what comes of it and serves you right. 'Fore God, I don't know what got into you." What Pa would do or say she didn't know, but it would be like him to go to Mr. Mack and brave around and settle happy for a horse or ox, as if that was the price of her.

While she pulled fear in, she understood it was Aunt Bess who'd made her look on Pa for what he was—a windy man and no-account, "slack-twisted" in Aunt Bess's words, though she never out and gave that name to him. Aunt Bess had kept her when things went extra hard, which generally they did, and by voice and manner had made her eyes to see, so that, when she went back home, she saw the dirt and ugliness of it and Ma dragged out and shriller as the days went by.

If she could talk to Mr. Mack! If she could put her head on his chest and cry to him how it was! But he hadn't made a way to see her again, not but just one time after Laramie, which seemed so long ago it was something on the edge of dreams and she wouldn't think that it was real except that her stomach churned and her time was past. But still he was with her. Still she took him to bed at night and got up with him in the morning and traveled with him by day, her hands pushing back the black lock of his hair and smoothing the trouble from his face. And it wasn't body-hunger for him and never had been much, but just the wanting to find strength and kindness in him and to give them back. She watched for him in camp and along the trail, watched for the frowned face and the quick way of him, acting as if she wasn't watching. Sometimes when their eyes met, he would smile or say hello, and she wondered, seeing him so common, did he remember? Did he hold the secret and was it dear? Did he cry for her inside?

Her stomach queased again, bringing her to now, bringing her to this, and a prayer spoke in her. O God, let it not be so. I pray, help me, God, and forgive my trespasses and make it so I can talk to Mr. Mack. Please, God, make it not so, I pray Thee.

A voice spoke, Brownie's voice, saying, "How-de-do, Mercy. Why, you're cryin'."

She brushed at her eyes and went to get up and was suddenly so dizzy she had to let herself sink back. "It's this fizz water brings tears to my eyes. It's this fizz water I been drinkin'."

"Oh!" he said. She saw just the blurred feet of him, shuffling as if not knowing what to do. "Mind if I set?"

"I was fixin' to go."

"I wisht you wouldn't."

"You could set, though."

He sprawled on the ground. "I want someone to talk to."

"There's others besides me," she said. She had laid fear back. She had brought it in and laid it back, and it was just a heaviness in her, weighing on the heart.

"Better to talk to you than some I could name," he said. "Nice place, ain't it? Been to Beer Springs?"

"No."

"Pa says it tastes like old beer, with the life gone out of it."

"I wouldn't know."

"I tried it oncet. Made my stummick turn."

When she didn't speak, he asked, "Whyn't you and me take a walk down that way?"

"There's work to do."

"It'll get itself done."

With fear closed in, her eyes had dried, and she let them lift and see his face. It was an honest face, with sandy hair and freckles like stains underneath his tan and a gaze that wouldn't see inside her.

"Wisht you'd walk."

"And just let work go?" She tried to make her tone light. "That'ud be a purty thing."

"You're the purty thing." The words came out of him like a blurt out of one of the springs, as if they had been building up and wouldn't be held and so spilled out of his mouth in spite of him. The blood rising in his face drowned tan and freckles both.

Before she thought, she said, "Purty is as purty does."

"Purty does all right, I bet."

"You don't know nothin' about me, Brownie."

"Reckon I do. You willin' to walk?"

His eyes, she thought, were a little like those of the old dog, Rock, that had trotted up and sat by him and watched her with a round, slow-winking stare. Before the open begging in them she said, "Can't stay long."

He didn't give her a hand up, as Mr. Mack would have, but stood awkward and unsure while she got to her feet, but of a sudden she felt close to him and somehow in his debt, for here, in her aloneness, was a one that prized her. Would he prize her no matter what, she asked herself while she waited for the dizziness to die in her. Would he if he knew?

They walked downriver, beyond the camp, beyond the steamboat's breathing sh-h-h, and came to Beer Springs, and he tried the taste of it, and they sat down afterwards behind a white cone where water had stopped flowing. The crust that the springs had made showed whiter against a sun that was sinking toward the hills.

241

"You ever think what you'll do after you get to Oregon?" he asked.

"Just keep on helpin' Ma."

"I mean after that."

"Not so much."

"I think a heap of things. I aim to work hard and get along and own a nice farm and have time to hunt and fish."

He leaned back and put the heels of his hands at his sides to brace himself. "A heap of things. Like about you, f'rinstance."

"I ain't much to think about, Brownie," She was sorry afterwards for what she'd said, for the words were teasing words though honest-spoken.

He answered, "You are so. If I could just tell you—"

She wouldn't lead him on. She wouldn't help his tongue to tell. She didn't want him, and, even if she did, she had no right. She had no right—and fear marched in her again. She had held it in, underneath thought, and it had risen, heavy and terrible, and she wanted to run wild into the hiding wildness or to cry out and fall weeping and give herself to earth.

"I'm nigh eighteen, Mercy."

"I best go."

"Pa got hisself married younger'n me."

She kept silent, drawing fear in, putting it quiet in its secret place.

"I reckon you know what I'm set to say."

Now that the thing was out, he turned to her, and face and eyes and all of him were honest and humble with his wanting. "If'n I could just feel you felt the same as I do, there wouldn't nothin' hamper me, in Oregon or wherever."

She ought to say no to him, no, Brownie, don't talk that way, but the face was too much for her, and tears washed in her eyes. "I ain't ready to think about it, Brownie. I can't think about it. I do' know as I feel the same, but I thank you all the same."

She couldn't keep from crying. The crying started deep in her and wrenched up and broke out, and she put her hands to her face and felt his arm go across her shoulder.

"Why, it's naught to take on over, Mercy. Don't have to cry on account of I want to marry you." The hand lay gentle on her back. He held quiet, as if he knew she had to cry though the why of it was lost to him.

She wiped her eyes later, leaning over so as to use the hem of her dress. "I didn't mean to act the fool."

"You couldn't act the fool to me, Mercy." His hand came under her chin and lifted her head and turned it to him. There was concern in his face, and questions and kindness, and of a sudden he bent and kissed her cheek, kissed the kiss not of hunger but of care and good-wishing. "You allus look so sad," he said, dropping his hand and drawing his arm from across her back. "Wisht I could make it so you didn't. I'd do anything."

"You're good, Brownie," she said. "Whatever happens, I know you're good."

She got up because she couldn't talk without more tears, and they went back, saying little, and neared camp, and he said, "I hope this ain't the last time I'll get to walk with you?"

"I do' know," she answered and turned from him and walked and arrived at her family's wagon and heard Pa saying, "I swear, woman! Hurry up them victuals! This country makes a man all gut."

She waited in the dark. She made herself a shadow in the dark so that people, looking, would take her for a bush or for a cloud across a star. The stars were out, cold and distant before the moon that would come later. A breeze ran on the ground and touched her legs and went on, whispering the night's secrets, and she trembled to it, not from cold.

The sounds of a camp about to go to bed came to her—the late close of a lid over a cleaned kettle, the tired voice of Mrs. Byrd with her young, the rumble that was the quiet, man-to-woman talk of men before they gave themselves to night. They mixed with other sounds, with the sh-h-h of the spring, with the thin sky-crying of coyotes far off, with the moo of a milch cow over a lately-born calf that the Gorhams had carried in their wagon.

She was alone with sound. She was nothing but the ear for sound, and sound wouldn't be except for her, or she be but for

243

sound. She could lose herself, if the ear would close to it, and be nothing at all except a stray remembering in people's minds.

She pulled her coat around her neck and told herself to wait. Wait for the last look around. Wait for the last chore before people took themselves to bed.

Once she thought the stars were wishful. Once she asked the stars to watch, the close, warm, happy stars that drew off now to shame her. Music had sounded then, and feet skipped in a dance, and it had sounded tonight and other feet had skipped, making of the fiddle's wail the opposite of sorrow, and Hig had sung a song of love and death that smiling people said was mighty pretty.

Lost echo of music and sh-h-h of the spring and cold eyes of the stars. I declare, Mercy, you're off your feed and what upset you so and it was that fizz water likely. Cry of coyotes and the moo of the calved cow and the springs giving birth and sh-h-h. Tan and freckles and I'd do anything. Black lock against a wrinkled brow and say no, Mercy. Nothing but the sounds of night and nothing but the night around and fear and the lunge of fear. I'm scared I'm in a fambly way, Mr. Mack. Sh-h-h. And wait and wait.

A dog came up, unseen, and nosed her hand, and she started and calmed and felt him to be Rock and held him with her while she waited.

She knew him when he stepped out, knew him by the thin, clean shadow that he was against the shadowed night, and boldness died in her and her legs trembled to run; and then she thought he'd go about his business before he knew that she was there and she would have to hold still or creep off in the dark and so not shame him with her knowing. She said, "Mr. Mack," and heard her voice as no more than a whisper, drowned by the sh-h-h of the spring. "Mr. Mack."

"What's that? Who is it?" Then, lower-voiced, "Oh, hello."

"It's Mercy McBee."

"I see now. How are you?"

"Mr. Mack?"

He came up to her, not answering. In the cover of the night

244

she let herself search his face, seeing the peaks of his cheeks and the pockets of his eyes in the starshine.

"Mr. Mack?"

"You're up late."

"Don't reckon I could sleep."

"Good night for sleeping."

"Mr. Mack?"

"Yes."

"Could we get away a piece, so's to talk?"

He took her arm without answering and led her out from camp, down toward the steamboat spring. "It has seemed best not to try to see you, Mercy."

"I wouldn't try to see you but—but—"

"What is it?"

"I'm afeard, Mr. Mack. I'm so afeard."

His voice sharpened. "Afraid?"

She only could nod, feeling from his tone the blame lay all on her.

"Of what?"

"You know."

"For God's sake!" he said. Then, "It's probably just your imagination."

"I been tryin' to tell myself that."

"Well?"

"Tellin' don't make it so."

"I can't believe it, Mercy."

"What if worst is worst?"

"It won't be. I'm sure it won't be."

"But if it is?"

"If it is, it is."

"What kin I do? Must be you know somethin' I kin do."

"What do you think I can do?"

"Nothin', I reckon, except go back to camp."

"Don't you see I can't do anything?"

"I didn't aim to cause you trouble."

"Cause me trouble?"

"I didn't mean I was holdin' it over you."

245

Of a sudden his voice softened. "I'm sorry, Mercy. It's just that I don't know what to do. I just don't know."

"Nothin' at all?"

"Nothing but wait and see."

"I've done done that," she answered, and it seemed strange to her that her voice was steady. It came thin but steady, from some lean, raw, lonely strength that wouldn't bow to tears.

While she wondered at it, he asked, "Have you thought about marriage, Mercy?"

"To who?"

"Well—to anyone?"

"An' never let on?"

"I don't know."

The voice in her said, "Talk don't seem to be no use. Must be your wife's expectin' you."

He cried out then, cried fierce but soft so that she felt the misery in him. "Mercy! I'm sorry. All I can say is I'm sorry."

He left without patting her, without touching her, without the kiss that she had thought would give her comfort; and she knew, while the knowing tore her to the lonely strength beneath, that he had wanted her only for the time, only for what his body found in her, and never again would come to her even to get more of the same.

Sound came back, the river complaining along the shore, the steamboat hissing, the coyotes crying louder as the moon flushed up, and, listening, she asked herself if she could wrong a boy like Brownie.

Curtis Mack didn't go immediately to his tent. He walked away from Mercy, toward it, and thought Amanda wouldn't be asleep as yet, and turned and wandered down the valley, his mind aware but motionless before the fact.

Ahead of him the hills bulked huge, lined against the sky by the rising moon, and, nearer, the waters of the river ran troubled under the long moon-slant that took them from the dark.

There was nothing to do, nothing he could do, nothing but wait, nothing but return to his tent as the girl had said when

246

anxiety had edged his words. "Nothin', I reckon, except go back to camp," she had answered with a bleak, offended courage that wrenched him more in recollection than event. She hadn't wept. She hadn't blamed him. She hadn't threatened. She had asked, humbly, and been answered in a way, and had dismissed him with her young, brave, hopeless dignity.

Thinking of her, he hated himself, hated his shabby answering to her need, hated the cheap suggestion that she marry. He could have given her of his strength. He could have tried to reassure her. He could, at least, have shown her tenderness. But to what end? To continue and compound a situation already made impossible? To give her false hope? Asking, he knew he argued late to justify himself. The reasons might be good enough, but at the time they hadn't been defined. What had moved him was a male's annoyed alarm, the wish to wiggle out, the half-aversion bred by disagreeable responsibility. It was a wonder he hadn't asked how she could be sure he was the one.

He stumbled and said, "Goddam it!" and caught himself and went on. He was a fool and a villain, or a man made villainish by circumstance, by the crazy, contrary, mindless unorder of life. There was yeast in him, not willed there by himself, and yeast would out, in the murder of a Kaw or the ruin of a girl. Preachers could talk about morals, as if all men were born and situated similarly, but morals were particular to every man, dependent on his stuff and state.

And yet a man felt guilt. He couldn't master self and circumstance, but still the fool felt guilt. It was senseless, senseless as the self-reproach of an idiot for being born that way, but it existed, wrought by hymns and texts and fierce mouthings about rewards and punishments. Long after reason came, the feeling stayed. Forever after. A man could deny God, knowing the afflictions that were a contradiction of Him, but still he felt accountable beyond the facts. Sinning sins that the Great Sinner forced upon him, he wanted to atone, to humble and flagellate himself, to promise to do better. That way he found comfort, as he, Curtis Mack, had found comfort in hard work and unaccustomed patience with Amanda after the killing of the Kaw.

It was in the nature of things, he thought, that now, with a better understanding reached between his wife and him, the consequences of misunderstanding should arise. Too late, if ever, one fell upon the answer to his plight.

It had been simple, so simple, if so wise, that he wondered at his blindness. Hot and swollen with his need there near the Southern Pass, he still had kept his voice in check, saying to Amanda while they lay in bed, "I wish you would. I wish you could, Amanda."

"I wish so, too."

"I understand the fear, but it isn't fear alone, not just of pregnancy."

"No," she said and waited for his words.

"Part must be resentment, and I understand that, too, I guess. No one likes to answer to demand."

"No."

"Do you know what it is?"

"Only that something gets in the way. Only that I feel I can't."

"Always?"

"Not always. You know that."

"Don't you feel desire? Ever?"

She didn't answer, and he thought he felt her stiffen in the bed and knew the line of inquiry was wrong. The old, hot words came to his mouth, and he shut them off, making himself think about the Kaw and himself and the chastening regrets, about Amanda and the strangeness that she couldn't alter. It was no less inviolable because it tortured him. He said, "We can wait. Maybe, if we just wait—" and turned over in bed.

"I wish I could, Curt."

"I've been wrong," he said, knowing suddenly it was true. "I've fixed the idea of demand in your head. If I had it to do over again, it would be different."

"How, Curt?"

"Maybe, if we had another try, I could make you see I need you, not your spirit alone or your body alone but all of you. And I wouldn't demand. I would try just to let you know that I stood in need of your help and that you could help me, and that I couldn't help it that I needed help. I guess that's what I mean. Good night, Amanda."

For a long time she lay still, and then her arm slipped around him, almost shyly, and her hand found his and asked him to turn over.

He wasn't fool enough, he reminded himself now, to think their troubles entirely at an end. The difference in their appetites was too great to allow of miracles. But they had made a start, and more than just a start. They were coming to adjustment, each trying to keep in mind the other. And he felt fulfilled and knew he loved his wife beyond all women.

So it would have to be in this, God's world, he thought, that an accident should come between. It wasn't in the scheme of things for happiness to last.

He stopped and faced about and started back. Too long an absence might call for explanations if Amanda kept herself awake for him. It was fear, he knew, that underlay his other feelings. Not fear of the lash. To hell with it and the shame of it! And not fear of Amanda, quite, but of the loss of her, and not of the loss of her, for he felt she wouldn't leave him, but of the loss of love which was the loss of her. He hadn't known till recently, till now, how much it meant to him.

And so, he thought, walking heavy-footed under the big moon, his worries were for self and not for Mercy. She was a girl-child and pregnant and alone, and he worried for himself. That was the scheme of things, too—self-preservation—but it was ugly just the same. And repentance and remorse and pleadings for forgiveness, what were they if not concern for self? Would he regret his act but for the consequences?

He tried to see the question honestly and didn't know the answer. Then he thought no, he wouldn't regret, if no harm at all had come to Mercy, no harm beyond the act if that was harm, no pregnancy, no disclosure, no shame, no heartache, no making of a trollop of her. He wouldn't have regretted even his own faithlessness, for there were reasons for it then.

There was the hitch, there was the kernel, existing whether there was God or not—had a man been right with man? He saw the girl again, standing small, standing brave, standing with that piteous dignity in her ruins, and he knew what his reply must be.

He said, "O Christ!" and shook himself and quickened his step, as if a man could outpace thought, and came to his tent and went in.

Amanda's voice said in the darkness, "I almost went to sleep, Curt."

"It's such a grand night out." He sat down and started taking off his shoes.

It was also in the nature of things, he thought as he crawled into bed, that she should be waiting for him tonight. Far off, the wry manipulators of affairs must be grinning to themselves.

Long after Amanda was asleep, he lay sleepless, hearing the murmur of the river and the singing of coyotes. He wondered if Mercy McBee, age fifteen or sixteen, also lay awake, kept from her young girl's dreams by the beat of fear. He wondered if the Kaw he'd killed was happy in the happy hunting grounds.

One thing he knew. Whatever happened, wherever he was, as long as he lived, he would bear the wound-stripe of his guilt.

"**Y**OU'LL HAVE YOURSELVES a spree, I'm thinkin'," the old mountaineer said. "This nigger's been that way, and it's some, that's what it is."

He was, Lije Evans thought, about the age of a hill—allow a hundred years one way or the other—and he sat on the ground with the solid ease of a hill, as if he never needed a chair or back-rest for his carcass. Greenwood, his name was, Caleb Greenwood, and he was green like an old, gray tree that still put out leaves.

"Ain't I right, Cap'n?"

There were eight or ten of them squatted around in the Fort Hall yard, outside the dried-mud building that Captain Grant used for office and home. The yard was in shadow, for the sun had fallen below the walls of the fort, and the beginning feel of night was in the air.

Captain Grant was the only one who stood. Seen from the ground, he looked even bigger than he was. He had England written all over him. He brushed his beard with his hand. "The Hudson's Bay Company never has tried to get a wagon train through," he answered.

"Why not?" Gorham asked.

Captain Grant shrugged, putting into the movement more than tongue could say.

Evans asked himself whether he was ready to dislike the man just because he was British. He had been good enough to the train, good enough to be better than you might expect from a damn Britisher. He had welcomed the company and traded with it—and made himself some money, which, still, was what he was in business for. You could buy flour from him, brought by boat and horse from the Oregon settlements, at twenty dollars a hundred, or horses at from fifteen to twenty-five each. If you didn't have money, he would take your sore-footed oxen and allow five up to twelve dollars for them. Good man or bad, though, he was British and so didn't want Americans taking over Oregon. That stood to reason. What he had to say about the trail ahead had to be taken with salt.

"Some of you'll git through, and maybe some wagons," the old man said and took the pipe from his mouth and looked around. "Ain't likely the whole kit and b'ilin' of you will, but some will, an' have a heap of fun."

"How?" Tadlock asked.

"Why, to look back on. Starvin' an' thirstin' and nigh drownin' makes rich rememberin', if so be it you live to remember."

"We done all right so far," Evans put in.

"Shore you did, boy. Done smart, this nigger says. Ain't quite the whisker of August, and here ye be."

"Well?"

"More this nigger thinks to it," Greenwood said, and stopped while his old lips kept his pipe alive, "more he almost wishes he was trailin' along. Californy way is too by-jesus tame. Nothin' the whole length of her to test a man. Nothin' to remember 'cept easy goin'."

He had smoked his pipe down, and now he tilted the ash from it and packed in more tobacco so's to smoke it back up without having to relight. "Shorter, too, to Californy, but this nigger's got to point that way. Said I would an' I by-jesus will."

Summers had been sitting quiet, the lines of inside smiling at the corners of his mouth. He said, "This child's been yan side of the Big Salt Sea, with the Diggers. Seems like it sticks in mind."

"Sure enough?" Greenwood answered as if he didn't understand.

The look of thinking ahead was on Patch's sharp face. "What did you say they raised in California?"

"Nothin'. Nothin' 'cept what's sot in the ground and whatever chews on grass. She's a soft country, she is, and so goddam sunny a man wonders ain't there ever no weather there. It ain't like Oregon thataway."

"Let's talk straight," Tadlock said, hitching forward on the ground. "Why do you think we can't make it to the Willamette?"

Old Greenwood spread his hands. "Did this nigger say that, now? Said some of you would. Shore. There's the Snake to ford twice, 'less you cross it here at Hall an' run into hell's trouble like Wyeth done, Dick, in 'thirty-four or sometime, an' the Snake ain't no piss-piddle of a river even if you might think so, seein' it from here, but you'll git over, most o' you, and maybe some wagons. An', oh, man, but it'll be fun. Do' know as I would try the wagons, though. There's plenty wagons for sale at Oregon City, I reckon. What you say, Cap'n?"

"I'd leave the wagons here."

"Ain't wagons gone through before?" Gorham asked.

Greenwood answered, "Some."

"Tell us some more of your fun," Tadlock said.

"Ain't so much more, but damn me fer a liar if fer days you don't roll along her rim and no drink for man or brute, and there she flows, so goddam far and steep below you couldn't leg it down and back from sunup to sundown."

In the thinking quiet Evans smelled the smoke of dying cook fires inside the buildings flanked around. The fires would be dying at camp, too, which was pitched south and west of the fort about a mile, and Rebecca would have the plates and kettles cleaned, for the camp had eaten early, and Brownie would be watching out against the friendly, thieving Snakes. There were other smells here, the smells of smoked meat and fish and hides and tobacco, the sour aftersmell of Indians, the smell of a bucket of milk that a half-breed carried by. The milk put him in mind of Independence and home and the cowshed and the Missouri flowing not so far away. He said, "We know somep'n about rivers."

"Shore, boy," old Greenwood answered. "The Missouri or the Mississippi, I'm thinkin'. Nice water. Come to think on it, what you aim to do with your cattle?"

"Take 'em along."

"Oh! An' then after the Snake, or Lewis River like sometimes we call it, you come to its pappy, an' there's more fun. You kin say you seen the chutes and falls of her and the black, by-jesus rocks smotherin' in foam. It's a sight, I tells you. Wuth seein'."

Evans let his gaze go from man to man, wondering if they felt like him, wary of this grandpa of the mountains but still fazed by the word of trials ahead. The company just yesterday had finished a toilsome stretch, through the black rocks and black dust this side the Bear, and had come down into the valley and seen water and woods and grass and bobolinks and kill-deers, and he didn't guess anyone wanted to move again, much less tackle what Greenwood was putting into words.

"I reckon you all know Meek," Evans said. "He swears he's learnt a better way to Oregon. Up the Malheur River. Said it 'ud save a hundred and fifty miles and more."

Captain Grant nodded. "Steve Meek. He broke with the train he was piloting and hurried here to talk himself into another. I wonder that you didn't see him when he passed you. What did you tell him?"

"Told him we had Summers."

Captain Grant said, "Right. I wouldn't care to try that trail, would you, Summers?"

Dick just shook his head.

Greenwood started up his song again. "You got such a smart start, maybe you'll git to the Willamette afore snow flies. Could be you will. Course, you'll have rain, one day on another, fer the rainy season's nigh here. What was it you said you aimed to do with the cattle?"

"Take 'em."

"Oh! They's a passel o' Injuns 'twixt here and there, an' I hear they've blacked their faces agin white parties, but fish-eatin' Injuns ain't much, like Summers'll tell you. They ain't likely to cause much harm."

Mack raised his eyes from the ground, which he had been worrying with one finger. "We got by the Pawnees and Sioux."

"Shore. Shore."

Evans was glad when Summers spoke. It was only Summers who knew Oregon and so could speak against the man, and when he didn't it was as if he couldn't because the said words

254

were truer and wiser than he could say himself. Summers asked, "Who's payin' you, Caleb?"

"Now as fer fevers," Greenwood said, giving Summers just the corner of his eye, "there's some as hold there's fever on the lower river, an' this nigger 'lows there's some but not as much as claimed. There ain't that much, or I don't know white from Injun. You say you aimed to take your cattle along, Evans?"

Captain Grant had gone inside. He came out with a jug and cups. It was good whisky, better than old Hitchcock sold at his store back in Independence. The captain passed it with a manner. You had to say the British had manners, if you liked manners.

Evans didn't know how McBee had kept quiet so long, unless it was because of Tadlock. He rolled a swallow of whisky around in his mouth and gulped it down and spoke up. " 'Y God," he said with the bright look of a man expecting a second to his motion, "I didn't set out for the West hopin' to live hard. I done lived hard enough already."

"Aw, don't let this nigger scare you off," Greenwood told him. "You ain't got more'n eight hundred miles or so to go. Could be you'll do smart." He emptied his cup with a throw-back of his head. "An' then you can say you seen all them dead Injuns down from the Dalles, too. Man, it's a sight to see! Dead'uns floatin' on rafts an' laid in pens an' all, along with little scare-devils. You'll never set your eye on more good Injuns than right there."

Tadlock asked, "Was there a fight?"

"Not as fur as this nigger knows. They just up and die, I reckon. Eh, Cap'n?"

Grant had seated himself with the rest. He nodded his big, British head. "Starvation and fevers, I suppose. I never stopped to think. At any rate it wasn't a fight."

"As fer cattle," Greenwood went on, "you can dicker fer 'em when you git there. There's a heap of cattle bein' drove from Californy to Oregon."

There was sorrow on Brother Weatherby's face, sorrow, Evans guessed, from the cursing that he heard. He guessed, too, that it was more to get God into the open than to argue with

Greenwood that he said, "We're in the Lord's hands, remember."

"Now that's good," Greenwood answered. "That there is smart. There's places you need prayer. Ain't nothin' like a good prayer-sayer from here to Oregon City, I allus say."

"Are there markets in California?" Tadlock asked.

"Well, if you want to talk Californy, there's no trouble about markets, stiddy markets, wheat a dollar and corn fifty cents and sheep a dollar or two."

"Who buys?"

"Hudson Bay Company, H. B. C., ol' Here Before Christ, that's who. Git to the ports, like Saint Francisco, and you'll see ships aplenty, makin' up cargoes to go with what they found in Oregon."

"Whose beaver you earnin', Caleb?" Summers asked again.

Tadlock had another question. He put it before Greenwood got around to Dick's. "I suppose they need men in California?"

Greenwood studied Tadlock with eyes the years had crowded around. Watching him, Evans thought he was a wise and tricky old varmint who would know how to play to Tadlock. He felt suddenly glad that Greenwood hadn't been on hand when the train pulled in yesterday but had just showed up today from a hunting trip or someplace. Give him time, and he would talk everyone into California, especially the women.

"Now as to that," Greenwood answered Tadlock, "she needs good men all right, and no denyin' it, but not just anybody. There's too many by-jesus anybodies everywhere to this coon's way of thinkin'. Needs 'em, I reckon, more'n Oregon does. Oregon's spillin' over with good men."

"What about the Mexicans?"

"Them Spaniards? They're all right. Leave 'em their blackrobes and the Pope, and they're right as Irish. Same time, I look fer to see Californy white men's country."

"And that's why you're eggin' us on?" Evans put in.

The old man spread his hands as if to show the all of him, heart and gizzard and mind and all. "You're readin' the sign wrong, son. Ain't I said Oregon's all right? But if so be it you point Californy-way, that's all right, too. An' it ain't no harm to think it belongs with the States. This nigger don't reckon you're goin' to Oregon just so's to be British?"

It was a good question, Evans thought, honest-seeming and with a point to it.

Captain Grant stirred at the words. "There are worse things than being a British subject."

"No offense, o' course," Greenwood said. "Every man to his mind, Cap'n. Every nigger to his nation."

"And whativer is wrong with the Irish?" Daugherty asked, pricked out of his silence by the old man's words.

"Niver a thing," Greenwood said back. "Niver a by-jesus thing."

"And you'll lead a train to the Sacramento?" Tadlock asked. Already, Evans knew, his mind was making up—and it was all right. Let Tadlock go, for he couldn't stand the Oregon train now he wasn't captain and had been whipped to boot. And let McBee go. Let him and his family go, and Mercy that Brownie had started to shine around. Let Brewer and his thick head go. The train didn't need numbers for safety any more.

Old Greenwood rubbed his hands and said, "Well, I don' know as you could call it a train. This nigger's got a busted wagon or so, and his stick points that way. Reckon I'll hang around a day or a dozen and see does any of the companies follerin' in your dust want to jine with me. There's a few early birds already has said yes?"

"I still say Oregon," Evans told him, and looked around to see what answer the words brought to the faces.

"Shore. Don't blame you a mite. You're big and stout. I bet you git there. An' prob'ly you'll like it. I know folks as does. Course, for the weak and ailin', I got to say maybe Californy's better, for the way's short and easy and 'pears like no one ever dies there."

"Damn if I can't believe that," Summers said. "What was it you heerd Lewis and Clark say to their mammies?"

Greenwood laughed an easy laugh. "You ain't so far wrong, young'un, but don't git it into your head I'm done fer. Whisky's stouter the longer she sets. You ain't sayin' the Snake ain't a by-jesus river, Dick, ner the Columbia, ner that a man don't go froze for meat and water?"

"Nup. Who's payin' you, Caleb?"

"Glad you asked me that. It's a honest question and desarvin' of a honest answer. Cap'n John Sutter down in the Sacramento valley, he figgered maybe some would want to come his way—not throwin' off on Oregon—and he says, 'Caleb, here's a little piece of money fer your old age, and whyn't you traipse to Hall so's to show any poor folks the way?' There's a good man, and one to make you welcome."

Evans said, "Tell him I'm obliged, but that them that goes with me will go to Oregon." Patch nodded to the words, and Daugherty and Mack and Gorham and Weatherby, and he understood with a little gush of good feeling that they were committed to Oregon like himself. The reason for it he didn't quite know. Was it just because they'd got their necks bent? Was it because they mistrusted Greenwood and kind of disliked Captain Grant, him being British? Was it because the thought of change just didn't set with them? It didn't matter. "I figger we'll make it," he said.

Captain Grant's voice had in it a touch of dander and a touch of giving up. "You Yankees will do whatever you set out to do, I suppose."

"We kin try."

"What is it you aim to do with the cattle?" Greenwood asked.

"Swim 'em. Didn't I tell you? Swim 'em down from the Dalles."

Summers stood up. Evans saw then that Brownie had come into the fort and stood back from the circle. He thought he saw trouble in the boy's face until he told himself it was just the darkening twilight putting shadows there. "Want me, boy?"

"No. There's—there's someone wants to talk to Dick."

Before Summers went to Brownie and walked with him to the big gate and disappeared outside, he grinned at Greenwood. "Caleb, them California beans sure work up a blow."

Chapter - - - - - - - - - - Twenty-Four

BROWNIE'S SAD-EYED, half-hound dog was waiting by the gate. He gave a slow wag of his tail as Summers and Brownie came out and fell into step behind them. "That your dog or your pa's, you figure?" Summers asked. He went on when Brownie didn't answer. "Or maybe Mercy McBee's. I see he's claimin' her, too. Where's this hoss wants to see me?"

Brownie walked on, silent, away from the fort.

"Where you say he's at?"

"Dick?"

"Uh-huh."

Brownie shuffled to a stop. He slid his eyes up to Summers and down to the ground. "You got time to talk to me?"

"Sure, boy. Time aplenty. Train don't roll till tomorrow."

"I got no business botherin' you, I reckon."

"You catched a party that loves to palaver. Jus' name your subject."

Brownie's lips tried a word or two, not making any sound. Not until then had Summers noticed the worry in his face.

"This is poor ground for talk, I'm thinkin'. Too all-fired open. Let's set somewheres."

Brownie nodded.

"Me, now, I can't hardly think to speak unless it's by water or a tree. River ain't so far."

Summers had thought maybe the boy would loosen up, walking, but he didn't. He just lagged along, his head bent as if from the weight in it. It could be he was waiting for the dark that was settling on the land. Words sometimes came easier when the mouth that made them couldn't be seen working. They passed a Shoshone lodge, and a fat-faced squaw watched them as if sight was the only life in her, and two ribby dogs ran out growling and held up at Rock's fierce answer.

"Glad you come and got me," Summers said. "It tired my tail

to hear ol' Greenwood talk of this an' that, as if naught but a cross of bird and beaver could make it to the Willamette."

Brownie asked without interest, "Is that what he was sayin?"

"Roundabout. Caleb allus comes up from behind. He snorted some of them hosses, too."

"Nothin' skeers you, I reckon, Dick, nor frets you."

"A heap of things, but not Greenwood."

They came to the river where the bank was open and sat down by it. Brownie picked up a piece of dead branch and tossed it in the water. It stayed in sight for a minute, and then the dark roll of the river took it. Rock sniffed along the shore, and, out of sight in the falling night, a fish leaped clear and smacked the water coming down.

"Fish'll do to live on in a fix," Summers said, "but they ain't like buffler. That's a trouble with Oregon, no buffler to speak of." For all the answer he got, he might as well not have spoken, but he let his voice run on, thinking words would lead to words. While he talked, he wondered what was in the boy to make him act so heavy. Nothing much, maybe. Young ones could build a pimple to a peak. "One day you'll want to foller up the Snake. That country's some, now, Jackson Hole and the Tetons and all, and Henry's Fork and the Yellowstone close by, that we used to call the Roche Jaune from the French. It's high land, top of the world, and pinched up so that water runs nigh any way you face. There's snow on her, and b'ilin' springs, and thunder underground. You best be thinkin' about a trip to her."

"Can't think of that, Dick. Not now."

"No?"

"I been thinkin' on marriage." The words came tight, the leanness of strain in them.

"Ain't nothin' wrong with that." Now that night had decided to set in, it had set in quick. From the corner of his eye Summers could see just the dim white of Brownie's face and the outline of his body, the shoulder slacked and the head down-turned.

"I don't know the answer to it."

Here was a spot for silence, Summers figured. Silence was the best come-on.

"I didn't know no one but you to come to."

Summers picked a grass stem and nibbled at it while he waited. There was the taste of fall in it already, the taste and toughness of fall.

"Maybe I got no rightful business talkin', to you or anybody. On'y I had to talk."

The night had taken in the far shore, so that land and water were just one. Rock came out of the darkness and smelled around them and snuffed away, following a trail in the grass.

"This can't git out, Dick."

"I allus forget to tell."

"I wouldn't be tellin' myself, except for thinkin' you could help me to the answers."

"It's yes or no, ain't it?"

"There's other things."

Answers, Summers thought while he waited. Brownie wanted answers. Always people wanted answers, the full and final, everlasting answers, not learning that answers answered only for the time, and none too well at that. His mind followed the idea along. What seemed true and right today was changed tomorrow. It all depended. On time and age and accident, and were your bowels all right. Brain and bowel went together, brain and bowel and body heat and the dream dreamed the night before. The brain made up its mind according but gave the credit all to self, standing high and prideful with its answer, not thinking that what it was thinking wouldn't be thought but for some outside partnership.

"Supposin', Dick—?"

"Just supposin'."

"Supposin' there was a girl, and a man aimed to marry her if she said yes?"

Again Summers held his tongue and waited for the tight, hard-spoken words.

"Supposin' he found out somethin' about her?"

"I'm follerin'."

"And might be she would have a baby?"

"Found out from who?"

"From her. And she didn't know if she cared for him and she

261

didn't know if she didn't, but she had to marry up with some-one?" Beyond the leanness of the tone, Summers caught a cry that stirred him the more because it was held in, the cry of hurt, the cry of not-understanding, the cry for help, the cry for answers.

"What about the man that done it, Brownie?"

"Goddam him, Dick! I'll kill him. I swear I'll kill him."

"Easy, hoss."

"Or tell the train and see him whupped for it."

"Easy."

"You think I won't!"

"I think you won't."

"Whatever do I do, Dick?"

"Might as well lay it open. I know it all but for the man."

"It's Mack."

"Wasn't none of my business to ask, Brownie. The who of him don't make no difference. Let's think on it." Summers searched for what was right to say. He tried to put himself in Brownie's place, tried to put there the him that used to be, not the him of now, worn hard and doubtful by the knocks of liv-ing. You couldn't tell a boy how few were the things that mat-tered and how little was their mattering. You couldn't say that the rest washed off in the wash of years so that, looking back, a man wanted to laugh except he couldn't quite laugh yet. The dreams dreamed and the hopes hoped and the hurts felt and the jolts suffered, they all got covered by the years. They buried themselves in memory. Dug out of it, they seemed queer, as a dug-up bone with the flesh rotted off of it might seem queer to the dog that had buried it.

And the rules that people set and broke and suffered from in the breaking? Like the rule against naturalness that animals had more sense than to deny? Like the rule that a girl couldn't lie with a man unless a preacher said amen? Big as it was now, how big would the lying seem to Brownie when the years had rubbed the fuzz off of him? How would Mack seem then? A man was a man by the nature of him and, grown up, knew himself in secret for what he was, unless he had an extra-sore religion. When a chance came, he took it, or, not taking, thought he was half a fool. The boy he had been came to look so soft and starry-headed that he shook his head and laughed, thinking of the good things he had missed.

Into the silence Summers said, "She didn't have to tell you, Brownie."

No matter, though, what the grown man learned, the dream was in the boy, like a green, high-growing shoot, the dream of goodness and happiness and never-ending love and true, right meanings. When a man lost it, he lost something that went to make life worth living. He lost something good, if foolish, and half his grown-up scorn of it came out of disappointment and half came from the buried doubt that the man was equal to the boy. So let the dream be dreamed, Summers thought. Let the shoot stand. He wouldn't cut it down, even if he could. Let time do it. Let life do it. It was work too dirty for a man.

"She didn't have to tell you, Brownie," he said again.

"I already told myself how honest it was of her."

"And she could've made out she took to you, 'stead of sayin' she didn't know."

"Maybe she never will take to me."

"I ain't in doubt about that."

The boy's voice had a kind of eagerness in it. "Ain't you, Dick?"

"Not a mite."

The voice sank back. "Even so, I don't know. A man don't like less than what he'd hoped."

No, thought Summers, leaving the words unsaid, a man didn't like to take less than he had hoped, but he had to take it. Maybe that was the big lesson, maybe that was all he'd learned and all that anyone could learn—always settle for half.

"Kin you git along without her, Brownie?"

"I don't feel so. Don't feel like I ever could. On'y—on'y—"

"There's your answer then," said Summers, and knew that there it was. Closer than his fool thought, closer than the wide ranging of his mind, there it was, plain as day. There it always had been, and he had seen it from the first but still had passed it by.

"How is it, Dick?"

"By God, take her!"

"You mean it?"

"An' never hold agin her what she's done. Put it out of mind. She'll make a smart wife."

"You think she's all right, don't you, Dick?"

It was confidence the boy wanted, and Summers tried to give it to him, saying, "Goddam it, why you ask a fool question like that! She's tip-top. She just ain't been favored in her pa or ma, and maybe thought what was the use, or maybe was carried beyond herself just because a nabob played up to her. Forgit, and take her, and count yourself lucky."

"Dick—?"

The one word wrenched out of Brownie, and Summers moved to get up, made uncomfortable and sorehearted by the tone of it. "That's all. Let's go. I done forgot what you told me."

"Didn't aim to be a baby. It's just what you said."

"Le's go!"

"And what if there is a baby?"

"It ain't hard to take up with a baby, no matter whose."

Brownie got to his feet. "I got to tell Pa that I'm marryin'."

"Lije'll be all right. He thinks just of you."

"I know't. I'm thankful to you, Dick."

"No cause fer it."

"Here, Rock! Where'd that dog go?"

"He's foolin' around somewheres."

"Maybe to see Mercy."

Walking back, Summers thought how mixed up was a man. Here was a bad thing, and he knew it for a bad thing, and yet, remembering the girl's grave face and the young and rounded lines of her, he could understand, with Mack, how the thing had come to be.

Chapter - - - - - - - - - - *Twenty-Five*

LIJE EVANS kicked his horse out ahead of the train, which was readying to roll. The wagons were supplied and repaired. The gab was gabbed. The marriage was done. So come on! Get started! Time to move. Can't spend the livelong day on a wedding and a lost dog. Snow'll be flying in Oregon before you know it. Follow along, Mr. and Mrs. George Brown Evans!

He set himself in the saddle and kicked Nellie again. The day was gray, and the wind blew cold, and it might rain before night, the driving, small-dropped rain that was different from a shower. Good day for a wedding. Good day for one wedding, anyhow. Good day to hook up with a McBee.

But there wasn't any point in stewing, or any point in thinking more. The milk was spilt. He would think about the trail or about the life ahead and the house he would build or about California and the folks who'd stayed behind to follow Greenwood—Tadlock and Brewer and Davisworth, and here was McBee in his thoughts again, in-law Hank McBee and his in-law brood. There was one thing, anyhow: he wouldn't have to put up but with one McBee. The picture wasn't all black. There was a little lining on the cloud, like on the blown rain cloud ahead.

He had cut McBee off when, just before the wedding, McBee had shown he might change his mind about going to California. "Never can tell what'll happen," McBee had said. There was a flicker in his muddy eye that Evans took for an invitation to be asked to trail along. "Pret' near wisht I hadn't quit the train."

"Prob'ly you'll like it in California."

"Oh, sure, sure. That's a good girl your boy's gettin'. Like I was sayin' "—the eye flickered again, this time, Evans thought,

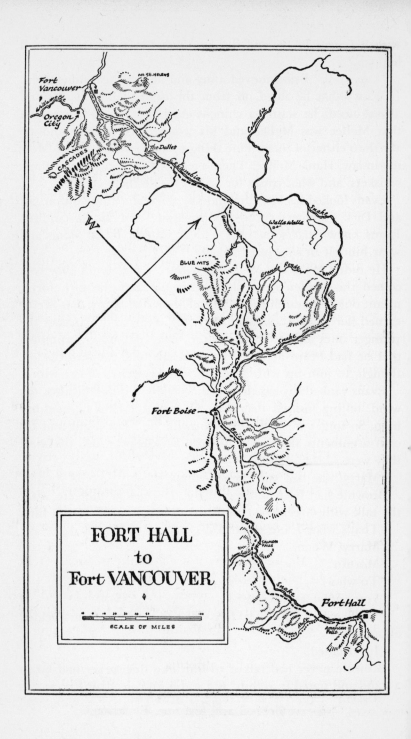

FORT HALL
to
Fort VANCOUVER

SCALE OF MILES

with a return of the old dislike—"you never can tell what'll happen."

"Can't tell." Evans moved away and figured he'd done right. It wasn't that he shied off from the help that McBee would always need; he wasn't a chinchy man, he hoped. It was just that McBee was McBee and his woman his woman, and no worth to either of them. Fine thing to have them around! Meet my in-law, Hank McBee. There's a face, I reckon, behind them whiskers, and what passes for a man inside them clothes.

Evans looked back of him and saw the train lining out at last and Dick Summers riding by the lead team, understanding, Evans knew, that sometimes a man wanted to be alone and wear himself in to a hurtful fact.

He didn't guess the McBees felt hurt. Like as not they welcomed the sudden news about Brownie and the girl, for it meant one less mouth to feed, though he had to say that Mercy earned her keep. She helped with the meals and managed the younger ones and often drove the team and never grumbled that he had heard about. Likely her ma and pa were tickled, though, to join up with a family that kept their noses wiped.

Evans yanked his hat tight and cocked a shoulder against the wind, telling himself that what he couldn't help he couldn't help. So forget it. And forget Brownie and last night and his own arguments that came to nothing. Spent wind, that's all they were.

"Marry!" he had said, unbelieving.

Brownie had been waiting in the darkness at the gate, after the talk with Greenwood, and had drawn him off to tell him.

"That's what I aim to do, Pa."

"Marry! When?"

"Mornin'."

"To who?"

"You know. To Mercy."

"Well, now, wait—look, boy—it ain't a thing to be decided all at once."

"It's decided."

Brownie never had talked to him like this, never had taken a stand and stated it so thin- and stubborn-voiced as if no words could budge him. Evans found himself wishing for light, so he could see the boy's face and the boy could see his. In the dark they were just two voices. He grabbed at what came to mind. "Them McBees—old Hank, now—"

"It ain't him I'm marryin'."

"That's what you think!"

"It don't matter, anyhow."

"You talked to him?"

"Not yit."

"Or the girl?"

"She's waitin'."

"She know her ma and pa's goin' to California?"

"That don't matter, either. But I won't be marryin' ol' Hank then, like you said I would."

"You ain't but a long seventeen."

"I'm older'n you was, and it worked out good."

"Can't get a license here. Can't do it proper."

"We kin sign a paper, I reckon, and there's Brother Weatherby."

Everything he said, it seemed to Evans, was made to turn against him. He tried to fight down the anger that grew out of his helplessness. "Just wait'll we git to Oregon, and if you feel the same then, we'll do it up right."

"Unless I marry her, she won't be goin' to Oregon, for you said her fambly wasn't. Anyhow, I ain't willin' to wait. Neither of us."

"You been talkin' to Dick. I seen you go out with him."

"Don't hold it agin him, Pa. It was bound to come."

"How you know this girl is what you want? Don't hardly know her but to pass the time of day."

"Don't say nothin' bad about her, please, Pa. I just know. She's all right, an' more'n that. It's just you can't see her for her fambly."

"Cats breeds cats."

"Please, Pa!"

"That's the way it is."

"Don't say nothin' to come between me and you!"

Evans asked what he wouldn't have asked if he had had time to think. "You mean it's her over me? And over your ma?"

The answer was a long time coming, but it came solid. "If I got to choose."

Evans made himself hold silent. Out of the thoughts that ran inside his head, he tried to catch a good one, one good enough to make the boy consider. While he tried, anger died in him, leaving just its ashes. "You owe it to your ma to talk to her, Brownie."

"I got to see Mercy."

"Not meanin' you won't talk to Ma?"

"Not about if I do or don't—but I'll talk to her."

"There's no changin' you, I reckon?"

"I'm sorry, Pa, and sorrier it riles you."

"It's you I'm tryin' to think of."

"Then don't be upset. I'm doin' what I want."

"I can't feel you're sure of that."

"I'm sure."

"You fixed things up with Weatherby?"

"Not yet."

"And got no tent or anything?"

"We kin sleep out, or under a wagon."

"Just married and sleep under a wagon!"

"Well—"

Evans found himself hurrying to say, "Never mind," knowing by the boy's voice that he was mortified and being somehow mortified himself.

"We'll make out somehow."

"If nothin'll hold you, I'll trade for a tent."

"Pa!"

"You're a man now, I reckon, and I ain't got the eye to see it, rememberin' baby days. An' I'll see Weatherby if you're still sot come mornin'."

Evans turned away, feeling heavy-footed. "Where's Rock?"

"He went off somewheres."

Thinking back, Evans couldn't make up better words than those he'd said. There wasn't a word that would have stopped the wedding, no word or way or reason, unless it was the outright no he couldn't bring himself to use. The boy wouldn't be drawn back from where his will had taken him. He wouldn't come to call any more than Rock would. Where in tarnation was the dog?

Evans glanced behind him, half expecting to see Rock loping up, but all he saw between him and the train was the grass running patterns before the wind. He wasn't anxious, though, not very, for Rock would show up in course of time. Probably he had come on a bitch in heat, which was about the only thing that would keep him gone so long, from night before to going on to noon.

Maybe, Evans thought, he should have hunted more, but the morning already was halfway gone, thanks to the wedding, and the company had to roll out miles. And he hated to own up to it, but he had felt a little foolish and exposed, whistling around the fort and by the outside of Indian lodges while Tadlock looked on, smiling wise, as if to say I told you, way back at the start, that dogs would hold you up. It wasn't Tadlock that forced him on, though. It was time and time a-passing and last night's talk of snow, and he already sore inside at what his boy had done. The dog would turn up. That's what he had told Brownie, who wasn't so carried off by marriage as to forget about old Rock, and that was what he looked to happen. Rock would just turn up, his mouth open in what went for a grin, his eyes remembering from the night. Meantime the train must move. You couldn't ask the folks to keep on waiting just for a misplaced dog, no matter if the dog was Rock.

Evans slid over in the saddle and cocked the other shoulder to the wind. Except for the weather coming at him, a man wouldn't think that hard miles lay ahead. The road looked pretty open, as if swift crossings and rough mountains were just dreamed up in Greenwood's head. Three hundred miles to Boise, or something close to that. More by way of Walla Walla, which way they wouldn't go since Summers said it wasn't needful. Eight hundred miles to the home they hadn't seen. Eight hundred to the new life. Giddap, horse.

Take away the gray sky, take away the wind, and things looked gentle—cattle grazing, horses grazing, a bunch of Indians bound for Hall, their horses dragging poles on which their goods were loaded, green grass growing, tall grass growing, trees fringed along the Snake. But the gray sky was here, and the wind, and they put a man in mind of winter. Winter would be along soon. The smell of it was in the air, like the smell of a thing out of sight, beyond the bend. It made a man feel half like saying enough, half like staying the season out in the grassy Fort Hall bottoms and maybe staying longer. Cattle could be grown here, and horses, and probably crops, though not a spade of earth had been turned; and the Indians would get over being meddlesome and pecky. Just what pushed people on? Evans asked, and didn't bother thinking why, for reasons seemed no good today. It was enough to answer that Oregon had put a spell on them.

It had put a spell on all of them except for Tadlock and Davisworth and Brewer and McBee except for one McBee, and he would try to act like real kinfolks to that one McBee like Rebecca told him to. Rebecca had taken the news quiet, as if she'd seen it coming, and hadn't argued that he knew of, or scolded, or asked Brownie to wait. She had talked with him a long time, while Evans kept himself away, not trusting himself to speak more about it. He had gone to bed finally and had heard their voices a piece off from the tent just as a murmur. Rebecca didn't speak when she first came back but undressed quietly and came to bed and by and by put her hand on his shoulder, knowing somehow that he didn't sleep. "Maybe it ain't the way I might hope, Lije," she whispered so that Brownie wouldn't hear.

"It ain't the way I'd hoped."

"But still it might turn out to be. You hold yourself in, Lije."

"I told him if he was sot, all right."

"I recollect when you was young. Think on it, Lije."

"I got me a real woman."

"Might be he has. She's a good young'un. Don't judge too quick."

"Seems like you think it's just fine."

Her hand patted him. "We got to take what comes and make the best of it and not the worst. You be nice to her."

What chafed him was he knew that she was right. He said, "I'd just as leave not talk tonight. I'm tired, and cranky too, I reckon."

But in the morning—it was just this morning, come to think of it—what worried her was what the girl would wear. Women were queer sometimes, even Becky. It turned out the girl was dressed all right. Had shoes on and a dress with a frilly collar. And she had twisted her hair up in a way that made her face look frail. And pretty. Prettier than ever. There was no denying the girl was pretty.

Weatherby had done the trick quick, knowing the train must move, but still the knot was likely tight enough—too tight, it might turn out. Weatherby had been pleased at a marrying, maybe because it was the opposite of the funerals he had had to preach, promising life instead of marking the end of it. How did it go? What God hath joined together, let no man put asunder?

The picture of the wedding stood in Evans' mind as he hunched into the wind that got inside his clothes and felt around his ribs—the men and women gathered in the Fort Hall yard, so's to be in shelter, and a few favorite Indians with them, wondering at the white man's medicine, and Brownie standing stiff and the girl indrawn and pale, and Weatherby asking in his preacher's voice if one took the other, come hell or heaven, and Ma McBee crying and her eyes red and her nose sharp standing between, and McBee acting important, as if, 'y God, except for him there wouldn't be any such big doings as now.

It was a friendly train, except for one or two, and good-wishing for the man and wife. Just wait'll we get to Oregon, they had promised, and we'll have a housewarmin' as is a housewarmin'. Mack had even tried to give a yoke of oxen as a wedding present, and Brownie had refused it, acting not polite enough, as if the gift would show he couldn't come it by himself.

So it was done, and there was winter in the air, or the foretaste of it. By the time it came, God willing, he would be in Oregon and have a cabin building. He could imagine himself

272

in it. He was sitting in it, and a fire was burning in the new fireplace, and outside the rain pattered or the snow flurried or the wind whined, and he was safe and snug, planning what to do when the storm let up. There he was, and Becky with him, and Brownie. And Mrs. George Brown Evans, who had been Mercy McBee. You remember the McBees? Hanks of homespun hung from the walls, and gourds sat on a shelf, holding seeds for the spring planting. There was the smell of roasting meat in the cabin, making Rock look hungry, and the sweetness of cookies, or was it bread a-baking. Right smart house we built, eh, boy? It'll do to keep the weather out. 'Member that wind leavin' Fort Hall? 'Member how chill we was? Makes this time real cozy, eh?

He sat in the cabin while he rode his horse, and he saw a thing far off, toward the touch of land and sky. A dead buffalo, he thought it was from the size of it, or more likely an elk or a cow or ox, and maybe not dead but only sick or resting. He studied it while his mind sat rocking in the new house on the Willamette. There were some skins on the wall, a bear that Brownie had brought down and a deer hide with the red of the fall woods in it. Come decent weather and we'll build you a cabin, Brownie, and put a floor in this one. Can't hardly wait on weather to start all the work that nudges to be done.

The thing wouldn't be as big as a cow, he saw now. Even on a gray day you couldn't trust your sight in country where a lark loomed hefty as a hen. Lying on the open flat where the wind could tear at it, the thing seemed lonesome. It made the world seem lonesome.

The could-be of it pinched him suddenly, and he pulled his horse up, not ready to believe, while his eyes said no and yes. They found the legs, the trunk, the head, the white-sprigged hair and put them all together. "Rock!" he said into the wind. "Hey, you, Rock!" He heeled his horse into a walk.

He sat still in the saddle when he had come to him, seeing, and numbed by seeing, the big head knocked in and one eye pushing from its socket and the old muzzle stained by blood. A bug crawled on the mouth, fighting the wind.

He took the sights in, one by one, but what he saw was Rock, the sprawly pup, Rock back at home and Brownie just a pup himself and the two growing up together, making the place cheerful with barks and cries and playful fracases. What he saw was Rock with age coming on him and wisdom in him and the graying muzzle resting on his knee.

He climbed down from the saddle and stooped and lifted a paw and knew by the stiffness of the lift that this was not a fresh-done thing.

Feeling ran far off from him, as if at something old in memory, while his mind worked at the how and why and who. He remembered Tadlock and his smile and looked back toward the fort and saw the ox train winding slow, a mile or so away. But it wasn't Tadlock. For all his faults Tadlock was too much a man for this.

Who, then? He didn't need to ask again. He knew as well as a man could know. "Never can tell what'll happen." The flicker in the muddy eye. They were McBee's way of letting him know, of making sure he wouldn't miss the knowing. They were the last laugh. They were the getting even for all the wounds to little pride. And he had taken them for something else, disremembering that he had warned himself to look out for sneaky tricks.

He brushed the bug off the mouth, feeling the blood hard and crusted against his knuckles. He closed the fist afterwards and studied it, recalling what it did to Tadlock, and he looked back again and saw the train still winding. He couldn't see the fort from so low on the ground, but it would be there, it and Hank McBee. In-law Hank McBee.

But anger wasn't in him yet, but just the far-off sorrow, and he waited for a what-to-do while his mind worked on to put the case together. McBee had thought it safe to do the deed, since he was parting from the train. Maybe he had walked from the fort last night, his mind made up for California, and seen the old dog dozing by his wagon, waiting for Mercy to come back from somewhere, and the scheme had broken on him like a sudden light, and he had used a hammer or an ax heel or a

274

club and had put the dead dog on a horse and packed him out and dumped him down where any eye would see. And then he had ridden back, smiling in his whiskers, thinking likely Evans wouldn't turn around, once started with the train, to push a point there at the fort that he had no proof about.

"Never can tell what'll happen"? What did that add up to? McBee was too sly to catch himself on words. It could even be, Evans thought without believing, that McBee was trying to excuse himself this morning, trying to say he'd've acted different if he'd known about the marriage at the time.

So what to do? Go back and fight? Beat the last laugh from the bushy mouth? Revenge old Rock, who'd been done in through no offense of his? Fight, and let the thing be known? Then what about Brownie and his new-wed wife and the damage possible to them? Brownie wouldn't blame her for a deed done by her pa, but still they'd know the shadow of it, both of them, and feel poor-mated, maybe, if their fathers fought.

Evans straightened up. The train had crawled closer, and there was just one thing to do. A poor thing but the best. Brownie mustn't ever know, or Mercy or even Becky or anyone but him and Hank.

He brought the horse around between him and the train and picked up Rock's stiff body and placed it across the saddle and got on behind, shielding it from any gaze that was sharp enough to see.

Down toward the river there was a thick patch of woods. He rode to the far side of it and got off and carried the body deep inside and laid it down. "I reckon you understand, Rock?" he said out loud, not caring if the words were foolish. He looked back afterwards and saw Rock didn't look quite comfortable and turned around and straightened out a leg.

Outside the woods the wind was blowing rain.

Chapter - - - - - - - - - - - Twenty-Six

IT SEEMED to Evans now that one day was like another and that all were bad. They were all work and worry and weariness, and dust and sun and wind and night and sun again and work again. He tried to whistle up the old, bold hope, but it had disappeared. It had ground out under the grind of wheels. It had lost itself in crazy heights and depths. It had thinned away in distance. Trying for it, the eye misted. Listening, the ear filled with the dry complainings of wheels and wagon boxes. Eight miles, fifteen, eight, twenty-three. It didn't matter. This sorry land was endless.

Day on day, dust on dust, pitch and climb and circle while the sand rasped under the worn tires and the rocks clattered and the wounded sage oozed out its smell. Where's grass? Where's water? Critters gant and hard to keep together overnight. Faces lank and eyes empty, or pointed suddenly, thinking forward to the ford across the Snake. Women cross, and young ones too, and men sharp-worded through their dusted lips, quick with whip and goad on teams too tired to care.

Violent country. Land of fracture and of fire, boiled up and broken when God first made the world. Range of rattlesnake and jackass rabbit and cactus hot as any hornet. Homeland of the poor and poisonous, and did Oregon really lie beyond? Mountains near and others far, sliding in and out of sight, plaguing people for their brashness. The great gorge of the Snake, the very gut of earth, the churning gut so steep below a horseman couldn't ride to it, so far a walker wore out climbing down and back. Eight miles, twenty, twelve. And still it didn't matter.

Evans knew this time would pass. He was right to try for Oregon. He had been all along. It was just that the country overpowered the mind. It was just that a man spent his hope in sweat. It was just that he couldn't think ahead for watching out against the here. It was partly that old Rock was dead and the place empty where he would have trotted. And partly it was Brownie's marriage, though not so much as once, and the manner of the man and wife, as if they had to take their state dead serious. Why, Evans thought, when he had first hooked on to Becky he was all laugh and prank and couldn't always keep his hands off her no matter if they weren't alone. No cause to take the thing so solemn even though the dog was gone. This was a time for frolic. For frolic, but for work for all.

He couldn't believe, back there at the fort, that the road would be so hard. For two days afterwards he couldn't believe it yet, while the train rolled to the Portneuf crossing and on to American Falls. There were springs above the falls and a river island that gave good grazing to the stock. But already, he remembered, the grassy bottoms of the fort had grown to sandy, sagy plains, and the Snake was scouring deep. The next day and the days that followed showed him what his mind's eye couldn't see.

No one day tired the outfit out, and no one thing. Day on day did it, and sand on rock on sage on drought. The sense of getting nowhere did it, the feeling that the train stood still in spite of straining wheels. The stingy treats of green and water, although welcome, served to make the gray miles worse. A man's mind turned back to them afterwards, as Evans' mind had turned back to the Raft. Here the California trail veered left, up a shallow valley toward a ragged peak a million miles away. Here Greenwood and Tadlock and their men would start the journey south. But it wasn't the thought of them that kept coming to him later, while grasshoppers clattered off on dusty wings. It was the thought of water and of grass. It was the remembered munching of the stock. It was the fresh wetness on the tongue.

He put the Raft with the marsh they'd bedded by one night, when he had heard the tear of grass to hungry mouths, far into dreams. He put it with a campsite that the Snake made, rising from its cut. He put it with Rock Creek and with Salmon Falls. They put a cheerless hunger in him while the sunken-sided teams dragged on to the crossing of the Snake.

A river out of hell, the Snake, or a river still in hell! A river making hell for burning souls who couldn't get down to it. Summers had called him off one day, and they had teetered on the great lip of its gorge and peered below and seen it like a frothy ribbon, so lessened by its depth away that Evans had to tell himself that here was such tormented water as he had never seen. A fair-sized falls and fair-sized water running white, sending up a fair-sized rumble—and what it was was sweep and plunge and thunder like nothing that he quite could believe.

He had pulled back, dizzy, and the question inside him must have shown, for Dick had said, "We'll ford her just the same."

Evans had asked, "We could go round the loop, like someone said at Hall, and so dodge both the crossings?"

"Could," Dick said while his eyes answered no. "Just as well drown as starve, though, I'm thinkin'. You want to lose your last damn head of stock?" He smiled. "The river calms down some. We'll make it, hoss."

It was hard to think so, though, remembering how they'd had to bed above. Once they'd pushed the stock away from camp a mile or more and found a way down to the river more fit for goats than cattle. But here was water and a little grass, and they'd left the livestock there, just lightly guarded, and had packed back water for the camp. And once, late starting after hunting wandered cows, they had camped entirely dry and found the stock more scattered in the morning.

That was a thing that bothered a man—the thirst and growing weakness and most of all the hunger of cattle and horses and teams. Driving, a teamster saw the sagging pockets beyond the hipbones of his oxen and the chained knuckles of their backs. When he unyoked, they looked at him softly, their eyes reproachful, as if to ask how he could treat them so. And sometimes under yoke they just lay down, and no goad or whip or fork could get them up again, and a man trying felt more brutish than his brutes. They left them where they lay, with what life remained in them, thinking they had earned the slim chance of a miracle, and sometimes put plunder from the wagons with them—a chest or favorite chair or grinding stone —for every pound now counted. Leaving such, Daugherty had scratched a sign and posted it close by for travelers coming later. It said, "Help yourself." It also said weariness and the sour humor growing out of it. It said help yourself, only you can't, you poor devil like me, and so the joke's on you.

Coming on to good campsites, on to grass and easy water, men and women always tried to believe the hardest miles were rolled. For a little while—until they pulled again into the waste of sand and stone—their spirits lifted and their voices rang out full. That was the way of them at Salmon Falls Creek, where everything was plenty, and at Salmon Falls. Though grass and fuel were scanty at the falls, the Indians had fresh salmon and cakes of pounded berries to trade for clothing, powder, knives and fishhooks. Most of all for fishhooks, which Dick had thought to bring aplenty of. Fresh meat tasted good, even salmon, after days of chewing on dried stuff, eaten stiff or mushed up in a pot, though Evans came to feel he'd just as soon not see a fish again if he could have red meat. And the berry cakes were better yet.

Seeing the Salmon Falls Indians, Evans knew why Summers spoke so low of the fish-eating tribes. They were friendly and talkative and sometimes funny, but childish-minded and dirty and naked except maybe for a lousy rabbit skin, and they ate anything—lizards and grasshoppers and pursy crickets that would gag a man. They lived in huts of grass and willow that were just half-circles, open to the south. The huts reminded him of swallows' nests, niched around the way they were, except that birds were better builders.

The camp had been a good camp anyhow, or not so bad as some, no matter if grass and wood were scarce and the Indians pretty sorry. A change of victuals helped the train, as did the proof that human life of sorts could live in such a country. And the great springs that burst out of the solid north wall of the Snake gave the people something new to talk about. Spring after spring, there was, like sunken rivers pouring out, which Summers called the Chutes.

More sand came afterwards, more sage, more rocks, more no-grass, more no-water, more worn-out stock, more of the hell of the Snake though they had borne out from it to cut across a bend it made.

Now when they were about to come to it again, to lower down the bluff and try the ford, Evans told himself that if any train could get to Oregon, this one could. It had the best pilot that he knew of, best man and pilot both. Its stock was poor but no poorer than would come behind. Its wagons were as good as others would be by the time they reached the ford. But it was the men he counted on, the men and women and spirit of the company. They had their faults, he knew. They had their differences and sometimes spoke severe, what with sand in their teeth and worries in their heads, but they wished well for one another and they hung together. Here where sometimes he'd heard the trains split up, old On-to-Oregon stayed one. Looking down the line from head to tail after the long drop to the Snake came into sight, he felt a kind of wrathy pride. Damn the Snake and all its sorry kin of sage and sand! Damn the crossing! They'd make it—he and Summers and Patch and Mack and Daugherty and Shields and Gorham and all the rest, clear down to Byrd. They'd make it or go down trying and still damn the Snake to do its damnedest.

Once he'd wondered if they'd keep him captain. That was when he'd outfought Tadlock and dared the other men to try to hang the Indian, but nothing came of it except they showed in little ways they didn't hold a grievance, maybe knowing without saying that they had been wrong. Only Daugherty had spoken open, saying, "I'm hopin' you'll forgit it, Captain. It was the divil in us, temptin' us to mortal sin." He had grinned and added, as if to give warning that he was his own man yet, "An' let us hope them Injuns quit their thievin' ways, or else to hell I'll maybe travel still."

They were for him, Evans told himself while he watched Dick coming into sight from below the brow of the bluff. They were for him and he was for them and each was for each other, and they'd get across the Snake and pull up safe in Oregon.

Summers rode alongside to say, "We can make it, I'm thinkin', without hold-back ropes or anything. Steep but not too bad."

"Hold up!" Evans called to Patch, whose two wagons were in the lead ahead of him. He lifted his hand for a stop behind. The rearward wagons closed up slow and came to rest, the oxen dragging to a halt without command and sagging afterwards as if from the little weight of yoke. He said to Summers, "Maybe we better hitch a rope to the first wagon and some of us walk along, just in case."

Summers gave a nod.

Evans faced down the line and yelled through his hands, "All out!" though nearly everybody was. The call was relayed to the rear by other voices. He waited, watching, until the last of them was down. The last was Mrs. Byrd, moving heavy with the child in her, and it occurred to Evans, seeing her, that he might as well have let the people sit until their turns came up. He stepped down the line, motioning to the nearest men. "Mack! Fairman! Carpenter!" Brother Weatherby came up with them, gray as a desert grasshopper from marching in the dust to save his horse. "Summers thinks we can drive down all right, but let's the bunch of us walk down with the lead wagon and see how it goes. We can stop her if she wants to run."

They followed him back to the head of the column, where Patch stood with his lead team and Summers waited to show the way. One of them had tied a rope to the rear axle. Mrs. Patch stood back with the second team, quiet as always and as always somehow noticeable. Evans thought while he spoke that you couldn't throw off on these two Yankees. They were cool and heady customers. He said, "All right, Dick. You ne'en to help, Brother Weatherby."

Weatherby said, "Why not?" as if there wasn't any answer, not even his sixty-four years.

Patch popped his whip and the oxen leaned into the yoke and the wheels turned and the front ones headed down.

The way was long and steep, but not so steep by Dick's meandering that two or three men, depending on the load and team, couldn't manage trouble if it came. Patch's outfit reached the bottom without real need of help. Still, it seemed wise to send men with each wagon.

The plan took time and wind but worked out safe. The loose

stock came behind, footing careful down the pitch and breaking to a heavy, stumbling run for water. Evans saw, before he went to look across the ford, that grass was scant here too. It added to his maybe-foolish load of worry to think that poor teams would make a poor out at getting through the Snake.

The crossing didn't look so risky, though, being broken by two islands that sat like low rafts in the stream.

"It's far across and swift," he said to Summers and the other men who'd lined up along the bank, "but it don't look so deep."

"Deeper'n you'd think," Summers answered. "Water's so clear it makes the bed look close."

"How deep?" Evans glanced up at Summers, sitting thoughtful on his horse.

Summers shrugged. "Not too deep. Way to look at it is, it ain't easy, but it ain't beyond doin', either. We'll make it."

Evans tilted his head and saw the white sun veering down. "Dick," he said, "there's grass aplenty on them islands."

"Plenty."

Evans spoke to the others as well as to Summers. "Let's push the livestock to 'em and let 'em get their bellies full and then line out in the morning. They'll be rested and fed both."

It was Byrd who answered first, saying, "Amen to that." In his fair, ungrown-up face Evans caught the shadow of alarm, and he wondered, as before, how the man had raised the spunk to start out in the first place. He belonged in town.

Summers was saying, "Good idee," and the rest were nodding.

"Let's circle up, though maybe there's no need of it, and git the work stock over."

While he and Brownie freed their teams, Evans thought again of Byrd, thought of him with a little of embarrassment, as if Byrd's weaknesses rested on him. Like some other unmanly men he'd known, Byrd must be a clever man in bed, judging by the flock he'd fathered. It was vexatious to feel responsible for him, and yet he did and more so maybe than with most, remembering the words that Mack had overheard and told him. Back there at Fort Hall Tadlock was working on

Byrd, arguing for California. Byrd had answered, "I'll stay with Evans and Summers. If any can, those two will see the train through."

To Evans there was a kind of womanish faith in that answer that, right or wrong, seemed to put an extra burden on him.

He laid the yoke down and let the team step out and saw his in-law daughter looking at him. "Wore out?" he asked, making himself smile.

She gave him just the ghost of an answering smile. "I'm all right."

Evans was up early. The dark still hung here in the bottom though overhead the sky was lightening. He stopped outside his tent and looked off to the water, seeing it as just a fluid dullness, without the shine of sun or moon or stars. The voice of it came to him, the whishing mutter of its strength. All night he'd heard it, even through his dreams.

He shook himself against the chill, against the inward funkiness of early morning, wishing with a sudden impatience that all the camp was up, ready for a try that weighed heavier with waiting. Right now, with the blood flowing weak in him after sleep and the dark cast of dawn lying on his spirit, damn if he wasn't as bad as Byrd, empty-chested before a danger built up in the mind. They'd get across, down to the last setting hen and chick. It was his being head rooster that put the foolish fidgets in him.

He walked down toward the water, flushing up a ground bird that rustled out of sight. Close up, the river still ran black. He couldn't see the bottom of it. Out in the stream the islands floated like clouds made out at night. The shapeless movement that he saw might be the livestock, getting up to graze.

They'd got the stock out there all right and afterwards, after food and coffee, had made light of the crossing, saying shoo, it wasn't anything. Critters now and then had had to swim and the current sure enough was swift, but still it wasn't anything. And, with grass and rest, the teams would be still stronger.

They'd soon see how it was, Evans thought, while there slipped into his mind the way the river reared against the horse he'd used to drive the loose stock over. The eastward sky was showing red. An hour or so, and they would see. There was just breakfast to get and eat and clean up after, and tents to strike and loads to load and the stock to push back and hitch. Then they'd see.

Except for being unloaded, the wagons were ready, or as ready as the place allowed. By Dick's advice the men had gone wood hunting yesterday and had found a little, mostly smallish-sized. Evans had thought it next to nothing, not much more than good enough for fires, and had said to Summers, "Them poles wouldn't float a cart."

"Don't aim to float the wagons, Lije. Not here."

"Don't?"

"Tide's too stiff. A floatin' wagon might draw the teams along with it."

"So what?"

"What we want is for the wheels to set solid on the bottom. We'll lay the wood on top the wagon boxes—that'll give us extry weight—and h'ist the flour and such on top of it, so's to keep it dry."

There wasn't wood enough to help out much. Here and there the men had found a small and lonesome tree and here and there a piece of punky drift. They laid their pickings over the wagon beds and, to piece them out and get the spoilables above the waterline, used plows and pack saddles and boxes emptied into others.

Evans turned away from the river, hearing sounds in camp, and saw Summers riding up. Behind him the arches of the wagons had divided from the dark.

"Got 'er figgered out, Lije?" Summers asked.

"Sure. All we have to do is cross and then think about the second crossing."

"Second ain't so bad. Close to Boise, too, where there's help if need be." Summers smiled while his eyes studied Evans' face. "You sleep any?"

"Sure."

"Ain't no sartain-sure way against accidents, Lije. If'n one happens, no one'll fault you 'less you do yourself."

"I know that."

"Know it but can't feel it," Summers answered, gazing off beyond the river. "That's what makes you a good captain, I reckon, but it's hard on the gizzard." His eyes came back to Evans. "I swear, Lije, back in Missouri I never thought to see you playin' mother hen."

"Me neither."

"Best put four yoke, anyhow, to a wagon, an' up to six to some."

"That'll mean usin' some teams twicet."

Summers bobbed his head. "With a long string of critters, enough will have footin' if others has to swim."

"I see."

"An', Lije, I'm thinkin' we need a rider at each side, upstream and down. Up man could have a hold-rope on the lead ox nearest him."

"Down man would have a poke, I reckon. Which side is dangerest?"

"Down, I figger. Yonder there's a ripple it would be bad to sag below. Let swimmers do the ridin', Lije."

"That's a job for me then."

"You're a fish," Summers answered, nodding. "Hig's hard to beat, I seen down on the Bear."

"I'll ask him."

Summers clucked to his horse. "Thought I'd scout acrost and find out how to go."

Evans watched the horse take to the river. He saw it splash in, unwilling but helpless under Dick's strong hand, and brace against the sweep and feel ahead for footholds while the water rose. At one place it had to swim, and Dick lifted himself to keep from getting any wetter than he had to. They came out, streaming, on the nearer island.

Evans faced around and made for camp. There was other work to do while Dick did his.

The sun was above the hills by the time the train was ready. Evans had put his own wagons first in line, six yoke to the big one, four to the small, thinking it his duty to try the danger first. The other wagons curled behind his, some prepared to go,

285

some waiting for ox teams to come back. People stood by them or perched inside or watched from on the bank, their talk littled by the thought of things to come.

Sitting his horse by the lead yoke, Evans squirmed around. His eyes met those of Brownie, who sat in the big wagon with Mercy by his side. He rode back toward them and pulled up and said, "I still don't like it. Let's have a try at her, with me up there, before you young'uns launch."

"We argued that out once, Pa," Brownie answered. "Lemme take the first team over. Me and Mercy ain't afraid. We got to go over sometime."

"Later's better, after we see."

"If all was to wait, you'd have to bring the wagons back to carry 'em across. Three crossings, that'ud make."

Evans flicked the end of the bridle reins against his opened palm, weighing one thing against another though he knew the choice was made. Young ones were hard to scare, believing they would live forever. Danger was a tonic to them. Why, right now, this minute ahead of risk, there was a looking-forward in their faces, a keen excitement more fit for new-joined man and wife than the sober manner that he'd wondered at. His gaze traveled back to the second wagon, where Becky sat, anxious but contained, as if she told herself here was a thing they had to meet.

"Never won an argument in my life," he said to the couple while he grinned at them. "Keep on Dick's tail now."

He remembered then he had put aside his goad. He rode to the second wagon and picked it from the wheel it slanted against. "Goin' to make it, Becky," he said. "Goin' to get to Oregon."

Her eyes were solemn. "You be careful, Lije. I'm as scared for you as anybody."

He raised the goad, saying with it that he would, and reined around.

They were waiting for him, Hig mounted yon side of the string, the rope from the near leader's horns dangling in his hand, and Dick ready to lead away.

"Reckon we're set," he said to Dick and saw that Dick's gaze was fixed behind. Turning, he saw Byrd hurrying up.

"Evans," Byrd said, "I'm nervous—about the children."

"They'll be all right."

"I know, but do you suppose you could take them?"

"First trip?"

"Your wagons are better and your teams stronger."

"You kin use my oxen."

"I just have the one wagon, too."

"Makes a big load all right," Evans answered, remembering how Byrd's light and flimsy second wagon had gone to pieces on the Green.

"And I'm not much of a teamster." Byrd spoke as if he'd like to think there were other things he was pretty much of.

"Don't take a teamster. Just takes a setter."

"Still—"

"Whyn't you wait until we try her out?"

"I'd like for the children to go in your wagons," Byrd said simply.

There it was again, Evans thought, the womanish faith in him, the clinging confidence that made him feel half sheepish but somehow answerable. "Bring 'em up if you're bound to," he said.

There were nine Byrd children, not counting the one unborn. Byrd herded them up. The oldest in the bunch was Jeff, who was maybe twelve and fair and open-faced like his father. He climbed into Brownie's wagon and took the toddler that Byrd lifted up. Three others climbed in after him. The rest would wait for Becky's wagon.

"Ready," Evans said.

"Here we go, hoss," Summers said to Brownie. He kicked his horse and reined around. Brownie hollered at the team.

The oxen took to the water slowly, staring out across it as if to calculate their chances. Already the current was bucking against Dick's horse.

Here was the deepest part, from shore to nearer island, the deepest but not the swiftest or the riskiest. The water climbed fast, up the legs of the leaders, to their bellies, up their bellies, streaming around the little dams that their bodies made. Evans wrenched his horse close, so as to be able to use the poke.

The lead yoke sank into a hole and lined out, swimming, giving to the current, their chins flattened on the surface. Evans punched at them, shouting, "Gee! Gee!" above the washing of the water. He felt the cold climb up his legs and felt his horse change gait, from jolt to fluid action, and knew that it was swimming. He held it short-reined, angled against the stream, while he worked the goad. Across the swimming backs he saw Hig's rope tighten like a fiddle string.

The leaders caught a foothold and staggered on and drew the next yoke over, and Evans looked behind him and saw the wagon lurching and Brownie grinning wide and Mercy holding the Byrd baby like the mother of it.

The island neared. In the wide and busy water it was as if the island swam to them. The oxen pulled up on it and drew the wagon after.

"How's that?" Evans yelled to Brownie while the team held up to blow.

The answer had the tone of spirit in it. "Ought to be hitched to a duck."

"Watch them wheelers do their part."

Summers led them across the island and angled upstream, and the water bore on them again and the oxen leaned into it, pitching on the tricky bottom, fighting upward step by step while the wagon balked behind. The second island was close at hand before Dick made a leftward turn and led them out where wheel tracks scarred the banks.

They stopped again to let the oxen catch their wind. Summers said to Hig and Evans, "Next one's hardest, you kin see." He raised his voice to reach to Brownie. "We head well up for two rod or so and then quarter a little down for six or eight and then turn up again for fifteen or twenty. Then point for where the tracks come out. Heavy water, but not so deep as some we've crossed. Watch out for that there ripple. We got to keep above her." The lined face grinned at Brownie. "What skeers me is your pa will git hisself washed off. Can't swim no better'n a salmon."

Fighting the current, seeing the lunge and sway of the wagon and the oxen half falling in the holes, Evans thought that only mountain men would have called this place a crossing. Only they would have found it and, finding, thought it possible to get a wagon through. This wasn't a ford, this wild, deep, uneven-bottomed water. It was an invitation to drown. Let a team be pulled over the muscled ripple to his left, let even a saddle horse pass over! Go it, critters! Again it was as if the solid land swam to them while the current banked against teams and wheels and wagon boxes and boiled off white at front and back. It swam to them, and the oxen lifted to it, and wheels ground in the gravel of the shore.

"We done it!" Evans yelled across at Hig as the leaders found the bank. "By godalmighty, yes!"

Hig didn't answer. He didn't need to. His thin grin answered for him.

"Dick, we done it!"

" 'Lowed we would."

"Fun," Brownie put in from the wagon seat. "Man, it was fun."

"Take the outfit up a ways, Brownie, and you and Mercy mind the young'uns. Don't want 'em underfoot."

"Want to take the team back?" Brownie asked.

"Unhitch and leave 'em rest awhile. We'll git some more across, I reckon, before usin' 'em again."

Later, with Becky across, and Mack and Shields and Carpenter, Evans told himself the talk last night was right: there wasn't anything to it. The crossing had the looks of danger; it sure enough was danger, close-sweeping in the stout and angry tide; but with Dick to lead and him and Hig to ride, there wasn't anything to it, not if a man took care. They'd be across, the whole set of them, by noon or maybe sooner.

Back on the southern shore Evans changed his blown horse, taking Nellie in its stead. "You ready, Byrd?"

"Ready."

"Ain't much to do except set, you and your missus."

"I'm grateful to you. I felt the children would be safest with you."

"Wasn't nothin'. Say you're ready?"

Byrd nodded, sober and watchful as a cornered coon. His woman was the same. Summers had said once she put him in mind of a pigeon, but, looking at her now, Evans figured she'd swelled out to a duck.

Behind them were more wagons. The Patches weren't over yet, or the Daughertys. After the last of them had made the crossing, Insko and Gorham and Holdridge and Botter would push the loose stock over. The herd wasn't so big now that Tadlock had quit the train.

Evans rode to the head of the line. "Good for another trip?" he joked at Hig, who sat like a bent stick on his horse. A knobby skeleton of a man, Hig was, with a face like an old white potato, but he could ride a horse or swim a stream or mend a rifle, and, what was more, he had a think-piece behind that withered skin.

"Good as gravy," Hig answered.

"Lead away, Dick."

They had hitched six yokes to Byrd's wagon, for it was medium heavy and the oxen either partly spent or smallish for so hard a chore.

They took the first stretch fine, barely swimming here and there, for, after all the trips across, the best course had been learnt. Glancing back as the leaders pulled up the bank of the first island, Evans thought Byrd looked like a churchman facing sin, a proper banker-churchman for the first time meeting evil in the flesh.

The next stretch went fine, too, the critters slanting up the stream and bending left and coming out like other teams before them.

While the oxen caught their wind, Evans made his horse step back. "Just one more hitch," he said to Byrd.

"I honestly believe it looks worse than it is."

"It ain't so bad. Scare you, Mrs. Byrd?"

She said it didn't.

"Just hang on."

Evans walked his horse back and nodded at Dick, and Dick led off again.

It happened suddenly, close to shore. It happened all at
once, without warning or good reason, like something bursting
into an easy dream. The team was going all right, the wagon
rolling safe above the muscled ripple, and then a leader slipped
and thrashed for footing, and the hungry current took it and
wrenched its mate along.

They descended on Evans, their legs scrambling the water
into spray, the weight of them dragging the second yoke out of
line. "Gee!" he hollered out of habit and poked with his stick
and beyond the tangle of them saw Hig and the hold-rope taut
and Hig's horse floundering with the pull on it. "Gee."

Nellie wouldn't hold. She broke before the thrashing push
of them, frightened now and unsteady in the tear of water.
The line clear back to the wheel yoke skewed to the pull, slanting the wagon below the come-out trail, slanting toward the
ripple, slanting off to wicked depths.

The wagon began to skid, half sailing, half grinding over
gravel. It was swinging like the tail of crack-the-whip, dragging
the wheelers with it, bending the yokes into an arc that it
yanked to a straight line, angled up into the tide. The swing
squeezed Nellie toward the lower shore, into swimming water
she couldn't swim against.

Too late the leaders found their feet. Every yoke was off the
course, some trying to swim, some trying to set themselves, and
all of them wild and all being beaten back. The landing place
was drawing off.

Evans heard Hig shouting and Byrd crying out, in words
that lost shape in the rush of water. His eye glimpsed people on
the shore and Dick moving with his horse. And then the swinging wagon caught on an unseen boulder and the current tore
at it and the upstream wheels lifted. Wrenched between the
rock and wash, the wagon flopped over on its side.

For a flash, it seemed to Evans, things happened slow and
sharp to see—Byrd grabbing for his woman and missing and
she pitching out and he climbing like a squirrel up the side
and she floating feathery as a hen tossed into a pond.

It wasn't a pond, this water. It was power and muscle to
shame the power and muscle of a man. It was fury. It was the

cold fury of the offended land. It rushed at arms and legs and tried to wrench the body over—and ahead of him was just the opened mouth of Mrs. Byrd, the hen's beak opened for a final squawk above the dragging feathers.

The beak went down, but underneath his hand, underneath the rippled water, he saw the blinking blue of cloth. He struck for it and caught a hold and squared around and tried for shore. It wasn't far away. It was a hop, skip and jump without an anvil in one hand. It was the stroke of an oar on peaceful water. It was here. It was streaming here, almost where he could reach it, and he never could. He hadn't strength enough, or wind. He hadn't legs and arms enough to take him over. Beyond, above the waves that lapped his face, he saw the people huddled, watching, and the wagon washed close to the bank and the oxen struggling and one yoke safe on land and Nellie standing near.

He lost them as a wave washed up. There was the water around him and the near-far shore and the sunshine dazzling to wet eyes and heaviness in arms and legs and strangles in the throat. There was the water and the power of water and the voice of it and over it another voice, over it, "Lije! Lije!"

The voice of Summers and the person of him, busy with his horse, and his arm swinging and a rope looping out, and his own arm catching for it and missing and catching it lower down.

Summers pulled him in, easy so as not to break his holds, and slid from his horse and drew Mrs. Byrd farther up the bank. The folks came running, Byrd in the lead, crying, "Ruth! Ruth!"

"She can't be dead," Evans panted at him. "Ain't had long enough to drown."

"Ruth!"

Dick said, "Easy," and turned Mrs. Byrd over on her stomach and lifted her at the middle to get the water out.

"You all right, Lije?" It was Becky, scolding him with her eyes for he didn't know what.

"Winded, is all."

They stood by, mostly quiet, while Summers worked on Mrs.

Byrd. "She's comin' round," he said. "I kin feel the life in her."

He turned her over, and she opened her eyes, and Byrd leaned down and pulled her dress so it wouldn't show her leg. "Are you all right, Ruth?"

She didn't answer right away. Her eyes looked big and washed-out, and they traveled from face to face as if to ask what she was doing on the ground with people looking down on her. Of a sudden her eyes filled and her face twisted, and Evans switched his gaze.

She was all right, though, except for the crying. Directly she got up, helped by Byrd and Weatherby, and let them lead her toward the wagons.

"She'd best lay down awhile," Becky said, and followed them to spread a blanket. The women trailed off with her.

"Poor way you picked to git to Oregon," Summers said to Evans then. His smile said something different.

"What's the loss?"

"Ain't had time to count."

Hig shook his head, as if still unbelieving. "I don't think there's a thing except a cracked tongue and some plunder wet."

"Not a critter?"

"Don't seem reasonable, but that wagon kind of coasted into shore. I hung to the rope and the team done the best it could, and she kind of coasted."

"What did Byrd do?"

"Just rode 'er out."

"I swear! What's holdin' the wagon now?"

"Team's still hitched."

Byrd was coming back from the wagons.

"Anything wrong?" Evans asked as he came into hearing.

"No. I think she's all right. I forgot to thank you. I just came to thank you."

"Fergit it! Just happens I can swim."

"I can't forget it, ever. I want you to know that." When Evans couldn't think of more to say, Byrd faced around and walked away.

"Funny nigger," Summers said, watching him. "But still I reckon you got thanks comin', Lije."

"Owe some myself." He turned away from the faces fastened on him. Across the river the other wagons waited. "We'll camp here. There's more outfits to bring across and Byrd's wagon to haul out and fix, and the wood we put in the boxes'll give us fires. You all think that's best?"

Their heads said they did.

"And it'll give the stock another fill of grass," Summers added. "There's more hard goin' ahead."

Evans had the wide-eye, from being overtired and over-anxious, though anxiousness had eased. They'd whipped the Snake and mended Byrd's wagon and dried his things as best they could, and Mrs. Byrd was feeling fair.

He turned over in bed, trying to get from his head the picture of the water. Once he shut his eyes, it streamed by him. It tore at wagons and at teams, breaking white around them. It ran a shimmer over Mrs. Byrd's blue dress. The shimmer and the blue and the push of the current on his chest kept flowing into Rebecca's face and Rebecca's words said later. "I wouldn't trade you, Lije, for a passel of Byrds. You might remember that." He remembered, and the remembering streamed on into water boiling round him.

A breeze stirred outside the tent, mixing with the mutter of the river. A horse kept up for herding blew its nose. It seemed to him, listening, that if he listened hard enough he heard old Rock padding around the tent, the ghost of old Rock following on to Oregon.

How many nights, he wondered, had he lain and listened? How many nights had his mind done and done again what his body did by day? How many times had he traveled the trail besides the one real time? How often, waiting for sleep, had he heard bird call and wolf cry and the bawling of buffalo? Long nights, listening nights, thinking nights, nights of casting ahead, to Boise now, and the Blue Mountains and the Columbia and the Dalles. And what would they do with their cattle? He hadn't got around to asking Dick, feeling somehow backward, as if the asking would show a doubt Dick hadn't earned.

But still, while the water climbed against his horse, the question nagged at him.

He turned back and felt Rebecca stir to his movement, Becky who wouldn't trade him for a dozen Byrds, who stayed with him through thick and thin, the most of which was thick. Or was it thin? How did you name heat and dust and mud and rain and rocks and racing water? Thick or thin? He thought he must be on the shore of sleep to worm in such a subject.

Rebecca began to snore, to snore the light and easy snore that he had heard ten thousand nights. There was a thing now. Snoring was a puky sound except by her. How was it that he felt with her no ugliness in anything she did or had? Did other men find rawness in their wives or didn't they, or was he just a simple man and, being simple, different? He wished the same for Brownie and his wife.

Raw or not, the women did their part and more. They traveled head to head with men, showing no more fear and asking no favor. Becky. Mrs. Patch. Judith Fairman with her load of grief. Mrs. Mack. Mrs. Daugherty. And, yes, Mercy too. They had a kind of toughness in them that you might not think, seeing them in a parlor. So, on a trail, women came to speak and men to listen almost as if to other men. It was lucky for the pride of men that few traveled with their wives to Oregon. They'd never quite believe again a woman was to look at but not to listen to.

The breeze was busy again. It ran a little chillness along the ground inside the tent. Overhead, Evans imagined, the stars would be sharp, for the night had come on clear. They would be dancing in the water that kept rushing in his mind. The breeze brought the whisper of footsteps. A voice said, "Evans! Captain!"

"Who is it?"

"Byrd."

"All right."

"My wife—"

"What's the matter?"

Rebecca had quit her snoring. Evans knew as well as if he could see her that she was listening.

"I think she's in labor. It's—it's ahead of time."

"Becky!"

"I heard." Louder she said, "I'll be right over, Mr. Byrd."

"Please!"

"We'll be right along," Evans said.

"You'd best get a fire goin'," Becky said to both of them. She was getting out of the bed.

Evans heard Byrd's footsteps whispering off. While he hunted for his clothes he asked, "How fur along is she?"

"Goin' on six months." Evans felt rather than saw his wife getting into her things. "Not long enough for a live baby."

"Scared out of her, I reckon. Or maybe she got a bump."

"It ain't any one thing, Lije. It's bein' worked and worried for so long."

"She didn't mention any bump."

"See can you find a candle, Lije. There's a nubbin or two in the oak box."

He found the candles and walked with her to Byrd's tent, taking a brand from the fire there to light the candle with inside.

It was just flickering shadow he saw at first, and then the beds slung around and the eyes of two young ones fastened on him. It was a big tent, as it had to be, with four beds in it. Mrs. Byrd was lying with her youngest one, in a bed that was rumpled where Byrd had got out. Byrd was squatting by her. She breathed something to Rebecca. Evans lit a candle with the brand and stuck it to the bottom of a bucket.

Rebecca had knelt by the bed. She twisted her head toward Evans. "Get the chirren out, Lije. Some can go to our bed, and likely the Macks or Fairmans or Patches'll see the others have a place to lie."

Byrd said, "Get up, children! Get up! Elizabeth! Mother's sick. You don't need to dress."

They squirmed out of bed, big-eyed, it seemed to Evans, with some young wisdom that knew without being told. They straggled out, gazing back as they left the door of home, none of them speaking. As Evans stepped out, he saw Rebecca take the littlest Byrd from his mother's side and lay him in one of the empty beds.

He and Byrd got the children placed and came back and freshened the fire and put a second kettle on to boil. The night was darker than Evans had expected, or maybe it was just the fire that made the world seem black. There was the red light of it and the glimmer of the tent and the bulge of the wagon top, and nothing to see beyond.

While Byrd poked at the fire, Evans went to the tent and entered, stooping, and said, "We got everything fixed, and two kettles b'ilin'. Anything else, Becky? Mrs. Mack is comin', and Mrs. Patch and Mrs. Fairman if you need 'em."

As he spoke, a spasm came on Mrs. Byrd's face, and her body writhed under the covers. Becky nodded, saying Byrd was right, saying this was it.

The spasm passed, leaving the face loose and tired. Mrs. Byrd opened her eyes, opened them dead into those of Evans. In that instant, in that flash of knowing, Evans saw not Mrs. Byrd or Mrs. Anybody. He saw Rebecca and Brownie and Mercy and all the members of the train. He saw everybody. He saw himself. He saw the humble, hurtful, anxious, hoping look that was the bone-deep look of man.

He went out, meeting Mrs. Mack coming in. A fire was going by the Fairmans' tent and Mrs. Fairman was a shadow by it, cooking up a broth, he thought, to take to Mrs. Byrd. A little mist of steam was coming from the kettles on the fire close by. Byrd was putting on more wood. He gazed at Evans as if to ask a question. Evans couldn't think of anything worth saying. He sat down by the fire to give the man his company.

A pigeon, he had thought, and later on a duck, and later on a chicken, a woman mild as milk, with no inner force to fix her in the others' minds. Even the moaning that brought Byrd to his feet was a weak moaning. Had things gone right with her, who could call her name ten years from now? What was her name, they'd say, you know, that quiet, little woman?

But, for a breath, he had looked into her eyes and seen below and known that she was kin to him.

The child was born dead, like Rebecca said, an hour or two before the eastern sky warmed up. They buried it, unnamed, and Weatherby spoke a prayer, and they rigged a bed for Mrs. Byrd and dragged away for Boise. It was August 15. Who could say when snow would be blowing in the Blues?

"WE GOT to be decidin' things," Evans said to open the meeting of the council.

It was a changed council, with Brewer and Tadlock gone and Patch and Shields elected to their places—a changed council but a better one, it seemed to Curtis Mack as he rumped down in the circle with the rest of them.

Evans wasn't in a hurry to proceed. He had his jackknife out, whittling on his nails. Underneath his thin-worn shirt Mack could see the bulge of muscles. A balanced man was Evans, big, slow, balanced, growing in stature with the captaincy. Mack felt with a twist of envy that here was a person sure to make his mark in Oregon, sure to lead in the organization of the territory, sure to represent it in some major office. It wasn't the future of him, though, that excited envy. It was the man himself. It was the suggestion in his looks and manner that he was at peace with himself, at a kind of modest peace that won men to him. Did he have no inward weaknesses, no secret conflicts, Mack wondered; no faults beyond the doubtful fault of unsure confidence, beyond the disappearing fault of indecision? Did he know the outlaw impulses? Did he wake up at night and try to run from judgment?

Mack took his gaze away from the broad and downturned face. The sky was overcast, but without much threat of rain. Through the clouds to the west he could see the bright spot that would be the sun.

"First thing to decide is to get away from this goddam fort," Shields said. "Fish! Whew!"

They sat back from the corralled train, closer to the river. The fort squatted on beyond, but still the smell of fish was all around, the smell of fresh, dried, rotting fish, of fly-blown leavings from the riches of the Snake.

"Couldn't sleep last night for them fish slappin' the water," Shields went on. "Fish in the ears and fish in the nose and fish, by God, in the tobacco you chew. Worst fort we've saw."

Fort Boise was the worst, Mack agreed inwardly while the other men joined Shields in small talk. It was the smallest and the worst—the dirtiest, stinkingest, the least concerned with order. Indians swarmed around it, fish-fat, filthy, witless Indians who couldn't learn, the fort men said, to store up food against the starving winters. What was it Summers held: that war alone—that love of war—gave fiber to the Indians eastward? In any case the other forts were better, Hall for one, and Laramie. Laramie? How many trains of thought led back to Laramie?

Evans was saying, "We'll pull out tomorrow now we've done our tradin'. Got enough dried fish aboard to last me all my life."

"I'll be glad to put the Snake behind," Patch said. "Let England have it."

Evans bent the talk to business. "The big thing is, what do we do with the cattle? Like old Greenwood said, what do we do with the cattle?"

His words, it seemed to Mack, were like pebbles dropped into a pool, or like the afterwash of pebbles into quiet water. His own attention rippled to them and ran back to Laramie, to Laramie and night and the one night afterwards along the trail. And it flowed along to Soda Springs and the girl despairing and to Fort Hall and the marriage and Brownie giving his stiff no to the offered gift of oxen, to a gift that wasn't a gift but a cheap offering to peace of mind.

Patch said, "I imagine we can drive the cattle through. The trail from the Dalles to the Willamette can't be any worse than some we've traveled."

"Who's we?" Evans asked.

"Well, one of us. Some of us."

"There ain't any trail to speak of. Remember that. Got to find your own, and no one knows the way, except Summers has a good idee."

"What's wrong with Summers?" Shields asked Evans.

300

"He said he'd trail 'em."

"Well?"

"Don't think we ought to let him do it."

Daugherty asked, "And why not?"

"We paid him just to get us to the Dalles and didn't pay him much, and he's done all and more'n we could ask."

Mack put himself into the conversation. "There's nothing standing in the way of a new contract. We can offer him more money."

Evans answered quietly, "Ain't everyone well fixed like you."

The words seemed almost like a reproach. Mack said quickly, "I'll pay him myself then. I'll be glad to pay him, for all of us."

Again Evans spoke quietly, while in the eyes around him Mack saw the answer turning. "Wouldn't keer for you to do that."

Mack asked, "Why not?" but he already knew. Evans, being too stout for help himself, thought others just as proud. He wasn't penniless, or Patch or Fairman, either, but sided with the penniless to spare them the imagined shame of charity. And the two would go along with him, acting poor as Byrd and Shields and Daugherty while they refused his offer.

No, Mack thought suddenly. Always no. Brownie's no and Evans' no and the council's no—as if his very situation were a crime, as if it set him off from them. They wouldn't let him do a favor no matter how he wanted to.

"Just wouldn't keer," Evans answered.

"If you won't let me pay, all right. You can owe me. You can owe me for your share until you're better situated."

Before he finished, a barefooted, bare-bodied Indian ambled up, carrying a fish by a finger hooked through a gill. His other hand dug at his scalp. Evans shook his head and waved him off, "No trade," he said. "No trade. Maybe trade later." He gave the Indian a pinch of tobacco to get rid of him. "That's good o' you," he said to Mack, "but let's see if there ain't another way."

"Does Summers want to take the cattle through?" Shields asked.

"Not for hisself." Evans was quiet for a minute, as if the words, soaked in, would show they couldn't let themselves use Summers. "Like you all know, on a ways we could hit north for Walla Walla."

"Extra miles," Patch put in.

Evans nodded. "But it might be the fort there'll take our stock and give us orders for a trade at Fort Vancouver. I hear they done it before."

"But we can't be sure they will again?" Fairman asked.

"Not certain-sure, but the man here at Boise—what's his name? Craigie—Craigie said they might."

"Then we'd have the river trip from Walla Walla," Patch said. "That would take money, too—for boats and Indian navigators. Money or trinkets, if we had any trinkets left."

"I hate to be beholdin' to the British any more than need be," Evans told him.

"They seem all right. They've been hospitable."

"Not sayin' they ain't, though I notice they don't give nothin' away but a meal and charge ten prices when it comes to trade. The point is, this here ain't their country."

Heads bobbed to that, and a silence followed in which, it seemed to Mack, the issues stood as plain as cactus. They had their choice of Walla Walla and the chance of credits for their cattle and of the nearer Dalles from which Dick Summers, paid or not, could take the livestock overland. The man had said he'd go for nothing. Mack had said he'd pay him. But still the council hesitated, as if from out of nowhere would come the magic answer.

Evans spoke into the silence. "Cows has been got through, we know. Not sayin' how many was lost along the way."

"Hate to think of more hard goin'," Shields said. "Them last days comin' on to Boise River like to ruint me. Christ!"

"Like to ruint iveryone," Daugherty chimed in. "And thin the good God brought the river and the trees."

"What about the single men?" Patch asked.

"Who?"

"You know. Higgins. Botter. Insko. Moss."

Evans inquired, "What about 'em?"

"They're going on to Oregon City, aren't they?"

"That was the agreement with my men," Fairman said.

"Moss, too. And Insko, I think," Mack added.

"Can't they drive the cattle?"

"When the travelin's hard, it's easy to leave a critter behind, or all of 'em, if the leavin' ain't no skin off you," Evans answered. "Might work out, but it's a heap to ask of 'em, to take the whole thing on themselves." He had folded his knife and was turning it over and over in one hand.

Mack spoke even before the thought had come clear in his mind. "I'll go."

"You'll go?" Evans asked.

"I'll go."

"Ain't no more call for you to go than any of the rest of us."

"I've got more cattle, and just one person to look after."

"What o' her?"

"That will depend. Isn't it possible a whole train will be going overland? I mean from this company and others?"

"Not in wagons. Dick thinks it ain't for wagons."

"On horseback then, and one of you can float my property down. Or, if there's not a party overland, maybe Amanda can go with you."

"Course she could," Evans answered slowly while he picked a stem of grass.

"What do you say then?" Mack found himself speaking with a kind of urgency, as if, for reasons lying back in mind, it was important that he get them to accept. Their faces were thoughtful, tentative with the brain's trial of yes and no.

"Wouldn't like to ask it of you," Evans said.

"You didn't."

"Right handsome of you," Shields put in, low-voiced, as if embarrassed at the need of comment.

Evans moved his head from face to face. "What you say?"

They didn't speak at once, but, watching, Mack foresaw the answer. He thought without irritation, he thought with understanding that, while they wouldn't take his money, they would take his toil and sweat and time, for they had that to give. And it was right, right for them and right for him.

303

"It's generous," Fairman said to Evans, "too generous, but —if he will?"

Mack got to his feet, seeing others nod. "It's settled, then? I'll see them through. The single men and I will."

Later, lying in bed, listening to the salmon in the river, he thought about his case. He didn't believe in God, at any rate the God that other people seemed to. He doubted the moralities. He wouldn't say what constituted sin, if sin existed. He knew in honesty that, with provocation, he might offend the rules again. As for the deed, it was committed. He couldn't wipe out the fact. Not all his offerings, not toil or time or sacrifice, could undo what was done. The part of good sense was to forget. Soon enough, he thought wryly, a man made new regrets that crowded out the old. Was there some hidden purpose in his treatment of the girl, some wish to overlay with fresh remorse the dismal recollection of the killing of the Kaw?

No, he didn't believe there was. He had acted out of hunger, out of disappointment, out of anger, out of then insufferable fester. Out of them he had shot the Indian and seduced the girl. And was he to blame? Or was it circumstance? Or was it the God he couldn't credit? Pushed so far, a man knew strange compulsions. So forget! Just forget!

He hadn't succeeded in forgetting. No one so molded could, no man so haunted by the ghosts of faith, no mind so tied, beyond the touch of reason, to old admonishments. Be ye therefore perfect. Be ye perfect but ye can't, so be ye burdened with thy sins. Repent! Oh, sure, repent, and make atonement!

Well, the unbeliever had. The unbeliever was going to. The unbeliever would trail the stock to destination for the sake of his nonexistent soul. Repentance? Atonement? Restitution? The churchy words. The pious words. The solemn words of Weatherby. To hell with them! It wasn't to God he made his offering, to Jesus, God or Holy Ghost. It wasn't to the train. It was to self. Its purpose was to square himself with self, to equalize accounts and so walk upright in the sight of Curtis Mack. That much remained, that stubborn much, of what was taught him as the way of heaven.

He was ready for sleep, tired and ready for sleep, but it

struck him before he slipped into it that now he could follow thoughts like these with less of his old soreness. The singular, fresh-milk fragrance of Amanda came to his nostrils. Her gentle breathing sounded in his ears. He would see the herd across the mountains. He didn't know when he had felt better.

Chapter - - - - - - - - - - - Twenty-Eight

Hᴇʀᴇ, from Boise to the Dalles, was the windup of the trail, the finish of the test, the yes or no to Oregon. Here by slow wheel tracks at last was being written the answer to a question raised years ago last spring, raised so long ago a man lost its beginning across the plain-peak, sage-tree, sand-rock field of time. He lost it along with places, people and doings remembered from before, so that none of them came real to him and he asked himself if sure enough there was an Independence, a Missouri and a spot he once called home, or were they vapors in his mind.

Asking, he would ask if there was a Dalles, an Oregon, a Columbia that, unseeing, he still had seen, streaming richly to the sea. Was anything behind him or before, anything but rolls of land, anything in all his life but distance to be covered so more distance could be covered? All he could swear to was this walking by his team.

And yet the days of hardest doubt were gone. The days of any doubt were gone. Evans didn't need to tell himself that it was so. The truth of it was big in him. It filled his head and toned his muscles and gave cheer to his words. Not since boyhood had he felt this way, not since his home town of St. Charles had set itself for an illumination. He could hardly wait then, seeing in advance the great fires in the street, answering already to the pitch of celebration.

He had to hold himself in. He had to keep from pushing, from asking of the teams and people more than they could give. He had to keep in mind that he was born with strength that others didn't have. Soon enough, if not soon enough for him, they'd reach the rimming hills and see the broad Columbia below. While he drove and double-yoked and watched the weak ones over, he saw it in imagination, rolling with the sun, and a shout swelled in his throat, to be choked down to easy, easy. Easy to the promised land.

He counted each day's going against the miles ahead. The Malheur. Birch Creek. The leaving of the Snake, and no one sorry that it lay behind. Burnt River. The Powder. The rough ridge road he followed now to get to the Grande Ronde.

Burnt River. There was a place. Burnt River—the Brulé, as Summers called it—so shouldered in by mountains, so thick with brush and briers, that no one would have dared it, maybe, except for knowing someone had.

Two days of it. Two days of such hard travel that man and brute arrived at camp with no wish but to rest. Unyoked, the oxen dragged off, waiting on the strength to feed. Men worked slow-motioned, tiredness pulling at their muscles as they pitched their tents and struck their fires and did the little chores while they waited for the food that droopy women fixed. The children quarreled, worn down to orneriness. Their whiny voices filled the air.

But still the days of doubt were gone. Still Evans felt the climb of celebration. They'd whipped the trail. They'd whipped it all but for a few mean miles, whipped the Platte and Green and Snake, whipped the deserts and the mountains, and they would whip the rest.

Sometimes he thought of cost, of Martin dead and Tod Fairman buried with his poisoned leg and Mrs. Byrd delivered of the too-soon child and old Rock rotting who used to trot at heel. He thought of other costs, of his fight with Tadlock, of oxen down and left to die, of losses from the Indians, of strength spent and juices sweated and courage whittled to a nub. Each reach of trail had taken toll—Platte, Sweetwater, Green, Bear, Snake. And yet—and yet—the thing was worth the cost. No prize came easy. Free land still had its price. A chance at better living had somehow to be earned. A nation couldn't grow unless somebody dared. The price was high, but who would say it was too high—except for those who'd paid so dear?

Byrd might think it, though without much right. None could mourn deep at a stillborn child, seen but for a moment and as a stranger then, with no life in it to leave a memory.

307

But Byrd might think it, being beaten down. Byrd, born timid and out of luck to boot.

It would have to be his wagon, Evans thought, that wrecked along the Brulé, his one-remaining wagon that broke a wheel the second day.

The first day had been bad enough, on a narrow, crooked, stony trail that crossed the river only to cross back, that pushed through stubborn thickets, that crept sidelong on ridges shooting into mountains. They'd made twelve miles or more that day and pitched their camp and fallen into bed, each hoping that the worst was past.

It wasn't, though. The worst was still ahead. Evans, in the lead, had stopped his team where the trail wormed through a tangle of cottonwood, alder, brush and briers. Beyond, the mountains squeezed the stream. He wiped his forehead with his sleeve. "I swear, Dick!"

"Don't look possible," Summers said from his horse, meaning that it was.

"Ain't room, hardly, for a pony cart to go through here. Bush looks liable to wipe off the wagon tops."

Summers nodded. "Others has been through."

"A teamster's got to get aboard, for there's no room for him by the side. Wisht whoever cut the trail had cut a road and not a mole run long as they were doin' it."

Summers was silent, looking beyond to the high, straight-rising mountains.

"And when we get through, we got them tarnal hills. Be more broke wagon tongues today, or I'm a nigger."

"Want to turn back?" Summers' mouth had twisted to a grin.

"Not yet a while, I reckon."

Behind Evans the other wagons were beginning to pull up. "This ain't makin' hay," he said to Summers and climbed up to his seat and spoke to his team while Summers led off.

It was, Evans thought, like pushing a hole through the growth. Branches laced over the team and parted to the bulge of the wagon and ripped along the covered bows while the wheels jolted on the stumps. All he could see was the oxen stumbling and the thin trail and the brush coming at him and squeezing to the sides like water to the bow of a boat. The sound of it along the wagon top was like hard-driven rain.

Beyond, the trail led down a wash and up the other side and lifted from the river bottom to teeter along the shoulder of a mountain.

Up from the wash Evans stopped again. They called this slanted scar ahead a trail! The wagon wasn't built that wouldn't lose its balance on it and fall over on its side. While he looked at it, Summers turned his horse around. "What you thinkin', hoss?"

"I ain't thinkin'. I'm just seein' wagons keel over."

"She's sidelong, sure enough."

"Wisht I had a wagon high-wheeled on the down side."

"An' sidehill critters, too, built to stand even on a slant."

"I'll pull forward a ways to where she starts so's to give the other wagons room behind, and then we'll take 'em over one or two at a time, with two-three men standin' on the up side. Reckon that'll work?"

Summers said, "Sure. Must've worked afore or the trail wouldn't be there."

Evans poked his team and stopped again and waited for the others to come out of the brush. He walked down the line then, telling how they'd try the slant. "Best all get out when your time comes. Don't want a woman or a young'un in a wagon that tips over. We'll try mine first, and if it works then we'll take two or maybe three at once. All right? Carpenter? Gorham? You feel like helpin'?"

They stepped up, their faces lined already from the morning's drive, their eyes narrowed on the trail against the hard glint of the sun.

Evans said, "Whyn't you whack the team, Carpenter? I'm heftier'n you. Watch you stay ahead of the wagon. Don't want no one mashed."

They got it over. They roosted on the side and got it over, though the up wheels tried to lift once and barely skimmed the ground.

"Good enough," Evans said. "We'll know better how to go

309

next time. You take the team on a ways, Carpenter, and tie it up somewheres, and we'll go back for more." Already he saw another wagon starting, with Patch walking by the side.

It was slow and sweaty work, made the worse because ahead, where Evans had hoped to see the bottom widen, it still ran pinched. It was just a stream-cut through the mountains, a stream-cut choked by brush. Beyond the little resting place they brought the wagons to, the trail squirmed out of sight.

Tramping back with Dick and Gorham to bring more outfits over, Evans wished that hard times, if they had to come, came early in the morning when men and teams were lively. Along toward noon the spirits started down and so made heavy travel heavier. Not that he felt whipped. Not that. Leave it to him and they'd roll longer than they ever thought. The Columbia was just beyond the Blues, or leastwise not so far.

The air stirred lazily, and he took off his hat to get the good of it. "How much more of this kind of goin' would you say, Dick?"

"Ought to be over the worst of it by night, barrin' trouble."

"Hope so," Gorham said. He tilted his head upward. "Ain't it time to eat?"

Some of the women and children were following behind a wagon that Daugherty drove, making a ragged line against the mountain slope. Evans and the two with him stepped out of the trail to let Daugherty go by. Daugherty had covered the worst of the slant. He spit over the wheel of his wagon. "And 'tis said the road to hell is steep!"

Rebecca was among the women, along with Judith Fairman and Mercy and Mrs. Gorham. "We'll noon up when we get 'em over," Evans told them. The thought came to him and slid away that Becky was the natural leader of the women. It was as if she had strength enough for all, a quiet, long-enduring strength. Without it, he didn't know what Judith Fairman would have done. "Tuckered?" he asked, just to be saying something to her.

Two of the young ones—Jeff Byrd and George Carpenter, it was—had stopped to tug a rock on edge. "Look out!" they shouted and gave it a turn. It started slow, as if half minded to lie down, and picked up speed and flew thudding down the mountainside and tore into the brush, flushing a flock of ducks off the hidden river.

"Don't you wish you had time to roll a rock, Lije?" Summers asked as the three of them started on. "I knowed you when you did."

"Reckon I do."

The little smile went from Summers' face, leaving just the mark of thought. "No time to roll a rock," he said as if speaking to himself.

Evans wasn't of a mind then to pry into what Dick meant. "Not till we git the rest across," he said.

Byrd was waiting for them. He stood faced up to the trail. It occurred to Evans that age had come on him, age without age's gumption, giving him the appearance of an old boy. "It ain't nothin'," Evans said to Mrs. Byrd, who had sat down to catch the shade a scrubby cedar made. She looked well enough, sitting there quiet with two of her children by her. She looked as she had at first, a milk-mild pigeon to the eye that hadn't seen beneath. "We'll put enough men on her so she can't tip over. How about it, Dick? You and Gorham and me?" They climbed up. "Push 'em across, Byrd."

Things would have gone well enough if the outfit had been sound. The team eased onto the sidelong trail, pulling slow but steady, and the wagon canted to the slope and the three of them held it down. They were maybe halfway across when the downhill front wheel hit a rock. From his place on the wagon Evans couldn't see it, but he felt the jolt and heard the splinter of overweighted spokes. The wagon dropped like a cow on one knee and hung for an instant and lifted and crashed over.

Perched on the upper side, holding to the wagon box underneath its cover. Evans couldn't think to jump until too late. He circled over with the wagon and cracked against a bow and skidded off and hit the ground sprawled out. He scrambled up. "Dick?"

Gorham had gone over, too. He got his knees under him and stood up. "Goddam it!" he said.

"You hurt?"

311

"No, goddam it!"

Dick was coming around the wagon. "All right? Whyn't you hosses jump?"

Evans said, "Sure."

"Christ, what a mix-up!" It was Gorham, looking over the wagon.

Evans hadn't thought of Byrd till then. Byrd stood silent by his halted team as if, of all the words, there wasn't one to say. He stood with a look of raw defeat that sharpened Evans' irritation. "Looks like trouble can't leave you alone, Byrd. Poor wagons you bought."

"I'm sorry."

The man was sorry. The unfit, pitiful damn man was sorry. Standing there with his wrecked wagon, with the wheel collapsed and the bows caved in and things messed up inside, what he was was sorry.

Of a sudden Evans was, too. "Never mind," he said. "We'll get it fixed up."

Mrs. Byrd was hurrying along the sidehill, carrying her youngest one. "Are you all right, Clarence? You're not hurt?"

From the other side people were coming up, children running first and then the men and then Becky and Mrs. Gorham. They gathered round.

Mrs. Byrd put the child down. Now that she'd asked if Byrd was all right, it was as if she didn't know words, either.

To all of them Evans said, "Let's git the pots a-b'ilin'. Time to noon." He bobbed his head to Becky's silent question about himself. "Let's git goin'. You, too, Mrs. Byrd. Would one of you unhitch Byrd's team, and some help unload the wagon?"

When they had it unloaded, he sent them on, staying himself to talk to Byrd a minute. "Didn't mean to sound like scoldin' you," he said. "I was just put out."

"You don't need to say anything."

"We'll git a saw."

"Saw?"

"To make a cart with. We'll saw your wagon in two."

"Oh."

"Other wagons has got room if you need some. Room for part of your plunder and your young'uns."

Byrd didn't answer. His eyes turned from the wagon to the brush of the creek below, to the loose stock that were beginning to foot it across the sidehill, to the mountains rising, to the far curve of sky.

"So you ain't in such bad case. Hig'll know how to make a first-rate cart."

Byrd's gaze was still lost in distance. "It's a long way back."

"Sure is. We got time to do some sawin' before we eat."

Weatherby walked off from camp, giving a last long stare at the little ring of card players. The train needed rest, he knew, but ways of resting could be wicked. Better to be toiling on the trail, better to be pushing the footloose stock, better to wear the body out than to corrupt the soul.

The deed seemed worse, the hearty slapping down of cards more evil, because the hand of God lay on this place. The Grande Ronde, people called it. It was such a spot as even Adam, after the beauty of the Garden, might still have thought was beautiful. The walking feet trod through rich grasses. The roving eye saw clover and wild flax and timber on the watercourses, and all around, as if to shield the place, the noble mountains lifting heavenward. Here were deer and elk and bear, and fish enough to feed the multitude without a miracle. And still the men played cards!

Meditation, he thought. This was a place for meditation, for giving self to God, for partaking of His strength and love. He let his spirit flow, let it flow humbly with its Maker's. A man had only to do this much to feel the healing grace. He had only to acknowledge God, he had only to accept His will in meekness to know the Holy Presence.

Walking by himself, seeing the sun going to rest in a majesty of fire, Weatherby wondered at the perverse way of men and women. Card players. Sabbath-breakers. Swearers. Readers of romances. Wearers of finery. How could they choose the temporal, sinful pleasures when salvation was the price?

Sometimes he felt that he had failed. In spite of all his exhortations the train still broke the Sabbath, condoning the sin by saying it was necessary. Its people liked the fiddle's music. They danced. They swore. They played card games. Some talked like deists, as if God didn't care. Give me strength, Lord! he asked. Give me power!

And yet his self-doubts seemed unworthy. God had given him work to do. God had given his old body an endurance equal to his task. God had seen him safe through all vicissitudes. God had called him west. All glory to His name!

It wasn't within the right of man to question God. The righteous man accepted, and knew peace. The sinner scoffed or ranted and in the fire of soul got a foretaste of the hell to come. He had had his foretaste as a younger man. He had known the torments of the flesh, and yielded, and known the torments of the spirit. And then God had given him to see, and, lo, his passion was become a righteous passion and his lust the love of Jesus.

Even now, he thought, the devil lurked. He wasn't always free of wickedness after all his years of fighting it. Sometimes, off guard, he'd think of women yet, of Mercy Evans and her husband and the young flesh and the warm bed, and he would push the devil back and cry to God to forgive and strengthen him. It seemed to him afterwards that his preaching had an extra force, a special urgency for sinners to repent; and the force and the urgency were wonderful and mysterious and spoke the love divine.

Ahead of him an Indian came riding on a horse, a Cayuse Indian, doubtless, or perhaps a Nez Percé. Here again, he knew, was the living proof of faith, not in the single Indian but in all the Indians hereabouts. They were clean and clothed. They were good husbandmen and artisans, having wheat and corn and vegetables and dressed skins to trade for garments, calico and nankins, and good horses to exchange for cattle. Their squaws were modest and industrious, happy to make or mend moccasins for a simple gift. In these tribes had disappeared the savage heathenisms—and all because of Christianity. All because two consecrated men, Dr. Whitman and another—Spalding—

314

had established missions somewhere north to bring the truth to them.

He said, "Good evening," to the Indian.

The Indian smiled and said, "How do?" He brought his horse up. It had a homemade saddle on it, with skins tied on behind.

"Cayuse?"

"Christian, me."

The answer struck Weatherby as the proper one, as the answer to the question that he should have asked. "I am a Christian. I am a preacher."

The Indian nodded as if in halting understanding of the words. "Good man. Pray."

"Let us have a prayer. Let us talk to the Holy Spirit."

"Pray now?"

"Pray now."

The Indian slipped from his horse and knelt with Weatherby in the grass.

Weatherby tried to make his prayer simple. "We thank Thee, God, for Thy blessings. We thank Thee for life and health and all Thy loving bounty. We thank Thee for Thy love of all of us, white man and red man and all the men of earth. Help us to be worthy. Help us to do Thy will. We pray Thee, help us not to swear or worship false gods or idols or to drink firewater or commit adultery. Let Thy mercy rest on us."

While he spoke, he said an inward prayer, asking God for the strength and wisdom to do His will among the poor heathens of the Columbia as Whitman and Spalding were doing with their tribes.

He said, "Amen," then, and the Indian said, "Amen."

Weatherby felt refreshed when he got up. More than ever he felt chosen, and strong, adequate, sure that in this little meeting, in this little worship by a white man and a red, God had shown Himself.

"Me go to camp," the Indian said, motioning toward the idled train. He led his horse along.

The men were still playing cards, so intent on the game that

315

none but Summers appeared to notice their approach. They played with noise and violence, slapping down the cards as if force would rule the outcome.

Weatherby tried to guide his guest around. He was angry and ashamed at this example of the white man's way, and fearful that a strange temptation would fascinate the Indian.

The Indian wouldn't be herded. He stepped up to the circle, Weatherby trailing after him, and watched for a long moment. He caught Summers' questioning eye. Then, to Weatherby's surprise, to his satisfaction, to his immense delight, he said, "Bad! Bad!"

Weatherby liked to think the game broke up as a consequence. Summers said, "Party's over, hoss," and the others began to get up. Summers went on, "If this here's the worst you ever do, you'll be a heap good Injun." His eyes went to Weatherby. They were gray, smiling, skeptical eyes, and Weatherby might have felt compelled to answer them but for the continuing wonder of the Indian's words.

He moved away as the game stopped and Daugherty and the Cayuse began to dicker over a deer hide. But the "Bad! Bad!" stayed with him. Into the mouth of a simple savage God had put the truth. In His greatness, in His mysterious workings, God had put the truth there. It was too bad that Whitman and Spalding weren't Methodists.

For three days Evans let the train dawdle across the Grande Ronde, though he fretted to be really rolling. Man and beast could use a rest, and the two Byrds needed time to get their courage up. Here, too, Patch took sick, his bowels upset by something, and looked so peaked for a spell that Evans doubted he was fit to go. Other reasons, big and small, came in. The women had a pile of washing. The Cayuse Indians offered things for trade. Among a believing tribe, Brother Weatherby was as close to heaven as he'd get on earth. By idling here the train might make the miles ahead without another rest.

The days were fair, with no hint of snowfall in the Blues. That made the waiting easier, that and the closeness of the Blues, rimmed around to westward. Seeing them against a cloudless sky, Evans knew he'd been too anxious. Snow was a long way off.

But fall was here. He saw it in the crisping grass out from the watered bottoms, in leaves that, earlier than most, were turning waxy-yellow, in the shortened time of sun. The snow would snow all right, and rain would rain down on the lower river, and, after rest, they'd best be wheeling. The question wasn't if they'd get there. The question was how long it took to build a cabin, how long to raise a shelter against the cold rain blown in from the sea.

While they waited, hunting, fishing, trading with the Indians down to their final pair of pants, a train of wagons straggled by, looking lank and battered, and sent a rider to their camping place a half mile off the trail. It had been Captain Welch's company, the rider said, or part of it, now long since broken from the starting train and subtracted from and added to along the way. They'd had their griefs, too. One burying. The goddam Indians on the Snake, stealing horses for the pay of finding them! How many following behind? God knew. A passel. This train was traveling light and fast. No. Couldn't stop. No time to gab. They aimed to get to Oregon, but thankee just the same, and had they heard about the party short-cutting up the Malheur?

Evans watched the train string on. He didn't care that it had passed, not much. Ahead was likely grass enough. It didn't matter that he couldn't brag on being first. What mattered were the companies following behind, the passel of people, maybe running into thousands, the home hunters, the darers, the stouthearted, the long-suffering. If he closed his eyes he could see them ranked along the trail, gray with dust and leaned by hardship but with the light of purpose in their eyes. Men and women. Children. Sucking babies. Milk cows. Mules and horses. Oxen. Plows. Seeds to decorate a dooryard. Books for unbuilt schools. The little fixings for the home to be. Whose was Oregon? Here, England, came the answer!

But though he wasn't jealous of the men ahead, nor anxious any more about snow in the Blues, he was eager to roll on. A thousand times, he bet, the Columbia flowed across his mind, a broad sheet streaming to Vancouver and the mouth of the Willamette. If he could just stand by it, he would count the trip as good as done. He'd be there now except for sickness, deaths and accidents and halts made for repairs and rest. Tadlock was right about one thing: a man ran into enough delays without excusing more.

They pulled out on a balmy morning, rested now and full of go, and climbed up in the Blues, making light of a two-mile rise so stiff they sometimes had to use six yokes. Above was rolling country with groves of yellow pine. Over it the trail ran stony and dipped to cross the Grande Ronde River and led on to a bottom where they camped. Seven miles or eight, they'd made, as Evans counted it. Good enough, all things considered.

The next day they did a little better over country just as hard—up a mountain, along a ridge, down and up a dozen sharp-pitched hollows, over craggy rocks and into plains and groves again where deadfall lay. All around was such grand scenery that a teamster had to prod himself to watch out where he went. Mountains reared around him and bare stone lifted and distance fell away below the edging wheels. Trees sprang up as if for thinning, and here and there a sweet park opened with highland flowers in bloom. It was as if here God had put the leavings of creation, the bits and masses of the stuff He'd worked with. Ten miles. They pitched camp in a park.

The third day, though, was best of all, though no softer than the rest. Pulling up a slope, head raised to see what lay beyond, Evans whoaed his team, for yonder, yonder, blue and white and dizzy in the distance, rose the Cascade range and, like the queen of heights, Mount Hood, like the nippled queen, like a snowy cloud, like proof and promise. Hard by would be the river. Evans looked back and saw Rebecca looking and felt he couldn't speak for the crowding in his chest. They made nine miles that day, across the main ridge of the Blues.

Evans didn't hold in now. He doubted that he could, even if the train had wanted to. It didn't. Its people felt like him. Here on the final stretch they had a long, hard, driving strength, with Mount Hood and Mount Saint Helens like beacons in their

318

eyes. The wagons jolted to the Umatilla, down the long drop from the Blues, coming onto prairie land again, to cottonwood and chokecherry and balm of Gilead along the stream and cultivated patches grown by Cayuse Indians who wished to trade for clothes.

The train camped there and lost a strayed or stolen horse and rolled on down the Umatilla, crossing and recrossing it and climbing to the side, to rolling, open land bristly with dried-out grass. And now, besides the snowy peaks, Evans saw the valley opening, the valley of the Columbia with the shades of distance in it.

It seemed he couldn't think but of the river. It flowed beneath and over and around his other thoughts—the Columbia and the Dalles and the mission buildings there, and afterwards each family for itself, finding ways to get downriver. Except that would his family be alone? Could he cut loose from the Byrds and Fairmans, who in their different ways leaned so much on him and Becky? The question slid off in the tide. Other questions too. Like why were Brownie and his girl still stiff like new acquaintances. Mercy was all right. He had to say that much and more, and Becky swore by her. A quiet, willing, pretty girl with more heft to her than on her father's fare.

Ten miles. Good grass. Timber only on the stream. Walla Walla Indians with potatoes and venison to trade. Dirty Indians. Not like the Cayuses. Showed the lack of Christianity, if Weatherby was right. Byrd's cart rolling solid. Patch as good as new. Summers saying watch out for these measly Injuns; what ain't nailed down they'll steal. Sights, words, feelings, questions, all washing with the river, all sensed across the mind-heard murmur of it.

He reached it when the sun was down and dusk lay thin among the hills. He reached it after heavy going through wild and sandy land where prickly pear and greasewood tried to grow. Out from it was barrenness, holding like a grudge the wheel scar of their passage, out from it no water, wood or graze; and on the shore was just a strip of grass and cocklebur and sunflower blooming hardy.

A lonely, empty land where thought itself might echo. A

new, old, wide-flung, solitary country purpled by the coming night. A place to make a man feel small, to drive his thoughts to cozy memories, to barns and barnyards and a rooster crowing and victual-scented kitchens closed away from space.

. But here the river ran!

Evans brought his gaze in close and saw the pebbly bottom and the water flowing clear. He let it stream on with the stream, across the silver flat of it and down its course to where it met the night. Beyond, he knew, the channel narrowed into falls and rapids, and so they'd have to wheel below. Still, here was the river road, the wide and sweeping road, the final road to Oregon. Here like a known thing on the way to home it was, like a recollected shore, like home itself.

A shudder shook him, and he started at Dick's voice and looked to right and left and saw that he was not alone and remembered how they'd left the wagons to stand upon the bank.

" 'Bout four days to the Dalles," Dick said.

Chapter - - - - - - - - - - Twenty-Nine

Judith Fairman sat by the river, which here near the mission house flowed with a kind of quiet peace after the violence she had glimpsed from the trail. Only here and there, in a boil of water or a flung wave, were the sudden, sharp rememberings of anguish. A river, she thought, was either a sad or anguished thing, compelled in either case to run its journey to seas nobody knew. Each drop of water flowed away, here for an instant and gone forever. The drift—the broken sunflower blossom, the naked snag, the dead fish, the foam wheeling from an eddy—it flowed away. Only the sun, lowering now, held steady on the surface, waiting its own time to move.

Voices sounded behind her, muted by distance. From downstream came the knock of axes, swung by earlier arrivals now busy building arks for the voyage to the Willamette. She caught the voices of men and Indians and the cries of children not killed by rattlesnakes.

"You be careful, Bethany," she called out. "Don't go too close."

The Byrd child tried to throw a stick into the water and turned around, hair goldened by the slanting sun, a small, fair girl with childhood's open wonder in her eyes. "I am." She reached down for another stick.

Judith herself was, she thought, content, sad and content, waiting like a hen on eggs for the slow warmth of her to bring the chick out of its shell. She hadn't any wish to talk, though Charles sat by her, his gaze like hers fixed on the water.

Content? Eased? Forgetful in the day-by-day? Sometimes the memory of Tod was driven out, by cooking, driving, weariness, by the hard demands of life and travel, and she would come back to it guilty, resentful of the interventions, and, crying, hold close the treasure of her grief.

Or she would find herself escaping, in conversation, in talk of Oregon, in dreaming of the unborn baby, in offering to tend the Byrd child after the wrecking of the wagon, in washing the small face and combing out the tangled hair.

"Please, Beth, not so close."

"I'm careful." The child came up and made room for herself in Judith's lap. "I want something to eat."

"We'll eat before long." The young smell came to Judith, the young and tender smell that once had been the smell of Toddie. She might be my very own, she thought, and let her lips brush the bright head. She might almost be Tod.

"I ought to be seeing about a boat," Charles said, still looking at the water. "We'll have to buy or build or something, the two boats for hire are engaged so far ahead. They're high, too, though I guess we could afford them."

"We just got here today," she answered, not wanting him to leave. She wondered if he felt the same as she did. Did any two people ever feel the same? Did ever one soul know another, though they shared bed and fortune, though they talked at night, though sometimes in hunger and in isolation they sought to make their bodies one, the all-mother in her loneliness trying to take back home the lost child-man?

While she wondered, Bethany squirmed off her lap and went to sorting pebbles.

"I guess we can wait until tomorrow," Charles said, "but I'll have to get busy then."

He would have to get busy. Always there was busyness, always calls on mind and body, always interventions. For Charles did Toddie lie far off, across the waste of land and time, beyond the rivers, over the mountains, across the sands? Had the picture of him blurred, the sound of his young voice grown indistinct from others except sometimes at night when, unbearably, he lived again?

Charles' hand touched hers, braced back upon the bank, and she welcomed it but didn't speak. What was talk, she asked herself, but fumbling for thought? Why speak? Why try to say? Thought and feeling didn't come in words. What lived inside herself she had no self words for. Better to keep silent. Better to rely on the flow of heart to heart.

What was grief? What was this long sorrow? What had Becky Evans said, with compassion underneath the hard simplicity? That no one could afford grief very long? As if grief were a luxury, an indulgence not to be enjoyed if a woman met her duties. That was the rule, she realized when Becky stated it, the rule to Oregon, the rule of all frontiers, the rule perhaps of life, but still she hated it. Still she fought against it, feeling hurt and guilt for having lost Tod in a chore.

Well, she had done her duties. She had found strength. She had borrowed it from Rebecca. If she cried, she cried at night and got up in good time and met the day. She would refute the rule. She would do her work and hold her grief. Not now, not ever, would Tod be lost to her.

She heard the sigh she hadn't known was coming. She knew her thought was tangled. Work, baby and Oregon, and Tod—how could her heart and mind make room for all of them, and first of all for Charles? Only time could tell her, and God if He would be so good.

Beth came to give her a white rock she had found. "Pretty?" she asked while her fat hand laid it in the open palm.

"Very pretty."

"Will you keep it in your house?"

"It will be a present from you."

"Can I come to see you sometimes when I get home?"

"Of course. But you're not going home."

"Home to Oregon," the child explained and walked off to find more rocks.

Home to Oregon. Home to a home unremembered, never seen, still unbuilt. Home across the endless plains, over thrusting mountains, through sad or anguished streams. Home.

And yet the thought was somehow good, the thought of homes to be, reached by bravery and strength, wrought out of wilderness, earned by work and suffering. Judith could see the home they'd have—a cabin first, unless saw lumber could be bought, and maybe later on a house of brick. Its structure didn't matter yet. Around the doorstep played the child she carried. Here in new land they'd work their future out. Today was new, and new tomorrows waited, and new ones for her love.

She said to Charles, "Sometimes I feel disloyal."

"Disloyal?"

"Don't you know?"

He nodded slowly, "I do, too."

She knew he knew. She knew his mind had turned to his returning interest in Oregon, to deeds done and words uttered in forgetfulness.

"Is it right, Charles? Can it be right?"

"It must be, Judie. It has to be. It's the same with everyone."

She fought to keep the easy tears away. "I never want to forget."

"You never will. But still we have to go ahead."

"Sometimes I don't know whether I'm thinking about Tod or the baby." The baby, she thought. Boy or girl, dark or fair, thrifty or frail, it must be Tod again. It would be Tod, and itself too, and sorrow and joy and remembrance and forgetfulness and recompense. And she would have for it all the love God had put in her for Tod, all He'd put there for her unborn seed. But still she cried, "It can't take Tod's place! It can't! It can't!"

His hand came to her shoulder. "Don't torture yourself, Judie! Please!"

"It mustn't!"

"Don't be afraid. We will remember, always, but it's the living we can help."

"I know," she answered, wrung by the truth of what he said.

He raised his eyes from the river, to the sky in which one cloud sailed, and she guessed he was thinking that that was where Tod was. "He would want you to love the baby," he said.

Bethany came from the river's edge. "I'm hungry."

"We'll eat right away," she answered, but before she got up, while her hand steadied her and her foot placed itself, she thought she felt the first flutter of the new life.

324

From the fire she'd kindled Rebecca Evans saw the Fairmans returning from the river, with Beth Byrd hanging on to Judith's hand. She waved a greeting to them and stooped to lay some bigger sticks upon the growing blaze. "There's a good woman," she told Mercy, wondering when the words were out how often she had said them.

Mercy wasn't one to point out she'd heard so before. While she worked dough on a board she looked up. "Yes," she answered.

"She's comin' to herself. Once the baby's here she'll be all right."

Mercy's gaze slid down. She didn't talk much. What was in her mind stayed there. But still she wasn't sulky. Sober, yes, but not ill-natured. Quiet with a kind of watching quietness. Quick, hard-working, and sparing with her words as if she didn't dare to say much. "Wonder when the men'll come?" Rebecca asked. "Late, I reckon. No tellin' about Lije and Dick."

The two had ridden off an hour or two after the train had reached the Dalles, trailing a couple of pack horses that looked top-heavy with their loads of buffalo robes. Rebecca didn't know just what they went for. To trade, Lije said. No use to hang around the Dalles. You couldn't hire or buy a boat there.

She didn't press him. She wasn't worried as some women were about how to get downriver. Lije would manage. He always did, leaving her to worry, if she had to, over other things.

"Brownie ought to be here pretty soon," Mercy said. "I saw the cattle guards go out to spell him."

"There ain't much to come for. Fish again, and rice. That and bread, and we'll get out some sweetenin'. Wish we had some greens and jowl."

Things were ready, or ready enough—fish cleaned and sliced, water heating for the rice, bread fixed to bake. Rebecca was glad they still had coffee left and sugar for it. The fare was poor enough in these last days. "I'll put a pot of coffee on," she said, "and then we'd better wait. We could set a while."

"I'm not tired. We'll need more water."

"You will be if you do around all day."

325

They sat out from the fire, for the evening's cool was slow in coming. From her position Rebecca could see the wrinkle that led up to the flanking hills. The Dalles. This was the Dalles for which they'd strained so long, the Methodist mission, the dreamed-of end of wagon travel, the name that helped to charm them on when grass was poor and water scarce and hope shriveled in the breast. It was just a mountain niche, a piece of bottom and sidehill, a breathing place between the heights and river, unknown maybe but to Indians until the Methodists had built a mission now seemingly about to peter out. The buildings, along with scattered Indian huts, gave the spot the look of settlement, but church and school and missionaries hadn't changed the Indians. They were a dull and heathen lot. They stank with rotten fish and rabbit. They answered poorly to the prayers of Weatherby. They still went naked, most of them. Dick said it was because no fur grew on a salmon.

Rebecca thought this place had never seen the likes of now, with wagons arched around, men talking of the trip and of the voyage ahead, their children running, their women visiting, the new arrivals mixing in, asking were there boats, asking what to do then, saying pleased to meetcha, my home ain't far from yours. Like the wagons there already, those of her own train had wheeled in ragged with the miles, the work stock stringy, the paint of wagon covers coated gray or black, the women worn down to the final scraps of dress, the men to mended pants and Indian buckskin.

Here the trains divided out. Here the kinship of the trail was loosened, each company confused with others, each family knowing now it stood alone, each feeling somehow strange toward those who'd been so close. The tie had been untied, Rebecca thought. This was the end of something hard and good, of something that would stay in mind to death. She and Lije and Brownie and Mercy, there were just them alone, except they wouldn't cut loose from the Byrds and Fairmans yet. A kind of claim lay on them, she and Lije agreed, a duty to the weak and weakened.

"Won't hurt to put the rice on," she said and started to get up, but Mercy beat her to her feet and spilled the rice into the boiling water and thought to move the pot to where it wouldn't sputter over.

"I ain't so old," she said. "You don't have to fetch and carry for me." Watching the girl's quick movements, seeing the little smile, she felt again the squeeze of inner tenderness. Whatever Mercy's parents were, whatever she had done before, she was a winning thing. You had to say, regardless, she was that. She made a body want to do for her, to take her under wing, to cluck there were no hawks about.

Beyond the fire a woman passed, tugged by one child and heavy with another. It was a sight, Rebecca thought, the way the young ones came along. With every train or piece of train were children, some born along the trail. With every one were women big in front.

Hardly meaning to, she let her gaze slide to the girl-wife by her. What was it told her? The filling-in of shoulders? The rounding into womanhood? The glow of face? The secret lying in the eyes? No matter what it was, she knew and was troubled with the knowing.

July. Late July to September 21. A short two months. Not long enough to show unless—unless— The question, the sore wondering, wouldn't down. Sometimes as Brownie's mother she had a mind to ask, to up and ask as maybe was her right and have the fact to go on. Sometimes she felt she wasn't motherly to let suspicion lie. And sometimes, seeing Brownie and the way of him toward Mercy, she guessed he had the answer. She felt his hurt then and knew anger and the urge to hurt his hurter.

She had held in. She had calmed Lije, who was upset enough without this added reason. She had bragged of Mercy. She had tried to be a mother to her, too. She wasn't sure of all the reasons why. Was it, she wondered, that any woman felt sister to another, partner in need against the breed of men? Was it Mercy's being Mercy? Was it the belief they'd have to make the best of things regardless? Was it the chance that Brownie'd been the man himself, before their marriage?

She'd like to think so, but it was outlandish. He didn't know enough. He wasn't bold. Just a boy yet. Who then? Who'd shone around her before Brownie took her to the preacher? No one much. She hadn't teased the men on, not that Rebecca knew. Everyone had liked her, though, and Mr. Mack had acted extra nice.

"Brownie's comin'," Mercy said. "See, stakin' out his horse?"

Brownie walked up and said hello, and Mercy said hello, and Rebecca said, "Your pa and Dick ain't here yet. They'll be along, though. We'll get the things to cookin'."

Lije came in while she was frying fish. "You'll be where you want to be before you know it," he said, smiling with some good news in him. "How's the grass, boy?"

"Fair. We took 'em back a ways."

"Where's Dick?" Rebecca asked.

"Won't be in till mornin'."

"You mean he's lyin' out, without food or a bed?"

"Shoo! That ain't nothin'. Not for Dick."

Lije was feeling big. As they sat down to eat, Rebecca thought she would have known it from his looks, without a word being said.

"That Dick!" he said and speared a slice of fish.

She asked, "What about him?"

"Knows everything. Fixes for everything. We'll be afloat tomorrow." He paused, getting, she knew, a small enjoyment from their wonderment.

"I thought there wasn't boats."

"Ain't."

"Well?"

"You know them buffalo Dick had us skin and save the hides?"

"Out with it, Pa!" Brownie said.

"It's them we'll sail on, in a way." Lije let them figure for a minute. "These Injuns got canoes, but nary stitch of clothes. Gits cold in the winter, too. They sure like buffalo robes."

"You aim to sail in one of them rough dugouts?" Rebecca asked.

He shook his head. "That Dick! Wanted us to get busy, before the canoes was all traded off."

"I swear, Lije, you take a heap of coaxin'."

328

"We'll fix us flatboats. Take down the wagons and lay the side and bottom boards across canoes and maybe raise a sail. Then, hello, home."

"What about the rest?"

"What?"

"The Fairmans and Byrds?"

"That's why Dick went on. To trade for enough canoes. Come mornin' you'll see a fleet come in."

"Will it work, Lije?"

"Slick as grease, but no one would think of it but Dick. We'll have one carry, at what they call the Cascades, but like as not we can trade some Injuns into helpin' us. You seen Mack to talk to?"

"There's talk of goin' overland, south of Mount Hood. Someone—I forget his name—is takin' a look. Mrs. Mack says they'll go that way, with wagons if they can."

Now that the news had been exchanged, Lije and Brownie went to work on supper. Rebecca got up to get more bread, for once ahead of Mercy. It did her good to see her menfolks eat. Almost before she and Mercy could make a start, they were mopping up their plates. They wiped their mouths and sat silent while Lije puffed at the pipe he'd lighted with a coal.

Other folks were through with supper, and men were drifting off from fires to join with other men while the women tidied up and bedded down the children.

Lije grinned at Mercy. "Cat got your tongue? Yours and Brownie's?"

Mercy only gave a half-smile back. Brownie said, "Watchin' cows don't give you much to say."

Lije lifted himself from the ground. "Well, boy, I reckon you can work if you can't talk. There's light enough for us to make a start on them wagons."

They kept busy until after dark. Then, saying they'd be back directly, they walked off toward the noise of voices.

With the day's work done, Rebecca sat again. Sometimes, tired, she wanted more to sit and let her thoughts slide on than to fall thoughtless into sleep. She could make out from here the dark streak of the river, carrying the dim rememberings of the day, and the darker flow of hills beyond. A pale star winked above the rim of them.

After a while Mercy came and lowered by her. What she had been doing Rebecca didn't know, maybe making neat the bed that she and Brownie slept in. Neither spoke. It struck Rebecca that both were letting rest seep in, drawing on it with their breath, fetching it with eyes that found it in the softened dark.

She felt the presence by her. Mercy McBee. Mercy McBee Evans. Daughter-in-law. Coming mother—which, unless somebody told him, Lije wouldn't know until the blind could see. Men had no eye for that.

Knowing, Lije would holler, for he loved children. Knowing more, he'd raise a ruckus. He'd say no son of his would raise a wood's colt. Men got mighty righteous when girls were caught because of doing things the men had begged them to.

Beyond her soreness, beyond the roily tenderness she felt for Mercy, she saw Lije pawing up the dust, saw him with understanding, with another tenderness. Men were men, and he couldn't help that he was one, nor would she change him if she could. He was a better man than most, the best to her of any, and, barring trifles, she had never kept a secret from him.

A baby was crying out somewhere in the darkness, its voice a thin wail over other voices. "Sight of young'uns," Rebecca said to Mercy. "Don't look like it'll take long to settle Oregon."

"Ma," Mercy said. It was the first time she had used the name.

"Yes, Mercy," Rebecca answered, touched that she had done so.

"I—I think I'm going to have a baby."

"Whoever would have guessed it! Now, ain't that fine?"

"I'm pretty sure I am."

Rebecca turned and in the darkness saw Mercy's head bent and her shoulders drooping and such an air of young sadness there that her arm seemed to go out of itself to bring her in. She said, "Don't you fret. It's just fine." She clucked the little things that came to tongue and felt the girl's breath on her throat and heard the whispered, "I was afraid to tell you."

A sudden fear came on her, the fear of knowing without a

330

doubt, the fear that Mercy, out of misery and the decent need of owning up, would tell her how it was. She walled the chance away. She sealed it off, forever beyond Lije, beyond herself, and with it sealed for good and all, she hoped, the painful wondering. She said, "A baby born to you and Brownie is bound to be a good one."

Mercy was in bed when Brownie came back. She heard him say good night to his father and listened for the soft press of the moccasins he wore. She heard him brush against the tent pole and slide inside, to the rustle of the flap, and begin to take his things off, working quietly so as not to rouse her.

She might as well be watching him, she thought. With her eyes closed in the dark she still saw, saw him walk the space between the tents and stoop to enter and loosen up his breeches and let them fall. She saw his gangly figure, the lightish hair unruly on his head, the look of seriousness out of place on so young a face.

A greeting started in her and died somewhere inside. "I'm here," she felt like saying. "I'm awake." If she could say that much, she thought, she could say more. She could tell him that Rebecca knew, though not the whole of it. If she could make a start, maybe they could talk the thing out, maybe talk it clear away, and come to easy footing.

But she couldn't, and, listening to the little sounds of his undressing, she thought she never could. Always in between would rise the past, always the life that she was being mother to, always Mr. Mack, seen by both of them, her seeing seen by him and his by her, so that they couldn't speak.

She felt the covers lift, felt the movements of his coming into bed and straightening out and drawing the covers back and putting a hand beneath his face. But there was no company in him, no help for loneliness. They might as well be strangers.

The night was quiet, but still she heard, as if in loneliness the ear reached out for lonely sounds—the bare breathing of the air, the pulse of night, the careful stir of some small animal, the tired heart-echo on the pillow.

She knew that Brownie was awake, maybe lying wide-eyed

in the dark, his mind like hers fixed on their trouble. He was good, too good for her, and Rebecca was good and Lije was good, and why, then, did she have to stand apart, with even gratitude locked in? Why must she feel unwifely?

It wasn't Brownie's fault and, since the marriage, not her own, she hoped. It was what she'd done before. It was the shadow falling in between. It was the baby that she carried, the small and fearful stranger. And all of it was too much for them. Not since she'd gone to him and said she'd marry if he'd have her had either spoken of it, as if agreeing silently it was too sore for words. They'd hardly talked of anything or known a minute's happiness except once when the fun of danger drove the cloud away.

Not her fault? Not since the marriage? Didn't Mr. Mack return to mind? The nights beside the Laramie? The quick and clever way of him? The lock that needed pushing back? Sometimes the dream slipped up of being with him again, of easing on his chest the silent loneliness, of whispering how it was with her to him who ought to understand.

She had wanted the man and had to take the boy, she thought, and wondered if that was the everlasting way of things; and it struck her, wondering, that she was being unworthy. Brownie was a man, a good and even gentle man for all the stiffness of his manner toward her. She ought to thank God for him, thank God and him and Lije and Rebecca and the luck that made them meet. She wasn't deserving of so much. What she deserved was nothing.

If only she could talk to him, if only he would let her, if only she could know the hand-touch of forgiveness! She couldn't swear he really cared for her, not any more, not since she'd told him and he had answered that they'd marry anyway. The doubt of him was like the loss of something not prized until too late.

It was then, it was right then that Brownie turned in bed and, having turned, made sure the cover still lay snug about her neck. His hand came out and smoothed it back and brushed her throat and went down by his side.

In believed-in secret he had done it. While he thought she slept he'd shown himself and answered her.

The act and meaning of it wrenched her. She held the knowledge tight, along with uncried tears, and tried to breathe as if she were asleep. She felt come alive in her a sympathy for Brownie, a pity that, earlier, she'd had to tell herself she ought to feel. It swelled in her, truer than the promptings of the mind, better than her self-concern, and choked up to words that must be said. Brownie, in his way, had had to take the boy, too.

Without thinking more, without letting herself hesitate, she said, "Brownie?"

"You awake?"

"I just this minute woke up. Brownie?"

"Uh-huh."

She came out with it. "I'm—I'm learnin' to care for you."

He didn't answer right away. Waiting, she came to know he couldn't.

"I hoped you'd want to know," she said.

Chapter - - - - - - - - - - - - - Thirty

FIFTY MILES maybe from the Dalles. Maybe forty still to go to reach Vancouver. Six miles then to the Willamette.

Evans wiped the sweat out of his eyes. Nothing to it now, he told himself, unless a spell of weather came; nothing but to rig the flatboats up again and climb aboard and wait on wind and river. Behind them lay the final hindrance, the Cascade Falls that from the portage looked like a field of snow. Ahead the water gentled, lazing on its final hitch.

He breathed deep and raised his elbows to let the air come in. The portage had been long and hard, but it was over. The last loose wheel had been rolled, the last board carried, the last pot and pan and dab of food lugged along, the last canoe brought over. Everyone was here and in good fettle—Byrds, Fairmans, Mercy, Becky, Brownie, Dick, not to mention the Indians hired to help out with the carry. Here where the path led back to water the Indians stood around, looking simple and pleasant, curious about the white man's doings. One of them had a blanket pinned at his neck with a stick. A squaw had trailed along with them, a young one who wore a skirt of beaten cedar bark. It covered part of her.

"Might as well make camp," Evans said, looking to the sun now swimming misty in the west. "Reckon we can get the boats back together before dark."

He didn't go to work, though, so that others would. He loaded his pipe and hunted up his tinder box and sat against a tree and smoked, content to rest a while and let the others rest. It had been a portage sure enough—four miles almost of heavy carrying and part of it across an Indian cemetery where bodies had been dumped in cedar pens or laid on rafts that floated in a pond. Rough statues sat around, of birds and brutes and little devils. Weatherby would have called them idols and

334

preached a scolding to the Indians. . . . It looked like Weatherby had cut himself a piece of work.

Evans drew deep on his pipe to get the remembered stink out of his nose. Byrd was fiddling with a fire. Mercy and Becky were talking by the water's edge where Fairman stood, his eyes set on the river's roll. Byrd had traded an old shirt to an Indian. It was the only thing the Indian wore, but he wore it as if it was enough, as if it was an outfit in itself. Every time young Jeff Byrd looked at him he had to giggle, but the Indian didn't care, being like a child himself. Dick was making talk to a couple of other Indians, maybe telling them to run along. The smell of Indians didn't help a meal.

Weatherby had cut himself a piece of work all right. He had known it, too. In looks and speech he'd owned up to the size of it when he'd said goodbye to Dick back at the Dalles.

"Better come along," Dick had said. "We'll make a place for you."

Brother Weatherby wagged his old head in a no. Looking at him while he and Summers talked, Evans thought he had shrunk to bone and string. He stood more stooped than ever, as if from the weight of sin and duty.

"There's heathen a plenty lower down," Dick said. "It ain't like you'd run out of work."

"I'll come later. I want to spend some time here at the mission. It needs help."

Dick said, "Yep. Don't look like religion has struck these Injuns very deep."

Weatherby nodded sadly. "I have talked to the Methodist brothers here. Brother Perkins is discouraged."

"Can't say I blame him. Ain't you?"

"I do the Lord's work. I thank Him for it."

"And so you're stayin'?"

"For the present." Weatherby looked up from the ground he had been studying. "Brother Summers?"

Dick waited for what came next.

"You have seen all along that I had the bread of the body."

"That's all right."

"I wish I could give you the bread of the spirit."

Dick held out his hand. Evans saw friendliness in his face, a liking for this man so different from himself, and at the same time the hint of ticklement. "I'll look you up if I get hungry," he said.

With all the goodbyes spoken, the little fleet had cut loose, one boat for the Evanses, one for the Byrds, one for the Fairmans. They were odd but slick contraptions, cabined by the wagon boxes, light-riding on the underneath canoes, pushed by scraps of sail when the wind was right, urged on by makeshift sweeps when it was not. They sailed on a river of little current, among tall stumps sheared off as if by giants, through mountains crowding high. Evans saw pine trees growing great and felt the sea wind in his face and told himself that here was Oregon. Here at last it came, strange to him yet and awesome, but dear for all of that.

Of those who stayed behind him at the Dalles, some, like Mack, would try their wagons overland. Some, like Patch, would wait their turns at hired boats. Daugherty had started working on a raft.

Evans had said goodbye to all of them and felt no wrench in saying it, for he would see them later. It was the goodbye coming up that bothered him, the goodbye that would come up unless a final talk would stop it. He'd argued Oregon with Dick. He'd told him he'd best come and settle like the rest. Dick had only smiled or said small things that added up to no. And now they didn't need him. Now his work was done and more than done. He'd just as good as said he'd leave them here.

Evans got up, uneasy with the sense of loss, and pocketed his pipe and went to help set the canoes in the water and fix the boards across. The Indians had straggled away, bought off with fishhooks or tobacco, he imagined. The women were doing around the fire that Byrd had built. They'd have just one or maybe two fires tonight. No need of more. Two of Byrd's young ones had climbed a tree. Judith Fairman was watching out for Bethany.

They had red meat this night—a deer that Summers had hunted the day before, saying salmon gagged him—and with it bread without butter and coffee without sugar or cream.

The night drew on softly, hazed a little from the sea, filled with the steady whispering of water. Now that the trip was almost done no one seemed to have very much to say. Even the children were quieter than usual and not balky about going to bed. Mercy and Brownie sat off a little from the rest, in some new-won closeness that Evans thought was good. He was silent himself, with only half his mind upon the here and now. The other half was hunting arguments to use on Dick.

He waited until Dick got up, then trailed off after him. "Dick!"

"What's up, hoss?"

"Nice night, ain't it?"

"If you like sea country."

"What's wrong with the sea?"

"Nothin'. I just like my country high."

"You'll git used to it here. You'll come to like it."

"Not me."

"You'll give it a try, though, Dick?"

"I reckon not."

"What you aim to do?"

"Hit back."

"To Independence?"

"Not that, Lije."

"When?"

"Tomorrow's as good a time as any."

"How you goin' to hit back with no horse or anything?"

"I got my rifle and flint and steel. I'll pick up a horse somewheres."

"Damn it, Dick, I wish you wasn't that way! A man can't just traipse on forever."

Dick took a minute answering, and when the words came they seemed to Evans not an answer but a fling at some thought Dick held in a far corner of his mind. "After a while he meets the ocean, Lije."

"Why don't you come with us, sure enough?"

"It ain't a thing for me, Lije."

"There's free land for you like everybody else." Evans

337

waited, and then added what he knew. "You could be an important man in Oregon." In the half-darkness he thought he saw a little smile twist Summers' mouth.

"It ain't importance that I'm after."

"What is it?"

Again Dick took time to answer, and again the answer troubled Evans. "I'm bound to chase my tail, I reckon, like a pup."

"You could live with us, an' double welcome."

"This child knows that, Lije. Your way's cut out, and it's a good way—for you. Mine's different."

"You just got it in your head that it is."

"That's mostly what counts."

"Where would you point then?"

"Maybe back to Bridger. Maybe to the Bear. Maybe north to Blackfoot country. Can't tell."

"There'll be snow in the mountains before you can git across."

"Likely."

"Dick, for a smart man you ain't got a lick of sense."

"Not a speck. But it ain't that I don't like you and your woman and Brownie, Lije. It ain't that." Summers turned and stepped away. "Right now you're interferin' with business. I came out here to make water."

Evans couldn't find anything more to say. It seemed he couldn't think beyond the feel of loss, beyond the knowing that it was a shame for a man like Dick to waste himself. What was it in the past that pulled him back, that put the lines of wanting in his face sometimes when he didn't know that anyone was looking? Trapping? Indians? Buffalo? The wild and empty country? Evans could understand a love of them. He liked open land himself. But still a man must live ahead. And such things didn't count for much compared with Oregon and the life now opening up. Besides, those times were gone or going.

When Dick turned back, Evans asked, "Don't it mean nothin' to you, Dick, for Oregon to be America's?"

"You'll tend to that, Lije. I kind of want to see the Popo Agie again."

338

Evans didn't ask what or where the Popo Agie was, or why Dick wished to see it. It didn't matter now. What or where or why would be just words to go along with other words that, hearing, he couldn't quite make sense of. "See you in the mornin', anyhow," he told Dick as they walked back to camp.

"Sure thing."

He didn't though. Before he roused, before any others did, Dick had slipped away.

Mountains walled on either side, mountains hanging over, mountains bare and mountains treed, their rims high-dizzy in the blue of sky. The broad-beamed river, salted from the touch of ocean, barely flowing in between. Waterfalls along the southern wall like frills of snowy ribbon. Moisture in the air, the damp outbreath of sea.

Time running slowly with the slow-borne boats. Shadowed morning, glinty noon, shadowed afternoon. Nights broody with the feel of mountains, broody with the sense of loss, the campfire sparking small against the greatness of the dark. Rice. Bread. More fish. Sleep. The lap of water on the narrow shore.

And wind. Wind out of the west, sea wind, fighting oar and current. Wind that guarded Oregon. The Cape Horn wind that drove the boats to shore. Wind that changed its mind, that eased or turned and bellied out the sails and streamed the lines of bank behind.

A fort bateau, up-bound to the falls for passengers. Hello and goodbye, and we're all right and how far yet to go? Emptiness afterwards, a greater loneliness, the loneliness of water, wind and mountains, of all the might of earth against three flimsy boats.

The touch of lostness, the touch of sorrow, the inward asking if gentler shores would come, the thought of Dick, called backward by some whisper in his mind.

But, under all, the waiting flush, the singing of the blood when hills would roll away, and real and fair to sight would come the hard-held dream. This time was short. These wind and mountain troubles were the last. Around the turn! Beyond the quiet stretch!

Hardships, sorrows, partings? But the heart still ready to beat high? Without troubles, Evans thought, rejoicing would be a puny thing, with no roots in the soil of life. How much would he prize Brownie if he hadn't lost another child? How much would he like Oregon except for sweat and grief along the way? Grief bowed the heart but made it richer, so that joy was rich. Some night on the banks of the Willamette he'd hear Rock's throaty growl and would like Oregon the more. Some night he'd see Tod Fairman and his swollen leg. Sometime he'd bend again and find in pigeon eyes the kinship to himself. In some remembering silence he'd hear Dick Summers say, "Take it easy, hoss!"

He held tight as the mountains fell away. He said not yet, not yet, while in his gaze a softer country swam. Not yet, not yet, and then ahead, beyond a grass-green prairie, mellow in the sun, the lines of Fort Vancouver with a great ship standing by! Across from it, unseen in the wooded flow of land, the waters of Willamette!

Once, long ago, he had come to the Platte and felt greatness. He had reached the Columbia and shuddered to the flowering hope. And now he looked on home. A tide rose in him, so fierce, so bursting in the breast, so close to women's tears, that he feared to meet the others' eyes. Yonder it was, yonder was home, yonder the rich soil waiting for the plow, waiting for the work of hands, for the happy cries of children. They'd made it. They had rolled the miles. And back of them came others. Crossers of plains. Grinders through the dust. Climbers of mountains. Forders of rivers. Meeters of dangers. Sailors at last of the big waters. Nation makers. Builders of the country.

He let himself look around and saw the Byrds' and Fairmans' boats lapping close behind and, on his own, Brownie idle with his sweep and Becky with the home-gleam in her eye and Mercy sitting by her. Mercy who, Rebecca said, was going to have a child. Sweet Mercy who would bring a baby to the house. Blood of his blood, Evans thought. Blood of his blood once removed.

He winked at his woman and spoke loud above the tremble in his throat. "Becky," he said, "hurrah for Oregon!"